# FIVE
# YEARS GONE

## MARIE FORCE

Five Years Gone
By: Marie Force

Published by HTJB, Inc.
Copyright 2018. HTJB, Inc.
Cover designer: Kristina Brinton
Interior Layout: Isabel Sullivan, E-book Formatting Fairies

ISBN: 978-1946136473

www.marieforce.com

# PROLOGUE

*Ava*

We met in a bar, of all places, a dingy hole-in-the-wall favored by military members from the nearby Navy base in San Diego. I went with a friend from school who was interested in one of the military guys. Before that night, I'd never been there, and I've never been back. John was celebrating the promotion of one of his buddies. He crashed into me as I left the ladies' room and kept me from falling by grabbing my arms to steady me.

Just like in the movies, our eyes met, and my spine tingled with the kind of instantaneous awareness I'd only read about but never experienced personally.

"I'm so sorry," he said, gorgeous and fierce in his fatigues.

I noticed gold on his collar, a hint of late-day scruff on his jaw and the name WEST in bold black letters on his chest. Intense electric-blue eyes made it impossible for me to look away, even when I was safely back on my feet.

"Are you all right?" he asked.

Realizing I'd been staring at him, I blinked and reluctantly broke the connection. "I… Yes, I'm fine. Thank you for the save."

And then he smiled, and the tingling began anew.

"I'm John."

I shook his outstretched hand. "Ava."

Keeping his hold on my hand, he tipped his head. "You come here often?"

"Never," I said, laughing. "I'm a first-timer."

"What do you think so far?"

"I wasn't impressed until about thirty seconds ago."

As if he had all the time in the world to give me, he leaned against the wall. "Is that right? What happened thirty seconds ago?"

I thought about taking back my hand but didn't. "I was saved from certain disaster by a man in uniform."

"The guy in the uniform is the reason you needed saving in the first place, because he wasn't watching where he was going. Least he can do is buy you a drink."

"I wouldn't say no to that." I was proud of my witty responses and got the feeling he could more than hold his own in the wittiness department. Across the crowded room, I noticed my friend talking to the guy she'd come to see, and her brows lifted in interest when she saw me with John. He guided me to the bar, placing a proprietary hand on my lower back, and told one of the guys to give me his stool.

"Yes, sir." The younger man bowed gallantly to me as he took his beer and moved along.

"Do people always do what you say?"

"If they know what's good for them." His teasing grin kept the comment from being overly cocky. "What can I get you?"

Deciding to live dangerously for once, I asked for a cosmopolitan.

"Go big or go home," he said with admiration.

"That's my motto." I was so full of shit. I wondered if he could tell I was all talk or what he'd think of me if he knew I usually err much closer to the side of caution than the wild side. I wondered if he could tell I was just barely old enough to drink. I'd turned twenty-one only six months earlier.

When my cosmo and his Budweiser had been delivered, he offered a toast. "To new friends."

I touched my glass to his bottle. "To new friends."

"So, where're you from, Ava?"

"New York."

"I thought I heard New Yawk in your voice."

I batted my eyelashes at him. "So four years at the University of California San Diego didn't scrub the New York out of me?"

Laughing, he said, "Hardly. I know some guys from New York. One of them is from Staten Island, which is about as New York as it gets. I know New York when I hear it."

"I'm from Purchase, upstate from the city. What about you?"

"I'm from all over. My old man is a retired general. You name it, I've lived there."

"Where's home?"

"Right here." He turned that intense gaze on me, and I went stupid in the head. I couldn't see anything but him. We might as well have been alone in the crowded bar for all I knew. Unlike my friend, who loved men in uniform, I was never turned on by the uniform. Until then. Until John. "You want to get out of here?"

I swallowed hard. It wasn't like me to leave a bar with a man I'd just met. "And go where?"

"Somewhere we can talk."

"What do you want to talk about?"

He leaned in so his lips were close to my ear. "Everything. I want to know every single thing there is to know about you."

That's how we started. We were intense from the first second we met until the last time I saw him five years ago today. I can't believe it's been five years since I looked into those incredible blue eyes or woke to him on the pillow next to me or heard his voice in my ear, whispering words that're permanently carved into my heart as he made love to me.

The worst part is I have no idea where he is. I don't know if he's alive or dead, being held captive or if he's living his life somewhere else with someone else. I don't know, and the not knowing is the hardest thing I've ever dealt with.

I love him as much today as I ever did. No amount of time could ever change that simple fact of my life. We had two beautiful, magnificent years together, caught up in our own little bubble. He never met my family. I never met his. We didn't make couple friends. We didn't talk about the future. We didn't need to. Our future was decided that first night, and it would take care of itself in due time. I honestly and naïvely believed that.

Now, with hindsight, I realize the bubble was strategic on his part. He gave me everything he had to give, including no promise of tomorrow.

Five years ago today, we watched the horror unfold on live television. A US-based cruise ship blown up by suicide bombers. Four thousand lives extinguished in a heartbeat. Our world permanently changed once again, our country declaring yet another war on terrorists. After 9/11 we thought we'd seen everything. We were wrong.

"I have to go," he said, grabbing the duffel that stood ready in the front hall closet. He called it his "go bag." I'd thought nothing of it.

"Where're you going?"

"I don't know."

"When will you be back?"

"I don't know that either." He held my face in his hands and gazed at me, seemingly trying to memorize my every feature. "I love you. I'll always love you." Then he kissed me as passionately as he ever had and was gone, out the door in a flash of camouflage.

I never saw him again.

I'm not his wife or even his fiancée, so no one notified me of his whereabouts. And three months after he left, when I found a way onto the base in a desperate quest for information, no one there could tell me anything either. I tried to locate his parents and other people he mentioned, but it was like they didn't exist. I could find no record of a retired general named West in the Marine Corps, Army or Air Force.

Furthermore, an exhaustive search for information on the John West I had known led nowhere. No high school, no college, no military service, no nothing.

Sometimes I wonder if I dreamed the two years we spent together, doing mundane things like grocery shopping, cooking, watching TV and sleeping together after long days at work. But then I'd remember the blissful passion, the scorching pleasure, the desire that ruled us from the beginning, and I'd know I didn't dream him. I didn't dream us. We were real, and he was everything to me.

Sitting on the floor in our apartment, surrounded by boxes, I take a few minutes before the movers arrive to memorize every detail of the place where we lived together. I've packed his things along with mine, and I'm moving home to New York. Today was my deadline. I gave it five years, and I simply can't do it anymore. I can't sit in our home among our things, waiting for something that's never going to happen.

It's over. It's time for me to move on. It's probably long past time, if I'm being honest with myself. And though I know it's the right move at the right time, that doesn't mean my heart isn't shattering all over again as I dismantle the place where we were us.

My sister is getting married next month. I promised her I'd be home in time to hold her hand through the festivities. Other than occasional trips home for holidays and other occasions, I've been gone more than ten years. I bear no resemblance whatsoever to the girl who left home at eighteen seeking independence from her overbearing family at a faraway college out West.

I accomplished all my goals, finishing college, landing a decent job and falling in love with the man of my dreams. I found out what happens when dreams come true and how painful it is when they blow up in your face.

It's time now to set new goals, to start over, to begin a life that doesn't have John at the center of it the way it did here. It'll be nice to be back with people who love me and care about me, even if they tend toward smothering at times. That's looking rather good to me after years of loneliness and grief.

The intercom sounds to let me know the movers are here. I pick myself up off the floor and steel my heart for the day ahead. I can do this. I've been through worse, and I'll survive this the same way I've survived everything else. Despite my resolve, my eyes fill with tears as I press the button that opens the door downstairs to the movers.

It doesn't take them long to pack my belongings into their truck. I keep with me the things that can't be replaced—precious photos, gifts he gave me, the clothing he left behind. After taking a final look around the apartment, I pack those boxes into my car, turn my apartment keys into the leasing office and head east, feeling as if I'm leaving behind everything that ever mattered to me.

It's like I'm losing him all over again. I cry all the way through the desert of Southern California and well into Arizona. I relive every minute I can remember, every conversation, every special moment. I think about what it was like to make love with him and wonder how I'll ever to do that with anyone but him. Maybe I won't. Maybe that part of my life ended with him, and even though I'm only twenty-eight now, I'm okay with that possibility. Once you've experienced perfection, it's hard to imagine settling for anything less.

The tears finally dry up somewhere in northern Arizona, but the ache inside… I take that with me all the way to New York, where I will try my very best to pick up the pieces of my shattered life and put them back together into some new version of myself.

After all, what choice do I have?

# CHAPTER 1

*Ava*

My sister, Camille, doesn't do anything halfway, including get married. She's one of those girls I'd love to hate if she weren't my beloved sister. Three years behind me in high school, she was class president, captain of the cheerleading squad, valedictorian and homecoming queen. I'm sure the teachers who had me first wondered how the same genes could've produced two such different sisters. Why do you think I moved so far from home to go to college and stayed there afterward? At least in San Diego, no one ever compared me to my rock star little sister.

A few weeks ago, she graduated from Yale Law School, at the top of her class, of course, and made *Law Review*, had offers from every big firm in the country and sported a three-carat diamond on her finger from the son of the New York governor.

Like I said, she doesn't do anything halfway. So here I am at the Waldorf Astoria in New York City, standing beside my sister as she marries Robert James Tilden III in a lavish ceremony. Did I mention she's also freaking gorgeous? Well, she is, and never more so than today. She's glowing with happiness and excitement and unfettered joy that serves as a bitter reminder of everything I've lost.

Pass the champagne.

If ever there was a time to get rip-roaring drunk, this is it. Rob arranged for hotel rooms for every member of the wedding party, so no one has to drive or even function after the reception. I plan to take full advantage of my new brother-in-law's generosity up to and including room service breakfast.

Camille grasps my arm as we make our way from the rooftop where the happy couple exchanged vows to the ballroom where the reception will be held. "Help me pee," she whispers.

I follow her to the restroom, where an attendant greets us and congratulates the bride.

"Thank you so much," Camille says with a gracious smile for the woman.

"Use the handicapped stall," the attendant says. "There's more room."

"Good call," I say as we enter the roomy stall where Camille teaches me how to bustle her dress. I get it pinned up as best I can and then hold it out of harm's way while she hovers over the toilet to take care of business.

"This wasn't in my maid-of-honor job description."

She laughs. "Sorry, but this is what sisters are for. And I'm *so* glad you're here."

"Me, too." And I mean that sincerely. "I love seeing you so happy."

"I am happy, but I'll be even happier tomorrow. I'm so ready for a vacation after planning a wedding during the last year of law school. If that doesn't kill me, nothing will. Two weeks of sand, sun, sex and booze. Bring it on."

My heart aches with envy, making me feel small and petty. What I wouldn't give for two weeks in the tropics with John. What I wouldn't give to simply know he's alive. I shake off those thoughts. This isn't the time to wallow in the past. Today is about Camille and Rob, and I'm determined to keep my focus on her.

She stands and hurls herself into my arms. "I love you so much, Ava. I'm so glad you're back home where you belong."

Blinking back tears, I return her embrace. "Love you, too." It's good to be home. Whether I'm back where I belong is questionable. I have no idea anymore where I belong, but I'm going to figure that out. "I wouldn't want to be anywhere else but with you today." That much is certainly true.

After she washes her hands at the sink inside the stall, she hooks her arm through mine to lead me out of the restroom as the attendant looks on with amusement. "Let's get this party started."

We line up outside the ballroom, and I'm paired with the best man, Rob's brother, Eric. My sister has married into a rather fantastic gene pool. Not only are the Tildens wealthy and successful, they're incredibly good-looking, too. Rob is a triplet, having shared the womb with Eric and their sister Amelia, whom they call Amy. They make a striking trio—Rob and Amy resemble their father, with dark hair and eyes, while Eric favors their blonde, hazel-eyed mother. Despite their different coloring, there's a definite resemblance among the three of them as well as their younger sister, Julianne, a blonde spitfire who's kept us laughing all weekend.

I instantly love the Tildens and can see why my sister is gone over Rob, who dotes on her to the point of nausea for the rest of us. I'll give them a pass since it's their wedding weekend, but the words *get a room* have frequently come to mind during the festivities.

"For Christ's sake," Eric mutters while we wait to be introduced. "Save it for the honeymoon."

I glance over my shoulder to see Rob and Camille engaged in yet another passionate lip-lock and laugh at the look of disgust on Eric's handsome face. "They can't help themselves."

"I need a drink. The wedding party is allowed to drink, right?"

"God, I hope so."

"You're up," the wedding coordinator, a peppy woman named Mimi, says after Julianne and Rob's cousin Nate are introduced.

"Ready?" Eric asks, extending his arm to me.

I tuck my hand into the crook of his elbow. "Ready."

"Please join me in welcoming our best man, the brother of the groom, Eric Tilden, and our maid of honor, the sister of the bride, Ava Lucas." The DJ draws out every syllable of my name, making me Avaaaaaa Luuuuuucasssss.

We walk in to thunderous applause from the nearly five hundred guests in the ballroom. I'll admit to being intimidated by the crowd and the noise, both of which have me hanging on to Eric a little more tightly.

As if he can feel my tension, Eric covers my hand on his arm with his free hand, and the gesture comforts me.

We stand on the side of the huge dance floor with the rest of the wedding party.

"And now, please welcome our bride and groom, Rob and Camille Tilden!"

The applause is deafening as the happy couple makes their way into the room, stopping for hugs and kisses from friends and family. They've been deliriously happy for two years now, ever since they met at a fundraiser for Rob's dad when Camille was finishing her first year of law school. Rob managed his father's campaign and runs his New York City office.

"Can we drink yet?" Eric speaks close to my ear so only I will hear him.

"Counting the minutes." I glance up at him and realize he's focused on me, not the bride and groom. The subtle, rich scent of his cologne surrounds me, making me want to lean in closer to him. This is, I realize in a moment of despair, the closest I've been to any man since the day John kissed me goodbye and disappeared from my life.

I shiver even though the room isn't cold. If anything, it's overly warm.

"Are you okay?" Eric asks.

I nod, but my heart aches. What I wouldn't give to have the man I love with me today, to celebrate my sister's marriage, to meet my family, to dance the night away. Even in the midst of so much happiness and joy, grief overwhelms me.

"It's kind of disgusting, isn't it?" Eric asks as he twirls me around on the dance floor after the wedding party is invited to join the bride and groom as they dance to "The Best Is Yet to Come" by Frank Sinatra.

"What is?"

"How perfect they are." He points his chin toward Rob and Camille, who are so caught up in each other, the hundreds of other people in the room might not exist for all they care.

"It's not disgusting. They're perfect for each other."

He pulls back ever so slightly to look down at me with an impish twinkle in his eyes. "You don't think it's the *tiniest bit disgusting* that any two people can be that gorgeous *and* that successful?"

I'll never admit to having had a few of those thoughts myself. "No, of course not. She's my sister. I'm very proud of her—and happy for her."

"Uh-huh. Okay. If you say so."

Why is he trying to bait me? "I say so."

"You don't think it's the *tiniest bit unfair* that they got it all—looks, smarts, true love, great jobs *and* a fab apartment? How much you want to bet they're going to have ugly kids?"

It's such an outrageous statement that I can't contain the gurgle of nervous laughter that erupts from my chest.

"Ah-ha! I knew it! You totally think their kids will be ugly."

"I do not! Don't say that. He's your brother. You're supposed to love him."

"I do love him, but sometimes I want to punch his lights out. Everything comes *so* easily to him. He's never had to really work for anything in his life."

"And you have?"

"I've worked hard for everything I have. Still do."

"What do you do?"

"I spend years researching a single company for the fund I work for, only to be shot down when I bring it to the acquisitions team. Then I have to find another company, spend years working on that proposal and hope it doesn't get shot down, too. I'm one-for-four over three years."

"That sounds rather..."

"Depressing?"

"Is it?"

"It can be. It's a major bummer to invest all that time and effort only to be shot down at committee." He leans in a little closer, again closer than any man has been to me since John left. "I'll let you in on a little secret. Those companies I spend all that time researching?"

I nod, intrigued by his secret.

"I've invested personally in every one of them, and they've yielded *spectacular* results."

"Then the time wasn't wasted."

"Not at all." He gazes down at me, seeming to take a visual inventory of my features in a way that reminds me of John doing the same thing the night we met—and again on the day he walked out of my life. The memory hits me like a punch to the gut, stealing the breath from my lungs. "You're very pretty, but of course you know that."

*The most beautiful girl I ever met.* John's husky, sexy voice pops into my head, and I'm transported right back to the bedroom we painted a light gray, the bed we chose together, the sheets tangled around our bodies as he made fierce love to me, whispering sweet words I've never forgotten.

"Ava? Are you okay?"

Eric's voice startles me, sucking me out of memories I wish I could wallow in. They come less frequently than they used to, and I live in fear of losing them forever at some point.

"Ava?"

I glance up at him, embarrassed to realize he's stopped moving and is looking at me with concern.

"I… I'm sorry."

"I didn't mean to upset you."

"You didn't."

The rest of the wedding party, including the bride and groom, are looking at us, wondering why we aren't dancing the way we're supposed to.

"Let's get a drink," Eric says.

"But the dance…"

"Screw the dance." He takes me by the hand and leads me to one of five bars strategically positioned around the massive ballroom. "What's your pleasure?"

"Just ice water, please."

He orders my water along with bourbon for himself. "Let's get some air."

We take our drinks to a balcony where the warm June breeze is a welcome relief after the stifling ballroom.

"Did I screw up by saying you're pretty?"

"No, of course not." I'm mortified by the episode. Right when I think I'm regaining my footing, a memory of John appears to show me otherwise. Sometimes I think I'm no further along on this journey than I was the day he left.

"Well, just for the record, you *are* very pretty. More than that, really. Gorgeous is a far better word. That was my first thought when I met you at the rehearsal."

"Thank you." He's flirting with me, and I'm so out of practice, I have no idea how to respond.

"You're sure you're okay?"

"I'm better now. It was hot in there."

"Yes, it was. Camille said you just moved back to New York from San Diego. What'd you do out there?"

Fell in love with the most extraordinary man who disappeared from my life five years ago. "I… I worked in PR."

"Is that right? Julianne is in PR. She knows everyone. I bet she can help you find a new job. If you're looking, that is."

"I am, and that'd be great. I have feelers out all over the city, but I have a feeling it's more about *who* you know than what you know here." My goal is to live and work in the city so I can get out of my parents' house in Purchase as soon as possible. After one month at home, I already know I've been gone too long to go back to living at home long-term. My parents are lovely, and they mean well, but they dote on me like I'm twelve rather than twenty-eight, and I'm wounded enough that it would be easy to let them take care of me indefinitely.

"We'll set you up."

He says that with the easy confidence of a man with connections. As the son of the governor, he's probably fat with connections, and I'm not above taking advantage of who his family knows to jumpstart my life in New York City.

After a few minutes outside, we rejoin the party. We're seated together at the head table, where we enjoy a delicious meal of tenderloin and shrimp. Eric entertains me with hilarious stories about growing up Tilden and how their parents had to ban practical jokes between the siblings out of fear of them burning the house down.

Despite the crowded room and the revelry all around us, in some ways I feel like we're on a date by ourselves. He gives me his full attention, except when someone comes up to say hello to him. Then he introduces me as Camille's sister, Ava, and includes me in the conversation. He's charming and fun and funny and handsome, and I'm not sure if it's him or the champagne that has me slightly dazzled, but whatever it is, I'm having more fun than I've had in years.

Mimi, the wedding planner, shows up after dinner with a cordless microphone that she hands to Eric. "You're on."

"Oh crap," he says to me. "I forgot I have to make a speech. What should I say?"

"*Seriously?*"

"Nah," he says, chuckling at my horrified expression. "I got this."

He stands and loudly clears his throat into the microphone. "If I could have your attention, please." When the room goes quiet, he says, "This is the part of the program where the best man is supposed to humiliate the groom with embarrassing stories that make the bride wonder what the hell she was thinking marrying such a jerk."

Laughter ripples through the big room as Rob glares at him.

"Sadly for me and the rest of you, Rob doesn't do embarrassing things. I know… It's not fair and sort of wrong that someone could live to be thirty-two without a truly embarrassing story to his name. But that's our Rob. Focused, brilliant and, despite a startling lack of flaws, fun to be around. And from all accounts, he's found in Camille someone who's just like him." Sobering, he says, "Rob, we've been together a long time."

More laughter follows that statement.

"And even though you're only five minutes older than me, you've been an awesome big brother and best friend. I love you, and on behalf of everyone here, I wish you and Camille the best of everything. Congratulations."

Rob stands to hug his brother while everyone else applauds.

Watching them together makes me feel emotional, which is odd because I'd never met either of them before two days ago. Still, their obvious affection for each other—and the multiple glasses of champagne I've consumed—made it a sweet moment to witness.

"Your turn," Eric says, handing me the mic.

Taking the mic from him, I stand and wobble ever so slightly, cursing the champagne.

Eric's hand on my back steadies me. I give him a grateful smile. "Unlike Rob," I say into the mic, "Camille had an awkward stage."

My sister groans, laughs and drops her face into her hands as her husband puts his arm around her.

"She got a big idea to cut her hair super short right before middle school started. That was an unfortunate decision. She was also the girl who'd come out of the restroom in a restaurant with a trail of toilet paper attached to her foot."

"No!" Camille cried. "You did not just mention the *toilet paper* on my wedding day!"

"That's all I've got," I reply. "Like your husband, you're too freaking perfect and obviously perfectly matched to each other. We can only hope that the six children you're sure to have will be high achievers like their parents."

"Ain't *nobody* having six kids," Camille says, cracking everyone up.

"I just want to say that you're a wonderful little sister and friend. I love you, and I wish you and Rob a lifetime of the kind of joy and happiness you're feeling today."

"Hear, hear." Eric raises his glass to the bride and groom, who're indulging in yet another passionate kiss.

"And," I say, before surrendering the mic, "on behalf of the entire wedding party, I'd like to add one more thing… Get a room. *Please*, get a room."

The comment, fueled by champagne, is met with wild applause from the rest of the wedding party.

"Got one," Rob says with a dirty grin when the ruckus dies down. "Gonna use the hell out of it later."

"Shut *up*, Rob!" Camille cries, punching his chest.

That leads to more kissing.

"Booze," Eric says, standing. "We need more booze."

"Take me with you. Please, take me with you."

"You got it."

# Chapter 2

*Ava*

I'm sloppy drunk. That's the only possible explanation for why I'm slow-dancing with Eric and clinging to him like he's the last lifeboat on the *Titanic*. If there's any upside to being sloppy drunk, I'm too busy laughing and dancing and partying to think about anything other than the massive headache I'm going to have tomorrow.

I should've taken up drinking years ago.

Eric tightens his hold on me, and I sink into his warm embrace. He shed his tuxedo jacket hours ago, and I've discovered he's one of those guys who smells good even when he's sweaty from dancing. I like the way he smells and the way his muscles move under the fine linen of his shirt and the way he seems to realize that if he lets go of me, I'll land in a puddle on the floor. So, he doesn't let go.

I'm not sure exactly when I become aware of the fact that he's hard and his hands are moving on my back with a certain sort of familiarity that doesn't put me off the way it would have before I'd spent a delightful day with him.

His presence comforts me. I felt safe letting go today because I knew he'd be there to catch me if I stumbled, which is crazy since I met him only two days ago. But I already know I can trust him, and letting go feels so good. Tomorrow will be a cold dose of reality, but tonight, anything feels possible.

"Eric..."

"Hmm?"

"I think I'd better call it a night."

"Not yet."

"There's a good chance I might pass out."

Without losing his grip on me, he straightens and takes charge. Although how he can still stand after drinking as much as he did is a mystery that doesn't need solving right now. "All righty, then. Let's get you out of here."

I have no idea how he does it, but Eric manages to half carry me out of the ballroom and into an elevator with minimum fuss. Rob and Camille departed more than an hour ago, so no goodbyes were needed, and no one paid much attention to us leaving together.

At least I hope they didn't…

He props me up in the back corner of the elevator and unleashes a potent smile. "Good?"

"So far, so good." My words are slurring. This is worse than I thought. Please, God, don't let me puke.

Eric watches over me until the elevator dings on the thirtieth floor.

My brain suddenly comes alive. "My purse!"

"Got it," he says, producing it from under his arm.

"You're a lifesaver."

Winking, he says, "Always happy to assist a damsel in distress." He scoops me into his arms, again with hardly any fuss, and carries me down the long hallway.

He's charming, handsome, fun. If I were capable of caring about another man, he'd have my interest. But I'm not capable. I'm barely able to walk, which is why he's carrying me.

"Can you get out your key?"

"Uh-huh." I'm all thumbs as I open the purse and dig out the key from the inside pocket where I stashed it earlier.

Outside my door, he puts me down but doesn't let go. He takes the key from me, opens the door and picks me up again, carrying me inside and placing me on the bed.

The minute I sink into the pillows, the room starts spinning wildly. I sit up quickly—too quickly—and a wave of nausea overtakes me. God, why did I drink so much?

"Are you going to be sick?"

"I really hope not."

"Sometimes it's for the best."

"I never drink."

"I figured as much. Didn't take much to make you tipsy."

I wonder if he's teasing me, but when I glance at him, I see only care and concern. Then he reaches down to help me out of my three-inch heels. He gets up and retrieves a T-shirt I tossed on the bed earlier. "Want to change? I'll help you, and I promise not to look."

Since the dress is tight, I'd love to take it off even if I'm not sure he'll keep his promise not to look. "Yes, please." I turn my back to him, contend with another sickening room spin and wait for him to unzip me. I wrestle my way into the T-shirt before I take his hand to stand and shimmy out of the dress. "Gotta pee." I stagger into the bathroom and manage to take care of business and brush my teeth without falling. I hear Eric talking in the other room, but I can't make out what he's saying.

I leave the bathroom and return to the bed. As I perch on the edge of the mattress, I wish the room would quit spinning.

Eric comes and sits next to me.

"Were you talking to someone?"

"I was ordering up a cure for what ails you. It'll be here momentarily."

"A cure sounds really good."

He nudges my shoulder. "Stick with me, kid. I'll fix you right up."

Because it's there and because I need it, I rest my head on his shoulder, comforted by his presence, his easygoing disposition and his willingness to help me. It's been such a long, lonely time since I could lean on anyone, and as I lean on him, I realize how much I've missed having that.

Then he makes it even better by putting his arm around me.

I luxuriate in his warmth, his strength and the appealing scent of him. I doze off and come to with a start when a doorbell rings. My hotel room has a doorbell. I find that unreasonably funny.

"If I let go, will you fall over?"

"Nope."

"Okay, here goes…" He releases me in increments, making sure I'm steady before he gets up to answer the door.

I hear him exchanging words with the delivery person as the mouthwatering scent of pizza fills the air.

Eric returns carrying a small pizza box, a brown bag and two bottles of water, all of which he puts on the desk. He comes over to the bed, arranges the pillows behind me so I'm sitting upright and helps me get settled. Then he brings me a slice of pizza on a paper plate and opens one of the bottles of water for me. "May I present the time-tested pizza cure?"

I take a bite of the best-tasting cheese pizza I've ever had in my life. I'm not sure if it's because the pizza is that good or it's just that I'm starving, but whatever the reason, I devour that first piece and ask for another.

"Feel better yet?" he asks.

"So much better."

"The pizza cure works every time. The bread acts like a sponge and soaks up the booze."

"Where did you learn of this cure?"

"I was a frat boy in college," he says with a wink and the charming grin that's been unleashed on me repeatedly during our day together. "That's where I learned all the most important life lessons."

I snort out an inelegant laugh. "I'm sure the lessons were memorable."

"Indeed, they were." From the brown paper bag, he produces a bottle of pain meds and shakes two of them into my hand. "Take them and drink all the water."

I follow his directions and settle into the pillows, watching him as he eats the rest of the pizza and guzzles the other bottle of water.

"Thank you." I'm grateful for his cure and his company.

"My pleasure." He wipes his face with the napkin and comes over to stretch out on the bed next to me. What would've been unimaginable only this morning is now comforting and intriguing... The sleeves of his tuxedo shirt were rolled up hours ago to reveal strong forearms with golden-blond hair. "You look much better."

"I *feel* much better. Sorry to be high maintenance."

His laughter transforms his face from handsome to devastating. "You call *this* high maintenance? Sweetheart, you wouldn't know how to be HM if you tried."

I'm rattled by the compliment as much as the term of endearment. "Still... You didn't want to spend your brother's wedding night tending to a sloppy drunk."

He reaches across the mattress for my hand. "My brother's wedding day was one of the best days I've had in a long, long time."

I squeeze his hand. "Me, too." It was the best day I've had in five years, and that's all because of him.

"I'm going to want to see you again, Ava. Would that be okay?"

Would it? Am I ready to start something new with someone other than John? How can I start something new when I still have no idea what became of the man I love? Am I willing to risk another heartbreak, or would I be better off alone?

"Wow," he says on a long sigh. "I didn't expect that to be a complicated question."

"It wasn't. It isn't... I just..."

"Is there someone else?"

Is there? I don't know, and I experience a flashpoint of rage directed at John for doing this to me. How could he leave me in this state of purgatory? How could he have let me fall so deeply in love with him, knowing it was possible he'd have to leave me this way? "No, there's no one else."

"So..." That smile is irresistible, as I'm sure he knows.

"I'd like to see you again." I have no idea what I want from him, but today was fun. I need more fun in my life, and Eric Tilden could be just what I need to jumpstart my new life in New York.

I don't recall falling asleep with Eric, but he's still there when I wake the next morning, feeling surprisingly well rested and refreshed thanks to his miracle cure. He moved closer to me in his sleep, and his arm is stretched across my waist, which means I can't move without disturbing him.

He slept in his clothes on top of the covers, a perfect gentleman when he could've been a typical guy and taken advantage of my drunken state. That he didn't even try earns him big points. I take a closer look at his handsome face, noticing the fine laugh lines around his eyes, the golden whiskers, the strong jawline and the lips that move adorably, as if he's having a conversation with someone as he sleeps.

A frat boy of all things. It's all I can do not to laugh. Most of the frat boys I met in college weren't people I wanted to spend time with. My friends dated a few here and there, and they'd lived up to their reputations. I try not to stereotype people, but most of the frat boys I've met in my life wouldn't have fed a drunk girl pizza to make her feel better.

Eric has great hair, the kind that doesn't require product to look like he just stepped out of a photo shoot. I wonder if it's soft or coarse, and I reach out to touch it.

His eyes open, startling me. For a long, charged moment, he stares at me, and then his face softens when he smiles. "Caught you," he says in a teasing tone, his voice rough from sleep.

I feel my face heat with embarrassment. "You have nice hair."

He twirls a lock of my hair around his finger. "So do you. You have nice everything."

"Are you always this charming first thing in the morning?"

"I do some of my best work first thing in the morning."

He's dangerously appealing. He makes me want things I thought I'd never want again. In one spectacular day, he showed me just how lonely I've been. I'm tired of being lonely and sad. I'm tired of mourning a man who's been gone so long, it's like he never existed. I like Eric and feeling as if I matter to him.

He's still holding my hand when he says, "Do you remember saying you'd like to see me again?"

"I remember." I have no idea if I'm capable of moving forward with someone else, but I had a nice time with him, and I like the way I feel when I'm with him, like someone has my back. I've missed that.

His smile reminds me of a little boy on Christmas who just got everything he asked for from Santa. "My parents are hosting a brunch for the family today. You want to come with me? Camille and Rob will be there, and Amy and Jules, too, so you'll know a few people."

"They won't mind an unexpected guest?"

He kisses the back of my hand. "They won't mind."


When we walk into the room where the brunch is being held, Camille grabs my arm and steers me into a corner. "Tell me the truth. Did you have sex with Eric last night?"

I wrestle my arm free from her tight grip. "No. I didn't have sex with him."

"Amy saw him coming out of your room this morning and told Jules, who told Rob. Welcome to the Tilden family, where nothing is a secret for long."

I'm mortified to have been the subject of family gossip. "I got a little drunk, and he stayed to make sure I was okay. That's all it was." That's all she needs to know, anyway.

She gives me the cagey stare that'll serve her well as a lawyer. "Rob says Eric is into you."

"Okay…" Where is she going with this?

"Are you into him, too?"

"We had a nice time together yesterday, and he helped me out when I got drunk. No need to make it into a middle-school drama."

"I don't mean to do that. But there're things about him… things you should know. If you are into him…"

"What things?"

Camille nods to her mother-in-law, who's waving her new daughter-in-law over to meet someone. "I can't talk about it here. Later." She takes off to deal with her new family, leaving me to wonder what "things" she needs to tell me about Eric.

He's with his brother and some other men, each of them handsome and well-dressed. When his gaze collides with mine, he smiles and waves me over to join them. I cross the room to stand next to him, and he places his hand on my back, a possessive move that has me leaning in a little closer to him. "This is Camille's sister, Ava. Ava, you know my cousin Nate, and these are his brothers Tyler and Justin."

I shake their hands. "Nice to meet you both. Which side of the family are you guys on?"

"Our fathers are brothers," Eric says.

I end up sitting with Eric and six of his male cousins. I learn his father is one of seven brothers, each of whom has at least two sons. The Tilden gene pool has been kind to the men in his family. Eric, the only blond, stands out among his dark-haired cousins, who share his charm and sense of humor. I'm thoroughly entertained by them even as I wonder what Camille will tell me later.

Eric's arm is across the back of my chair, as if he's telling his cousins I'm off-limits. I'm not sure how I feel about that, but I'm having too much fun to quibble about where his arm is. Mrs. Tilden comes over to say hello and zeroes right in on the location of his arm.

"Ava," she says, "I'm so glad you were able to join us."

"Thank you for accommodating a last-minute addition."

"No problem at all. Any friend of Eric's is a friend of ours."

"Easy, Mother." He never loses the affable smile that's so much a part of who he is even as his eyes harden ever so slightly.

Mrs. Tilden squeezes his shoulder. "Nice to see you smiling again, honey." She moves on before he can reply, but the exchange leaves me with more questions.

"Aunt Sarah Beth is looking rather *hopeful*," Jack, another of Eric's cousins, says.

"Aunt Sarah Beth needs to learn to mind her own goddamned business," Eric replies sharply, so sharply it startles me.

"Easy, Skippy," Tyler says. "Now that Rob is married, all the focus shifts to you and Amy. You had to expect that."

Eric turns to me. "Let's get out of here."

Since I came as his guest, I take the hand he offers and follow him from the room, noting Camille's stunned expression as I walk faster to keep up with him. He keeps moving down two flights of stairs to the lobby, where he heads right for the main doors. Once we're outside, he stops, takes a couple of deep breaths and glances at me.

"You want to tell me what just happened there?"

"My mother happened. She drives me nuts."

"You want to walk?" I left my suitcase at the bellman's stand before brunch and can go back for it later. I'm planning to take the Northeast Regional train back to Purchase this afternoon.

"I'd love to walk."

# CHAPTER 3

*Ava*

We stroll up Park Avenue and over to Central Park, past the Wollman ice rink and along winding leafy paths that almost make me forget I'm in the middle of one of the biggest cities in the world. "This is so pretty," I say, breaking a long silence.

The air is filled with the scent of flowers and freshly cut grass and hot dogs, a thought that makes me laugh.

"What's so funny?"

"How this entire city smells like hot dogs."

He laughs along with me. "Yes, I suppose it does. Since we didn't get to eat, you want one?"

"A hot dog for breakfast?"

"Why not? Think of it as hair of the dog—literally."

I laugh at that. "Sure, that actually sounds good."

"Coming right up."

While I take a seat on a bench, he fetches hot dogs for both of us and icy cold bottles of Coke. "Mustard," I tell him when he points to the condiments.

He sits next to me, hands over my hot dog and the soda, and we eat in silence.

"This might be the best hot dog I've ever had," I tell him.

"Street hot dogs are the best. I haven't had one in years."

"Neither have I."

He hands me a napkin that I use to wipe the mustard from my lips, and I think once again how easy he is to be with. I feel like I've known him much longer than two days.

"I was engaged," he says, breaking a long silence.

I'm not sure if I should say something or let him speak. Before I can decide, he continues.

"She ghosted me." He glances at me to gauge my reaction. "You know what that means?"

I shake my head. I'm not familiar with the term.

"She ended our relationship without telling me. She quit her job, moved out of her apartment and basically exited our life together without a single word to me."

I can't contain the gasp that escapes my lips. He probably thinks I'm expressing shock over what was done to him, but what truly shocks me is how similar his situation is to mine.

"Did you ever find out where she went?"

He nods. "Amy and Jules hunted her down, confronted her, got her to admit that she'd met someone else and wasn't sure how to handle me or our family or all the expectations that come with being 'engaged to a Tilden.'" He puts air quotes around those last four words. "They demanded she return the seventy-five-thousand-dollar engagement ring I'd gotten her—and made her pay for the canceled wedding."

"I'm so sorry that happened to you." The hot dog sits like a brick in my belly. I should tell him something similar happened to me, but John didn't "ghost" me. He'd been called to duty in service of our country. He could be dead for all I know. It's not the same thing.

"Thank you."

"Did you love her?"

"I really did. And when she dropped off the face of the earth, I went crazy trying to find her, thinking something awful had happened to her. People covered for her, including people I'd considered friends. They said they didn't know where she was. I called in the NYPD, made a fool of myself looking for a woman who wanted out of our relationship badly enough to fake her own disappearance. Do you know what kind of planning it takes to disappear in the age of social media?"

I swallow hard. Emotion rushes through me, making me feel weak and sick. I should tell him that I understand, that I get how painful it is to lose someone you love with little or no explanation. But I haven't told anyone what happened to me, and I probably ought to tell my sister before I tell her new brother-in-law.

The thought of telling anyone, of having to relive it, makes me dizzy, nauseated and sweaty.

Naturally, Eric notices because he pays attention. "Are you all right?"

"I'm fine." I understand the courage it took for him to share his painful past with me. I can't make it about me. I shake off my emotional reaction so I can focus on him. "What happened just now with your mom?"

"Any time she sees me so much as *talking* to a woman, she gets all excited, thinking this is going to be the one to save me from myself." He gifts me with the lazy grin that would indicate he hasn't a care in the world to anyone who doesn't know better. "I couldn't subject you to that, and I was in no mood for it myself after such a good day yesterday. That was the first really good day I've had since everything happened, and it's all thanks to you."

"It was a good day for me, too."

"I'm glad. If I promise to keep my mother and her expectations far, far away from you, do you still think you might be persuaded to see me again?"

I smile, because he's so adorable and charming. And he's fragile, just like me. "I could be persuaded."

### Camille

I cozy up to my new husband, having raised the armrest between us in the first-class seats. After waiting so long to get to this day, I don't want anything standing between me and Rob. There were times in the last year of finishing law school and planning a wedding while I was in New Haven and he was in the city that I questioned my sanity. But yesterday had made it worth all the sacrifices and sleepless nights. It was the best day of my life.

Rob's head rests against the seat and his eyes are closed, but his hand is wrapped tightly around mine.

We're exhausted after the best kind of sleepless night. We partied with our guests until the wee hours and then went upstairs to our suite and made good use of the king-size bed. Wanting our wedding night to be special, I'd suggested we stop having sex a month ago. Pent-up Rob was a wild man, not that I'm complaining.

I know exactly who I married, and wild or not, he's the right man for me. Of that I've had no doubt since the day we met at the fundraiser for his dad two years ago. We've been together ever since.

We have ambitions, big ambitions, plans we've shared with no one, except his father, who's vowed to help us get where we want to be. Bob Tilden understands ambition. It took him all the way to Albany, but unlike his son, Bob doesn't seem to have higher aspirations for himself. He certainly has them for the eldest of his four children. Yesterday was much more than a wedding. It was a merger of sorts between two New York families that traced their roots back to the *Mayflower*.

Like me, Rob was raised to believe that anything is possible, and we plan to ride the wave of possibility as far as we can. We have a twelve-year plan that includes him running for office within the next two years, and the wheels will begin turning in that direction upon our return from Hawaii.

I'm going to start my career as general counsel to an organization that provides aid to children in crisis.

In pursuit of our goal, I turned down huge offers from major law firms. Rob told me that every move we make will be scrutinized later, so we're determined to make every move count, starting with the job I accepted as a top graduate of Yale Law.

"You could've done better," my dad had said, his disappointment apparent.

Yes, I could've done a lot better, but Rob is paying off my law school loans as a wedding gift. His family has money. Lots of it. Since we don't need to work for a paycheck, we will work toward the goal.

"How about Eric and Ava?" Rob asks, the gruff timbre of his voice indicative of a hangover.

"I know! How cool would that be?"

He opens his eyes and looks over at me. "She won't hurt him, will she?"

"Ava? She's a lamb. She couldn't hurt a fly."

"From the little time I spent with her, she seems very sweet."

"She is very sweet. What you see is what you get with her. Don't worry." Though Ava is three years older than me, I often feel like the elder sister in our relationship. Where Ava is quiet and reserved, I'm outgoing and determined. People have often joked about whether we have the same father, and the jokes have hurt Ava on more than one occasion.

I hate that, because I love my sister, even if I struggled to maintain a relationship with her while she was in San Diego. Now that Ava is back in New York, I hope we can be closer than we've been in the past.

"I do worry about Eric," Rob says. "After what happened with Brittany the bitch, he can't handle another disappointment."

"You're getting a little ahead of things by making them into a couple. They hung out yesterday because they were paired together. That might be all it is."

"Don't forget he spent the night in her room."

"Because she got drunk, and he took care of her. She told me nothing went on, and I believe her. Something happened when she was in San Diego. I don't know what it was, but it was something."

"How do you know?"

"She's different. Quieter, even more reserved than she used to be, which is saying something. I've tried to get her to talk to me about her life out there, but she never would."

"Keep an eye on the situation with Eric, will you? I couldn't bear to see him go through another disaster like Brittany."

"I'll keep an eye on it, but Ava's not a bitch, and she could *never* do something like what Brittany did. You have nothing to worry about. Besides, how much fun would it be if your brother and my sister got together?"

"Lots of fun."

A flight attendant comes by to offer drinks. Rob orders a Bloody Mary.

"That sounds good. Make it two, please."

"Coming right up," the attendant said.

"A little hair of the dog, my love?" I ask him.

"Let's hope it works. I feel like death warmed over."

"Two weeks in Hawaii will fix everything."

He brings our joined hands to his lips. "This is the part I've been most looking forward to."

"Me, too. The wedding was amazing, but the honeymoon…"

He leans in to kiss me. "Will be epic."

# CHAPTER 4

*Ava*

Eric doesn't waste any time asking Julianne to get involved in my job search. A week after the wedding, I've already been on four interviews with top PR firms in the city—two of them I got on my own and two were thanks to her help. The fourth one, the most promising of the interviews I landed on my own, appeals to me the most because one of the partners, Miles Ferguson, lost his fiancée on the *Star of the High Seas*.

If anything, that should make me not want to work there, but I'm drawn to the place like the masochist I've become in the last five years. I'm sure I'll have little to do with Miles if I get the job, but the connection, however fleeting, makes his firm that much more interesting to me.

Yeah, I know… It's insane, but there you have it. I've given up on trying to make sense of how my brain works in my post-John reality.

I text Eric to thank him again for his help and ask if I can buy him a drink while I'm in town.

He replies right away. *Happy to help, and I'd love to meet you. Where do you want to go?*

*I have no idea. You tell me.*

He suggests a hot spot in the Financial District, and we agree to meet in an hour when he finishes work.

With a little time to kill before I have to head downtown, I duck into Bloomingdale's to check out a big sale on suits. I'm elated to find two that I could never normally afford, one red and the other black. I ask the clerk to bag rather than hang them, so I can carry them on the train home without a hassle.

We've nearly completed the transaction when I notice the pin on the saleswoman's lapel that indicates she lost someone on the *Star of the High Seas*. Right in the middle of a rather great day is a reminder that sucks the air from my lungs and brings tears to my eyes, the reaction as involuntary as the ache in my chest. "I'm sorry for your loss," I say when I recover the ability to speak.

The clerk reaches up to touch the pin, caressing it lovingly. "My parents," she says softly. I figure her to be roughly my age. My heart breaks for her.

With her eyes full of tears, she gets busy folding and bagging my new suits.

I want to ask if she's okay, if she has a support system, if she has people who love her. I want to know who her parents were. I'm sure I've read their story. I've read every word ever published about the unbearable tragedy. I don't ask any questions as I take the bag from her. "Thank you."

"Have a nice day."

"You do the same."

The encounter rocks me and reminds me of why John had to leave. It was for people like the sales clerk and her parents. In the first few months, the memorial pins were produced and sold by the family member survivor group, which raised money for a memorial to the victims that has yet to be built. Infighting among the group about how the victims should be remembered has slowed the process. I've read every word about that, too.

From the beginning, I've made a point to stay up-to-date on the investigation, the war that was declared on the Al Khad terrorist group that claimed responsibility and the survivor group struggling to cope with staggering loss. I still scour the internet every day for news of the war, hoping to catch a glimpse or a clue or anything to tell me what became of John. But there's never been anything. Not one single thing.

My elation over the deal on the suits is long gone as I trudge to the corner to flag down a cab. I wish now that I hadn't made plans with Eric. I just want to go home. However, I can't blow him off after everything he's done to help me, so I give the cab driver the address of the bar and try to find my game face. You'd think by now I'd be an expert at pretending to be fine when I'm anything but.

At times, I wonder if I'll ever be fine again, or if there will always be a cloud hanging over my life, an asterisk next to my name. I also wonder if there are other people like me out there somewhere who have no idea what's become of the men and women they love. Unlike the families of the victims, there's no group for me to join. I've walked this journey alone and will continue to do so, no matter where that journey might take me.

With my forehead pressed against the cab's window, I watch the city go by in flashes of light and glass and stone and people. So many people. Why can't one of them be the man I love?

Tears roll down my cheeks, making me feel weak and powerless, the way I did for so long after he first left. I don't cry over him as much as I used to, and when I get low enough for tears, I can usually expect a rough couple of days.

As we get closer to the cross street Eric told me to look for, I make an attempt to pull myself together, to wipe away the tears, to repair my makeup, to put on that game face. I brush my hair and apply lipstick, hoping I'll appear cheerful and upbeat. I can pretend for a few hours, until I can be alone again with my memories and my grief.

Dragging the shopping bag behind me, I enter the crowded bar. On the way through the throng of happy-hour revelers, I note polished wood and brass, mirrors and velvet-covered barstools. I scan the faces of young, attractive, ambitious professionals, but I don't see Eric among them. I'm about to turn around to leave when hands land on my shoulders and the familiar scent of his cologne fills my senses.

"Here I am." His voice is comforting and familiar. He takes the shopping bag out of my hand and steers me to the back corner, which is all but deserted. Apparently, no one wants to be back here, preferring to see and be seen in the front.

"I feel like I just passed an endurance test," I say to him as we take seats at a table.

His grin lights up his face.

I'd forgotten just how handsome he is. The navy suit he wears fits him as if it was cut just for him, which it probably was. He's the picture of up-and-coming success, and I'm happy to see him. Happier than I expected to be.

"You passed the Wall Street happy-hour test."

"Is that a thing?"

"It could be an Olympic sport. Lots of business gets accomplished in these places."

"Lots of hookups, you mean."

"Those, too," he says with the easy grin that I remember from the wedding. Despite the heartbreak he suffered at the hands of his ex, he's still quick to smile, to joke, to appreciate life's lighter moments. I admire that he can be lighthearted. For the first two years after John left, I didn't smile or laugh about anything.

"What can I get you?" a frazzled waiter asks as he plops a bowl of Chex Mix on the table.

"Bourbon for me and...?" Eric crooks a brow at me.

"A cosmo, please." Why not? I'm not driving. Then I hear John's distinctive voice: *Go big or go home.* I wish I could tell him and that sexy voice to leave me alone.

"The interview went well?" Eric asks, diving into the bowl of Chex Mix.

"Really well. If they make me an offer, I think I'll go with them. They're working on some fun projects."

"Like what?" he asks with genuine interest.

I give him a rundown on the hip clients the firm represents, from bakeries to five-star restaurants to Broadway actors and actresses, one of the country's hottest comedians and a celebrity chef who made himself into a household name by appearing on a cooking competition that scored huge ratings last summer.

"That's like a who's-who of pop culture," Eric says.

"I know! How much fun would that be?" It's the kind of job I could throw myself into, and that's what I need. "Plus, the salary is decent enough that I could live in the city if I can find a roommate."

He snaps his fingers. "Speaking of that..." Withdrawing a piece of paper from a pocket inside his suit coat, he hands it to me.

I unfold a flyer created by a woman with an apartment in Tribeca who's looking for a roommate.

"I saw that on the board at work and grabbed it for you."

"You're supposed to grab one of the tabs at the bottom, not the whole thing."

"If I hadn't taken the whole thing, the place would be gone already. You should call her."

"I haven't got the job yet."

"You'll get something soon." He nods to the paper. "Go for it. We'd be neighbors."

I like the idea of living near him, this new friend who's been so kind to me in the short time I've known him. I pick up my phone and dial the number the woman listed and wait for her to pick up.

"Hello?"

"Um, hi, I'm calling about the apartment. Is it still available?"

"It is. Some asshole took my flyer at work, so I haven't gotten any calls."

It's all I can do not to lose it laughing. "Oh, well, my friend took a photo of it and sent it to me."

Eric's eyes dance with mischief that makes me smile along with him.

"Can you tell me more about it?"

She describes a two-bedroom loft with a shared bathroom, living room and kitchen. "It's nothing special, but we have an elevator and a doorman, *and* there's a gym and laundry in the building." She tells me her name is Skylar, she's a first-year attorney at Eric's company, and her roommate moved in with her boyfriend, leaving her in the lurch.

She asks what I do. I tell her I'm job-hunting but getting close to landing something, and after some friendly back-and-forth, she says, "Are you interested?"

"I'll take it." Maybe I'm being impulsive, but it feels good to be moving forward, especially after the setback I suffered earlier. Besides, I have some money saved, at least enough for three months' rent. If I don't have a job at the end of three months, I'll have bigger issues than whether I can pay my rent.

"Oh, that's great. I was worried about swinging the rent by myself."

I hope I haven't made a huge mistake committing to the apartment before I land a job or even see the place, but I have a good feeling about this. Good feelings have been in short supply in my life of late, so I'm running with this one.

"I'm on the lease, so you can send me a check for the first month's rent and move in whenever you want. Just let me know when. I'll get you keys and clear it with the super."

I thank her, we say our goodbyes, and I end the call.

Eric raises his glass. "Welcome to the neighborhood."

I touch my glass to his. In the ten minutes we've been together, he's made me feel better—again. I could get used to this, a thought that scares me as much as it excites me. "Thank you."

"I like to see you smile. You're even prettier when you smile."

I like the effortless, charming way he flirts with me, even if my better judgment warns me to proceed with caution.

"How was your day?" I ask him.

"Actually, it was very good. I pitched a new client to the acquisition committee, and they seemed far more interested than they usually are."

"When will you know?"

"Next few days."

"Ugh, the waiting must be *torture*."

"I try not to get too wound up about it. I get paid whether they take on the client or not." He grabs another handful of Chex Mix. "That helps me to keep it in perspective."

"Still, it would be nice to score a win."

"It'd be very nice." He leans in closer to me, so close I feel his breath brush against my cheek.

I break out in goose bumps.

"If I score a win, will you help me celebrate?"

I shoot him a playful look. "Depends on what this celebration entails."

"Dinner, dancing, drinks. Somewhere fancy with candles and cloth napkins."

I'm utterly charmed by him, and I find myself rooting for a win so we can celebrate together. "That sounds lovely."

"*You* are quite lovely." He tucks my hair behind my ear, and for a brief, terrifying second, I think he might kiss me.

But he doesn't.

And when he backs off, I'm caught between regret and relief. That's when I realize Eric Tilden poses a threat to the heart I've patched back together, and I need to be very careful where he's concerned.

"I'm starving," he announces when he finishes off the bowl of Chex. "Want to get dinner?"

I'd planned to go home and do my nightly scour of the news sites, looking for any sign of John. But more time with Eric is much more appealing than that dreadful task. "I'd love to."

# CHAPTER 5

*Ava*

Two weeks later, Eric, Rob, Camille, Amy and Jules help me move into my new apartment in Tribeca. I got the job I wanted and am due to start at FergusonMain on Monday. As I can't bring my car into the city, my parents drive me in, along with the possessions I brought home with me from San Diego. I stash the priceless boxes full of John's belongings in my bedroom closet and try to forget about them.

If Eric is curious after I insist on carrying them in myself, he doesn't say so.

Skylar already has living room furniture, so I decide to keep my things from San Diego, including the bed I shared with John, in storage for now and buy a new bed for my room. New home, new beginnings, new bed. If my heart breaks a little at the thought of starting over without him, I stuff those feelings into a box inside my heart and seal it up so I can continue moving forward rather than dwelling on the painful past.

When I'm unpacked and settled in, my parents head back to Purchase, and Camille suggests the rest of us hit the town for dinner and drinks. I invite Skylar to join us. I've gotten to know her by text over the last few weeks and have learned she's focused on her job to the point of distraction. Tonight is no exception.

"I wish I could," she says, eyeing Eric with barely concealed interest that rankles me for reasons I don't dare explore too closely. Apparently, they've never met at the firm where they both work. She's tall and striking, with dark hair and eyes. "I have a huge presentation on Monday that I'm in no way prepared for. I need every minute of this weekend. But you have fun."

We say our goodbyes and take the stairs to the street level, making more noise than we probably should. The Tildens are a rowdy bunch, and my sister fits right in with them. She and Rob are tanned and happy after their Hawaiian honeymoon and still can't keep their hands off each other for more than a few minutes at a time.

We bring up the rear, behind Rob and Camille. Eric nudges my shoulder, nods to bring my attention to Rob's hand on his wife's ass and rolls his eyes dramatically. *Get a room*, he mouths.

I cover my mouth so I won't laugh out loud and nudge him in the ribs. "Stop it."

"I don't have to." He's been flying high after the firm's acquisitions committee approved his latest recommendation. Camille told me he earns a big bonus for a successful recommendation. He hasn't said anything about that to me. In the weeks since we had dinner, we've chatted by text almost every day.

I've learned that he's as witty and entertaining by text as he is in person, and I've found myself looking forward to hearing from him. I appreciate that he didn't doggedly pursue me after our first memorable weekend together. Rather, he's allowed a comfortable friendship to develop between us, one text at a time. I've tried not to read too much into the flirtatious banter or the time he spends texting me, but I like knowing that behind the texts is a man who is also familiar with deep pain.

As much as I'd never wish something like what he went through on anyone, it puts us on somewhat of a level playing field, even if he doesn't know what happened to me, and never will if I have anything to say about it. Part of me feels like I'm being unfair to him, especially after he told me about Brittany. But I'm accustomed to not talking about John, and I prefer it that way.

At the beginning of our relationship, John told me that due to the sensitive nature of his job, it would be better if I didn't tell people about us. I gladly went along with that because I loved existing inside the bubble with him. I kept my family away by going home a few times a year so they wouldn't feel the need to come visit me, and I didn't talk about him with anyone.

With hindsight and tons of research into the lives of Special Forces officers, I realize he was probably part of a unit that wasn't supposed to have romantic entanglements, and that's why he asked for my discretion. That's just another reason to be infuriated with him and the web he drew me into, knowing it was possible he might have to disappear from my life, perhaps permanently. I wish I could hate him for that. It would make everything so much easier. But I don't hate him. Quite the opposite.

Eric nudges me out of my thoughts. "Where'd you go?"

I look up to see we've walked ten blocks from my apartment. "Nowhere. I'm here."

"Everything okay?"

"Of course." My new life is falling into place. I have no reason to be anything other than thrilled by my new apartment, new job and new friends, all of which were the goals when I left San Diego. But I'm learning that even though I left our old life behind, I brought John with me. There's no leaving him behind, as much as I wish I could.

"Sometimes you seem so sad, Ava," Eric says, his voice low so he won't be heard by anyone but me. "I wish I knew why."

His astute observation rattles me. "I…"

"It's okay." He puts his arm around my shoulders. "You don't have to explain yourself to anyone, least of all me."

I appreciate him more than he could ever know, and when he keeps his arm around me as we walk toward Times Square, I don't try to shake him off. Why would I when I enjoy being around him so much?

As always, Times Square is a mob scene, and we briefly get separated from the others. I'm trying to spot them in the crowd when my eye is drawn to a crawler with the day's headlines. In bright red letters, I read, "David Dawkins, who lost his daughter and new son-in-law on *Star of the High Seas*, and family group file suit against the federal government as well as former National Security Advisor

Kent Hartley and several other former government officials, claiming they ignored a terror threat in weeks before attack."

I stop walking so I can keep reading. "Dawkins, the outspoken leader of the SHS family group, says the suit is a class action that seeks answers on behalf of the more than fifteen thousand immediate family members impacted by the terrorist attack on the cruise ship that left four thousand people dead."

I've read about Dawkins. Three days before the ship was attacked, he walked his only child down the aisle at her wedding. From the beginning, his story and that of so many other family members touched me deeply and has stayed with me ever since.

"Ava?"

I look over at Eric and blink him into focus. I can't believe I forgot where I am and who I'm with as the report about Dawkins takes me right back to day one of the nightmare.

"Are you okay?" Eric's brow furrows with concern as he takes note of what I'm staring at. "What did it say?"

I force the emotion aside and try to sound matter-of-fact in my reply. "Dawkins and the other *Star of the High Seas* families are filing a class action against the government and several former federal officials."

"Oh, damn. On what grounds?"

"They've been claiming for years that the government ignored a credible terror threat in the weeks before the attack. They're going after people who would've been in the know at the time."

Eric's deep sigh says it all. "Did you know anyone on the ship?"

I shake my head. "Didn't matter, though. I've been obsessed with it ever since it happened."

"My college roommate lost his brother-in-law and sister-in-law. It was so horrible for their family."

"So many people were affected by it. When we were kids, my parents took us on cruises all the time. And now..."

"You wouldn't step foot on a cruise ship if your life depended on it," he says bluntly.

"Right."

"Me either. I've only been on one, years ago with our grandparents. I felt confined and queasy the whole time. Never wanted to go again."

I tell myself that it doesn't count as a lie, because what I've told him is true. We did go on cruises every year growing up. My mother is a travel agent who once specialized in cruise vacations and got freebies all the time from the various cruise lines. Her business was decimated by the attack, and she changed her focus to European and Asian vacation packages in the last few years.

Eric doesn't need to know I have a whole other reason for being devastated by the *Star of the High Seas* tragedy.

Again, he puts his arm around me as we navigate the crowds in Times Square. I assume he knows where we're going, so I let him lead me. It's astounding to me that no matter what I do or where I go, the grief and sorrow still find me. All it took this time was seeing Dawkins' name and the news of the lawsuit to interrupt what had been another good day.

Will it always be this way? Is there no escaping it no matter what I do? Sometimes I feel like I'm inside a gilded cage as I lead my nice, quiet, safe life, but I'm surrounded by bars that keep the grief trapped with me. It's always there, no matter what I'm doing, who I'm with or how desperately I wish to put the past behind me so I can get on with the future.

John told me every day we were together that he loved me more than anything. If he truly loved me, *how* could he do this to me? Tears sting my eyes, and it takes everything I have to fight through the emotional overload. I'm done crying over him.

"You still want to go?" Eric asks, tuned in to my struggle.

I force a smile for him and curl my hand around his arm. "Of course. I'm celebrating a new apartment and a new job and your victory at work."

"You know," he says tentatively, "I really hope we're going to be very good friends, and friends are there for each other in good times and in bad. I'd hate to think you were suffering over something and didn't feel that you could lean on your good friend Eric."

In five long, lonely years, I've never been more tempted to unload on anyone than I am with him in this moment. But something stops me… I'm so accustomed to keeping John to myself, and Eric's brother is married to my sister. If Eric were to mention it to Rob… Within minutes, my entire family would be involved, and I just can't have that.

"I appreciate that more than you know."

"It's a standing offer."

"You're a good guy, Eric Tilden."

"Thanks," he says with a small smile. "I've had reason to wonder if I'm as good as I think I am."

We arrive at our destination, a funky contemporary restaurant and bar with an A rating and a name I can't pronounce.

I stop him from going in with a hand to his arm. "Don't let her do that to you. She's not worth it."

"No, she certainly isn't." He holds the door and gestures for me to go in ahead of him. "Let's drink."

Hours later, Eric and I stumble back to Tribeca, laughing, singing off-key and generally acting like fools. Once again, I wonder why I didn't turn to alcohol a long time ago, because it provides a temporary respite from my troubles. I've had the best time tonight. I've felt normal again, like I did at the wedding, and that's due in large part to Eric and his thoughtful attention to me.

That attention didn't go unnoticed by the others. Eric's siblings are cautiously optimistic about what they see happening between us, whereas Camille is like a bull in a china shop, cornering me in the ladies' room to ask if we're officially seeing each other. I had to let her down easy and tell her we're just friends, but I could tell she didn't totally buy that.

"He likes you," she said. "A lot."

"I like him, too."

"Sooooo…"

"Do me a huge favor, will you? Please leave us alone. If something is going to happen, it will. If everyone is on us about it, that makes me less interested in him."

"I don't get why you have to be so private and hush-hush about everything." Three vodka tonics loosened her tongue. "I know something happened to you in San Diego, but you never talk about it, not even to me. That kind of hurts me, Ava."

"I'm a private person. That's the way I've always been, and it's not intended to hurt you or anyone else."

"So, what're you and Camille fighting about?" Eric asks as we walk arm in arm on the way home. He seems to know where we're going, which is good, because I'm clueless.

Surprised by the question, I say, "We aren't fighting."

"Seemed that way to me, and Rob said something, too. You guys came back from the bathroom bringing obvious tension."

"Truthfully, she was bugging me about you, and I told her to cut it out."

"Ahhh, I wondered if she'd done that, because her husband was all over me while you were in the bathroom. Amy and Jules told him to back off and leave me alone."

"That's basically what I said to Camille, and she didn't take it well."

"Their intentions are good."

"I guess. I'm sure it's exciting for them that we met at their wedding and have become friends, but they need to take a step back and give us room to breathe." I no sooner say the words than I trip over a crack in the sidewalk.

Eric stops me from taking a bad fall by wrapping his arms around me and pulling me into his embrace.

I look up at him as he looks down at me with care and concern that I want to wallow in. He's just so damned sweet.

"Are you okay?"

"Uh-huh. Sorry about that."

"I'm not."

For a second, I think he's going to kiss me. I hold my breath, not sure if I want him to. But the moment passes. He clears his throat and tightens one arm around me, directing me toward home. At least I think that's where we're going.

A few blocks later, I see my building. At the bottom of the stairs, I turn to him. "Thanks for walking me home."

"My pleasure. You going to be all right, or do you need the emergency pizza cure?"

"I'm totally stuffed from dinner." We had sushi and delicious Asian-fusion cuisine.

"Go out with me tonight."

For a second, I'm confused, but then I realize it's after two in the morning.

"Just us." He tucks a strand of my hair behind my ear and caresses my cheek. His touch gives me goose bumps. "You promised me a celebration if I scored a win at work, so technically, you owe me."

"You're calling me out on a technicality?" I ask, teasing.

"Whatever it takes to get you to go out with me." There's nothing teasing about the intense way he looks at me.

"I did promise to help you celebrate."

"Yes, you did. Tonight, then?"

"What time?"

"Eight?"

"That works. What should I wear?"

"Let's get dressed up."

"Okay."

He leans in and kisses my cheek. "I'll wait until you get inside."

As I go up the stairs, I'm breathless from the brush of his lips against my face. I greet the doorman as he lets me in.

When I turn back, Eric waves from the sidewalk.

In the elevator, I'm giddy from the alcohol and looking forward to seeing him again. It's been so long since I had anything to look forward to, and now there're so many things—my new job, my new city, my new friends. One new friend, in particular…

Inside the apartment, I move around quietly so I won't disturb Skylar. I use the bathroom, go into my room and close the door. I withdraw my phone to send a text to Camille.

*Sorry to be bitchy earlier. I know you're just curious, and that's ok, but give us a little room, please? If there's anything to tell you, I will. When I can.*

It's late, and the text goes unread for now. I'm sure she'll reply when she sees it. We don't usually let shit fester between us, and I want to be closer to her now that we live near each other for the first time in a decade.

In bed, I scroll through my Twitter feed and gasp at the sight of an AP headline: SEAL Team Ambushed in Pakistan. I click on the link and devour every word of the story, which includes the dreadful news that two US service members have been killed. My heart sinks, and I'm filled with sadness, knowing that two families will soon receive dreaded news. It'll be ten to twelve hours, if not longer, before their names and photos are released to the public after their families are notified. I know this because I've had to endure that wait every time I've read about a dead American service member overseas for five long years now.

I know I'd be better off to avoid the news, and I've tried many times in the past to quit my obsessive scouring of the headlines. The most I've lasted is a full day before I'm back at it, watching, surfing, reading, devouring anything and everything about the ongoing effort to bring down Mohammad Al Khad, elusive mastermind behind the attack, and his terrorist organization.

I know more about US Special Forces and Special Operations than most civilians ever will. I've thoroughly researched Navy SEALs as well as Army Green Berets, Rangers and Night Stalkers. I've discovered a dazzling number of units John could've been attached to but have narrowed his branch to the Marines or Navy, as both have units that deploy out of San Diego. I know it's somewhat unbelievable that I don't know which branch of the service he was in or that he didn't tell me, but we never talked about his work. And by never, I do mean *never*. The only time I saw him in uniform was the night we met, and the details of the fatigues he wore that night have grown fuzzy over the years. I don't know if they were Navy fatigues or Marine Corps.

This is another thing I've realized with hindsight was strategic on his part. The less I knew, the better as far as he was concerned. It was fine by me, because I didn't like to think about the possibility of him having to deploy for longer than a week or two here and there, which happened frequently during our two years together.

My research has also yielded hints of groups within the military so secret that there's literally no information anywhere about them, which has me thinking John is involved at that level. I have no way to know if he's still alive, or if he's attached to one of these top-secret units. A long time ago, I had to accept that I may never know for sure. After years of scouring the internet, Pentagon websites and other military-related sites, I've never gotten the first clue as to what these groups are called, let alone how to find a military member who might be attached to one of them.

I've learned that service members are fiercely loyal to their branches, and that if John was a Marine, he might've had a Semper Fi tattoo or sticker on his truck. He had neither. I didn't hear the term Semper Fi until long after he was gone.

I blame myself for not paying closer attention, but mostly I blame him for leaving me in this torturous state of limbo. And as I pass a sleepless night, waiting for the Pentagon to identify the latest fallen service members, it's clear to me that while I might've changed my address, I've brought the nightmare with me, and I'll never be able to fully escape it.

# CHAPTER 6

*Ava*

I wake to my phone buzzing under my face. I fell asleep on top of the covers, and the air conditioning has me shivering. Pulling a blanket up and over me, I reach for the phone and read a text from Camille in response to mine from last night.

*It's okay. Rob is worried about Eric bc he seems to really like you. He's been through a lot...*

I shouldn't encourage this friendship or flirtation or whatever it is with Eric. Camille is right—after what happened with his ex, the last thing he needs is to get involved with me when my life is such a mess. Except being with him is fun and easy, and his obvious interest in me makes me feel special after being alone for such a long time. I like him. I like him *a lot.*

Staring up at the ceiling, I think about the time I've spent with Eric and how he makes me laugh. I remember the way he cared for me when I had too much to drink at the wedding and stayed with me, risking gossip from his family, to make sure I was okay during the night. After witnessing the way his mother reacted to us being together at the brunch, I have a new appreciation for the sacrifice he made to spend that night with me.

I ought to text him and tell him I can't go out with him tonight, that it wouldn't be fair for me to allow him to get involved with someone who's as messed up as I am. But as the day progresses, I never send that text. I want to see him. I want to feel the way I do when I'm with him. I like the attention he gives me, the way he listens when I speak and how he watches over me. Maybe it's wrong to allow this to happen, but I'm so tired of being alone. Eric makes me *feel* again, and God help me, I don't have the strength to turn my back on him.

During that torturous day, I decide it may finally be time to seek out therapy to deal with everything that's happened. I haven't done that before now because it was too painful to think about, let alone talk about to a stranger. But last night made me see that the only thing that's changed since I left San Diego is my address. If I'm truly to have a chance at a whole new life here, I need help.

As I straighten my hair, I study the reflection of the woman staring back at me. Her eyes are haunted, her brows furrowed and her mouth pinched by the strain of grief that's taken an awful toll. It would've been easier, I know, if John had been killed. At least then I'd have answers. But this endless purgatory has added years to my face that weren't there when I met him.

Accepting that I can't continue to do this alone comes with overwhelming relief. Tomorrow, I'll try to find someone who can help me and take that first important step toward true healing. It's long overdue. Tonight, however, I have a date to look forward to with a fun, funny, handsome, sweet man, and I'm going to push aside the grief and despair and allow myself to enjoy the time with him.

I've certainly earned the right to enjoy myself again.

*Eric*

I like her more than I probably should, especially in light of my recent history with women—or I should say *one* woman in particular. Ava is hesitant and a little skittish and deeply troubled by something she hasn't shared with me. I've had to resist the temptation to ask Camille if she knows what's up with her sister. I suspect Camille has been so absorbed in finishing law school and planning a wedding that she hasn't noticed her sister is troubled.

But I've noticed. The day she met me for a drink after work? She'd been crying. She said it was allergies, but allergies don't leave a person looking as devastated as she looked when we met at that bar.

I've always been a perceptive kind of guy. I see things others don't. Sometimes I wonder if I missed my calling. I should've been a globe-trotting TV news reporter. As an astute people-watcher and more than casual observer of the human race, I think I would've been good at that. But I'm too much of a homebody to travel the way I'd have to for that career. I like being around my friends and family—most of them, anyway—and my current career keeps me close to my siblings and friends.

The first time I met Ava, I *saw* the pain she tries so hard to keep hidden from others. It may as well have been lit up in blinking neon: This girl is suffering. Naturally, being the masochist that I am where women are concerned, her suffering sparked my curiosity. The fact that she's simply stunning didn't hurt anything, but that's almost secondary to my desire to know what happened to her.

I sniffed around a bit with Rob and Camille when they were first home from their honeymoon. Walking the careful line between showing too much interest and trying to find out more about her, I tried to bring it up casually when I had dinner with them, Amy and Jules the day after they got back.

As I put on a gray suit for my night out with Ava, I think back to that dinner with my siblings, which was before Ava moved to the city from her parents' home in Purchase.

Camille gave me the perfect opening when she said Ava and I seemed to hit it off at the wedding.

"We did," I said. "We had a great time." I didn't mention that I'd been texting with her regularly since the wedding because that's no one's business but hers and mine.

"I *loved* her," Jules said over sushi and fancy drinks at a midtown place Amy recommended. "*Such* a fun girl."

Our youngest sister likes everyone—literally every person in the world. She's never had an enemy or met anyone she didn't want to befriend, from homeless people on the street to millionaire clients. Jules has the kindest heart I've ever experienced, and because of that, the rest of us worry endlessly about her safety. Fortunately, along with her compassion is a healthy dose of street smarts—and pepper spray Rob bought her attached to her keychain—that keep us from losing sleep over her.

"You think you'll see her again?" Rob asked casually.

A word about my "older" brother here—he doesn't do anything casually, so there's nothing *casual* about his probing question.

"Of course I will," I told him. "Her sister is married to my brother. I expect I'll see lots of her."

Rob scowled at me. Most people don't see right through him, but his siblings always do.

"Leave him alone, Rob," Amy said, sipping from an overly full martini glass. "The last thing he needs is everyone up in his grill because he had a good time at your wedding."

"Thank you, Amy." I raised my beer mug in tribute to her. They'd made fun of me for ordering a beer when the rest of them went the fancy cocktail route. I had stuff to do the next day, and beer never leaves me feeling like shit after a night out. I adore bourbon, but beer and I are *old* friends. "What's her story, anyway?" I asked Camille, in the same casual tone, only mine was much more effective than his because Camille took the bait.

"I'm sure she told you she's lived in San Diego since she left for college and only recently moved home. She's hoping that's very temporary because my parents are super excited to have one of us back at home. They're giving her a little *too* much attention, and after ten years on her own, they're going to quickly drive her nuts."

None of this information was new to me. Ava told me this much herself.

"No serious boyfriends?" Amy asked, glancing at me with a knowing look in her eye.

I appreciated her saving me the trouble of having to decide if I was willing to ask that question.

"None that I know of, but Ava is super private. She never said much about her life out there, and I was too busy with law school to pry. All I know is she wants to find a job and an apartment in the city."

"I put out some feelers with my contacts for her," Jules said. "She'll find something soon."

"Thanks for that," Camille said. "I'd love to have her living close to us."

I want that, too, not that I shared that thought with them. I've learned to hold my cards close around my overly involved family. I failed to do that with Brittany. I was so crazy about her, I wanted the whole world to know. Think Tom Cruise on Oprah's sofa after he met Katie Holmes. That was me with Brit. After waiting my whole life for *the one*, I went all in like a madman on steroids.

Months after the disaster, I still miss her and actively hate myself for that. More than anything, I miss the *feeling* that had me higher than I've ever been in my life. But I've learned that when you're higher than you've ever been, the crash is that much more excruciating.

In thirty-two blessed years, I'd never been disabled by grief or disappointment, but I was after she left me—or, I should say, after she *ghosted* me. To this day, I can't get my head around how someone could do that to the person they've professed to love. It boggles my mind. And when I think about the way I freaked out trying to find her, calling in the police and sounding the alarm with everyone we knew… I shudder as a wave of nausea has me wondering if I'm going to be sick—again. I've puked more since she left me than I did in my whole life before her.

Only after Amy and Jules tracked her down and came back with the true story did I fall into the deep pit of true despair. Before then, I'd had hope to cling to. Surely there had to be an explanation that made sense. I'd pictured her in a hospital suffering from a head injury that had stolen her memory. What other reason could there be for seven days without a word from the woman I loved?

Turns out there was a reason, and after I heard it painfully delivered by my sisters, I went underground for a full month. I didn't go to work or leave my apartment even once. I refused to talk to my siblings, my friends, my parents… The only one I wanted no longer wanted me. What else did I need to know? Luckily, my employers value my contributions, so I didn't lose my job, but even if I had, I wouldn't have cared. I was lower than I've ever been, and nothing as trivial as losing my job could bring me lower.

I haven't been out with anyone since disaster struck eight months ago. I haven't wanted to—until I met Ava at the wedding. Since then, I find myself thinking about her quite frequently, which is a welcome relief. The more I think about her, the less time there is to dwell on Brittany and the mess she made of my otherwise charmed life.

Adjusting my gray suit coat over the white dress shirt I've worn without a tie, I try to mentally prepare myself for my first real date after the worst breakup in modern history. With Ava's sister married to my brother, there's too much at stake to risk taking a step with her that I'm not ready for. I'm ready for this, or I wouldn't have asked her. I wish I'd met Ava before Brittany did a number on me. I think Ava would've liked the guy Eric Tilden was before Brittany Kerns ruined him.

The new Eric Tilden is cautious and jaded and cynical. This Eric will never again put himself in a position to be flattened by a woman. The days of jumping on sofas are over forever for this guy. Funny enough, I don't miss sex, and I used to have a lot of it, before Brittany and with her. Since she left me, I've lost interest. It's like my sex drive shriveled up and died along with my heart. She broke me in more ways than one.

I dab on a hint of cologne—something I've never worn before, because I got rid of everything that reminded me of Brittany—clothes, cologne, music and the bed I shared with her. I destroyed every photo of her and us together. I threw out clothing she left at my place—even the five-hundred-dollar jeans she treasured—and smashed the turntable she gave me for our first Christmas into a thousand pieces before I dumped it down the trash chute in my building. I wanted nothing of her left in my life, and I succeeded in purging her from my home. If only I could do the same with my memories.

I'd like to invent a device that can rid your brain of things you no longer want or need to remember. Wouldn't that be something? A way to wipe clean the hard drive and reboot your internal system. Sign me up. I'd willingly volunteer my brain to develop such a thing, especially if it meant I'd never have another thought about Brittany for the rest of my life.

"We're not thinking about her tonight," I remind myself. "Tonight is for Ava. Brittany is dead to us." *Keep saying it, old man. Keep saying it until you succeed in purging her from your brain the same way you've gotten rid of her in your home.*

I grab my wallet, phone and keys off the kitchen counter and head out to pick up Ava, determined to look forward rather than backward. I want to get to know her better. I want her to trust me with whatever haunts her, but that's not going to happen overnight. If she's never told her sister, what makes me think she'll tell me?

Maybe she won't, but that doesn't mean I'm not going to try to get to know her. I have a feeling she might be worth the effort.

If someone had asked me before my brother's wedding—which I'd been dreading, by the way—if I was ready to get back to dating, I would've said no way. I had zero interest in anything having to do with women or dating. In fact, before the wedding, I might've replied that I'd rather have a vasectomy without painkillers than go out with a woman, and it would've been the truth. But then I met Ava, and suddenly, I was intrigued by a woman again.

Not that I'm looking to plunge into another relationship. Not even kinda. I like Ava, and I enjoy spending time with her. That's all this is, I tell myself as I walk the short distance from my place to hers. It's a diversion. Something to do. A new friend to get to know.

Another thing I like about spending time with Ava is that she doesn't know Brittany, didn't know me with her and doesn't look at me with sympathy or empathy or pity the way everyone else in my life does. I'm tired of being on the receiving end of everyone's good intentions. Even the people I work with, the fucking *partners*, for God's sake, know what happened to me, and I hate that. But that's what happens when you take an unscheduled month out of work. The bosses find out your fiancée ghosted you, and everyone feels terrible for you.

It's time to rewrite the narrative but to proceed with utmost caution.

As I arrive at Ava's building, I text her.

*Be right down*, she replies.

The doorman admits me when I tell him I'm here to see Ava. A few minutes later, she comes off the elevator, wearing sky-high heels and one of those sexy, clingy dresses that tie at the hip. Miles of creamy white leg is on display, and her auburn hair falls in silky waves around her shoulders. Her golden-brown eyes have been given a smoky look with artfully applied makeup. Tonight, she seems a little less haunted than she was on our previous encounters. I'm hypnotized by her, and then she smiles.

Holy shit, she's stunning, and for a moment, I'm rendered mute and paralyzed while I watch her come to me.

"Hi," she says, sounding a little breathless. "You look nice."

"You look… Wow. Beautiful."

"Thank you."

I extend a hand to her, and she takes it, our eyes meeting in a charged moment of awareness.

She looks up at me. "Where're we going?"

"Brooklyn."

"Oh, cool. What's there?"

"Come and I'll show you." I lead her out the door that the doorman holds for us and down the stairs, moving slowly in deference to her heels. On the street level, I hail a cab, help her in, and when I'm settled next to her, I give the driver the address of our destination.

My eyes are drawn to her sexy legs, and I remind myself I'm not allowed to touch. But for the first time in a very long time, I want to. I really, really want to.

# CHAPTER 7

*Ava*

Sitting in the backseat of a cab with Eric next to me, I have butterflies in my stomach. Something is different tonight, from the way he looked at me when I came off the elevator to how he held my hand and helped me into the cab. The easy banter is gone, replaced by the kind of tense expectation I haven't experienced since the night I met John.

Eric looks so sexy in a gray suit, and he smells delicious. I want to lean in closer to get a better handle on the scent he's wearing.

I've never been nervous in his presence before, but now I am. I have no reason to be afraid of him, not physically, anyway. He's never been anything but a perfect gentleman around me, from the night we met when he slept on the other side of my bed so he could be there if I needed him. Nothing breeds trust with a new guy quite like a platonic night in the same bed, especially when I was drunk and vulnerable.

I liked the way he held my hand and helped me into the cab.

I love the suit he's wearing and the way it hugs his lean but muscular body.

I like the way he looked at me when he saw me coming toward him, and I marvel at how everything between us seemed to change in those first few seconds.

I'm unnerved by the unusual silence between us. Even when we'd just met, we've always had plenty to talk about. The silence isn't uncomfortable, but rather, charged with the weight of expectation. I try to remember the last time I truly looked forward to anything, and it was before John left. I used to look forward to getting home to him after work each night, especially on Fridays when we'd have an entire weekend to spend together.

I don't want to think about him when Eric is sitting close enough for me to touch him, not that I do. But I could, and I'm quite confident my touch would be welcome.

"Are you okay?" I ask him, more to break the silence than anything.

"I'm great. You?"

Smiling, I nod. "I'm excited to be going out tonight."

"I'm excited to be going out with *you* tonight." He reaches across the small bit of seat separating us and takes my hand.

As the breath catches in my throat, I curl my fingers around his hand. His gaze meets mine, and I can tell by the way he looks at me that he's feeling the same way I am. This casual night out with a friend has taken on all-new significance, and how did that happen in the span of a heartbeat?

The taxi darts through traffic, horn blasting, stopping, starting and swerving to avoid disaster at the last second.

"I feel like I'm in a video game."

Eric laughs. "Such is life in New York. And why do we never put on seat belts in cabs when they drive the way they do?"

"Safest drivers in the world," the cabbie says in a thick New Yawk accent that makes us laugh.

We lurch to the left, and I grasp the door handle with my free hand. The driver lets loose with a string of profanity and lays on the horn. I love every second of it. Even with my life in danger, I feel more alive than I have in years. We cross the Brooklyn Bridge, take an exit that leads to the waterfront and pull up to The River Café, situated adjacent to the bridge.

Eric hands the driver cash, helps me out of the cab and keeps an arm around my waist as we're ushered into a cozy, elegant dining room. Our table looks across the East River to Manhattan.

"This is fabulous," I tell him when we're seated.

"I've heard great things and have always wanted to come here."

I like knowing he's never been here before, that it's not somewhere he went with his ex. Not that I think he'd bring me to a place he went with her, but I'm glad just the same that we can share this new experience with each other.

"I had to call in a favor from a friend to get us in on short notice. A guy I went to college with is friends with the general manager."

"Well, thank you for calling in a favor on my behalf."

"What looks good to you?"

We discuss the menu and settle on salads to start with as well as the salmon for me and the halibut for him. Then we look over the drink menu.

"Mmm, the dark and stormy looks good," he says. "I wonder if they'd do that with bourbon rather than rum."

"You don't like rum?"

"I got sick on it once." He makes a face. "Never again."

"That's me and gin. Never again. I might've had to add champagne to my never-again list if it hadn't been for your emergency pizza rescue."

"I'm glad I was able to preserve your relationship with champagne."

The waiter says they can do the dark and stormy with bourbon, so we each order one, and when he returns with our drinks, Eric orders dinner for both of us. He does it so smoothly that it never occurs to me to tell him I could order for myself.

"How do you like the dark and stormy?" he asks.

I take a sip of the drink that was served in an iced glass. "It's got an interesting flavor."

"Ginger beer."

"Ah, that's what that is. I like it." The bourbon makes me feel warm on the inside as it seeps through my system.

He leans his elbows on the table and gives me his full attention. "Tell me more about you."

His interest in me is a refreshing change of pace. Most of the men I've dated are far more interested in talking endlessly about themselves. The only other guy I've ever met who was truly interested in me... *No, we're not thinking about him tonight.* "You know most of my story. During a rather average childhood in Purchase, I played the flute in the high school band and piccolo in the concert band. I ran track and cross country and was a representative on the student council."

"Do you still run?"

"Not really. I do need to get back to the gym, though."

"What made you decide on a college so far from home?"

"I wanted to experience another part of the country, and I needed some independence. My parents are wonderful, and I adore them, but they hovered. I felt a little claustrophobic under all that parental concern, and I knew if I didn't go far away, I might end up letting them call all the shots for me."

"What did they say about you going to San Diego?"

"My mom went on anxiety meds, and my dad bought me pepper spray."

He laughs, and the warm, rich sound feels like the bourbon as it washes over me.

"Are you getting a better sense of why I wanted to go away to school?"

"You paint a rather vivid picture."

"San Diego was perfect—too far for them to pop in any time they wanted, and a nice, relaxed atmosphere that allowed me to blend in and do my thing under the radar."

"You like it there? Under the radar?"

I nod. "It's my favorite place to be. I'm not as outgoing or social as my sister or worried about keeping up with the Joneses the way my parents are. I hate being the center of attention. That wedding my sister planned?"

"What about it?"

I curl up my lip. "I'd never want a big public thing like that. I'd break out in hives at the thought of it."

"Funny how two siblings can be so different, right?"

"I've marveled about that since the day my sister was born. She's always been exactly the way she is now, and I adore her. Don't get me wrong."

"I can tell you love her whenever you guys are together."

"We're just very different people."

"Ever come close to getting married?" he asks as our salads are delivered.

The question strikes a little too close to home, and I'm thankful to turn my attention to the salad so he can't see that. "Not really," I answer truthfully. John and I never discussed getting married. At the time, I thought we were too busy enjoying the present to talk about the future, but with hindsight, I realize that, too, was intentional on his part.

"Surely the guys in San Diego were interested in you."

"A few. Here and there." It's hard to eat when there's a lump in your throat the size of a grapefruit.

"Nothing serious?"

"One." I take a sip of my drink and fight back the surge of panic that would have me running from this conversation if that were an option. "He's my Brittany."

"Ah, gotcha. Say no more."

I offer a small smile in appreciation of his willingness to drop it. I hope I can bring myself to talk about John to a therapist, but not anyone else. What would be the point? It happened, it's over, and I need to move on.

"Life can be a bitch sometimes," Eric says, a rueful expression on his handsome face.

"Indeed, it can."

He holds up his glass in a toast. "Here's to moving on."

I touch my glass to his. "To moving on."

After a delicious dinner, we share a dessert called the Chocolate Brooklyn Bridge. I take a few bites and then push the plate closer to him. "All yours. I'm done."

"You're wimping out on me?"

"If I eat another bite, I might explode."

"Well, we can't have that, so I'll take one for the team and finish this."

"The team thanks you."

This has been the most relaxing, enjoyable evening I've had in years, and it's thanks to him and his easygoing charm, entertaining stories and quick wit. I can't imagine how any woman could ever treat him the way his ex-fiancée did.

"What?" he asks, catching me gazing at him.

"Nothing." My face heats with embarrassment.

"Oh, come on. What're you thinking about over there?"

"I don't want to bring old hurts into our good time."

He puts down the fork and wipes his mouth with the cloth napkin. "It's okay. You can say anything to me."

"I just wonder how she could've treated you the way she did. You're a good guy, Eric. A really good guy. How did she not see that?"

"I have no idea. I was good to her. I treated her right." He shrugs. "Who knows?"

Before I can think too much about the possible implications, I reach across the table and lay my hand on top of his. "I'm sorry she did that to you, and I want you to know…"

He turns his hand so our palms are touching and wraps his fingers around my hand. "What do you want me to know?"

I swallow hard. "That I understand, better than most people would, what it feels like to be abandoned the way she abandoned you."

He tips his head ever so slightly, looking at me with new appreciation. "Do you?"

I nod, but I don't say anything more. I can't. I've already said more than I ever intended to.

"How do you feel about jazz?" he asks, surprising me with the sudden shift.

"In general, or as a religion?"

His face lights up when he smiles. It's a good look on him. "Do I take that to mean after-dinner drinks at a jazz club would work for you?"

"Absolutely."

He signals for the check and uses a black American Express card to pay it.

"Next time is on me," I tell him.

"I'm thrilled to hear there's going to be a next time." He guides me to the exit with his hand on my lower back. Using his phone, he summons an Uber, and we step out into a beautiful, clear evening to wait for our ride. "I love nights like this when there's no humidity."

"Reminds me of San Diego. The climate there was lovely."

He keeps an arm looped casually around my waist while we stand outside the restaurant. "We should go there sometime together. I'd love to see it through your eyes."

"That would be nice," I say, but I don't want to go there with him. That was my place with John.

I'm not sure if it's the bourbon that makes me do it, but I lean into Eric's embrace, slightly, but enough that he draws me in even closer to him. Then I feel his lips brush against my hair. The surface of my skin tingles in awareness, and desire, the first I've experienced in years, makes me want to squirm. Somehow, I manage to remain still even as my body awakens from a long, dark winter of despair.

The car arrives, and Eric holds the door for me, waits for me to get settled and then closes it to go around to the other side. When he gets in, he reaches for me. "Come back where you were."

I slide across the seat, and he wraps his arm around me. "Tell me something…"

"Sure." I hope I can be truthful with him, because he deserves that much.

"Has there been anyone since the important one?"

"No."

"How long?"

"Five years."

All the breath seems to leave him on one long exhale. "Ah, Ava... God."

My eyes fill, and I close them, determined to fight through the emotional storm I've been battling for years now. "How about you? Anyone since her?"

"No."

We don't say anything more during the ride across the bridge into Manhattan, but the weight of the things we've said hangs heavy in the air between us. So much is at stake for both of us. And with our siblings married to each other, the potential for further catastrophe isn't lost on me.

The car arrives at Columbus Circle. Eric holds my hand in the elevator to the fifth-floor location of Dizzy's Club Coca-Cola. He exchanges a few words I can't hear with the guy working the door. The man nods and gestures to a corner table.

Eric pays the cover and shakes the man's hand, slipping him a tip. At the table, he holds the chair for me until I'm settled and then takes the seat next to mine. "We're just in time for the eleven-thirty show. Check out the stage. Pretty cool, right?"

Behind the stage is the New York skyline. "What're we looking at?"

"Columbus Circle and Central Park."

"It's beautiful."

"One of the best views in the city, and the music is excellent, too."

"I can't wait."

Another couple named John and Carlene are seated at our table. His name is John. Of course it is. Thankfully, he looks nothing at all like my John. They're nice enough, but Eric keeps his focus on me.

We order another round of dark and stormy with bourbon and sit back to enjoy the Mardi Gras band that takes the stage right at eleven thirty. They're electrifying—and loud. So loud that Eric slides his chair closer to mine and puts an arm around me, making it so we can hear each other. We don't say much, but his hand on my arm has my attention divided between the music and him. Then his fingers begin to move, sliding subtly from shoulder to elbow and then up again.

He's barely touching me, but that doesn't lessen the effect of being caught up in the moment with him—and that subtle caress makes me realize how much I've missed being touched by a man. I've been so caught up in the grief of losing the person I loved most in the world that I haven't given much thought to the secondary aspects of losing him. Who has time to think about sex when you have no idea whether the man you love is alive or dead or ever coming back?

With Eric sitting so close to me and his touch setting off fireworks inside me, the woman in me is reawakening to things I haven't wanted in years. While I'm not sure I'm ready for a new relationship and everything that goes with it, I can't bring myself to stop something that feels so damned good. I watch the show, listen to the music and wallow in the sensations that remind me I'm still very much alive and still very much a woman in her prime.

# CHAPTER 8

*Eric*

Tonight has been… I struggle to find the word to describe how it feels to be back on track after nearly a year in complete hell. I want to thank Ava, and I want to kiss her, but more than anything, I don't want to mess this up by acting like a fool. I'm a lover of live music in any form, and normally, I'm completely absorbed by a show. But with Ava sitting so close to me, the fragrant scent of her hair filling my senses and her soft skin under my fingertips, I'm distracted rather than absorbed.

I'm trying to remember my plan to keep things casual and not get overly involved, but I can't deny that something changed during that moment in her building earlier, and I think she'd say the same thing happened to her.

I want to get out of here so I can spend more time with her, but the show doesn't wrap up until close to one.

"That was amazing," Ava says in the elevator. "I loved it."

"I'm glad you did."

"Didn't you?"

"It was great. I've seen them before. They're always fantastic."

I haven't touched her since we left our seats, and I'm almost afraid to touch her now. What was so easy and natural a few hours ago is now fraught with implications. The bubble we've been in since those first moments earlier seems to have burst since we left the club. I have no idea how to play this next part of the evening, and the uncertainty grates on my nerves during the cab ride to Tribeca.

I'd give anything to know what she's thinking. Has she been as affected by this evening as I have? What happens now?

I never used to have insecurities with women until Brittany gave me reason to doubt myself and my instincts. That's just another reason to hate her for what she did to me, but I don't want to think about her, especially not with Ava sitting a foot from me after the wonderful evening we've had.

Long before I'm ready, the cab pulls up to Ava's building. I pay the driver and go around to help her out of the car. The second her hand curls around mine, I feel settled again, the way I did in the club. I'm still thinking about what I want to say to her when she looks up at me. "Do you want to come up for a drink?"

"Sure." I try to sound casual, but I'm filled with relief to not have to figure out how to end this evening on the right note. Not yet anyway. I follow her into the elevator and then to her apartment.

"I'm not sure if Skylar is home, so we need to be quiet."

"I can be quiet."

She smiles at me over her shoulder and opens the door to the dark apartment. After turning on a light, she checks the other bedroom. "She must be pulling another all-nighter."

"Better her than me."

"What goes on at that firm of yours that requires attorneys to work all weekend?"

"They're acquiring a couple of other companies. That might be what it's about. Nothing to do with me, thank goodness. I haven't done an all-nighter since college."

"Me either. I need my sleep. I'm a raving lunatic without it."

I follow her into the kitchen. "I can't picture you as a raving lunatic."

"You haven't seen me sleep-deprived. It's not pretty."

"I can't imagine you as anything other than pretty." I curl a length of her gorgeous hair around my finger, and when I shift my gaze from her hair to her face, our eyes meet in a moment of supercharged awareness. "Ava..."

She licks her lips. "Yes?"

It's been a long time since I asked a woman for permission before I kissed her, but something tells me I need to ask Ava before I take that step. "Would it be okay if, instead of a drink, I kissed you?" I cup her cheek and move my thumb ever so slightly.

She hesitates a second before nodding, but I can see that it costs her something to give her permission. I proceed with utmost caution, brushing my lips lightly over hers and making sure she's with me before I do it again. As she curls her hands around my wrists, I'm not sure if she wants to keep me close or push me away. Her eyes are closed, so I can't gain any insight there.

"Ava..."

"Hmm?"

"Look at me."

She slowly opens her eyes, and I see they're full of unshed tears that break my heart.

"Sweetheart... We don't have to... Not if you don't want to."

"I want to. Please don't stop." Her arms curl around my neck, and she brings me down to her for another kiss. This time, her lips are parted as she kisses me.

The tears have rattled me, but I have a feeling that rejecting her advances would do more harm than good, so I follow her lead and fully participate in the kiss. I slide an arm around her waist to bring her in closer to me.

Her tongue touches my bottom lip, and for a second, I almost forget my plan to be careful with her, to go slowly, to let her set the pace. She's so sweet and sexy and timid... The combination of those things is endlessly appealing to me after having been bulldozed by a woman who's never had a timid moment in her life.

Before things can progress too far, I withdraw from the kiss, even though that's the last thing I want to do. "My parents are having a party tomorrow. Come with me?"

She seems undone by the sudden change of direction. "Are you sure you're willing to risk getting your mother's hopes up?"

"I'm sure you're worth the risk." I kiss her again. "I had a great time tonight."

"I did, too. Thank you for dinner and the show."

"You're welcome. Pick you up around noon?"

"What should I wear?"

"It's casual. Shorts or whatever's comfortable. And we have a pool, so bring a suit if you want to swim."

"Sounds like fun."

"I'll let you get some sleep." I reluctantly release her, and she walks me to the door. "Thanks again for tonight."

"Thank *you.*"

I kiss her one last time and head down the stairs, my step lighter than it's been in eight months. There was a time, not that long ago, when kisses in the kitchen might've led to something more in the bedroom. But with Ava, those chaste kisses feel like a victory for both of us—and right about now, I'll take the victory.

*Ava*

I kissed him. I kissed him, and I didn't fall apart. But my heart... It splintered into a thousand pieces. My chest aches and my stomach is queasy. None of this has anything to do with Eric, who is wonderful and sweet and sexy. He's everything anyone could want in a man. But he's not John.

After the lovely evening with Eric, I hate myself for thinking that. I hate myself for comparing them, for kissing Eric when I'm still in love with John, and mostly I hate John for the impossible mess he made of my life when he let me fall in love with him, knowing he might have to leave the way he did.

I kick off the heels and claw at the dress, wanting it off right now. In the bathroom, I scrub my face free of makeup and brush my teeth.

I can't do this. I can't be with someone else when my heart still belongs to John.

I thought I could do it, and I wanted to. I really did. I was all in until he kissed me. Until it got real. Until I remembered the last time a man kissed me, on the way out the door and out of my life.

I break down into grief-stricken sobs, sinking to the floor of the bathroom and curling myself into a tight little ball, arms around my legs, head on my knees. I have no idea how long I'm there, but I'm still there when Skylar comes home and finds me.

"Ava?" She gets right down on the floor with me and puts her hand on my arm. "Are you hurt?"

I'm mortified to be caught in this condition by my new roommate. I wipe the tears from my face and force myself to look at her. "I'm…" I was going to tell her I'm okay, but I'm not. I'm exhausted. But she's been at work all day and all night, and the last thing she needs is a roommate she barely knows having a breakdown in her bathroom.

"What can I do?" she asks.

I shake my head. There's nothing anyone can do.

She sits next to me, her shoulder against mine, letting me know she's willing to wait me out. Her compassion triggers another wave of despair.

"Did someone hurt you?" she asks, her tone gentle.

"No. Nothing like that." I need to check online to see if the Pentagon has identified the service members who were killed. I haven't gotten around to checking because I was too busy kissing Eric.

"I know we've only just met, but I'm a good listener. All my friends say so."

I'm not sure why her or why now, but the words come pouring out of me. I tell her everything. I have no idea if I'm making the biggest mistake of my life by sharing it with her or whether I can trust her not to tell anyone, but I can't bring myself to care. The relief at finally, *finally* telling *someone* is so overwhelming that it leaves me weak in the aftermath of the word storm I unleash on her.

"Ava... Oh my God, you poor thing." At some point during the verbal tirade, she put her arm around me. "Why in the world have you endured something like this completely alone?"

"I don't know. It just sort of happened that way." My eyes are so swollen from crying that I may not be able to show my face in public again for days.

"What happened tonight?"

"I went out with Eric, the guy from your firm."

"Did something happen? Did he do something?"

"No, nothing like that." I wipe the dampness from my face. "He's wonderful, and we had the nicest time. And then, when we got home... He asked if he could kiss me, and I said he could."

"Afterward, you felt guilty," she says.

"Yes."

"Ava... You didn't do anything wrong by kissing Eric or enjoying the night out with him. You know that, don't you?"

"If that's true, why do I feel so awful?"

She's quiet for a long time, and then she begins to speak. "I lost my little sister in a car accident when I was in law school. The loss about broke me. I had to leave school for a semester, and for a while, I didn't think I could go back to the life I'd been leading before I lost her."

"I'm so sorry," I whisper.

"Thank you. It was the worst thing that's ever happened to me. The pain was just... excruciating. I wished I could die, too. That would've been easier than living without her."

I know that feeling. I know it all too well. "How did you survive it?"

"One day at a time, and a lot of grief therapy. That saved my life."

"I've been thinking that I need to find a good therapist and get my life back on track. More than five years is long enough to live like this."

"I can set you up with mine. I still see her every now and then, and she takes patients right away, even on weekends. She says grief doesn't keep regular hours and neither does she. You want me to text her?"

"I would really appreciate that, but isn't it kind of late?"

Skylar pulls her phone out of her back pocket and sends the text. "She has a phone that she answers regardless of the time."

I'm sitting close enough to her to see what she says: *I have a friend in bad need of what you do best. When could you squeeze her in? The sooner the better.*

The response comes almost right away. *9 in the morning?*

"As in *this* morning?" I ask, incredulous.

"I told you. She doesn't mess around when people need her. Should I tell her you'll be there?"

"Yes, please."

*She'll be there. Her name is Ava Lucas. Appreciate this.*

*Anything for you. Tell Ava I look forward to meeting her.*

*Will do.*

"You're all set. Her name is Jessica Trudeau. I'll text you the address."

"Thank you so much, Skylar. I'm so sorry you had to come home to so much drama."

"I don't mind at all. I'm glad I could help, and I'm honored to be the first person you've told." She rests her head against the vanity. "I know how hard it can be to share this sort of thing with someone, especially when you're possibly starting a new relationship. I had a boyfriend when my sister died, and he stuck it out for a year afterward, which was about nine months longer than he should have. He tried, but there was nothing he could do, and after a while, he gave up and moved on. I've yet to get far enough into another relationship where I felt comfortable telling a new guy about my sister."

Sighing, I say, "I'm not sure why I never told anyone. Probably because he wanted me to keep it between us when we were together, which, with hindsight, should've been a red flag. But what did I know? I was twenty-one and madly in love for the first time in my life. If he'd asked me to skydive without a parachute, I would've done it because he asked me to."

"Plus, you said you went away to school to put some distance between yourself and your family."

"Yeah, and they would've swooped in and tried to fix everything for me, and I didn't want that either."

She turns her head toward me. "Remember this—you don't owe anyone an explanation for how you chose to deal with this. Anyone who would hassle you about *how* you handled it has never dealt with anything like this, or they'd know to keep their fat mouths shut."

"I think I might love you a little bit."

Her laughter rings out in the small bathroom. "That's good news, because I was expecting to hate you after you showed up with all the governor's kids in tow."

"They're my sister's new family, and they're actually really nice."

She nudges me with her elbow. "Especially the brother, huh?"

I think of Eric and the evening we spent together and smile. "Yeah, especially him. He's been so great to me since the day we met when I got drunk at my sister's wedding and he took care of me." I tell her about his pizza cure and how it saved me. "And he risked having his whole family up in his business by staying in my room in case I needed him during the night." I fill her in on what happened with his ex and why it was such a big deal for him to step up for me the way he did.

"You know, I heard he was out on an extended leave of absence earlier this year, but I never found out why. The poor guy. Who could do that to someone they supposedly love?"

"I have no idea, but because of that, I'm extra concerned about getting involved with him if I'm not really ready to take that step."

"Jessica will help you figure it out. She's the best."

"I'm so relieved to have told someone and to have a plan in place to try to feel better about everything. I can't thank you enough."

"Happy to help. What do you say we get the hell out of the bathroom?"

Laughing, I let her help me up, and then I hug her.

She returns the embrace and pats me on the back. "Try to get some sleep."

"You, too."

"I finished everything tonight, so I actually get to sleep in tomorrow."

"Enjoy that. Good night."

"Night, Ava."

I go into my room, close the door and get into my bed. I'm about to reach for my phone to see if there's any news from the Pentagon, but I stop myself. I can't take any more tonight, and tomorrow will be soon enough to find out if he's among the casualties.

# CHAPTER 9

*Ava*

I sleep surprisingly well and awake at eight when my alarm goes off. For several minutes, I lie in bed thinking about everything that happened yesterday. I told someone about John, and nothing terrible happened. In fact, several good things came of it, including the referral to a therapist and a new friend. Skylar was amazing—supportive, understanding and helpful. When I pondered the possibility of telling people about John and what happened in San Diego, I always imagined I'd tell Camille and my parents before I told anyone else.

Telling Skylar was much easier than telling them would've been. No question about that. In addition to sharing my pain, I'd have to deal with theirs when they heard what happened with John. They'd want to know why I didn't include them at the time, and that would make it harder on me.

I get up and go straight to the Keurig for a cup of coffee that I take with me into the bathroom, where I shower and dry my hair. I leave the apartment with plenty of time to get to the address on Third Avenue that Skylar gave me. In the cab, I expect to feel nervous or unsettled, but I don't feel either of those things. I'm still reveling in the relief of having shared my story with someone and to have found a therapist who can help me forge a path forward.

It's been a long time since I've had so many positive things to focus on. I hope Jessica can help me navigate my new life in a way that keeps the old life in the past where it belongs.

Jessica's office is in a brick-fronted building that's just as Skylar described it. The street level is a bustling deli with scents coming from it that make my mouth water. I'll stop for a closer look at what they have after my appointment. I press the button next to Jessica's name, and she buzzes me in. She's on the third floor and is waiting for me when I reach the landing.

Right away, I notice she's a lot younger than I expected. She has curly blonde shoulder-length hair and wears cat-eye leopard-print glasses that make her look smart and hip at the same time. She's wearing a black top with jeans and black wedges.

She extends a hand to me. "You must be Ava."

I shake her hand. "I am. It's so nice to meet you, and thank you for seeing me on a Saturday."

"No problem. Grief doesn't keep nine-to-five hours, and neither do I." She ushers me into a cozy space with plush, oversized easy chairs and lots of pillows. The walls are painted a dark shade of orange, and the artwork consists of soothing beach scenes. "Coffee? Tea? Water? What can I get for you?"

"A coffee would be awesome."

"How do you take it?"

"Just cream, please."

"You got it." She gestures to a clipboard on the coffee table. "If you could fill out the usual forms, that'll take care of the paperwork."

I complete the forms and fill in my credit card number since my new insurance at work won't kick in for another month.

Bringing two mugs of steaming coffee with her, she sits across from me and places my coffee on the table between us. Holding her mug in both hands, she settles into her chair, curling her legs under her. "Tell me a little about you, and then I'll tell you a little about me. We'll go from there."

Her easygoing demeanor puts me immediately at ease, and I try to summarize what's brought me to her in as few words as possible. "In the five years since he left, I haven't told anyone about him until last night when Skylar came home and found me in a heap after my first real date with another man."

Jessica winced. "That's an awfully long time to deal with something so traumatic on your own."

"With hindsight, I think I basically followed his lead from when we were together. 'Let's keep this to ourselves,' he'd say. I know now that was probably because he wasn't supposed to be so involved with anyone due to his job, but I didn't understand that at the time."

"Before we delve into that, I want to tell you about me, if that's okay."

"Of course."

"Like you, I had a rather idyllic childhood. I married my high school sweetheart when I was still in graduate school. We had our first child two weeks after I completed my master's degree. A boy named Liam."

I experience a sense of dread that's confirmed when she continues.

"He was nine months old when he contracted meningitis. We lost him three days later."

"I'm so sorry." The words feel incredibly inadequate, but I don't know what else to say.

"Thank you. I tell you this so you'll know I understand where you're coming from in here. Liam's death twelve years ago changed everything about my life, and I decided to specialize in grief counseling because I wanted to help other people who were going through what I did when I lost my son. A therapist put me back together, and during that process, I found my professional calling."

I have so many questions. I want to know if she has other children and if she and her husband stayed together. She doesn't wear a ring, but that doesn't mean anything. I don't feel comfortable asking, but I'm sure Skylar knows. I'll wait and ask her.

"We're going to talk a lot about John and what happened in San Diego five years ago. But first, I want to talk about Eric and what's happening right now in New York City, okay?"

I nod, intrigued by her approach, but willing to follow her lead.

"Tell me what happened last night."

I recount our evening, ending with the kisses in my kitchen that sent me into a guilt-induced spiral.

"When he asked if he could kiss you, did you feel guilty when you gave permission?"

I think about that. "No, I didn't feel guilty until after he left."

"So, in the moment, you enjoyed kissing him?"

"I did. I've enjoyed everything with him. He was a good friend to me the day we met and has been every day since then. Last night was a really great night."

She sits back and eyes me shrewdly. "You're suffering from a lack of closure in your relationship with John. If he'd broken up with you before he left or, God forbid, been killed, then you'd have closure. But when he left, he told you he loved you and walked out of your life, leaving you in this state of limbo that has kept you from moving forward. Do you agree?"

"Definitely. I've begun to feel anger toward him about that."

"You've only just recently begun to feel anger toward him?" she asks, incredulous. "Most people would've been furious long before now."

"I really, really loved him."

"I know."

"And he left me to serve our country, to go after the people who attacked the cruise ship. It's hard to blame someone who's trying to get retribution for so many people."

"At least you think that's what he's doing. You don't actually know that for sure, right?"

"No," I say, sighing, "I don't know anything for sure."

"If John were to walk into this room right now, what would you want to say to him?"

"Oh jeez." I exhale on a nervous laugh. "I wouldn't know where to start."

"Humor me. He comes strolling in here, back like he never left. What's the first thing that comes to mind?"

"I'd probably be too busy hugging him and kissing him to say anything."

"That's your first impulse? To hug and kiss him? Not to ask him why he did this to you if he loved you as much as he said he did?"

I think about that. "Yes, that's my first impulse—to hug and kiss him."

"I give you credit. I'd probably want to stab a guy who did to me what he did to you."

"We were so incredibly good together. So very, very good. My relationship with him was the most perfect thing in my life."

"Except for the things he kept from you, of course, like the fact that he might have to deploy, potentially for years, without a word to you."

"Maybe he didn't know that was possible. I mean, who expected terrorists to blow up a cruise ship?"

Jessica uncurls her legs from under her and leans forward, elbows on knees, her expression intense. "*He* expected it—or something like it, Ava. He trained for years for a scenario just like the one that transpired, and he knew—every minute he spent with you, he *knew*—it was possible he'd have to leave you the way he did."

"You... you don't know that for certain."

"Yes, I do, and so do you. You know it. A man in the military doesn't just disappear off the face of the earth for *five* years. That doesn't happen. Unless he's in a unit designed for just that kind of mission."

"I... I think maybe this wasn't such a good idea."

"Because you don't like what I'm saying about the man you love?"

God, she's so blunt! "In part."

"It's the truth, and I think it's going to be really important to your ability to move forward for you to accept that what he did to you wasn't honorable. It wasn't what a man does to the woman he loves."

I'm so hurt by what she's saying and furious on John's behalf that tears roll down my cheeks. I make no move to deal with them, because I'm frozen in place.

She hands me a tissue, forcing me to react, to take it from her and mop up the flood.

"I'm not saying these things to hurt you, Ava. I'm saying them because you need to hear them. You've put him on a pedestal he doesn't belong on."

"Even if he's spent the last five years sacrificing his own life in service to our country?"

"If that's what he's been doing, then we all owe him a tremendous debt of gratitude, but that doesn't change the fact that what he did *to you* was shitty."

"Is this how you coped with the loss of your son? Did you find someone to blame?"

"There was no one to blame. We don't know how or where he contracted the virus, and the doctors did everything they could to try to save him."

"I'm sorry. I shouldn't have said that."

"You're more than welcome to ask me about how I dealt with my grief. I'm happy to share anything that'll help you deal with yours."

"I can't find it in me to blame him when he was just doing his job."

"Fair enough, but I want you to really think about the concept of *intentions*. What were his toward you when he got involved with you? Did he go into your relationship knowing there was a possibility that he might have to leave you in this state of purgatory for *years*? Did he know that was possible, and did he do it anyway?"

I don't know the answers to those questions, so I don't respond.

"What about his friends and family? What do they say about where he disappeared to?"

"I... I never met any of them. We kept to ourselves. We liked it that way."

"You both liked it that way, or *he* did?"

"We both did. We had everything we needed in each other."

"So not only did he keep from you that he might have to leave you indefinitely, but he kept you isolated so you wouldn't have a support system in place if what he knew might happen actually did. Is that correct?"

"It wasn't like that." I dab at my eyes, which are aching. It's been years since I've broken down the way I have in the last two days.

"What was it like, then?"

"We were happy. *I* was happy."

"You were also young and naïve and far away from your home and your family. That made you the perfect girlfriend for a man who maybe wasn't supposed to have a significant other."

"This isn't helping me. I didn't come here to dismantle the character of the man I love."

"Why did you come?"

"Because! I'm tired of being stuck. I want to move on with my life, but I don't know how."

"I'm trying to show you how, Ava. You've got to let him go, really let him go, or you'll never be anything other than stuck. What he asked of you is more than any man has a right to ask of any woman, no matter how much you loved him or he loved you. It was unfair of him to allow you to fall in love with him. If you can find a way to accept that, I think you might be able to get unstuck."

I take another tissue from the box on the table and wipe away more tears. "Did you have other children?"

"Three."

"Did it help?"

"It really did. No one can take Liam's place, but his little brothers and sister have filled our hearts and our home with love and light and laughter. They give me a reason to get up in the morning, and we all need that."

I'm happy for her that she has other children, and her use of the word *our* gives me hope that she managed to hang on to her marriage.

"Let's talk some more about Eric."

"What about him?"

"You said you like him and he's been very good to you?"

Nodding, I say, "From the start."

"And you feel guilty that you're attracted to him?"

"Yes."

"Why?"

I stare at her. "Do I honestly have to spell that out for you?"

"I guess you do, because frankly, I don't understand what in the world you have to feel guilty about."

"I feel guilty," I say through gritted teeth, "because I'm still in love with John."

"Who left you five years ago and hasn't been in touch with you since, correct?"

"Not because he doesn't want to be. He could be dead for all I know!"

"Yes, he could be. Let's look at the various scenarios, shall we? A. He's dead and took no steps whatsoever to ensure you'd be notified of his death. B. He's choosing to remain out of touch with you for reasons only he knows. C. He's somewhere in the world where he can't get in touch with you. D. He's part of an operation where contact with the outside world could sacrifice the mission he signed on for long before he met you. Have I missed anything?"

"No," I mutter, infuriated with her—and with him.

"Ava."

I glance at her and see only care and compassion in the way she's looking at me.

"If you had told a friend or family member about this years ago, they would've said the same things I'm saying now. Anyone who cares about you would be furious about what he's put you through."

I wipe away tears that keep on coming even as I wonder how there can still be more.

"Do you want to see Eric again?"

I nod.

"Then you should. You should do whatever it takes to be happy and feel better. If he makes you happy, run with it. You owe John nothing more than the five years of grief you've already given him. He didn't marry you or ask you to marry him or ask you to wait for him or anything that binds you to him in a way that would require you to feel guilty about moving on with someone else. Do you hear me on that, Ava?"

"Yes," I whisper.

After a long pause, she says, "How do you feel?"

"Devastated." It's the first word that comes to mind.

"That might actually be a good thing."

"*How* is that a good thing?"

"You're devastated because I'm forcing you to face the truth of what John did to you and continues to do to you all these years later. I'm telling you it's time to let him go and move on with someone who is right here, right now and obviously interested in you."

"Do I tell him about John?"

"Do you want to?"

"I feel like I should because he told me about what happened with his ex, but I wouldn't want him to tell his brother, who's married to my sister. I don't want to bring my family in on this."

"From what you've said about him, he seems like an upstanding kind of guy. Ask for his discretion beforehand. If you tell him it's important he not share what you're going to tell him with his brother and get his assurances that he won't, then it should be fine."

"Should be..."

"What's the worst thing that could happen if your sister and parents find out?"

"They'd be all over me, hovering and worrying and..." I shudder at the thought of it.

"And that'd last a couple of days, a week at most, and then they'd move on when they see that's what you're doing." She leans in. "If you want Eric to know about John, *tell him*, Ava. Just tell him and be done with it. And remember, as big a deal as this has been for you, it won't be as big a deal for him or anyone else. Everyone has their own crap to deal with."

Over her shoulder, I see the clock edging toward eleven. I can't believe I've been here almost two hours. Time flies when your soul is being flayed open and examined.

"If you're still speaking to me after today, I'd be happy to set up another appointment. We made great progress, but it takes time and a lot of work to really move forward."

I didn't like a lot of what she said to me, but I can't deny that she made valid points. "Another appointment would be good."

"Excellent."

Because I'm starting my new job this week, we make an appointment for this coming Thursday at seven p.m. Then I stand on legs that feel rubbery and extend my hand to her.

"I want to hug you," she says. "Is that okay?"

"Sure."

She comes around the table and embraces me. "I admire your strength, your loyalty, your courage and your fortitude," she says. "You have more than earned the right to be happy by yourself, with Eric or with someone else if he's not the one for you."

Her kind words bring more tears to eyes that feel gritty and tortured. "Some of this was hard to hear, but I appreciate your time and your perspective."

She hands me a business card. "My cell number is on there. I'm here for you any time you need me."

"Thank you so much."

"I'm rooting for you, Ava."

I leave her with a small smile and head for the door. I go downstairs and out into the warm summer day, taking deep breaths of the fresh air. I can't imagine how red and puffy my face must be. I retrieve sunglasses from my purse and put them on, hoping to hide some of the carnage. The deli that smelled so good to me on the way in makes me queasy now, so I walk past it to the corner and hail a cab.

After I'm in the car, my phone buzzes with a text from Skylar. *Got called into work—grrrrr. Just checking to see how it went with Jess.*

*She was great—and very, very blunt.*

*LOL! That's my girl. She says it like it is.*

*Yes, she does. She said a lot of things I needed to hear. Still processing it all. Sorry you got called into work.*

*Just for a few hours. I'll see you later.*

*Thank you again for everything. I can't tell you what it means to me…*

*Any time. xo*

:)

# CHAPTER 10

*Ava*

This has been the most traumatic twelve hours I've had in years, and yet I feel strangely… calm. Settled. Relieved. I told someone. I told *two* people, and nothing bad happened. In fact, something good came of it. I feel like I've made a new friend in Skylar, and her referral to Jessica was just what I needed, even if it was hard to hear a lot of what she had to say.

I'm also determined to be honest with Eric. He deserves the truth about my past before we get any further into whatever this is that's happening between us.

When I get home, I go right to the freezer and make an ice pack to put on my eyes, hoping to repair some of the damage before Eric arrives. I stretch out on the sofa, ice pack on my eyes and think about the things Jessica said. I try to reconcile them with the image of John I've carried with me all this time.

As much as I might want to, I can't deny she's one hundred percent right about John. I've always known, on some level, that what he did was anything but heroic, even if the reason he left in the first place is the epitome of the word.

A short time later, my phone buzzes with a text from Eric. *Just leaving the garage and on the way to your place. Can't wait to see you.*

A zing of excitement goes through me. I can't wait to see him either. I get up from the sofa, toss the ice pack in the kitchen sink and head for the bathroom to repair the damage with concealer. My eyes are still red, but not as puffy as they were earlier. If anyone asks, I can use allergies as an excuse for the redness—and thank goodness for sunglasses that cover a world of hurt.

I quickly pack my swimsuit, sunscreen, a cover-up and denim jacket into a beach bag before changing into shorts and a white top. I'm sliding my feet into leather flip-flops when the doorman calls to tell me Eric has arrived. "I'll be right down."

I'm in no mood for a family party today, especially someone else's family. But I'll put on my game face for Eric's sake, and then afterward, I'll ask him if we can talk. I'm going to tell him about John and why it's so complicated for me to be starting something new with him. It's complicated for him, too, so we have that in common, but Jessica has helped me see that it wouldn't be fair to go forward with him without giving him all the information he needs to understand what he's getting into.

As I toss my bag over my shoulder, lock the door and head for the elevator, it occurs to me that I never checked to see if the Pentagon released the names of the dead service members.

## Eric

Something is different today. I can't put my finger on it at first, but she's quiet. Not that she's ever super chatty, but her silence feels unsettled. I hope she'll relax as the day unfolds, but I wonder if she's regretting what happened last night. I really hope not, because I woke up today feeling better than I have in months.

Not only did I have a great time with her last night, but today I get to drive my Mercedes AMG GT. I pay a ridiculous monthly fee to keep her garaged in the city, and any chance I get to drive her is welcomed.

It would've been easier to take Metro North, but as I navigate heavy traffic heading out of the city on the Henry Hudson Parkway, I'm glad I didn't go for what's easier. I love living in the city—most of the time—but I miss driving. I've got the sunroof open to let in the cool summer breeze.

"This is a really nice car," Ava says, breaking the long silence.

"Thanks. I bought it with the bonus check I got for my first successful pitch." I merge onto the Sawmill River Parkway heading north toward home. I've been gone from there for fifteen years, but Croton-on-Hudson will always be home to me and my siblings.

In fact, Rob and Camille recently bought a condo down the street from where we grew up, so they have a place to escape to when they need a break from the city. It's forty-one miles from my building to the house where we grew up, but that forty-one miles may as well be forty-one hundred miles for how different the two places are.

After another long silence, I glance over at her. I'm struck once again by how lovely she is. The sun is picking up the red highlights in her hair, and her skin has taken on a rosy glow. Her eyes are hidden behind sunglasses, and I notice she's gripping the handle of the beach bag she brought as if someone might take it from her.

After another long silence, I can't take it anymore. I have to know what's up with her. "Are you okay?"

She glances over at me but doesn't say anything as she seems to wrestle mightily with something. "Can we talk later? When we get back to the city?"

My stomach drops. Not again. I knew it was a mistake to kiss her last night. From the beginning, I've sensed a fragility to her that has had me proceeding with caution as friendship became something more, at least for me.

"About what happened to me five years ago," she says. "I want to tell you."

While I'm relieved she apparently doesn't want to tell me that this—whatever it is we're doing—is over, I'm not sure how I'm supposed to wait hours to hear what she wants to say. "We don't have to go to my parents' house. We can turn around and go back if you're not feeling it today."

She places her hand on my arm. "Later is soon enough."

*Ugh.* Patience has never been my best quality and having to soldier through an entire day to get to later may just kill me. "Did something happen?" I ask her. The curiosity is already making me spin.

"Yes," she says softly. "You happened."

I have no idea what to say to that. "Ava…"

She slides her hand down my arm to clasp the hand that's resting on my leg. "It's nothing bad. In fact, it's actually a good thing that I want to talk about it. It's nothing to worry about. I promise."

"If you say so."

"You're cute when you don't get your own way."

The playful comment makes me laugh and gives me hope that she's not about to tell me why we can't possibly continue something that feels so damned good. I also take comfort in the fact that she continues to hold my hand.

"Are you worried about what your mom will say when you show up with me?"

"Not particularly."

"You were so upset the last time…"

"I probably overreacted a little. It's just that she's so damned predictable sometimes. The minute the three of us turned thirty, she was all over us about getting married and pumping out grandchildren, like we were suddenly going to run out of time if we didn't hop to it. Part of me thinks that's why I was so over-the-top when I met Brittany. I played right into her hand. That's for sure."

"You were happy with her. That had nothing to do with your mother."

"*She* was happy with Brittany. She started planning the wedding the first month we were together. I don't want her pulling that crap with you. If she says anything inappropriate, feel free to tell her to mind her own business."

"I'm not saying that to your mother."

"Then tell me, and I'll say it. I don't want you to feel pressured by her or anyone."

"Don't worry about me. I can take care of myself."

"I don't want you to have to take care of yourself when you're with me or my family."

"It's very sweet of you to be concerned, but I've been taking care of myself for a long time."

"What if I want to take care of you in certain situations, such as when my mother wants to sink her claws into you?"

She laughs, and the tension that's been gathering in my chest thankfully relents somewhat. That feeling reminds me far too much of the desperate days I spent searching for Brittany, not knowing she'd left me.

Ava squeezes my hand. "Why did you just get all tense?"

I don't want to admit that I was thinking of Brittany. "Just worried about my mom driving you away."

"I won't be easily driven. You've got nothing to worry about."

Her assurances comfort me, but I won't let my guard down around my family today. The last thing I want, when I'm finally getting back on track, is for Ava to feel pressured into something she isn't ready for. I already know I'm going to have to take it slow with her, and if slow doesn't work for my mother or anyone else, too bad.

*Ava*

I absolutely love the Village of Croton-on-Hudson—never on *the* Hudson, as Eric tells me when we drive into the quaint town. "Your parents don't live at Albany?" I asked.

"Only during the week. They come home on the weekends."

The Tildens' home is a Shaker-style riverfront "cottage" that Eric tells me has twenty rooms. Despite the size, the house has a comfortable, lived-in feel to it and is decorated in a coastal theme. We receive a warm welcome from Governor and Mrs. Tilden, both of whom are casually dressed and busy in the kitchen when we arrive.

"Ava!" Mrs. Tilden drops her knife, and it lands with a clatter on the stone countertop. Wiping her hands on a towel, she comes around the island to hug me like we're old friends. "It's so nice to see you again! I didn't know you were coming, but I'm so glad you did. Your parents are on their way, too."

"Take a breath, Mom," Eric says, extricating me so he can hug her. He rolls his eyes at me behind her back.

A word here about Eric's mom. She's *stunning*. That's the only word I can think of to describe her. She's youthful and fit with a blonde bob that falls right below her jawline. You'd never know she has four children, three of whom are in their thirties. Out of all her offspring, Eric and Jules look the most like her. She's the kind of woman who leaves even the most confident of other women intimidated, and I'm no exception.

"I'm so excited to have everyone home for the day," she says, keeping one arm around Eric.

"What can I do to help?" I ask her.

"Oh, nothing. Bob and I have it covered. Go on outside and enjoy the day. Eric, Dad has the Jet Skis ready if you want to take Ava for a ride before we eat."

"Our part of the Hudson is the clean part," Eric says, smiling. "Want to take a spin?"

"Sure, that sounds like fun."

"Show her where she can change in the pool house, Eric," Mrs. Tilden says before she goes back to chopping cucumbers.

I find it interesting that other than hello, the governor doesn't say anything to us.

"Is your dad always so quiet?" I ask Eric when we're outside on the huge deck that overlooks the Hudson. The artfully arranged seating areas remind me of a Frontgate catalog, right down to the outdoor carpeting, pillows and copper fire pit.

"He can hardly get a word in edgewise when my mom gets going." He leads me around an in-ground pool to a smaller shingled building. "You can change in there and leave your stuff there, too."

He's wearing board shorts and a T-shirt, so he doesn't need to change.

"I'll be quick."

"Take your time."

I change into the bikini and cover-up I brought and slather on sunscreen so I won't be bright red by the end of the day. I capture my hair into a ponytail and put a Yankees ball cap on over it.

I find Eric sitting with his feet in the pool while he waits for me.

"Ready."

He turns to look up at me. "Oh no. *No, no, no.*"

"What?" I ask, alarmed.

"*Yankees?* No. Just no. We're Mets people."

"Um, your dad is the governor of all of New York, including the Yankees part."

"No, he asked them not to vote for him."

"Shut up," I say, laughing. "He did not."

He stands and faces me. "I knew there had to be something about you that wasn't perfect."

My face heats with embarrassment and the tingle of desire I'm becoming used to when he's around.

He tugs on my hat, playfully scowls at me and then takes my hand to lead me to the dock where a gorgeous wooden sailboat is tied up. We go down a ramp to a floating dock where two Jet Skis are tied next to a rubber dinghy with an outboard engine.

Eric removes his shirt, giving me my first glimpse at a muscular chest with a fine coating of gold hair. He hands me a life jacket and gets on one of the Jet Skis.

I remove the cover-up and don the life jacket.

"You have to hold on tight so you don't fall off," he says with a grin.

"Are you in cahoots with your mother to get my hands all over you?"

"Hardly, but if the result is your hands all over me, I'm good with that."

I laugh a lot when I'm with him, even when my heart is heavy and burdened by the things I need to tell him later. Attempting to be somewhat graceful, I take the hand he offers, get on the Jet Ski and let him direct me on where to put my hands—under the lower edge of his life jacket on his abdomen, which ripples under my palms.

"You ready?" he asks over his shoulder.

"Yep."

"Don't let go."

"Wouldn't dream of it."

Laughing, he fires up the Jet Ski, unties it from the dock and accelerates into the river. The ride is thrilling. I lose all sense of time as we fly over the water, jumping waves from other boats and having a complete blast. It's the most fun I've had in years, and it gets even better when Rob and Camille join us on the other Jet Ski and we race over the water next to each other.

Eric jumps a wave, and I scream as we catch air. We land with a huge splash of cold water.

"That," he says, "was awesome."

"Oh my God! I almost peed my pants!" I forget this is a new relationship when the words fly right through my filter.

He loses it laughing. "Glad you managed to hold it in."

"Just barely."

Rob sends a wall of water our way, and when we can see again, he and Camille are hysterically laughing.

"Bastards," Eric shouts. "This is war."

I'm not sure how I feel about being part of a Jet Ski war, but I'm not consulted before Eric takes off in hot pursuit of his brother.

We arrive back at the dock some time later, soaking wet and weak from laughing. Eric ties up the Jet Ski and gets off, extending his hand to help me. As I take his outstretched hand, I realize I haven't thought of John in hours, and surely that must be a record. It's nice to have something else—and someone else—to think about.

Eric helps me out of the life jacket and takes a good long look at me in the bikini. Leaning in so he won't be overheard by Rob and Camille, who've arrived right after us, he says, "So very, very lovely." He leans over to retrieve the cover-up I left on the dock and hands it to me.

Undone by his compliment and the hungry way he looks at me, I fumble my way into the cover-up and go ahead of him up the ramp to the dock.

Once again, the sleek wooden sailboat catches my attention. "That's a gorgeous boat." It's all white paint and gleaming varnish with cranberry sail covers and canvas.

"The *Sarah Beth*—my father's pride and joy. That's my mom's name. He restored it himself when they were first married and takes immaculate care of it."

"I used to sail with my grandfather when I was a kid."

"So you know how?"

"I haven't done it in years, but if it's like riding a bike, then yes, I know how."

"It's something you never forget once you know how. I love to sail. Maybe we can go out later."

"I'm not sure I trust you after the Jet Ski incident."

Laughing, he puts an arm around me. "Is that what we're calling it?"

"Was it or was it not an incident?"

"For me, it was just another day on the Hudson. For you…"

"An incident in which I nearly peed my pants in front of this cute new guy I've been seeing."

He pulls me in closer to him and kisses my temple. "Is it later yet?"

I nudge him with my elbow. "If your mother is watching this, you're filling her with hope."

He releases me so suddenly that I nearly stumble. Only his arms around me stop me from falling.

"You did that on purpose!"

"You can't prove that."

Oh, I like him. I really, really do. I like the way I feel when I'm with him—hopeful and happy and optimistic. And then I remember what I have to tell him, and I ache at the thought of him saying it's too much for him to take on. Who could blame him? It's my life, and it's too much for me.

# CHAPTER 11

*Ava*

Rob and Camille follow us up the dock, and we join Amy, Jules, their parents and mine on the deck.

Camille sits next to me on a wicker love seat. "Looking rather cozy with my BIL."

"Am I?" I'm intentionally vague because I know it'll drive her nuts.

"You know you are. I'm not going to say anything more than it's nice to see you both happy and having fun."

"Awww." I lay my head on her shoulder. "Is my baby sister growing up?"

"Nah, that'll never happen. I'm still curious as all hell, but Rob told me I need to leave you alone."

"Thank God for him. He's now my favorite brother-in-law."

"Very funny."

Our mother gets up from her spot on the other side of the deck and comes over to sit next to us. "I love seeing my girls back together again." She's petite and shares my coloring. Camille got her almond-shaped eyes.

"It's nice to be back together," I say.

"Do you see a lot of each other in the city?"

"As much as we can," Camille says.

"With my job starting on Monday, I'm about to get really busy again."

"Me, too," Camille says. "The party is officially over on Wednesday when I start my new job and classes to prepare for the bar exam." She wrinkles her nose in distaste.

"Daddy and I are proud of you both for landing great jobs that you're happy about."

"Thanks, Mom," I say.

"Do you know yet who your clients will be?" Camille asks me.

"Not yet, but I'll find out more on Monday. I can't wait to dig in and be busy again." Staying frantically busy at work was my salvation after John left, not that I tell them that.

"I don't mean to pry, but you seem close with Eric," Mom says, leaning in so she can't be overheard while prying. "Have you seen him since the wedding?"

"Here and there. My sister is married to his brother."

"I know that, silly. I was just wondering if maybe there's more to it than your sister being married to his brother."

"We're friends."

"Honestly, Ava," Mom says. "You can take your need for privacy a little too far sometimes."

I stare at her, incredulous that she would say that out loud when I know she's been thinking it for years. But since this isn't the time or the place to argue with my mother about boundaries, I choke back the retort that would tell her to mind her own business. "When there's something to tell, you'll be among the first to know. For now, we're friends."

"Leave her alone, Mom," Camille says. "She has the same right to privacy we all have."

"I never said otherwise. You misunderstand me. Both of you. I just want you to be happy, Ava. That's all."

"I'm doing well. It's all good. No need to worry about me."

"Carol," Sarah Beth says to my mom. "Come see the pictures I have from the wedding." Sarah Beth has brought her iPad onto the shaded side of the deck.

My mom gets up and goes to sit with her.

"Thanks," I say quietly to Camille.

"No problem. I meant what I said to her, but I still get the feeling there're things you're struggling with. If you need a friend, I'm always here for you."

I look at my sister with all-new respect. She's grown up a lot in the years we spent apart, and I want to be close to her now that we're adults. "There is something I'd like to tell you about. When the time is right."

"I'm here whenever you need me."

"That means a lot. Thank you."

Camille has always been my beloved baby sister, but sitting together on her in-laws' deck, I feel like we just became friends as well as sisters. I will tell her about John, but not until I've had the chance to talk to Eric. It's funny to me that before last night, I hadn't told anyone about him, and by the end of today, three people will know, and soon I'll tell Camille, too.

I'm relieved not to be carrying my burden alone anymore. I can only hope that what I need to tell him won't drive Eric out of my life.

I can tell he's going crazy trying to get through this casual day with his family. After we eat the burgers his Dad cooks on the grill and enjoy a relaxing lunch, Amy and Jules want to play volleyball, but Eric declines.

"Hey, Dad," he says, "would you mind if Ava and I took the boat out for a sail?"

"Of course not. Have at it."

"Thanks."

"I want to go," Rob says.

"Not this time."

"Eric, I was hoping for some family time," his mom says, seeming antsy.

"We won't be long. Ava?" He holds out a hand to me and doesn't seem to care that everyone is watching us.

I take his hand and let him lead from the deck through the yard to the dock. "Way to be subtle. For a guy who doesn't want everyone up in his business, you just made a heck of a statement there."

"All right, then."

He gets on the boat and reaches for me, surprising me when he picks me up and deposits me on the deck. "I don't mean to be abrupt, but I'm going a little mad wondering what you want to talk to me about. This was the best way I could think of to get some alone time with you right now."

I'm completely charmed. How could I not be? "Well, why didn't you say so?" I ask as I place a hand on his chest and look up at him.

He's got his sunglasses pushed to the top of his head, so I can see his eyes and the flash of heat directed at me. "Are you enjoying tying me in knots?"

"Not at all. That wasn't my intention. I'm sorry to have done that to you."

Right there, out in the open with everyone probably watching us, he kisses me. It's a quick kiss that packs a major punch and makes me want more.

"Hold that thought," he says. "Make yourself comfortable while I get the boat ready."

"I can help."

"Sounds good."

Working together, we remove the sail cover, prepare the mainsail, untie the tiller and prepare the jib. When we're ready, Eric asks me to remove the bow line while he sees to the spring and stern lines. I watch with fascination as the current carries the boat into the channel, which is when Eric releases the stern line and raises the mainsail and jib.

When we're under way, I join him in the cockpit, sitting across from him. "Very smooth, Captain."

"I've done it a few hundred times. That's how many times I had to do it before my dad would let me take her out by myself."

The sails catch the wind, and we take off, the boat slicing cleanly through the calm water. After a long silence, he says, "You wanted to talk. I'm listening."

I dig deep for the fortitude to share my story again. This time, the stakes are so much higher. Even though my relationship with Eric is new, it has real potential. He's given me the best possible reason to move on, even if he doesn't realize it yet.

"When I lived in San Diego, I was in love with a man named John. He was in the military, and we were together for two years."

His hand is on the tiller, and his gaze is fixed on me. "What happened?"

"The *Star of the High Seas* happened."

He gasps. "He was on it?"

I shake my head. "No, but he deployed the day it happened, and I've never seen or heard from him again."

"That was more than five years ago."

"Believe me, I know."

"Ava... God. All this time... You were alone and waiting?"

"Pretty much. I gave myself until the fifth anniversary, and that's when I decided it had to stop. I needed to let it go—let *him* go—and move on, and that's what I'm trying to do."

"I... I don't know what to say."

"I'd understand if this is too much for you to take on, especially after what happened to you."

"I'm surprised I haven't caught wind of this already. My family isn't known for its reticence."

"No one knows. You're the third person I've told, all within the last twelve hours."

"Why now?" He no sooner asks that when he says, "Because of what happened last night."

"That was the first time since him, and it was... I was..."

"Can you come over here?" He reaches for me, and I take his hand to move to his side of the boat, where he settles me next to him, his arm around me. "I'm so sorry if anything I did caused a setback for you."

"It wasn't your fault. It was bound to happen, and it actually led to a soul cleansing of sorts." I tell him about unloading on Skylar and her referral to Jessica.

"Did you feel better after you told someone?"

"Strangely, I really did, even if I was wrecked emotionally."

"Why did it take you so long to tell someone?"

"I've always been a very private person, and John was, too. I know now that he was probably more secretive than private, but after a while, it seemed like too much time had gone by to involve my family, and most of my friends in San Diego were work colleagues. One year became two and two became five, and I just didn't tell people."

"I hate to think of you being so alone with something so painful for such a long time."

"It was my choice to be alone with it, but it's easier to manage now that I've decided to share it with a few select people, including the roommate I just met, who was amazing, by the way. I have you to thank for connecting me to her."

"I'm glad she was there for you when you needed someone, but you could've called me. I would've come back."

"I know, and I so appreciate what a good friend you've been to me, but I think it happened the way it was meant to. Skylar led me to Jessica, and I already know she's going to be a great help to me even if some of what she had to say was hard to hear."

"Like what?"

"For one thing, she said that while John is a hero for presumably going after the people who blew up the ship, he's not a hero for how he handled me and our relationship."

"I can sort of see what she means. Can you?"

"I guess. After all this time of loving him and longing for him, it's hard to think of him as less than what I've built him up to be in my mind. But she's right. It was wrong of him to get so involved with me, knowing it was possible he might have to leave me the way he did."

"Although it's hard to fault someone who may be off fighting terrorists."

"Which has been at the heart of my dilemma."

After another period of silence, he says, "We need to come about."

I look up to see we're a long way from where we started out. The dock in front of the Tildens' home is a speck in the distance behind us.

Eric turns the boat, and we switch sides. "Come back," he says, raising his arm to put it around me.

I settle in next to him and enjoy the feel of the warm sunshine on my face and the rare moment of contentment. He knows, and he still wants me close to him. That feels like a victory. "You must have questions."

"A few."

"You can ask me anything, Eric. I promise to be honest with you."

"That means a lot to me, as you can imagine."

"When you first told me about Brittany, I realized there were similarities between your story and mine."

"Except the one you loved didn't launch an intricate plot to exit your life."

"Didn't he? When you think about it, that's exactly what he did. He knew the whole time we were together that it was highly likely he could get called to duty that would take him away from me indefinitely, and he never told me. Probably because he couldn't, but that doesn't make it right. Perhaps his reasons are more honorable than hers were, but the carnage left behind is quite similar."

"Yeah, I guess it is." After another long pause, he says, "Are you ready for something new, Ava?"

"I want to be." I promised him the truth, and that's what I give him.

"Me, too."

"Well, to quote a country song I used to like, that's a real fine place to start."

"Yes, it is. What do you see happening now?"

"I'd like to spend more time with you and see how it goes, but only if that's what you want, too."

"It's what I want."

"Even after everything I told you?"

"Even then." He runs his fingers through my hair, making my scalp tingle with awareness. "When I woke up this morning, my mind was full of thoughts of you and last night and how much I enjoy being with you. It's such a welcome relief to be thinking about something positive. It's a welcome relief to have found *you*."

"I feel the same way."

"Almost all I've thought about since kissing you last night is how long I'll have to wait until I can do it again."

"What're you doing right now?"

"Right now as in *right now*?"

I laugh at his boyish befuddlement, which I know is all an act. He's a man in every sense of the word. "Unless you're too busy, of course."

"Never too busy for you." He leans in slowly, keeping his eyes open and fixed on my face as he touches his lips to mine in the lightest possible caress. Pulling back, he studies me intently for a long, breathless moment before he comes back for more. He hooks a leg over the tiller so he can keep the boat on course while he uses both hands to frame my face and kiss me more intently.

I'm not thinking about anything other than him when I open my mouth to his tongue and moan from the desire that reawakens within me.

As if a switch has been thrown, I'm suddenly dying for more. With all my senses on full alert, I realize how numb I've been for all this time until Eric kissed me and touched me and made me feel alive again. Our kisses are desperate and needy and deliciously carnal. After sharing my story with him, I'm no longer burdened by the things I've kept to myself. I'm set free from my painful past. I'm ready for this. I'm ready for *him*.

"*God*, Ava," he says when we finally come up for air. His face is flushed, his heated gaze full of emotion. "*Where* did you come from?"

"I believe it was your brother's wedding."

He smiles and caresses my cheek. "I'm feeling a sudden, urgent need to get back to the city."

"Funny, because I seem to have the same urgent need."

The sound that comes from him is a cross between a tortured groan and a fierce growl. "Who the hell had the big idea to go *sailing*?"

I can't help the gurgle of laughter that comes out of me, earning a glare from him as he directs the boat toward home.

He keeps his arm around me, but we don't say anything in the forty minutes it takes to get back to the dock. Working together, we drop the sails, secure the boat and clean up as quickly as possible. With each minute that passes in charged silence, the tension between us seems to multiply.

I'm buzzing like I've consumed an entire bottle of champagne, but I'm remarkably clearheaded when I take his hand and let him help me off the boat. He keeps a tight grip on my hand as we walk up the dock to rejoin the others. I keep waiting for him to let me go before we get to where they can see us holding hands, but he doesn't let go.

I'm so caught up in what's happening between us that I don't immediately notice that something's amiss on the deck.

Eric stops short and releases my hand. "What's going on?"

# CHAPTER 12

*Ava*

Amy brushes at tears, Jules stares at the deck, and Camille, looking stricken, is holding Rob, who seems gutted. What the hell happened? There's no sign of my parents or Sarah Beth, but Bob is sitting among his other children.

"Could someone please tell me what the hell is wrong?" Eric says when we arrive on the deck.

I want to run away. Whatever it is, I don't want to know. For the first time in forever, I feel good. I don't want to lose that feeling. I don't want to hear what they're going to say.

Amy gets up, wipes her face and comes over to hug Eric.

He bristles. "What the fuck, Amy?"

"Mom and Dad are getting divorced."

He goes completely still. "What?"

"Come have a seat, son," Bob says.

"I don't want to sit. I want someone to tell me what the hell happened in the last two hours."

I want to put my arm around him or do something to comfort him, but I sense it wouldn't be welcome, so I stand awkwardly at his side, feeling as if I'm watching a slow-moving accident happen right in front of me.

"We were hanging out," Jules says, "and this guy came. He said he was a friend of Mom's and needed her to come with him. He… he acted like he had some kind of right to be here." She swipes a hand across her face, angrily swatting at tears. "She said she loves us all very much, but she can't live a lie anymore. She… she left with him."

Oh. My. *God.* I can't believe this is happening. I shouldn't be here. It's none of my business, but my feet are anchored in place. I can't move or breathe or do anything other than ache for Eric and his family. I catch Camille's gaze and see that my sister is similarly affected. The euphoria I experienced on the boat suddenly seems like it happened days ago when it was only an hour.

"It's been going on for a while," Bob says.

"You *knew?*" Eric stares at his father.

"I knew."

"This is why you aren't running for reelection, isn't it?" Rob asks in a dull, flat tone that sounds nothing like him. "I couldn't figure out why you won't meet with the party about the Senate race or the reelection campaign. This is why."

"Yes," Bob says.

"You're just going to *let this happen?*" Eric asks his father.

"What would you have me do?"

His quiet dignity in the face of catastrophe touches me deeply. I wish I had the right to hug him. The poor guy.

"Is this why we're here today?" Eric asks. "So you guys could drop this bomb on us?"

"I had no idea he was going to come here today," Bob replies. "I never would've subjected any of you to such a spectacle. Camille and Ava, I apologize that you and your parents had to be part of something like this."

I can't bear that he feels the need to apologize to me.

"Please don't worry about us," Camille says. "I'm so sorry this has happened to you."

Bob shrugs. "It's not the first time, but it will be the last time."

"*What?*" Amy cries. "She's done this *before?*"

"Several times," Bob says. "But this one is different, apparently."

Rob stands so abruptly, he nearly displaces Camille from her spot on the love seat next to him. "I can't hear any more of this." He takes her hand and heads for the stairs.

Camille looks over her shoulder and catches my eye. She looks haunted as she scurries to keep up with her husband's stride.

Jules goes to sit next to her father. "Why did you put up with it, Dad?"

"Because I love her. I've always loved her."

Jules rests her head on her father's shoulder.

Eric takes a step back. "I... I need to go." He starts toward the stairs and then seems to remember he didn't come alone. "Ava, please. Let's go."

I feel like I should say something to Bob, but what could I say that would matter to him? I follow Eric down the stairs. "I need my bag from the pool house."

"I'll be in the car." He takes off toward the driveway.

I move quickly to retrieve my bag and join him in the car so he won't have to be here any longer than necessary. I can't begin to imagine what he's feeling. As I walk around the house, I dig my phone out of my bag and find a text from my mother.

*Holy God*, she wrote. *What we just witnessed at the Tildens'... Be glad you were sailing. Call me when you can.*

The second my door closes, Eric guns the car into reverse and leaves a cloud of dust on the dirt road in his haste to get the hell out of there.

I have so many questions. I want to know if he had any idea his parents' marriage was in trouble or that his mother was a serial philanderer. I want to know what he's thinking and how I can help, but the tension in the car is so thick, I can barely breathe, let alone talk.

His tight grip on the wheel turns his knuckles white, and a pulse in his jaw ticks wildly. He barely blinks as he focuses on the road, driving faster than he should. He doesn't say a single word on the hour-long ride to the city. We're getting close to Tribeca when I can't bear it any longer.

"Take the car to the garage. You don't need to be alone tonight."

"I'm not up for company."

"Too bad. I'm not letting you deal with this alone."

"Ava…"

"Would you let me be alone tonight if this had happened to my family?" I already know him well enough to be certain he'd never leave me alone with something like this.

His jaw shifts from one impenetrable expression to another, but he doesn't argue the point. A few blocks later, he takes a series of turns that put us in front of a metal garage door. He uses a keycard to gain access, and the door opens with a loud clatter of metal. Inside, he drives down a couple of levels and parks in an assigned spot. We gather our belongings, he locks the car, and we walk toward a stairwell that delivers us to the street level.

He takes my hand, and we head in the opposite direction of my apartment.

I have more questions, but I bite my tongue and decide to follow his lead. Whatever he needs tonight is what he'll get from me.

Hurt rolls off him in waves that make me ache for him. He's had enough hurt to last him a lifetime, and now this. I want to wrap my arms around him and make him feel better. If he'll let me.

*Eric*

This can't be real. If someone had told me this would happen today, I would've laughed. My mom the adulteress. It's *preposterous*. Except… There've been signs over the years that their marriage wasn't what it could be, but never in my wildest dreams did I imagine anything like *this*.

I realize Ava is having trouble keeping up with me, so I slow my stride.

Ava… I don't want to expose her to this, especially not after we took such a huge step forward in our relationship today. When we returned from sailing, all I wanted was to get her home as quickly as possible so we could continue what we started on the boat. But then we walked into the disaster unfolding in my family, and now… Now, I don't know what I want.

This reminds me far too much of the horror that followed Brittany's deception. I'm sick and sweaty and disgusted. Why do people hurt the ones they claim to love? I'll never understand that. Maybe thinking like that makes me a pussy, but to me, loving someone means you *stay*. You put in the time and do the work. You don't leave or cheat or plot your own disappearance.

We arrive at my building, and I hold the door for Ava to proceed inside ahead of me. If I'd had my way, I would've delivered her home and then come home alone, but she wasn't having that. While I appreciate her support, I'd rather be alone with the bottle of vodka chilling in my freezer.

This is the first time she's been to my place, but I don't take the time to show her around. I head directly to the freezer to retrieve the icy bottle and pour a healthy glass for myself and down half of it before I offer some to her.

She shakes her head.

I pour another glass. By the time the second dose reaches my system, I begin to settle somewhat. I refrain from pouring a third round. With my hands on the counter, I let my head drop, hoping to relieve some of the pressure that's gathered at the base of my neck.

And then Ava is there, massaging my shoulders and soothing the ache inside me with her special brand of sweetness. "What can I do?"

"More of that would be good." I appreciate that she continues to massage my neck and shoulders but doesn't feel the need to fill the silence with useless platitudes the way some women would have. The way Brittany would have. She couldn't stand long silences. They made her uncomfortable. With hindsight, I've come to see they made her feel insecure. "Feels good." Then I turn to her, and she wraps her arms around me. I cling to her like a life raft in a stormy sea. "I'm so sorry you had to be part of such an ugly thing."

"Please don't apologize. You had no way to know that was going to happen. None of you did."

"She totally staged it so we'd all be there to witness the spectacular end to her marriage. I must've disappointed her when I left to go sailing."

"She acted kind of strange when you said we were going. Antsy was the word I thought of at the time."

"She wanted us all there to see it go down, but what I don't get is why. What did we ever do to her to warrant that kind of cruelty?"

"If I had to guess, she's so caught up in her great escape that she's not thinking about anyone but herself."

"That would certainly be true to character." I withdraw slightly, just enough so I can see her face. "I'm sorry our plans got derailed."

"Please don't apologize to me. There's no need for it."

"So, this is my place," I say with a weak smile.

"I sort of figured that when you had the key. It's nice. I like it."

I used to like it, too, before I spent time here with Brittany, and she ruined it for me. "Thank you." I take her hand and give a gentle tug. "Come sit with me." The loft is one big open room, with twenty-foot ceilings full of industrial piping and beams. A bedroom and bathroom are hidden behind a half wall on the far side. I lead her around the kitchen island to the living room, where a flat-screen TV is mounted to a brick wall above a working fireplace. Still holding hands, we sit close to each other on the sofa.

I wish more than anything we could've gone right from the boat to the car and skipped the family drama. I want to recapture the magic I experienced with her on the boat, but the bubble has burst and left me riddled with emotional shrapnel so overwhelming, I can't begin to process it.

"You want to talk about it?" she asks.

"I wouldn't know what to say."

"You had no idea they were having problems?"

"Not this kind of problem, but I don't spend much time with them these days. I've always been closer to my dad, but he's been crazy busy since he was elected, and I work so much… When we are together, it's usually a family thing. If there was something amiss, it'd be hard to notice it under those circumstances."

I review every gathering from the last year—holidays, birthdays, the rare political event I attended to show my support, the wedding…

"The wedding."

"What about it?"

"She waited to get past it to make her move."

"You think it was that calculated?"

"I absolutely do. Amy always says she plans everything down to the last potato. She's the queen of spreadsheets and checklists. There's no way this was some random occurrence that wasn't fully thought out ahead of time."

"I don't understand why anyone would do that to the people they love."

"No, you wouldn't, because you aren't calculating like she is." My phone is blowing up, and while I'd prefer to ignore it, I suspect my siblings are talking to each other about what went on today.

I unlock my phone and find thirty-six unread messages in our group chat. As expected, my brother and sisters are in full-on meltdown mode and are wondering where I am. I'm glad to see Jules and Amy decided to stay with Dad tonight, even if he insisted he'd be fine if they left. Rob is in a rage and wants to know who the guy is. What difference does it make, I want to ask. I refrain from sending the text and turn off my phone. The new nightmare will still be there in the morning.

I return my attention to Ava. "I hate that this got in the way of what was a rather great day."

"There'll be other great days. Don't worry."

I rest my head against the back of the sofa and turn my gaze to her. "You promise?" She's curled up with her legs under her. I like that she's made herself comfortable in my space. "You probably want to go home."

"I'd rather stay here with you."

"You would?"

Her gaze never wavers when she nods.

"I'll probably be crappy company."

"That's okay. Unless you'd rather be alone…"

"No." I cover her hand with mine. "I'd much rather be with you than be alone. I even have an extra toothbrush you can have."

"That's very nice of you, but I never leave home without my toothbrush."

"*Ever?*"

"Ever."

"That's very… obsessive…"

"I always have floss with me, too."

"You think you know a girl…"

She laughs, and the sound is one of the sweetest things I've ever heard. "I wouldn't mind borrowing your shower."

"Didn't bring yours with you?"

"It doesn't fit in this bag."

Smiling at her witty reply, I meet her gaze. Her gorgeous face is quickly becoming my favorite thing to look at. "I feel bad that our day got hijacked. You shared something very important with me, and we need to talk more about that, but then this happened, and now…"

"Breathe, Eric. It's okay. I'm talked out on my crap after last night and today. It was important to me that you know, and now you do."

"It means a lot to me that you shared it with me."

"It meant a lot to me when you told me about Brittany. I felt bad afterward that I hadn't been able to do the same. I guess I wasn't ready yet."

"Don't give that another thought. I'm painfully aware of how difficult it is to bring up these things in casual conversation." I kiss the back of her hand. "How about that shower you wanted?"

"Show me the way."

# CHAPTER 13

*Camille*

Upon arriving home, Rob went directly to the sofa, where he is stretched out, dealing with a flood of texts, presumably from his sisters.

I watch over him, uncertain of what to do. He hasn't said a word to me since we left his parents' house. I go into the kitchen and fix myself a glass of wine, drink half of it and then pour one for him. From my vantage point, I can see him texting. At least he's talking to someone.

I sit on the coffee table and offer him the glass of wine.

He sits up and takes the glass, downing most of it in one big gulp. "Thanks."

"What can I do?"

"Nothing." He continues to respond to texts while I sit there feeling stupid and impotent.

I get up, put my glass in the sink and go take a shower. The new-wife handbook didn't include a chapter on what to do when your in-laws' marriage implodes right in front of you. And when your father-in-law is the governor of New York, there needs to be an additional chapter on how to navigate what's certain to be a huge public relations challenge on top of the personal disaster.

Good times.

As I wash off salt water and sunscreen, I relive the scene on the deck. At first, I couldn't figure out who the guy in the light blue oxford shirt was or what he wanted with us. And then, when the pieces began to fall into place, the shock ricocheted through the family like a poison arrow, permanently changing each person as the realization set in.

Sarah Beth Tilden was never a warm or fuzzy kind of person, but I wouldn't have thought her capable of the sort of callousness she exhibited today. The man she left with was younger than she was, handsome and clearly intent on leaving with his prize—if you could call her that.

The aftermath of their departure reminded me of the way people look on TV after an F-5 tornado levels their home. And Rob... God, he's a mess. He wanted to go after his mother, but his father stopped him. "Let her go," Bob said. "It's what she wants."

That's when Rob, Amy and Jules realized their father knew about the affair, which only served to multiply their shock.

I shudder with revulsion. Watching people I love be steamrolled by someone who was supposed to love *them* made me sick. That woman will be my children's grandmother.

I get out of the shower, dry off and don a robe. My phone is alive with new texts from my mother and Ava. I read Ava's first.

*How's Rob? Eric is so shocked. I feel terrible for him. I can't believe someone would do this to their own family.*

*Rob is a mess. I sort of believe it... He's never come right out and used the word selfish to describe her, but I've picked up on things over the years. Are you with Eric?*

*Yes, didn't want him to be alone.*

*Nice to see you two together. You look happy.*

*I am. Or I was until this happened... Mom texted me. Did you talk to her?*

*Not yet. They left shortly after it all went down. I'll call her in the morning.*

*Check in with me after you talk to her.*

*Will do. Hope you guys can get some sleep.*

*Same to you. xo*

I change into one of the sexy nightgowns I received as a shower gift and get into bed, wondering if Rob will join me or fall asleep on the sofa. I think about going to get him but decide to give him some space. If he needs me, he knows where to find me.

Leaving the light on for him, I turn toward his side of the bed. Though I'm tired and drained, sleep proves elusive. How will the meltdown of the Tildens' marriage affect the plans Rob and I have made? Will the press go wild over the story of the governor's wife leaving him for another man? Probably… Imagining the sordid headlines apt to turn up in the *New York Post* disgusts me, because surely Sarah Beth anticipated them.

At some point, I must've fallen asleep. When I awake in the middle of the night, Rob is next to me, awake and staring up at the ceiling.

"Hey," I say, reaching for him.

He places his hand on top of mine.

"Are you okay?"

"Yeah, never better," he says with a bitter laugh.

I move closer and snuggle up to him. "I wish there was something I could say or do to help."

"I know, babe. I don't mean to take it out on you."

"It's okay. You can." I caress his bare chest, trying to offer what comfort I can. "What're you thinking?"

"I'm thinking about my dad. This is going to diminish him in more ways than one. The party has been all over him to declare his intention to seek a second term, and he hasn't been willing to even meet with them. Now I know it's because his wife is cheating on him, and he's trying to figure out how to handle that in the context of a reelection campaign."

"The poor guy."

"That poor guy has put up with this for a long time, apparently."

"Are you angry with him?"

"God, no. It's just going to create a nightmare for us at work. I can't begin to imagine the headlines."

"I was thinking earlier about what the *Post* would have to say."

A shudder ripples through his body and mine, too. "I feel like I'm going to be sick."

"Sit up." I help him up and rub his back as he takes a series of deep breaths.

"How could she do this to him? To us?"

"I've been asking myself that since it happened."

"It's like a gigantic 'fuck you' to her entire family. I hate that you and Ava and your parents were there, too."

"Don't worry about us. We're thinking only of you and your dad and siblings. No judgment."

"My mother texted us."

"What did she say?"

"That she's sorry but she can't live a lie anymore."

"Unreal."

He raises his head and looks over at me. "This could fuck up everything for us."

"Why would it? Your mother's actions are no reflection on you."

"Sure they are. The Tilden name is going to get run through the mud, and when the mudslinging is over, our political fortunes aren't going to look quite as shiny as they did before."

Disappointment and disillusionment color his every word.

"Whatever happens, we'll figure it out the way we always do."

He leans his head on my chest.

I run my fingers through his dark hair, wishing there was something I could say or do that would make him feel better, to assure him it won't be as bad as he thinks. But I can't do that, because when people find out about the dramatic way his mother chose to end her marriage, it will be an epic scandal.

*Ava*

I put my hair up in a bun and step into Eric's shower. I admire the tiny glass tiles that make up the shower, as well as the slate countertop and vessel sinks. His home suits him. It's classy and hip and sophisticated. Using body wash that smells like him, I wash up quickly so I can get back to him.

The events of the last twenty-four hours make me feel strangely removed from the reality that's been my life for the last five years. The woman standing naked in Eric Tilden's shower bears no resemblance whatsoever to who she was this time yesterday. I've taken a giant leap forward on my path toward a new life, and I'm proud of my progress, even if I'm sad for Eric and his family.

While I want to be supportive of him, I also need to stay focused on this positive new path I find myself on. Being here with him, overnight, is a huge step for me, and I want to enjoy it. I want to enjoy him and my newfound freedom and…

God, I'm a jerk for thinking of myself at a time like this. He's a mess, and it's not about me tonight. It can't be about me.

But maybe it can be about *us*, about taking that step forward together. I'm down with whatever it takes to keep moving in the right direction.

I turn off the water, towel off and change into a faded yellow T-shirt from a 5K road race that Eric gave me to sleep in. It smells like fabric softener and falls to my thighs. I brush my hair and teeth and take a minute to collect my thoughts before I join him in the bedroom.

He's sitting on the bed, wearing only a pair of gym shorts and staring off into space. When I emerge from the bathroom, he stands and comes over to me. "I'm going to take a quick shower, too. Make yourself comfortable." He kisses my cheek and disappears into the bathroom.

I sit on the bed and read an email from my new boss, giving me the rundown for my first day on Monday. His name is Trevor, and he seems like a nice enough guy. He ends the email with: *We've got an exciting project we want to bring you in on. More to come on that. Look forward to seeing you Monday!*

I write back to thank him for the information. *I'm looking forward to hearing more about the project. See you Monday!*

I'm contemplating checking to see if the Pentagon has released the names of the service members who were killed when Eric comes out of the bathroom, his hair damp and his face freshly shaven. My gaze travels over his bare chest and muscular abdomen.

He crawls onto the bed and lands next to me. "Everything okay?" he asks, nodding to my phone.

"Uh-huh. Just answering an email from the new boss." I put my phone on the bedside table and give him my full attention. "How're you doing?"

"Better because you're here." He smooths the hair back from my face. "I want to go back to where we were on the boat, before the shit hit the fan. Can we do that?"

"I can if you can."

"Remind me of where we left off," he says, running his thumb over my bottom lip, his gaze fixed on my mouth.

"I think it was something like this…" I lean closer to kiss him. "And this." I kiss him again. "Is it coming back to you?"

"Not quite yet."

Smiling, I kiss him again, lingering a little longer this time.

"Ava," he says, his hand diving into my hair to anchor me to him. "You're so sweet and so sexy."

As he kisses me more intently, I have a flashback of John saying almost those exact words to me in the same desperate tone. I don't want to think of him when Eric is kissing me so passionately, but there he is, smack in the middle of everything.

"What's wrong?" he asks, his lips hovering above mine.

"Nothing." I reach for him and bring him back to me, opening my mouth to his tongue and trying to lose myself in the moment. But I can't seem to get there, no matter how hard I try.

"You're all tense, sweetheart. Tell me what's wrong."

"I… I don't know." I do know, but I can't very well tell him that John is haunting me during this important moment with him.

He guides my head onto his chest and caresses my back. "Relax. It's okay. Nothing has to happen between us until you want it to."

"I *do* want it." Tears fill my eyes, infuriating me. I don't want to be this weepy, sad version of myself. I'm so sick of being sad. "I want you."

"I want you, too, but I'm not in any rush. I swear. It's all good." His hand moves in soothing circles on my back, and I begin to relax. "That's it. Nice and easy. We've got all the time in the world."

"I'm supposed to be comforting you tonight, not the other way around."

"You're comforting me just by being here."

"Eric?"

"Hmm?"

"I just want to thank you for being such a good guy. From the first time we met, you've been looking out for me, and I appreciate that more than you know."

"That's nice of you to say, but looking out for you is my pleasure. You can't begin to know how much it means to me to be moving on and to be spending this time with you. I don't care what we do. I just know that I feel better when I'm with you."

"Me, too."

"That's enough for me tonight."

I decide to make it enough for me, too, but always in the back of my mind is John's voice, telling me he loves me, that I'm the most beautiful girl he's ever known. I begin to actively hate him.

Eric and I spend Sunday together. We go to brunch at a place in our neighborhood where the people call him by name and greet me warmly. They seem happy to see him with a woman.

"Do they know about Brittany?" I ask him over Bloody Marys.

"*Everyone* knows about Brittany." Humiliation peppers his every word. "I handled it exactly the opposite of how you handled your situation. You told no one. I told everyone. I think I kept hoping if I told enough people, someone would help me make sense of it."

"There's no making sense of cruelty, Eric, especially when it's couched in love."

"You're right, and I've figured that out for myself over the last eight months. Once I realized it'd never make sense, I stopped talking about it to anyone who would listen. I was such a pathetic mess. I cringe to think of it now."

I take his hand. "You weren't pathetic."

He offers a cute smile. "How do you know? You weren't there."

"I know you, and I can picture you bewildered and hurt, but not pathetic. Never that. You survived. That's what matters."

"I like the way I look to you. I want to be this strong, resilient guy you think I am."

"We're a pair of emotional cripples learning how to walk again."

He laughs. "That's a good description."

"The way forward is one foot in front of the other."

"Very true."

"I want to tell you… I'm sorry for what happened last night. I… I don't mean to send mixed signals."

"Stop. You didn't. There'll probably be a few steps backward to go with many steps forward. You certainly don't have to apologize to me. I get it."

"The day after the wedding, when you told me about Brittany… I thought at the time that I was probably the worst person you could be interested in."

"Why would you ever think that?"

"Because of what I hadn't told you or anyone then. I didn't think it was fair for me to get involved with you after everything that happened to you. You needed someone who wasn't toting a million pounds of baggage behind her. But now…"

"What?" he asks, sounding slightly breathless as he stares intently at me.

"Now I see that maybe we're perfect for each other because we understand better than anyone else ever could what the other has endured."

"I couldn't agree more. There's comfort in knowing someone gets it, even if I wish you'd never been hurt so badly."

"Same."

We're so caught up in each other that we're startled by the arrival of the waitress with our food. We're further startled when Rob, Camille, Amy and Jules come strolling in, taking chairs from other tables and bringing them to ours.

"Um, hello?" Eric says. "Private party here."

"Too bad." Amy's eyes are rimmed with red, and dark circles under her eyes indicate a rough night. "If you shut off your phone during a family crisis, you run the risk of being hunted down."

"What the fuck, Eric?" Rob's testy tone makes Eric tense. "How can you just disappear at a time like this?"

He takes a bite of his eggs Benedict. "I'm an asshole because I choose not to be engrossed in the meltdown of my parents' marriage?"

"No one said that," Jules says. She, too, looks like she's been up all night. "But you can't just check out on us."

Camille bites her lip, a sign that she's nervous. Keeping a hand looped around Rob's arm, she meets my gaze with a grimace.

"Look, guys," Eric says, "I appreciate that everyone is upset. I feel terrible for Dad, and I'll tell him so when I get the chance. But I'm just emerging from my own personal nightmare. I don't have the fortitude to take on theirs. I'm finally feeling good again. I can't be dragged back down. I'm sorry if that makes me sound like a callous jerk, but that's how I feel. Leave me out of it."

"Easy for you to say," Rob says. "You don't have to work with him."

"Neither do you," Eric says. "You've got a law degree. Use it somewhere else if you don't want to deal with the meltdown."

"I can't walk away from him now," Rob replies. "He needs me and the rest of us to prop him up. When this gets out, the press will be ruthless."

"He has a team of people paid to handle that," Eric says. "I've got my own shit to deal with."

Rob explodes. "For Christ's sake, Eric! Brittany was almost a year ago. Get over it, will you?"

I gasp, and everyone looks at me. Moving without thinking, I take bills from my wallet, toss them on the table and stand. To Eric, I say, "Let's go."

# CHAPTER 14

*Ava*

Eric is robotic as he drops his napkin on the table and takes my outstretched hand.

"Eric… I'm sorry. I shouldn't have said that."

I glare at my new brother-in-law. "No, you shouldn't have. It's easy to be smug when you're sitting there happy as a pig in shit with your new wife by your side, never having survived anything *remotely similar* to what happened to him."

"I'm sorry," Rob says, and I believe him. "Forgive me, Eric."

"Sure," Eric says, his tone lifeless.

I head for the door, towing him behind me. I'm so fucking furious. Outside, I start walking. I have no idea where I'm going. I just want to get him away from there.

"Easy, tiger," he says after we've covered a couple of blocks.

"I can't believe he would say something like that to you. He's lucky I didn't punch him."

Eric laughs, and I stop walking to glare at him. "*What* is so funny?"

"You are." He slides his arms around me and gazes down at me.

"I am not funny! I'm pissed. How could he say something like that to—"

He kisses me into submission, right there on the street where anyone can see us. And oddly enough, I don't care if anyone sees us.

"He's my brother. He says stupid shit to me all the time. I say stupid shit to him all the time. It's okay. He doesn't mean anything by it."

"I'm sorry, but that was out of line."

"You're very sexy when you defend me." He kisses my neck and makes me want to purr from the sensations that travel through me like warm honey, heating me from the inside. "Especially when you take on your sister's husband."

"She's probably going to hate me for that."

"No, she won't. He was being a douche, and you called him out on it."

"I did put him in his place, didn't I?"

"Mmm, you sure did."

I realize we're walking again, this time in the direction of his place. He keeps an arm tight around me and continues to nuzzle my neck while steering us both through busy foot traffic on the sidewalk. In the short time it takes us to get back to his building, he has me practically clinging to him. Inside, he guides me up the stairs with his hands on my hips and his aroused body pressed to my back.

I'm reminded of a three-legged race I once did with Camille in which we moved seamlessly as one. Eric and I are like that as we go up the stairs to his second-floor loft. He reaches around me to unlock the door, guides me in ahead of him and keeps moving until we're in his bedroom, the bed still unmade from the night before.

I turn to him and he's right there, devouring me in a deep, passionate kiss. Then we're falling onto the bed in a mess of arms and legs and tongues and greedy desire. I'm so overtaken by him and the euphoria of the moment, I have no time to think about anything other than what's happening right now.

My dress disappears over my head. I tug on the hem of his T-shirt, trying to get it out of my way. He pulls my bra up to free my breasts and sucks my nipple into the heat of his mouth while his hand slides into my underwear. He groans when he encounters the slick heat between my legs. And then he pushes two fingers into me as he sucks on my nipple, and I come so quickly, it shocks us both.

The rest of our clothes are pushed aside, and I'm still coming when I hear the crinkle of a condom wrapper. Then he's pressing into me, taking it slow until he's sure I'm with him. I'm with him, even if I'm stretched to capacity as he pushes deeper into me.

"Ava," he whispers, "you feel so good."

I cling to him, breathe in his appealing scent and wrap my legs around his hips.

He keeps his arms tight around me as he moves inside me, constantly kissing me and never giving me the chance to punch out of the present to revisit the past.

It's good, so good... I'm on fire for him, swept up in the desire that pulses through me like a separate heartbeat that belongs only to him.

Reaching under me, he grasps my bottom and picks up the pace without breaking the never-ending kiss.

I'm completely lost to him and the need he's reawakened in me. I break the kiss when I come, crying out.

He's right behind me, pushing hard into me and letting himself go before collapsing on top of me, his sweat mingling with mine as aftershocks leave me breathless and spent. "Are you okay?" he asks right away.

"I'm surprisingly fine. You?"

"Same," he says, still breathing hard. "More than fine, actually. I'm quite spectacular, in fact." He raises his head and gazes down at me. "I figured the first time I did this after everything that happened would be..."

"Awful?" I ask, smiling.

"Yeah, but it wasn't." He kisses me. "It was amazing, because you're amazing."

With my hands on his face, I hold him there for more kisses. Now that I've started kissing him, I don't want to stop. Our kisses go from soothing to heated in a matter of seconds.

He groans as he pulls back from the kiss. "Hold that thought for one second." Grasping the base of his cock to secure the condom, he withdraws from me and gets up to use the bathroom. I watch him go, taking a good long look at his bare ass and the way his muscles flex as he moves.

I take a deep breath, hold it and let it out, waiting for pain that doesn't materialize. To use the bandage analogy, taking it off quick tends to hurt less, and the way this happened was exactly what I needed. No time to think. No time to second-guess. No time to mourn what used to be.

Eric comes out of the bathroom and gets back in bed, reaching for me and snuggling me into his warm embrace. "Hey there."

"How're you doing?"

"I'm great, you?"

"Very, very good."

"Mmm, I like that. Very good is *very* good." He drags his hand up and down my arm in a caress that's comforting as much as arousing.

I kiss his chest, and he tightens his hold on me. I'd forgotten what contentment felt like, and for a long time, I had good reason to wonder if I'd ever be content again. But then I met Eric, and one small step at a time, he has helped get me to the point where this is possible. I'm incredibly thankful to him for being exactly who and what I need.

"Did you have stuff to do today?" he asks.

"Nothing that won't keep."

"That's good, because I'd like to keep you here all day—and all night."

"I can do all day, but I have to get some sleep tonight. New job starts tomorrow, and I can't show up looking like something the cat dragged in."

"You couldn't look like that if you tried."

"Nice try, but I'm going home to sleep in my own bed tonight—alone."

"And here I thought you liked me."

"I *do* like you. That's the problem."

"It's not a problem. It—and *you*—may turn out to be the best thing to ever happen to me."

Wouldn't that be something?

*

I report to my new midtown office at nine o'clock the next morning, not nearly as well rested as I'd hoped to be. After Eric walked me home, he ended up spending the night, because I couldn't bear to send him away. I'm tired and sore, but it was so worth it. What a great day we had together, and even though I'm sleep-deprived, I'm also buzzing with excitement and anticipation.

FergusonMain, Inc. is one of the hottest PR firms in the city, and I'm delighted to have been hired because of my experience. Not that I would've said no to a job that came through the Tildens, but there's something extra satisfying in knowing I did this on my own.

Trevor, the senior account executive I'll report to, greets me in the reception area and walks me to the cluster of offices that make up his team. He introduces me to the others, and I try to memorize their names as he rattles them off. Everyone is nice and friendly and welcoming.

I fill out HR paperwork, set up my email account and record my voicemail message. They've got business cards already made for me, and I'm given files on their ongoing clients. I dive right in, and I'm working my way through the files when Trevor appears at my door, holding a coffee that he offers to me. He's tall and handsome with black-framed glasses and a serious demeanor. I figure he's about five or six years older than me.

I take the coffee from him. "Thank you."

"It's got cream but no sugar." He holds up sugar and artificial sweetener packs. "What's your pleasure?"

"Just cream is perfect, but thanks for the options."

He takes a seat in front of my desk. "How's it going so far?"

"I'm in PR heaven with everything you guys are involved with."

"It's never boring around here, that's for sure. I wanted to talk to you about the special project I mentioned over the weekend."

"Of course."

"As you may already know, Miles Ferguson, our managing partner, lost his fiancée and her parents on the *Star of the High Seas*."

Like a balloon hit by a pin, I deflate from the inside. I hope my despair doesn't show in the expression I try to keep neutral. Of course, I know about Miles and his tragic loss. I know his story by heart, but I hadn't expected to be confronted by his loss on my first day. I was prepared to have little to no contact with the big bosses, but as Trevor continues, I begin to realize the opposite will be true. Dear God, what've I signed on for?

"Miles has been very active in the family group, and now that they've filed suit against the government, they're looking to ramp up their activities to gain more exposure for their cause. That's where we come in." He pauses, tips his head and says, "Ava? Are you all right? You've gone pale on me. Oh God! You didn't lose someone on the ship, did you?"

A bead of sweat slides down my back, and for a brief, terrifying second, I fear I'm going to be sick in front of my new boss.

"Ava?"

I realize he's waiting for me to answer his question. "I didn't lose someone on the ship, but I was very much affected by it, as we all were."

"For sure. That was one of the worst days of my life, and I didn't know anyone who was killed."

"I... I had a... a friend... who was deployed after it happened. As far as I know, he's either still deployed or dead." The words are out before I take even one second to gauge the consequences of sharing such a thing with my new boss.

"God, Ava," he says, his voice little more than a whisper. "That's crazy. You don't have any way to find out what became of him?"

I shake my head because I don't trust myself to speak. I can't believe this is happening on my first day.

"I'll reassign you."

"No!" The last thing I want is special treatment. "No," I say again, less emphatically this time. "There's no need to reassign me. It will be a privilege to work for the family group."

"Are you sure? Because it's totally okay to say so if it's not something you feel comfortable doing."

"It's fine, Trevor, but thank you for asking." I absolutely *refuse* to come across as a victim on my first day. I'm not a victim. Not the way Miles and the other family members are.

"Okay, then. I'll walk you over to meet Miles."

"Could I ask one thing?"

"Of course."

"Why me? Why someone brand new to work on such an important account with one of the partners?"

His face flushes with embarrassment. "Um, well, you're the lowest-ranking account executive, so it costs us less to put you on a pro bono job."

"Ah, okay. I see."

"No offense or anything."

"None taken. Everyone has to start somewhere."

"It's also a great opportunity for you to wow the big boss with your awesomeness."

"No pressure or anything."

"None at all," he says, grinning.

Tamping down the panic that wants to overtake me, I gather the laptop that's on my desk and follow him down a winding set of hallways to the side-by-side offices of Miles Ferguson and Alexander Main. Since they founded the firm twelve years ago, they've built it into one of the city's premier public relations and marketing outfits while also earning a reputation for their philanthropic endeavors.

"Morning, Keith," Trevor says to the young man at the desk outside the two closed doors. "This is Ava Lucas, the new account exec on my team."

Keith stands to shake my hand. "Nice to meet you. Welcome aboard."

"Thank you. Nice to meet you, too."

"Miles is expecting you. Go on in."

"Thank you," Trevor says.

I follow Trevor into a huge office with a panoramic view of the Hudson River and New Jersey.

Miles, who has gone completely gray since I last saw a photo of him, gets up to come around the desk to greet us. The gray hair is in stark contrast to his youthful face. On his lapel, he wears the family member survivor pin.

"Miles, meet Ava Lucas. Ava, Miles Ferguson."

"A pleasure," he says. His eyes, I notice, project the kind of sadness I understand all too well. My heart goes out to him. "Welcome to the team."

"Thank you. I'm excited to be here."

"Come," he says, gesturing to a seating area with plush sofas. "Have a seat."

As I cross the room, I take a surreptitious look at the wall of awards and photos with celebrities. His has been an illustrious career. On the credenza behind his desk is a single framed photo of him with his late fiancée, Emerson Phillips.

When we're seated, Keith comes in with a tray bearing coffee and pastries.

"Thanks, Keith," Miles says.

"Yes, thank you," I add.

"Sure thing," Keith says, smiling as he leaves us.

"Help yourself," Miles says.

Though I've already exceeded my daily caffeine quota, I pour a cup of coffee and add cream.

"So," Miles says when he and Trevor have poured their coffee, "Trev told you about the *Star of the High Seas* family group project?"

"He did, and I hope it's appropriate to say that I'm sorry for your loss."

"Thank you."

I have so many questions. I want to know how he is, if he's found new love or if he's still single. I want to know everything about him and Emerson. I've read about them, but the details are fuzzy. As soon as I can, I'll refresh my memory.

I watch him try to shake off the grief and focus on the present. "You've heard about the lawsuit the family group has filed."

"Yes, I read about it." That moment in Times Square comes back to me in sickening waves that have me fighting to keep my composure.

"Over the next few weeks and months, the goal is to get as much publicity for the lawsuit as we can. We'll be booking Dawkins, myself and several of the other leaders of the family group everywhere we can. The goal is mass saturation to get people talking about this again and to drum up support for the lawsuit. We hope to force the government to own up to the mistakes that were made that led to calamity."

I open my laptop and begin to take notes as he speaks about the reasoning behind the lawsuit, the timing, the stakes, the hook to get the media on board and other aspects of the project. The activity helps to keep me focused on the present and not mired in the past.

"As you can imagine, this will be a difficult project at times, but I also believe it'll be very rewarding for everyone involved. We believe we have a slam-dunk case against the government that'll be settled long before it goes to trial. Former National Security Advisor Hartley has all but admitted in past interviews that they fucked up. They didn't take a credible threat seriously, and the result, as you know, was devastating."

Miles leans forward, arms on his knees, his expression earnest and intense. "This lawsuit is not about money. We want to hold these people accountable for their failure to protect four thousand American citizens. We want to put current and future officials charged with keeping us safe on notice that they *will* be held accountable for their actions—or inaction—while in office." He sits back, his shoulders losing some of their rigidity. "Their failures ruined our lives."

I swallow the massive lump that's lodged in my throat. It ruined mine, too, not that I can tell him that, because speaking would require breathing, and I'm having trouble with that. Rather than speak, I focus on taking copious notes. I'll do anything I can to help him and the other family members gain support for their cause.

He hands me a stack of paper. "These are all the requests for interviews we've received since the suit was filed."

I sift through them, noting that every major network, newspaper and web outlet is represented, as are the big morning broadcasts, late-night shows and even Ellen DeGeneres has requested an interview. This is going to be huge. The kind of PR campaign I could've only dreamed about in my old job.

"Here's the thing…"

I return my attention to Miles, who looks pained.

"Dawkins is a good guy, but he can be a loose cannon at times. I offered up my firm to handle the publicity at no charge to the family group in exchange for him agreeing to allow me to accompany him on all interviews. So you'll be setting these up for both of us and then coming along to handle any logistics. Assuming that's okay with you."

Accompany my boss to the *Today* show, *Jimmy Fallon*, *Ellen*? Umm… "No problem at all. How soon were you hoping to begin?"

"As soon as possible. I'll leave the coordination to you, but I'd suggest we start locally and handle the West Coast stuff all at once."

I've never handled a national media campaign on my own, but I figure with everyone clamoring for more of this story, it won't be difficult to get it done quickly.

Miles hands me another piece of paper. "Dawkins's contact info. He's standing by, waiting for his marching orders."

"I'll set it up and send you and Mr. Dawkins the schedule."

"Thank you. I know it's a lot to hit you with on your first day, but Trevor tells me you're more than up for the challenge."

"Absolutely. I'm honored to have been chosen to help with this."

Miles stands and extends his hand. "I look forward to working with you."

Juggling my laptop, I stand and shake his hand. "Likewise. Thank you for the opportunity."

"If you could update me at the end of the day, I'd appreciate it."

"Will do."

Trevor and I leave the office and return to our corner of the vast space. It's an open concept with each team grouped together in glass cubicles. "He liked you."

"I'm glad to hear it."

"Ava... I want to be sure this is something you feel capable of taking on in light of what you shared earlier. We aren't about emotional torture around here. I'd never hold it against you if you were to say it's not going to work for you."

"I appreciate your thoughtfulness, but I'm fine. I swear."

"Okay, then. I'll leave you to it. Let me know if you need anything. My door is always open."

"Thank you. I'll keep you both posted."

"Sounds good." He moves on to talk to others in our group.

# CHAPTER 15

*Ava*

I take a seat at my desk and pause for a second to catch my breath. Across the way, a woman on one of the other teams glares at me. What the hell is her problem? I return her stare and refuse to blink until she does. As she returns her attention to her computer, her lips are white with rage. I'll have to keep an eye on her.

"What's up?" a young Hispanic man asks as he leans against the door to my cube.

"Usual first-day madness. What's up with you?"

"Carlos Alvarez, at your service," he says with a low bow. "The woman who used to occupy your cube was my work wife, and I'm interviewing for a replacement. I wondered if you might be interested in the job."

I'm instantly amused by him. He's a total hipster in his skinny khakis, formfitting dress shirt and funky glasses. His dark hair is styled into a dramatic wave on top and shaved close on the sides. "What's the job description?"

He comes in and takes a seat in my visitor chair. "Coffee debrief in the morning, regular lunches, office gossip, Friday night happy hour and emotional support for all personal and professional drama."

"What number wife would I be?"

"Two," he says, his expression glum. "Tanya divorced me after a five-year marriage when she got a better offer from another company. She hit the road and never looked back."

I press my lips together so I won't be tempted to laugh. "Answer a question for me, and I'll consider your proposal."

"Anything for you."

"Blondie across the hall... No, don't look! She'll know I'm talking about her. I thought you knew how to do office gossip?"

"Darling, I am the *boss* of office gossip."

"Why's she glaring at me?"

He leans forward and lowers his voice considerably. "Because she wants to be the one to heal Miles's broken heart, but you were the one chosen to work on his passion project."

"So, they're dating?"

He snorts. "She wishes. To my knowledge, Miles hasn't dated anyone since Emerson died."

That makes me incredibly sad for him.

"Steer clear of Catty Caitlyn. She's a venomous viper."

"Good to know."

"About our work marriage..."

I already know I'd love nothing more than to be best friends with this entertaining, comical man, but I'm going to make him work for it. "I'll consider a thirty-day probationary period. Bring your A game, my friend."

"Oh, it's on like Donkey Kong."

I snort with laughter. "Get out of here. I've got interviews to line up at the *Today* show and *The Late Show with Stephen Colbert.*"

"I didn't realize you were a name-dropping bitch. Now that I've seen your mean side, I may have to reconsider my proposal."

"Or I could offer to bring you with me to the *Today* show... If you're willing to carry my purse for me, that is."

He grins widely. "How do you take your coffee, my love?"

"Large and full of cream."

He shudders dramatically before he sweeps out of my cube. "This'll be a match made in heaven."

So far, other than Catty Caitlyn, I love this place. I take one second to dash off a quick text to Eric.

*Guess what project I've been assigned to? Star of the High Seas family group lawsuit publicity. Can't make this up!*

He responds within seconds. *Oh damn. Are you sure you ought to be doing that?*

*Absolutely not, but it's a great opportunity, so I'm trying to stay focused on that.*

*Should you maybe ask the shrink if it's a good idea?*

*Yeah, probably. I'll hit her up.*

*Sounds like a plan. Can't stop thinking about you and the best weekend ever (not counting parental meltdown).*

*Me too.*

*Dinner tonight to celebrate your new job?*

*Sure, I'll text you when I'm leaving.*

*I'll be waiting.*

He leaves me feeling happy and excited to see him and moved by his concern for me. The relief of no longer having to carry my heavy burden alone continues to be pervasive days after I unloaded on three different people. I feel a thousand times better now that Eric knows, and I appreciate that he didn't run for his life from me after hearing about what happened with John. I wouldn't have blamed him if he had.

But he didn't, and no matter what happens between us, I'll always be thankful for that.

### Eric

I'm concerned about Ava being assigned to the family group project just when she's starting to show signs of having survived her own trauma. The weekend with her was nothing short of blissful. I haven't felt that good in well, ever… Even when things were fantastic with Brittany, it was never easy the way it is with Ava. I don't have to think before I speak with her or weigh the potential for fallout if I express an unpopular opinion.

It's a fucking relief to be completely myself with Ava.

And yes, I realize now, with the power of hindsight, that I was never completely myself with Brittany, which should've been a huge red flag. It's nice to think that maybe I learned something from that debacle, which would give it meaning it's lacked up to now. If the nightmare with Brittany was leading me to Ava, that also gives it meaning.

The phone on my desk buzzes with a call from my assistant, Taylor.

I hit the intercom button. "What's up?"

"Your brother is here to see you."

He is? Rob has never been to my office. "Send him in. Thanks."

I stand as Rob comes through the door, carrying two cups of coffee and wearing a conciliatory expression. He hands me one of the coffees. "I come in peace to apologize profusely for being a total asshole."

I take the coffee from him. I've already forgiven him, but that doesn't mean I'm going to let him off easy. What fun would that be? "I know you can't help it sometimes."

"That's what my wife said, too." He makes himself comfortable on the sofa by the window and props his feet on the coffee table.

I go over to join him. "I thought you'd be putting out fires at work today."

"The fire hasn't struck yet. The media hasn't caught wind of the governor's marital meltdown. I believe we're in what's commonly referred to as the calm before the storm." He glances at me. "I'm really and truly sorry for what I said about Brittany. It was totally out of line and uncalled for."

"Yes, it was, but it wasn't entirely untrue."

"No?"

I shake my head. "I've allowed myself to wallow in that pit far too long."

"What she did goes beyond egregious to downright cruel. You didn't deserve what she did to you."

"No, I didn't, but there were warning signs I chose to ignore."

"Please don't tell me you're blaming yourself in any way for what she did."

"Definitely not. I'm just pointing out that there were things I chose to ignore that with hindsight were a big deal."

"I didn't come here to force you to revisit that nightmare, and I'm sorry if something I said brought it all back. That's the last fucking thing I'd ever want to do to you. I hope you know that."

"I do. It was heat of the moment. I'm over it."

"I'd understand if you wanted to punch it out the way we would've back in the day."

"Nah. I've got better uses for my hands these days than beating the shit out of you."

"A. You never once beat the shit out of me. B. Does that mean you're using your hands on my sister-in-law?"

"A. Yes, I did, too, beat the shit out of you, and you know it. And B. None of your fucking business."

"I knew it. I told Camille you two were getting busy."

I smirk at him. "We weren't getting busy until my brother hurt my feelings, and she offered comfort."

He chokes on a mouthful of coffee and just manages to contain it before it would've gone all over the white dress shirt he's wearing with a blue pinstripe suit and red tie.

"So, thanks for that, and if you breathe a word of it to her sister or anyone else, I *will* beat the shit out of you, and I *will* make it hurt. *That* you can count on."

"I won't say anything. I promise."

I trust Rob, Amy and Jules more than anyone in this world, and I believe him when he says he won't spill my secrets.

"So look at us," he says, "married to and dating sisters. Kinda funny when you think about it."

"And a potential minefield."

"How do you figure?"

"I feel like the stakes are higher for Ava and me because of you and Camille."

"Don't put that pressure on yourself. We're thrilled the two of you are hanging out. If it doesn't work out, for whatever reason, that's between you guys."

"You say that now, but if I were to screw it up somehow and hurt your sister-in-law, that's apt to cause trouble for you with your wife."

"Are you planning to screw it up or hurt her?"

"Hell no. But we both know how these things can go bad."

"It doesn't always go bad, Eric. You know that as well as I do. Don't let one chick ruin your sense of optimism. Ava is a great person. She's nothing like Brittany. And you're a pretty good guy, too. I told my wife that her sister couldn't ask for better than my brother."

"You did? Really?"

"Of course I did. Ava is lucky to have you, and by now, I'm sure she realizes that."

"Do me a favor and don't add to the already considerable pressure on both of us by making it into something it's not. Not yet, anyway."

He holds up his hands. "No pressure from me."

"What's the latest with the parents?"

"Haven't heard a word from either of them. Amy was up there last night with Dad, and she said he's surprisingly fine. She thinks maybe he's known this was coming for quite some time and wasn't as blindsided as we were."

"Lucky him."

"I know, right? I just can't fathom why she would do it that way."

"Maybe she's tried the subtle approach in the past with no success."

"Maybe," he concedes. "It's not like it's a newsflash to any of us that they weren't exactly happy."

"At least we know why he isn't interested in reelection or higher office."

"That, too."

"How bad will it be when the press catches wind of this?"

"As bad as it gets."

*Ava*

I'm wrapping up my first day at FergusonMain when I get a text from Camille. *Call me 911.*

What the hell? I find her at the top of my Favorites list and put through the call.

"Thank God you got my text."

"What's wrong?"

"I just got a call from a reporter at the *New York Post* wanting to know if there's any truth to the rumor that my mother-in-law, the first lady of New York, left my father-in-law, the governor, for the tennis pro at their golf club."

"Oh shit. How'd they get your number?"

"I have no idea, but I'm freaking out. I can't reach Rob, and I have no idea what to do."

"What did you say to the reporter?"

"I hung up on him, but he's been calling me once every minute."

"Take the call and tell him you're not authorized to comment on the Tilden family or anything having to do with the governor. All inquiries will need to be directed to the governor's office. Don't say anything but that."

"Say it again. I want to write it down in case I brain-freeze."

I go through it again, slower this time so she can get it all down. "It's really important that you don't let him trick you into saying anything else."

"Okay."

"You can do this, Camille. Take some deep breaths."

"He's calling again."

"Take the call, tell him what I said, then hang up and block him." That won't stop him from calling on a different phone, but it'll eliminate the one he's calling on now. "Call me back after."

"Okay."

The line goes dead, and I put down my phone, wishing I could handle the call for her.

"Miles and Alex don't approve of us taking personal calls on company time." I look up to find Catty Caitlyn standing in my doorway. Her arms are crossed over her substantial breasts, and her mouth is pursed in a mean little sneer.

"That was a client in need of emergency media advice, not that it's any of your business."

"What client do you have who needs emergency advice? You just started."

"Wouldn't you like to know?"

"I'm sure Miles would like to know."

"I'll be happy to tell him that I represent members of the Tilden family in their dealings with the media, but if you want to tell him first, be my guest."

Her mouth falls open and just as quickly snaps shut before she turns and stalks off. Round one most definitely goes to me, but I have a feeling it'll be the first of many rounds with Catty Caitlyn.

My phone rings, and I pounce on the call from Camille. "Did you do it?"

"All set. My hands are still shaking, though."

"You need to find Rob and let him know about this ASAP. If one reporter knows, others do, too, and they need to be ready."

"I'm going to call him again right now. Thank you for your help."

"No problem. You helped me win a round of passive aggression with the resident bitch in my office."

"Didn't take long to get entrenched in office politics, huh?"

"In my defense, she started it."

Camille laughs.

"How was your day?"

"Much less eventful than yours, until the *Post* called."

"Let's catch up later. Go call Rob."

"I'm going."

I put down my phone and finish typing the report I promised Miles by the end of the day. So far, I've booked him and Dawkins on the *Today* show, *Good Morning America, CBS This Morning* and *Morning Joe*. I have emails into thirty other top media outlets and will be adding them to the schedule as I hear back from the various producers who book guests.

I send the email to Miles, copying Trevor, and then gather my belongings. On the way out, I stop at Trevor's open door to let him know I'm leaving.

"Hope you had a good first day," he says.

"I'm now on a first-name basis with a producer at the *Today* show. I think you could call it a good day."

"Excellent. Does this mean you'll be back tomorrow?"

"I'll be back."

"See you then."

I step out of the office into pouring rain and decide to splurge on a cab. On the ride home, I dash off a text to Jessica, updating her on the project at work and asking her opinion.

She responds by calling me.

"Hi there."

"Hey, I got your text and I'm on the run, so I figured I'd call. Can you talk for a minute?"

"Yes, I'm in a cab."

"Funny! Me, too. So tell me more about the project they've put you on."

I tell her about Miles, the fiancée he lost in the attack and the management of publicity requests for the family group since the lawsuit was filed.

"Did you know one of the partners had suffered a loss on the ship when you took the job?"

"I did. I told my direct supervisor, Trevor, that the guy I was involved with at the time of the attack was deployed that day and I haven't heard from him since. He offered to let me off the hook on the project with Miles, but I told him I didn't want that. I didn't want special treatment, especially on my first day."

"I can understand that, but are you sure this project is healthy for you when you've begun to make such positive steps forward?"

"In a way, it sort of feels like I'm contributing to the cause by helping out the family group, even in a small way. Does that make sense?"

"It does."

"But I don't want a setback at this point. Like you said, I've begun to feel better and... things with Eric have moved forward rather significantly."

"Is that right?"

"I told him about John, and he was so understanding and sweet. We slept together over the weekend, and it was great."

"I'm happy for you, Ava. These are all very positive steps in the right direction."

"It feels good to be optimistic again."

"I'll bet it does."

"So you don't think I'll be screwing things up by taking on a project that strikes a little too close to home?"

"Only you can decide that for certain. I would give it a few weeks to be sure it's not going to make anything worse for you. Your boss, Trevor, gave you an out. If you need it, don't hesitate to take it."

"I won't. I so appreciate your input."

"Happy to help any time. Are we still on for Thursday?"

"I'll be there. Thanks again."

After we end the call, I check my texts and see one from Eric. *Leaving the office. What's your status?*

*Almost home.*

*Meet you at your place?*

*Sounds good.*

*See you in fifteen.*

I take the elevator to my apartment and head straight for the bathroom to brush my hair and teeth before he arrives. I'm rubbing scented lotion into my hands and arms when the doorman calls to let me know he's arrived. Buzzing with excitement, I wait for him in the doorway.

# CHAPTER 16

*Ava*

He comes off the elevator and stops short when he's an inch from me. "Mmm, professional Ava is very, *very* sexy." His arm hooks around my waist, and he lifts me right off my feet to walk us into my apartment, kicking the door closed behind us. "Skylar…"

"Isn't home."

"Oh, good, because this might get loud."

I expect him to put me down inside, but he moves with determination to my room and kicks that door closed, too.

I frame his face and kiss him, thrilled to see him after the long day apart.

He seems equally happy to see me if the press of his erection against my belly is any indication. We're still kissing when he lowers me to the bed and comes down on top of me. "Mmm," he says, "I've been thinking about your sweet lips all day. I couldn't get a thing done, and it's all your fault."

"How is it my fault?" I look up at him with an intentionally innocent expression. "What did I do?"

Smiling, he kisses me again. "You did me. Really, *really* well."

I smack his shoulder. "I can't believe you said that!"

Laughing now, he buries his face in the curve of my neck and seems to breathe me in. "I love being with you, Ava, and every time we're together, I just want more of you."

Combing my fingers through his dark blond hair, I realize he just summed up exactly how I feel about him.

He raises his head to gaze down at me. "Tell me it's not just me who feels this way."

"Definitely not just you."

"That's very good news." Keeping his eyes open, he kisses me softly and tugs at the top button to my blouse.

My breasts feel tight and confined inside my bra, which he releases with the flick of his fingers over the front clasp. The relief is immediate but short-lived as he pushes both my shirt and the bra aside so he can run his tongue over my nipple. Sensation is like a live wire between my nipple and clit, and I wriggle beneath him, looking for more.

"Nice and slow this time," he whispers against my nipple. "I want to taste every inch of your sweet skin."

He's true to his word, and by the time he finally enters me, the room has begun to go dark. I've already come twice, and I'm hovering on the brink of a third.

I'm completely captivated by him. His tenderness shatters all my defenses, and as we move together, I can't deny I'm falling hard for him. Perhaps I have been since my sister's wedding, when he took such good care of me on a day that could've been torturous for me but wasn't because of him.

He's loyal and devoted and adorable and sexy. I know his family and his secrets, which means so much to me. With Eric, what you see is what you get, and considering my past, there's a lot to be said for that.

I cling to him as he moves in me, his lips soft against my neck.

"You feel so good, Ava. So hot and sweet."

His words and the heat of his breath on my neck make me shiver.

He picks up the pace, his fingers digging into my hips. He touches a place deep inside me that triggers the orgasm that's been building with every deep thrust.

I cry out as I come, and he tightens his hold on me, groaning as he comes, too.

I keep my arms around him under the suit coat he never took off, not wanting to let him go yet. He sags into my embrace.

"Ava…"

"I know. Me, too."

He releases a deep sigh of contentment that makes me happier than I've been in far too long.

"Thank you for being exactly what I need." I hadn't intended to say that out loud, but the words are out before I can stop them.

"Right back atcha, sweetheart."

*

Eric and I spend every night together that summer, except for when I'm traveling with Miles. The press coverage of Eric's parents' divorce is relentless, and other than having dinner with his father every other week or so, we do our best to stay far away from it. Camille and Rob aren't so lucky since Rob works for his father and is forced to deal with it far more often than the rest of us.

We support him with frequent nights out and regular dinners in which we "close ranks" around the four Tildens as they weather the storm their mother created. Story after story is written about the man she left their father for, who, it turns out, has a criminal record dating back to the eighties.

From all accounts, Sarah Beth is standing by her man, who she claims has been "clean" for a decade.

No one is surprised when Governor Tilden announces he won't seek a second term.

I feel guilty about being so happy in my life at a time when such chaos surrounds Eric's family. But he seems to be holding up okay, and the more time we spend together, the more in love with him I am. Yes, you heard that right. I'm in love, and so is he. Not that we've said the words yet. We don't have to. We both know.

I've all but moved into his place, where we have complete privacy, although I've continued to develop my friendship with Skylar with regular lunches and happy-hour meetups. I also see Jessica twice a month as kind of a check-in to make sure I'm still moving in the right direction.

I still have moments of grief and despair when I think of John, but they aren't as frequent as they once were, and I no longer spend hours every day scouring the internet, hoping to find news of him. With hindsight, I can see how unhealthy that behavior was.

In addition to my happy personal life, I absolutely *love* my job. Carlos has become my best friend as well as my work husband, and Miles… He's an absolute sweetheart of a guy. I've gotten to know him quite well during our travels over the summer, and I'd go so far as to say we've become close friends.

In mid-October, we're in Los Angeles having an after-dinner drink in the hotel bar when he opens up to me about losing his fiancée.

"I was supposed to go with them," he says, taking me by surprise when I realize he's talking about the cruise. Prior to this, he hasn't said much about it other than the snippets he shares during interviews. "My father had a heart scare, so at the last minute, I flew home to Minneapolis and urged Emmie and her parents to take the trip without me. She wanted to come with me, but I didn't want her to miss out on the trip she'd been looking forward to."

I haven't heard this before. Those details weren't contained in any of the stories that've been written about them. I'm riveted as the words seem to spill out of him, as if a dam has broken inside him.

"Funny, isn't it, that my father's health scare saved my life." His lightly spoken words convey a world of agony.

"What was she like?" I know from experience it will matter to him that I care about *her*, that I want to know *her*.

"She was…" He smiles, lost in memories. "She was life itself. Funny and outgoing. Klutzy and elegant at the same time. Athletic but not competitive. And beautiful. So very, very lovely, inside and out."

"I wish I'd gotten to meet her."

"Me, too. She would've liked you."

"That's nice of you to say." There are times, here and there, when I wonder if Miles would be interested in me if I didn't have a boyfriend he's met several times. This is one of those times. I ache for him and wish I could do something to ease his pain—short of venturing into inappropriate territory. "I want to tell you something about me."

"Okay…"

I've been wanting to tell him about John for a while now, and tonight seems to be a night for sharing. "I had a boyfriend in San Diego. A military officer named John West, or at least I think that was his name."

His brows furrow. "You don't know for sure?"

I shake my head. "I don't know anything for sure when it comes to him." I tell him the rest, the whole sordid tale, and he listens intently without interrupting.

"Jesus, Ava," he says when I'm finally finished. He sits back against the banquette and stares at me. "I don't know what to say. I'm so sorry you went through that all alone."

"I chose to do it alone. I still haven't gotten around to telling my sister or parents about him."

"Still…"

"It's nothing compared to what happened to you."

"It's certainly not nothing, and you're the last person who should've been assigned to publicity for the family group."

I rest my hand on his arm. "Trevor knows and offered me an out that I didn't want. It's been an honor and a privilege to work with you and the others. It's helped in my healing, believe it or not."

"I can't imagine living more than five years without knowing what'd happened to Emmie. How can you bear the not knowing?"

"It was unbearable for a long time, but I reached a point where I couldn't obsess about it anymore. I had to accept that I'll probably never know what became of him. Moving to New York helped. Meeting Eric helped. This job has helped. Thank you for that, by the way."

"You don't have to thank me. You've done a brilliant job for us."

"That's nice to hear. I'm so thankful to have been entrusted with such an important project."

"I had no idea we were getting someone so uniquely qualified."

"It's a hell of a club to belong to, isn't it?"

"One I'd never join willingly, that's for sure."

"Can I ask you something that's absolutely none of my business?"

He flashes a rare, genuine boyish grin that transforms his serious countenance and gives me a hint of what he was like before tragedy struck. "Why stop now? Go for it."

"Do you think you'll ever date again?"

"I wish I had a dollar for every time I've been asked that. I'd be able to retire to the Caribbean and live out my days in luxury."

"I don't mean to pile on."

He waves away the comment. "It's a fair question, and after five and a half years, you'd think I'd be closer to an answer than I am. If I met someone who interested me, I wouldn't be opposed to it, but I'm not about to start hitting the bars or anything."

"I have a friend…" The idea hits me with sudden clarity. Skylar.

He groans. "If I had a dollar for every time I've heard *that*, I could buy a private island."

"But this time is different because my friend Skylar is amazing. You'd love her. She's actually my roommate and was the first person I told about John. She came home to a full-on meltdown after the first time Eric kissed me, and I spilled the whole thing to her. She set me up with the therapist who's been such a huge help to me. Skylar… she understands loss. Her younger sister was killed in an accident when Skylar was in law school. It messed her up badly."

"That's so sad," he says, seeming genuinely moved. "If you think I'd like her, I wouldn't be opposed to meeting her. But not a blind date. Set something up with a group so it's not insanely awkward. And make sure she knows the point of the evening."

"You're really going to let me do this?"

He shrugs, but there's a helplessness to it that tugs at my heart. "Emmie's not coming back, and I am getting rather sick of my own company. It might be time to stick a foot into the shark-infested waters."

I clap my hands in unrestrained glee. "This will be so fun!"

He groans. "God, what've I gotten myself into?"

Two weeks later, Eric and I host a dinner party at his place. We've invited Rob, Camille, Amy, Jules, Miles and Skylar, who said she was willing to meet him if I thought she might like him. Naturally, she was deeply affected after hearing he lost his fiancée in the cruise ship attack.

"Has he dated at all since then?" she asked.

"No."

"Ah, well, at least you're not dragging me into a total emotional minefield or anything."

"Did I mention he's insanely hot and all pent up?"

She rolled her eyes. "Save the sales pitch. I'll meet your boss, but only because you're asking me to. No expectations, though, you hear me?"

"I hear you loud and clear. But I think you'll really like him."

"Ava! Stop. There's nothing in this world more awkward than a setup."

"Um, getting your skirt caught in your underwear is worse, or tripping over a grate and face-planting on the sidewalk, or—"

"Enough. I'm doing this for you, so don't make me regret it."

"Promise you won't regret it."

Now that the big night is upon us, I'm nervous for two people who've become friends. I want them both to be as happy as I am with Eric.

Speaking of the man who makes me so happy, I'm standing in his kitchen tending to the bruschetta I made as an appetizer when he slides his arms around me from behind, nuzzling my neck. He's fresh from the shower and smells delicious.

"My mouth is watering," he says. "It's like an Italian bistro in here."

"I'm worried I used too much garlic. If Miles offers to take her home, she won't want to kiss him if she stinks like garlic."

Eric laughs. "You've worked yourself into a panic over this evening."

"He's suffered *so* much. Imagine if they hit it off."

"Are you prepared for the possibility that they may not click?"

"No! Don't even say it. I want him to go crazy over her." I bite my lip as another thought worries me.

"What? Whenever you torture your poor lip, that means your wheels are spinning."

I push my ass back against his erection. "Quit acting like you know me so well."

"I do know you that well, so you may as well tell me what you're thinking."

"I'm just kind of worried that Sky looks a tiny bit like his late fiancée."

He goes stiff behind me, and not in a good way. "You're just thinking of that *now?*"

"It's not going to be a problem," I say with more bravado than I feel. "It's only a slight resemblance, and besides, Sky is fabulous. Anyone would love her."

"I hope you know what you're doing, sweetheart."

I turn to face him and slide my hands up his chest to link behind his neck. "Thanks for letting me use your place tonight."

"My place is your place." He kisses me. "You know that." He gave me keys months ago so I could come and go as I please.

"You told Rob and your sisters to act normal and not stare at them, right?"

"Yes, dear. I follow all your orders like the awesome boyfriend I am."

"I just want this to be perfect for them, but especially for him. He's *such* a nice guy, and he deserves to be happy again."

"If I didn't know better, I'd be worried about this guy Miles you think so highly of."

"You have nothing to worry about, as you well know. I'm just... invested in him after all the time we've spent together."

"Not to mention the similarities of what you've been through."

"That, too."

"I get it, babe, and I know I have nothing to worry about. His story is heartbreaking, and it'd be great if he found someone wonderful to start over with the way I did."

"And the way I did." I kiss him and toss in some tongue because he deserves it after letting me take over his home the way I have in preparation for tonight.

"That was very unfair," he says when we break apart, breathing heavily when the kiss turns into a passionate embrace as most of our kisses do. He rubs his hard cock against me. "You're going to let me walk around like this all night?"

I glance at the clock on the oven, see that we have thirty minutes before our guests are due to arrive and turn off the heat under the pots on the stove. Grasping his hand, I tug him along behind me.

"Um, excuse me. What's happening here?"

"Come with me, and I'll show you."

"You lead, and I'll follow."

In the living room, I push him down on the sofa, and he lands hard, making me laugh. I kneel before him, undo his belt and carefully unzip him, working around the huge bulge in his pants.

"*Ava,*" he says on a protracted groan. "You're *killing* me."

"We can't have that now, can we?" I bend to take him into my mouth and go for broke, determined to finish him off in under five minutes so I can get back to the stove. It takes only four minutes before he's gasping in the aftermath of an almost-violent release.

"*Holy shit.* That was… Holy shit."

I pat his leg, lean forward to kiss him and get up to fix my makeup before our guests arrive. "Zip up before you get caught with your dick out, babe." I love that his hands are shaking as he zips his pants.

I go into the bathroom to brush my teeth and reapply my lipstick.

Eric joins me, wrapping his arms around me like he did in the kitchen. "You are amazing, and I love you. Not just because you gave me the best blow job ever, but because you've become everything to me, and I can no longer imagine my life without you right in the middle of it."

My knees go weak under me, and only his arms tight around my waist keep me from sliding into a puddle on the floor. "Eric…"

"It's okay if you aren't there yet, but I've been there for a while now, and it's become almost painful trying not to say it too soon."

I meet his gaze in the mirror. "It's not too soon, and I love you, too. I have, probably, since the day I met you, and you saved my life with a slice of cheese pizza."

His smile is giddy and joyful. His happiness is mine, too. "You saved my life in a million ways, but especially with your sweet sincerity. You have no idea how much it means to me to know I can trust every word you say."

"I think I know."

"Yeah, I guess you do." He turns me to face him and gazes down at me. "I love you, Ava."

"I love you, too, Eric."

It feels more official this time, when we say it face-to-face.

He kisses me softly and sweetly. "And the blow job was fucking *epic.*"

That makes me laugh so hard, I mess up the kiss. But that's okay. There'll be plenty more of them to look forward to later.

# CHAPTER 17

*Ava*

Miles and Skylar hit it off like a house on fire while the rest of us spend the evening pretending we aren't watching them. I've never seen him so animated or engaged, and she looks positively gobsmacked. If this isn't a love connection in the making, then I'll hang up my matchmaking cape forever.

It's a fun evening all around. Everyone loves my lasagna, and the Tildens are entertaining as always, especially now that some of the dust has settled on their parents' breakup. For a while there, I wondered if they would ever be the lighthearted, fun-loving group they once were, but they're slowly getting back to normal, or what counts for normal these days.

"I had lunch with Dad yesterday," Jules says when we gather in the living room with after-dinner drinks. "He seems really good, better than he's been in a long time."

"I've thought that lately, too," Rob says. "Ever since Mom left and he announced he's not running for reelection, he seems unburdened."

"Imagine knowing for years that your wife is cheating and having to sit on that while you're responsible for the entire state of New York," Amy says, shuddering. "It's a wonder he didn't have a breakdown."

"I talked to him about online dating," Jules said.

"He can't do that!" Rob says, horrified. "He's the freaking governor."

"Not for much longer."

"For the better part of another year," Rob replies. "He cannot be on those sites while he's still in office, Jules. Seriously."

"I hear you. I was just planting the idea for later."

Rob relaxes, but only slightly. What he doesn't say, but we all know, is that some of the shine has gone out of the Tilden family name since the scandal hit. He thinks his siblings don't know that he wants to follow their father into politics. Their parents' messy split makes his path much more fraught with pitfalls than it was before. Eric told me that Rob has big plans, but he doesn't talk about them.

"Dad's had enough bad press to last a lifetime. The last thing we need is the *Post* catching wind of his online dating profile." Rob cringes. "I can't even imagine what they'd do with that—and I don't want to."

"I hear you, big brother," Jules says. "Loud and clear."

"Nothing says he can't try online dating when he leaves office," Camille says.

"Maybe he'll meet someone the old-fashioned way long before then," I offer from my perch next to Eric on the sofa. His arm is around me, and my hand is on his leg. His body heat keeps me nice and warm as the temperature drops outside and puts a chill in the loft. We'll have to turn on the heat before much longer. "Too bad there's not another family wedding coming soon. I hear that's a great way to meet people."

The others laugh as Eric tightens his hand on my shoulder.

Rob's phone buzzes with a text that has him sitting up straighter. "Holy fuck," he says in a tone that sends shivers down my spine. "They got Mohammad Al Khad in a Special Forces raid in Afghanistan."

Amy jumps up. "We need the TV. Where's the remote, Eric?"

Miles and Skylar, who were still seated at the dining room table long after the rest of us decamped to the living room, join us to gather around the TV to watch CNN. They report that an elite team of US Special Forces infiltrated the compound in a remote corner of Afghanistan where Al Khad, his family and closest associates were hiding out.

"The Pentagon is reporting several fatalities among Al Khad's family and associates," the anchor says, reading from a piece of paper. On the bottom of the screen, a breaking news crawler repeats the same news the anchor is reporting. "We don't have information yet on whether there were casualties on the American side."

I'm freezing. I'm so cold, my body trembles uncontrollably. I have no way to know for certain whether John was involved in the raid, but I tremble nonetheless.

Eric tunes in to my distress and wraps a blanket around me.

"What's the matter, Ava?" Camille asks, her brows furrowing with concern.

I can't speak or think. I can barely breathe as I wonder if I'm going to be sick.

"She lived with a guy in San Diego who was deployed on the day of the attack," Eric says, speaking for me when I can't speak for myself. I hear the uncertainty in his tone. He's not sure I want him to share this, but it's okay. I don't mind if he tells them something I should've told my sister long ago. "She hasn't seen or heard from him since."

"Oh my God," Camille says. "Do you think… Is he…"

"She has no way to know," Skylar says.

"*You* knew this, too?" Camille asks, hurt radiating from her. "Was it serious?"

"Yeah," Eric says, continuing to rub my arm. "It was."

Camille, who was standing, sits next to Rob, her expression bewildered. She has questions that thankfully she doesn't ask now when I have no answers.

I burrow deeper into the blanket and watch the story unfold on TV. They don't know the status of the soldiers who went in after him. They don't know how many people were killed. Because they don't have details, they bring in a progression of talking heads who offer speculation as the anchors ask one repetitive question after another.

"How much planning would be involved in a mission like this?"

"It could've been years in the making."

*Years in the making…*

The anchor interrupts with an update. "We're hearing now that at least two US service members were killed in the raid."

My stomach surges, and I'm running for the bathroom before I'm aware that I'm moving. The dinner I lovingly prepared for our friends and family comes rushing back up, the bile stinging my throat and bringing tears to my eyes.

Eric is there, holding my hair back and soothing me the way he has from the beginning.

The trembling is so violent, it makes me feel like I've been plugged into a machine that makes my body shake.

"Easy, sweetheart," Eric says when the vomiting finally stops. He runs a cool washcloth over my face and holds me tight against him. "Breathe. That's all you need to do right now. Just breathe."

I close my eyes and focus on getting air to my lungs. That's all I'm capable of.

Then Camille is there, too, squatting to brush back hair that's stuck to my face. How can I be sweating when I feel frozen to the bone? "What can I do for you?"

I shake my head. I don't know. I don't know anything. Was John part of capturing Al Khad? Is this what he's been doing all this time? Is he one of the dead service members? Will I ever get answers to these or any of my hundreds of other questions?

I remember Miles is here and probably more affected by this news than I have any right to be. I force myself to pull it together, struggle free of Eric's hold and stand on shaking legs. I brush my teeth and run a brush through my hair, my trembling hands making the simplest of tasks difficult.

Eric stands and places a hand on my shoulder. "Ava, honey… Give yourself a minute."

"I need to speak to Miles." On my way to the door, I squeeze Camille's arm and step into the main room of the loft, where Miles is sitting on the sofa, his eyes glued to the television while Skylar sits propped on the arm of the sofa next to him, seeming uncertain of her role here now that the Al Khad news has upended our evening.

I sit next to Miles and rest my hand on his arm. "Are you okay?"

"I'm kind of numb, actually." He glances at me, his gaze full of raw pain that tells me he's anything but numb.

He's my boss. My *big* boss. But he's also my friend. And that's why I wrap my hands around his arm and lean my head on his shoulder. Though we're in a room full of friends, we may as well be on an island by ourselves, survivors in a sea of people who can't begin to fathom the shared journey we've been on long before we ever met.

"Brings it all back," Miles mutters.

I nod because I understand. We were doing better, and now we're plunged back into the nightmare that never really left us, even as we did our best to push it into the past.

"Do you think he was involved?" he asks.

"I have no idea. I may never know."

We watch the coverage in strained silence for quite some time before Miles clears his throat. "I need to... I need to walk, get some air."

"Do you want me to come with you?" I ask him.

"That's okay." He gives me a one-armed hug and kisses the top of my head. "Thanks for dinner."

When he stands, Skylar does, too. "Would you mind if I walked with you?" she asks.

He hesitates, but only for a second. "No, not at all. It would be nice to have some company."

I fetch their coats and hug them both while Eric stands with me to see them off.

"I'll check in with you tomorrow," Miles says on his way out.

"Call me if you need to before then."

"I will." He shakes Eric's hand. "Thanks for having me."

"Any time."

Skylar hugs me, says she'll text me later and follows Miles out the door.

I close the door behind them and lean my forehead against it for a full minute before I turn to contend with the questions the others are sure to have.

Eric puts his arm around me.

I lean into him as we cross the room and sit together on the sofa.

No one says anything, but I know they're waiting on me. I try to find the words, but my brain is blank, my attention drawn to the unfolding drama on TV.

"Ava was with John for two years before he was deployed, the same day as the attack on the ship." Eric holds my hand and speaks in a low, soft tone that the others hang on. "As I said before, she's never seen or heard from him again."

"Ava," Camille says on a gasp. "All this time, you suffered over this *alone?*"

"That was how she chose to handle it until recently," Eric says. His firm tone puts Camille on notice that he won't appreciate her picking me apart. Not right now, anyway.

Camille glances at the TV. "Do you think that it might be…"

"She has no way to know that. She may never know for sure."

After a long silence, Jules says, "I'm really sorry that happened to you."

"Me, too," Amy says. "I can't imagine…"

"I wish I'd known," Camille says, subtly wiping away tears. "I would've tried to help in some way."

I smile at her. "That means a lot to me. There was nothing anyone could do."

"Um, we ought to go and give you some space." Rob stands and offers a hand to Camille, who takes it somewhat reluctantly, or so it seems to me. She probably wants to stay, but he's right. I could use some space.

I hug them all, saving my sister for last. "I'm sorry if you're hurt. That wasn't my intention."

"It's not about me," she says stoically. "Call me tomorrow?"

"I will."

While Eric walks them to the stairs, I go into the kitchen and start doing the dishes. I'm putting plates in the dishwasher when he returns.

"Let me do that, honey. You should go take a hot bath or something that'll help you relax."

"It's okay. I don't mind doing it."

He puts his hands over mine. "Let me take care of you." Giving a little tug, he convinces me to follow him as he walks backward toward the bathroom, where he draws a hot bath and fills it with my favorite bath beads that he bought for me after I mentioned my affection for the scent of lavender.

One of the things I love about him is how he pays attention to the little things, such as my favorite scent. After testing the temperature of the water, he helps me out of my clothes and into the steaming water, which feels heavenly.

When I'm settled, I reach for his hand. "Thank you."

"My pleasure."

"Sorry to cause so much drama tonight."

"You have nothing to apologize for. I totally understand how shocking that news would be for you to hear."

I give his hand a little tug. "You want to come in with me?"

He kisses the back of my hand. "You enjoy the tub while I clean up."

"Okay."

I watch him as he walks out of the room, noticing the unusual hunch to his shoulders that lets me know I'm not the only one who was undone by the news of Al Khad's capture.

*Eric*

I leave the bathroom and go directly to the bar we set up earlier on a side table in the living room. I pour a drink. I'm not even sure what exactly I'm drinking, but what does it matter? Seeing Ava come apart earlier has left me rattled and off-kilter.

My mind races with scenarios, each more dreadful than the next. What if John was involved in the raid and is now able to come home to resume the life he put on hold more than five years ago? What if he wants her back? Would she go? What if he was one of the people killed in the raid? Will she ever have a minute of true peace if she never knows what became of him?

I can't bear the speculating. I've been so incredibly happy with her these last few months. Even my parents' marital meltdown barely touched me because I was so busy being blissfully involved with Ava. Now that I know what it feels like to be in love with her, I've had reason to wonder if I was ever really in love with Brittany. There's no comparison between her and Ava, who is, quite simply, the best person I've ever known.

She is sweet and kind and funny and smart and so, so sexy, she makes me crazy with wanting her. My mind drifts to earlier when she dropped to her knees in front of me... I moan at the thought of losing her now that I've found her. I somehow managed to survive what Brittany did, but if Ava leaves me...

God, I don't know what I'd ever do without her. And I'm disgusted with myself for making it about me, when it's not about me. It's about her and the men who risked everything to capture the son of a bitch who killed so many innocent people. It's about the heartbroken families who'll once again have scabs ripped off wounds when they're forced to relive the horror. It's about the families of the soldiers who were killed and the country that'll be on edge waiting to see if the terrorists will retaliate against us for taking down their leader.

It is most definitely *not* about me. And yet, I ache anyway, trying to imagine life without Ava. We need more time. We've only had a few months. He had years with her...

"Stop. Just stop." I down the last of my drink—vodka, which almost always gives me heartburn—and take the glass with me to the kitchen, where I pour Sauvignon Blanc for Ava and take it to her in the bathroom. She's staring at the far wall as tears roll down her cheeks.

Her heartache guts me. I'd give everything I have, everything I am to spare her this new pain.

I don't want to intrude on her privacy, so I retreat, taking the wine with me. With nervous energy bouncing around inside me, I get busy cleaning the kitchen. I need to do something to keep from losing my mind as the frenetic coverage continues unabated hours after the story first broke. I should shut it off, but I don't. I keep it on and absorb each new detail of the raid as it's reported.

I've got the kitchen sparkling by the time Ava emerges from the bathroom, wearing a robe she brought here the third weekend we spent together. It's been here ever since, along with clothes and shoes and makeup. I love having her stuff all over my place and knowing she'll be there most nights when I get home from work, snuggled up on the sofa, watching the news.

Once I teased her about her obsession with the news, but when her face fell with dismay, I realized my error. She's obsessed with the news because she's looking for any sign of *him* that she can find. I never teased her about the news again.

She comes over to me, her face flushed from the heat of the bath and her hair damp at the ends.

"Feel better?"

"Much." She puts her arms around me, and I do the same, holding her close to me where I want her to stay forever. I can't tell her that. Not yet, and certainly not now when my motives would come into question. But it's true. I want to marry her and have babies and a life. I want it all with her, and I'm terrified that this man from her past is going to come back and take her away from me.

In that way, it's very much about me.

# CHAPTER 18

*Miles*

Skylar and I leave Eric's building and start walking through Tribeca with no destination in mind. It's a cool autumn Saturday night, and the streets are full of people out and about, smiling, laughing, on their way somewhere. I hear an occasional mention of Al Khad as people go by us. Someone tells us there's a celebration happening in Times Square.

His capture will be the story of the year and will reinvigorate coverage of the ship bombing right when life has begun to return to some semblance of normal—or the new normal I've found in the years since losing Emmie.

Tonight was a good night. A great night. Until the past resurfaced to remind me there's no escaping it.

I should say something to Skylar, but I don't know what. Our conversation flowed effortlessly for hours, and now I can't think of a thing to say.

"Look." She points to the Empire State Building lit up in red, white and blue.

The sight of that statement of support for our country, our military and the victims of the ship bombing moves me deeply.

"It's nice to know that people haven't forgotten," I say.

"We will never forget."

I nod to acknowledge her. Emotions storming around inside me make it impossible to speak.

Emmie would like Skylar. It's an odd thought, but my thoughts are all over the place.

We walk for a long time. Near Times Square, we hear the celebration under way and see the jumbotrons lit up with coverage of the raid that brought down Al Khad. I watch with a detached sense of awareness that people are happy with the news.

Skylar's hand on my arm directs me away from the fray.

"I've waited such a long time for this," I tell her. "I'm not sure what to do with the energy I've devoted to wanting revenge."

"You'll redirect it into something productive after you've had a chance to absorb it."

"I suppose."

"That's what you've done all along, right? You've focused on your business and your work and supporting the family group."

"I've tried."

"And succeeded, from what Ava told me about you."

"What else did she tell you?" I ask, amused by the thought of them talking about me before tonight.

"That she admires you greatly, and we have a lot in common."

"I was sorry to hear about your sister." We didn't cover serious topics earlier, but now that the tone of the evening has shifted, it seems appropriate to mention it.

"Thank you."

"What was her name?"

"Teegan. She was five years younger than me, and I adored her. Losing her nearly broke me."

"I know that feeling."

She looks up at me. "I should be honest and tell you I read about you long before I knew Ava."

"Is that right?"

Nodding, she says, "I read about you and Emerson and your admirable devotion to preserving her memory."

"She would've done the same if it'd been me on that ship."

"I'm so, so sorry you lost her the way you did."

"Thanks. I am, too. Whenever there's a development in the story, it feels brand new again."

"I don't know how you stand having to keep revisiting it."

"Sometimes I can't stand it. I'm happy they got Al Khad, don't get me wrong. But I didn't want to think about this crap tonight. I wanted to focus on meeting someone who interests me for the first time since I lost Emmie."

She glances down, but not before I catch the rosy flush of her cheeks.

"Was that too forward?"

"Not at all. It was sweet."

"I'm extremely out of practice."

"You're doing just fine." She takes hold of my hand and looks up at me. "For what it's worth, I'm interested, too. Just so you know."

"It's worth a lot, and I'm glad to know it's not just me." We cover another block, and I'm immensely thankful for her company and her honesty. "You want to get a drink?"

"Sure."

I look up to realize we've walked all the way to Murray Hill. We duck into an Irish pub and find seats along the wall. It's crowded, so we're forced to sit close to each other, not that I mind. After we order draught beers, I put my arm around her so she won't be shoved off her stool by the rowdy young men next to her.

"Not conducive to conversation," I say, my lips close to her ear so she can hear me over the trio loudly playing Irish music.

She smiles widely. "I'm not complaining."

At first I thought she resembled Emmie, but upon further scrutiny, I've decided that while their coloring is similar, that's where the similarities end. I breathe in the distinctive scent of Skylar's hair. This is as close as I've been to a woman since Emmie died. I hope she'd approve of me moving on after all this time.

Actually, she'd be furious that it's taken this long. My Emmie was nothing if not practical.

I notice the TV in the bar is set to Al Khad coverage.

Skylar sees me looking, places her hand on my face and turns it gently away from the television. "Look at me instead of that."

I gaze into her eyes, which are a golden shade of brown, and immediately feel a sense of relief from the madness swirling around the capture of Al Khad. The noise around us fades to a dull roar. I lean in closer to her, without consciously deciding to. My lips connect with hers, and her hand curls around my neck. For the longest time, we simply breathe the same air, existing in our own little bubble where nothing matters but the two of us.

She breaks the kiss but keeps her hand on my neck.

I note the rosy glow of her cheeks, the shine of her dark hair, the slick moisture on her bottom lip, and a surge of desire takes me by surprise. It's been so long since I experienced anything resembling desire that I've almost forgotten how it feels.

A second round is delivered, and we separate to take the beers from the waitress.

I hand her a twenty and tell her to keep the change.

Skylar and I watch the band, listen to the music and drink our beer, but all I can think about is kissing her again and how long I'll have to wait until I can.

When her mug is half empty, she puts it down. "You want to get out of here?"

I place my glass next to hers. "Very much so."

She stands and extends a hand to me.

I take it and let her lead me through the crowd. When we're back on the street, the cool air is a welcome relief from the heat of the bar. I look at where we are, and a thought occurs to me. "Do you want to see my office?" It's closer than either of our homes.

"I'd love to."

I tuck her hand into mine, and we cover the six blocks and two avenues in silence. In the lobby of my office building, I show my ID to the security officer, who unlocks the elevator for us.

"Thank you."

"No problem, Mr. Ferguson."

"If the night security people know your name, you probably work too much," Sky says in a teasing tone when we're in the elevator. We're still holding hands.

"I do work too much, but he probably knows me because of the publicity I've gotten since the lawsuit."

"I also work too much."

I like that she helps me keep the focus on the here and now. "I know why I do. What's your excuse?"

"Most of the time, it's because I have nothing better to do."

I take a step closer to her until our bodies are nearly touching. "What if you had something better to do? Would you still work too much?"

She looks up at me and shakes her head. "No way."

I've forgotten what it's like to be attracted to a woman. My body is like a leg that's fallen asleep and is suddenly coming back to life. Pinpricks of sensation trickle down my back and up my legs. My heart beats a slow, steady cadence. I feel breathless and lightheaded. And I'm hard. For a while now, I've wondered if my manhood died along with Emmie. It's a relief to know I'm still very much alive, even if I've had reason to believe that part of me died with her.

The ding of the elevator arriving on our floor ends the charged moment. I lead her from the elevator to the glass doors with our logo on them.

I unlock the door and disengage the alarm system. "This is where the magic happens." I lead her from reception to my office in the far left-hand corner. "My partner Alex's office is in there." I gesture to the closed door to my right. "But he travels so much, we rarely see him. He handles business development while I oversee campaign implementation."

The glow of lights from adjacent buildings makes it so I don't need to turn on lights for her to see my office. "Welcome to my home away from home."

"Where's your real home?"

"Chelsea."

"Not far from Tribeca."

"Nice how that works out, huh?"

I want her to see the view, but she's more interested in looking at me.

"I usually hate setups," she says.

"Is that right?"

Nodding, she says, "They're always a disaster."

"Always?"

"They *were* always a disaster."

"If you knew how many people have tried to fix me up since Emmie died, you'd laugh."

"People want to help."

"I know. I've been incredibly well supported by family and friends who helped me survive the darkest days of my life. I don't know where I'd be today without them."

"And where are you today?"

"I'm in the company of a beautiful, sexy woman who's reminded me tonight that despite my painful past, I'm still very much alive."

"Just how alive are we talking?"

I put my arms around her and bring her in tight against my erection.

"Oh, well. Very much alive indeed."

I've smiled so much tonight that my face aches, a further reminder of how long it's been since I had something to smile about.

She puts her arms around my neck and brings me down to her for another chaste kiss that makes me want to beg for more. As if she can read my mind, her mouth opens and her tongue comes looking for mine. I almost faint from the surge of blood to my groin.

My coat falls to the floor in a heap. She breaks the kiss to get rid of her coat, and it lands next to mine.

"Sofa?" she asks.

It takes a second for my blood-starved brain to catch up, but then I'm nodding and then we're landing on the plush leather sofa in a tangle of arms and legs and more tongue-curling kisses. I realize she's unbuttoned my shirt when I feel her hand on my chest.

I tremble under her touch, and memories come flooding back, the last night with Emmie, before she left on the cruise with her parents and I went home to Minneapolis to be with my dad. I don't want to think about that right now, but the memories are relentless.

I pull back from Sky.

"Miles? Are you okay?"

"I…" I don't know what to say to her. I want this. I want it badly, but I'm not sure if I'm ready for it.

"Come here," she says, holding out her arms to me.

I rest my head on her chest, and she combs her fingers through my hair in a soothing caress that helps to calm me. "I'm sorry."

"Don't be. I've thoroughly enjoyed every minute of this evening—or I guess I should say last evening, since it's after midnight."

"What're you doing tonight?" I ask her.

"I don't have any plans."

"You do now—if you want to, that is."

"I want to."

Knowing there will be more helps me to relax into her embrace. Rather than fighting the memories that intruded on our good time, I wallow in them. I want to remember Emmie and my fierce love for her. I want to feel that way again.

Maybe now that Al Khad has been captured, I can put my thirst for vengeance into something more productive, as Sky suggested.

Maybe I can invest that energy into a new relationship.

It's probably time. Long past time, if I'm being honest, and if tonight is any indication of things to come, I've finally found someone worth the effort it'll take to try again.

# CHAPTER 19

*Ava*

I'm not sure what I expected to happen after they captured Al Khad, but for weeks afterward, I've existed in a bizarre state of limbo, waiting for something. But nothing happens, and my life goes on as it did before that night. The names and photographs of the servicemen killed in the raid were finally released, and none of them is John. After a week of nonstop, round-the-clock coverage of the raid and the capture of the most wanted man on earth, even the news channels had to move on when there was nothing more they could say about it for now.

The United States government has refused to divulge where Al Khad is being held or what will happen next. Other than a ramped-up terror level and citizens on high alert against retaliatory attacks, nothing more is said about Al Khad.

I talk about the state of limbo with Jessica in one of our regular sessions. "Every time the phone rings with a number I don't recognize, my heart stops because I think, is this it? Will this be him calling me?"

"So you still expect to hear from him?"

"Intellectually, no. But my phone number hasn't changed. It's not outside the realm of possibility that he could call me."

"Do you hope for that, Ava? Do you want him to come back so you can be with him again?"

"No, I don't hope for that the way I once did. More than anything, I want answers. If he's still alive, I want to know where he's been for all this time, why he never told me he might have to disappear for years, or why he would get involved with me in the first place if that was possible."

I wipe tears that spill down my cheeks, infuriating me. I've cried more in the last few weeks than I have since I first told people about John. As much as I'd like to pretend otherwise, Al Khad's capture has been a setback for me.

Eric has noticed it, too, but he's been nothing but supportive.

"Those are perfectly reasonable questions," Jessica says gently. She's always so incredibly nice to me, even if she still says things that are hard to hear. "Anyone would want those answers. You're being far too hard on yourself if you think you're unreasonable for wanting to know those things."

"I'm worried about Eric."

"How so?"

"This is really hard on him. He tries to hide it, but he's afraid I'll leave him the way his ex-fiancée did."

"You'll never do to him what she did," Jessica says forcefully. When I first told her what Brittany had done to Eric, she'd been initially shocked speechless. "I hear a lot of awful things in this room, but that one is on a level all its own. He has to know that's not going to happen with you."

"I think he's worried about other awful things happening."

"Let me ask you this… If John were to call you right now and beg for your forgiveness, what would you do?"

"I… I don't know. I'd be so glad to hear he was safe that I'd probably lose my shit."

"After that… What then? Would you want him back?"

"I… No, I don't think so. No. Definitely not."

Jessica raises a brow. "You don't think so? Definitely not?"

"It's not going to happen, so what's the point of looking at hypotheticals?"

"What if it does happen, Ava? You should probably have a plan in place for how you would deal with it."

"It's not going to happen. The only thing he could've been doing for this long was hunting down Al Khad. They got him, and still no John. There's no point in playing the what-if game."

She gives me a skeptical look but thankfully doesn't pursue that line of questioning any further. I leave, feeling out of sorts and angry, not at her but at John. What would it be like, I wonder, to live a life in which the specter of John didn't hang over every minute? It's been so long since I didn't have to wonder where he is that the wondering has become like a part-time job. I'm so bloody sick of it and sick of him and sick of the entire situation. I'm tired of talking about it, which I've been doing a lot now that people know about him.

Camille begged me to tell my parents about him, which I did with extreme reluctance over Thanksgiving. My parents surprised me with their empathetic reaction.

"I knew something was wrong," Mom said. "A mother knows these things."

"I'm sorry you didn't tell us sooner," Dad said. "I wish we could've been more supportive."

"You didn't think to ask him about what he did in the military?" Mom asked tentatively.

"I was twenty-one years old and madly in love for the first time in my life. I didn't know I should ask questions."

I assured them there wasn't anything they or anyone else could've done to make this situation easier on me. But I went back to the city and back to Eric the next day with my emotions further shredded by the confession I made to my parents.

After having a fun holiday with his father and siblings, Eric was in a great mood and helped to once again put me back together without even appearing to try. Now we're staring down our first Christmas together and got a huge tree for the loft that we decorated together. We cohosted a Christmas party for our friends and family that was a huge success.

Miles came with Sky, who couldn't look at him without beaming with happiness. Everyone at the office is talking about the change in him, and only I know that he's found someone special. I love knowing something none of my coworkers know about the boss we all adore.

I asked him recently, over drinks after another long day on the publicity circuit, why he didn't want anyone to know about his new relationship.

"I've been such a public face of the family group," he said, sounding pained. "So many of them lost parents and siblings and children. People who can never be replaced."

"Miles, no one who knows you will ever think that you've replaced Emmie. They know that's not possible."

"Still, I'm happy again in a way that isn't possible for so many of them."

"They wouldn't begrudge you that, knowing how you've suffered right along with them."

"Maybe not, but I'd still rather wait to go public with Sky until after the buzz about the lawsuit dies down."

"That's likely to take a while."

"We're not in any rush."

I wonder if she feels the same way, or if she's going along with what he wants.

On Christmas Eve, we're invited to a party at Rob and Camille's apartment, and I'm thrilled that they also invited Miles and Sky, who've unofficially joined our city rat pack. We do something as a group at least once every weekend, which leaves Eric and me a night to spend alone together.

I love being part of a couple again, and I particularly love sharing my life with Eric. We're all but living together in the loft, and he's been making comments lately about me giving up my place and making it official. But we haven't actually made that decision yet, at least I haven't. Something is holding me back from fully committing to living with him. Maybe it's because the last time I moved in with a guy, it went so terribly wrong in the end.

Eric and I spend the afternoon wrapping presents and making love. At the last possible minute, we drag ourselves out of bed to shower and change for the party.

"Two hours max, and then we're coming home," he says as I pack up the appetizers I made earlier.

"What's your rush?"

"Santa can't come until we're asleep," he says with a wink. He's wearing a red plaid shirt that would look tacky on anyone else. On him, it's classy—or it is until he adds a tie with tiny Santas all over it.

"Did I know you're a Christmas geek? That seems like something I should've been told before now."

"Is my baby a secret Scrooge? Seems like something I should've been told before now."

I adjust his tie and fix the knot before placing my hands on his chest. "Christmas has been tough for me the last few years. I'm hoping we can make some new memories this year."

He hooks his arm around my waist and kisses me. "That's the plan."

We take an Uber to Rob and Camille's and arrive at the same time as Miles and Sky. Everyone is in high spirits as we exchange joke gifts and drink spiked eggnog that goes down way too easy.

"Don't get drunk," Eric whispers in my ear about an hour into the party. "We have plans later."

"What plans do we have?"

He kisses my nose. "I'll tell you later, but lighten up on the nog."

"Buzzkill."

"We'll see if you're saying that later." Against my ear, he says, "And P.S., that sweater is so sexy I can't even look at you or I'll embarrass myself."

"This old thing?" I bought the white cashmere cowl-neck sweater on sale at Nordstrom, and this is the first time I've worn it.

His low growl makes me laugh. I do that a lot these days. For a time there, I had good reason to wonder if I'd ever laugh again, but with Eric, remaining dour is impossible. He's so endlessly upbeat and optimistic and funny. I crook my finger at him.

"What's up?" he asks, tipping his head closer so he can hear me over the hubbub.

"I just want you to know I love you, and I wanted to thank you."

"For what?"

"Putting me back together this year."

"Aw, sweetheart," he says softly, "you did the same for me." He brings our joined hands to his lips and kisses the back of mine. "Let's get out of here."

"It's only been an hour."

"I can't wait anymore."

"For what?"

"Come with me, and I'll tell you."

Perplexed by his mysteriousness and on fire with curiosity, I help him make our excuses. We take some major abuse from our friends and family about our early departure. When we're outside, Eric puts his arm around me. "Let's walk."

I left the dishes I'd brought at Camille's, so we're traveling light on the way home. Though it's cold, the air is refreshing. A light snow is falling, adding to the magical atmosphere.

"What's not to love about Christmas in the city?" Eric asks, humming "It's Beginning to Look a Lot Like Christmas."

"I have to admit the festive windows, the greenery, the snow and the sense of expectation have been contagious."

"I want this to be the best Christmas you've ever had."

"It already is."

He kisses my cheek and picks up the pace until I tell him to slow down because I can't keep up with him. Shocking the living hell out of me, he swings me up into his arms and carries me the last block to his place, where he puts me in charge of doors and locks.

"Put me down before you pull something and ruin your holiday—and mine."

"Not quite yet," he says, carrying me into the loft and depositing me on the sofa.

He helps me out of my coat and tosses it with his over a nearby chair.

Then he gets down on his knees before me with the twinkling white lights on the tree providing the only light in the big room. Taking my hands, he kisses each of them and then my lips. "You're the best thing to ever happen to me, Ava. I've fallen so hard for you that you're all I think about, even when I'm supposed to be thinking about other things. There's only you. Right when I'd given up on ever finding you, there you were at my brother's wedding, so beautiful and sweet and everything I'd ever wanted."

Tears run unchecked down my face as I listen to him pour his heart out to me. I caress his face and hair and kiss him.

"I want this," he says, "just this, you and me, forever. Will you marry me, Ava?"

"Yes." I don't hesitate, even for a second, to accept his heartfelt proposal. "I love you so much, and I've loved every minute we've spent together."

He leans his forehead on mine and releases a deep breath.

"You weren't worried I'd say no, were you?"

"No, but I'm relieved you said yes."

"You have nothing to worry about where I'm concerned. I'm all yours."

We wrap our arms around each other and kiss like kissing is about to be outlawed. And when we finally come up for air, he gasps. "I forgot the most important part!" Reaching between the couch cushions, he produces a blue Tiffany box that he opens to reveal a stunning diamond ring.

I cover my mouth as more tears cascade down my face while I watch him slide the ring onto my left hand. "There. Now it's official. I hope you like it. If you don't—"

I kiss him. "I love it, and I love you. I can't wait to be married to you." My sister and I will be married to brothers. How fun is that? My parents will be thrilled. They adore Eric. We can share our happy news in person tomorrow when we go to Purchase for dinner with my parents as well as Rob, Camille, Amy, Jules and Mr. Tilden.

Eric hugs me so tightly, I can barely breathe, but I don't want him to ever let go. Then he joins me on the sofa, where we celebrate our engagement until the wee hours of the morning.

"Merry Christmas, sweet Ava," he whispers before I finally give in to the pull of sleep.

"Merry Christmas, Eric."

I fall asleep with a smile on my face, but I dream of a dark-haired, brooding soldier with intense blue eyes who chases me through a maze with no beginning, no end and no way out.

# CHAPTER 20

*Eric*

The definition of joy is "a feeling of great pleasure and happiness." I know this because I looked it up the day after Ava and I got engaged. I once thought I'd never again be capable of true joy, but Ava showed me otherwise. I'll be thankful to her forever for restoring my faith in humanity.

It's fitting that Rob and Camille are the first to hear our big news, since they're the reason we met in the first place. We pick them up for the ride to Purchase, and when they're settled in the backseat of my car, Ava turns and flashes her bling.

Camille lets out a bloodcurdling scream that makes us laugh.

"*Jesus*, woman," Rob mutters, rubbing his ear.

Reaching for Ava's hand, Camille takes a good look at the ring. "Well done, Eric. It's gorgeous."

"I love it," Ava says, beaming at me.

I'm so glad she's happy with the ring. I agonized over which one to get her, and I've had it for a month as I counted down to Christmas Eve. Guys are told to never give engagement rings for Christmas or birthdays because they count as gifts that the woman gets to keep if the relationship goes south. If this relationship goes south, she can keep the ring. That'll be the least of my concerns.

The last thing I want to think about today is my worst-case scenario. Today I want to wallow in the joy I feel at having found my soul mate, my perfect partner and the woman of my dreams.

Rob squeezes my shoulder. "Congrats, bud. Happy for you."

"Thanks," I say, smiling at my brother in the rearview mirror.

Ava and Camille chatter all the way to Purchase about weddings and wedding planners and wedding venues.

"Get ready," Rob mutters when they come up for air. "It's gonna be all-wedding-all-the-time until the big day."

"Be quiet, Rob," Camille says. "When all you have to do is show up in a tux and say 'I do,' you don't get to make fun of the process."

"Be glad you're not marrying a lawyer," Rob says. "At least you'll have a chance at actually winning an argument."

"Ava and I don't argue," I say, squeezing her hand. The biggest fight we've had since we've been together is over how to load the dishwasher. She's a sorter—in her world, the silverware must be separated by type into compartments while loading, which I think is a waste of time. What the hell does it matter if you sort going in or coming out? According to my beloved, it matters greatly. I refuse to sort. She refuses to throw the silverware in the basket willy-nilly the way I would if left to my own devices. I've caught her reorganizing my work, which led to more bickering.

Apparently, I also snore when I drink, which she handles by poking me until I wake up and turn over.

As you can see, being with Ava is a terrible hardship, but we've managed to work through our "differences." We agree on everything that matters. Our priorities are in alignment. We care greatly about our family and friends, our community and our careers. We both enjoy volunteering our time to worthy causes, such as the local food bank and after-school programs for underprivileged kids. Ava got her entire office, even Catty Caitlyn, to donate a Saturday to paint a community center that runs programs for at-risk youth. I helped, too, mostly because I didn't want to spend an entire day without her.

Yeah, I'm that far gone over her, but whatever. She makes me happy, and I like being happy. It's such a huge departure from where I was this time last year, when I didn't know which end was up or how I would survive what Brittany had done to me. After the months I've spent with Ava, Brittany feels like a bad dream that happened to someone else.

We arrive at Ava's parents' house and share our news with our families, who are overjoyed.

"Here's to sisters marrying brothers," her dad says, toasting us at dinner.

"Hear, hear." My dad raises his glass to us. "Happy for you both."

"When's the big day?" Jules asks Ava.

"We haven't talked about that yet, but maybe next summer?" She looks to me for confirmation.

"Whatever you want is fine with me."

"Careful," Rob says. "A sentence like that sets a dangerous precedent."

His wife smacks him upside the head, making everyone laugh. "Shut *up*, Rob."

"I'd better get back to dating," Amy says during dessert. "That's the only thing the two of you have ever done better than me."

"*Whatever*," Rob says, rolling his eyes. "We did *everything* better than you."

"Um, no," Amy says indignantly. "That's not true. Who graduated highest in our high school class out of the three of us? Who qualified for the junior Olympics in gymnastics? Who was the first to make enough money to buy her own car?" Amy holds up her hand to her ear. "What's that? No comments from my womb-mates?"

I grimace. "Don't talk about wombs over Christmas dinner."

"Christmas is *all about* the womb," Amy retorts.

"If we're going to talk about girl parts," Rob says, his eyes dancing with glee, "then—"

Whatever he was going to say is muffled by Camille's hand over his mouth. "I have no idea how that sentence was going to end, and I, for one, do not want to know."

Rob nibbles on her hand, and Camille dissolves into giggles.

It's a very good day—one of the best Christmases I've ever had, even if the glaring absence of my mother makes it a far different holiday from what I'm used to. Nothing can bring me down today.

Or so I think.

## Ava

I'm flying high from last night and a wonderful day with our families. The excitement of our engagement and the talk of wedding plans has consumed me today. I don't realize until we get home that I never gave Eric the gifts I bought for him, which have been under our tree for weeks now.

"Come open your gifts," I say, taking his hand to lead him to the sofa.

"I have some for you, too."

"You gave me a ring! That's more than enough."

"That was a life gift, not a Christmas gift."

He loves the photo frame I got him for his office that I loaded with tons of pictures of us together and wants to see every photo before he moves on to the next gift, which is a framed piece of artwork with the following words written in a beautiful script font:

*When I was at my lowest, there you were to raise me up.*

"I love this, Ava," he says in a hushed voice. "I could say the same for you."

"I thought we might find a place to put it where we can both enjoy it."

"In the bedroom."

"That works for me."

He puts an arm around me and kisses me. "Thank you. Not just for this, but for everything."

I smile and return his kiss. "Ditto."

My gifts to him include courtside seats to see his beloved Knicks play the Lakers at Madison Square Garden.

"How'd you score courtside seats?" he asks, clearly thrilled with the gift.

"One word: Miles."

"I love him—almost as much as I love you. This is fabulous. Thank you!"

His happiness is my happiness. It really is that simple.

He got me tickets to see "Hello, Dolly" on Broadway and my very first I Love NY T-shirt, which he said I had to have as an official New York City resident. The last thing he gives me is the sexiest lingerie I've ever owned, from La Perla.

"I can't wait to see that on you."

"I wouldn't dream of making you wait." Giving him a saucy look, I get up, take the package with me and go into the bedroom to change. The lavender-and-black-lace baby-doll nightgown leaves absolutely nothing to the imagination, which, of course, is the whole point. I don the matching thong and top off the outfit with a pair of spike heels. I put a little wiggle in my walk when I model it for Eric.

He stares at me with fire in his gaze. Twirling his finger, he asks me to turn and show him the back.

I smile at him over my shoulder. "What do you think?"

"I think," he says slowly, "that I have to be the luckiest guy who ever lived."

I saunter over to him, and propping a knee on either side of him, I straddle him and run my fingers through his hair. "The luck runs both ways."

He cups my ass and pulls me in tight against his erection. "Nah. I'm way luckier than you are."

"No way."

"Mmm," he says, kissing me. "Yes, way."

The "argument" ends in a draw, with both of us "winning" when we make love right there, with me on top of him. I feel his love for me in every kiss, every caress and every deep thrust of his cock. In his arms, I'm able to let go of everything and give myself to him completely. I can't believe it's possible that our lovemaking is even more intense since we got engaged, but there's something to be said for commitment.

Afterward, we lie on the sofa with the Christmas tree lights casting a soft, romantic glow over us. Outside, the wind howls and the snow that was predicted for tonight begins to fall.

"This was the best Christmas I've ever had," I tell him, smoothing my hand over his arm.

"I had that same thought earlier. We're going to have to work really hard to top this one."

"I'm up to that challenge if you are."

"We've got a lifetime of Christmases to look forward to, and I'll gladly take that challenge."

I'm on the verge of dozing off when my phone buzzes with a text that I ignore. Whatever it is can wait until tomorrow. Then it buzzes three more times in rapid succession, and I begin to fear that something is wrong. "Let me check that."

Eric releases me so I can reach for the phone on the coffee table. The texts are from Miles:

*Ava? Are you up?*

*Have you seen the news?*

*Ava?*

*Turn on the TV.*

I stare at the phone for a long time, torn between wanting to know what's up and not wanting to know. This has been the best day of my life, and I don't want anything to ruin it. Not that long ago, a text like that would've sent me flying for the remote. Now, I don't want to know. But Miles can see that I've read the texts, so I respond to him.

*On my way to sleep. What's up?*

He responds instantly. *Al Khad's associates released a recording of the raid to show how American service members attacked his family and other civilians. They've outed the US commandos who orchestrated the raid. It's all over the news. You can see their faces…*

"Ava?" Eric's voice is husky with sleep. "What is it?" When I don't reply, he pushes himself up on one elbow. "Sweetheart, you're shaking. What's wrong?"

I hand him my phone so he can see the texts from Miles.

"Oh my God. Do you want to see the video?"

"I... I don't know. Part of me does, but an even bigger part of me doesn't."

"Do you want me to look for you?"

I once showed him a picture of John, so he'd be able to pick him out. "I... I don't know what to do."

"I'll do whatever you want me to."

"Just hold me for now. That's what I need."

"There's nothing I'd rather do."

I turn to him and let him wrap me up in his love and warmth, which goes a long way toward alleviating the out-of-control trembling that makes me feel weak.

"I'm right here, sweetheart, and I'll always be right here, no matter what. I love you so much. Nothing will ever hurt you again, not as long as I have a breath left in me."

When I close my eyes, tears leak from the corners. I'm gutted by the possibility that I could turn on the TV and see him, that it could be as simple as pressing the ON button, that most of the questions that've haunted me for years could be answered in a matter of minutes. That possibility has me completely paralyzed with indecision.

"Tell me what I can do for you," Eric says after a long silence.

In a matter of minutes, it becomes clear to me that I won't have any peace until I look, even as I try to tell myself it can wait until tomorrow. Whatever it is will still be the same tomorrow. That may be true, but much as I might want to avoid this latest development, I can't. I have to know.

"Would you mind if I turned on the TV?"

"Of course not." He lets me up and wraps a blanket around us both as I reach for the remote.

My hands are trembling as I turn on the TV and switch the channel to CNN, where huge red letters announce Breaking News.

After a few minutes of listening to talking heads break it down, the anchor says, "For those who are just joining us, the Al Khad organization has released a security video that shows the commando raid on the compound where the terrorist was holed up with his family and closest associates. We have to warn you that parts of the video are hard to watch and are not suitable for children."

The network shows only snippets of the video, which is more aggravating than anything.

"I found the full video online," Eric says, turning his laptop toward me.

I watch the video with dread and anticipation pounding through me. I see men in fatigues with heavy vests over their chests, their faces covered with some sort of paint, weapons leading the way as they enter the building from all sides, a well-coordinated assault that takes the occupants by surprise.

Gunfire explodes in a fury of fire and sound.

Women scream and dive on top of their children.

A woman wielding a knife comes at the commandos and is shot dead.

More screams, words in a language I don't recognize, pleas for mercy that are recognizable in any language.

I reach for Eric's hand and hold on tight as I watch the raid unfold with a methodical search of every room, more gunfire, shouts in English, more screams… If I didn't know better, I'd think I was watching an action movie and not a real-life drama. It seems surreal.

I can't see the Americans' faces, only their backs. It's all happening so fast that I can't tell much of anything from what I see on the screen.

A woman shoots one of the US commandos, and she is quickly executed by one of his colleagues.

"Get him out of here," someone shouts.

Another of the commandos turns, and a face I don't recognize is exposed for all the world to see as he tends to his fallen brother.

The others continue forward, storming up a flight of stairs and returning gunfire with a barrage of bullets.

I'm so scared, I can barely breathe. Have I waited all this time to find out what became of John only to watch him be killed? I'm not sure I'd survive that. I want to look anywhere but at the television, but I can't bring myself to look away.

"Breathe, Ava," Eric says, his lips brushing the fevered skin on my face.

I force air into my lungs as I watch the systematic search of the second floor.

A shout goes out, more gunfire erupts, another of the commandos is hit, and someone yells, "I've got him! In here!"

For a few seconds, the only thing on the screen is fire and screams and explosions that rock the building and the camera that's filming the action below it. When the dust settles and the smoke clears, two men emerge from the room where everything happened. They're dragging a third man, who is Al Khad.

One of the two men with him is John.

I let out an anguished cry.

"Oh my God," Eric whispers, tightening his grip on me.

Sobs shake me as I watch him and his colleague wrestle Al Khad through the hallway to the stairs, where more gunfire greets them.

John goes down, and I scream.

Eric is there, his arms around me, his words soft and supportive even if they don't permeate the fog in my brain.

Did I just watch him get killed? Is he dead and they never released his name? Is John West even his real name? I can't bear to look anymore. Hysterical and inconsolable, I bury my face in Eric's chest.

In the background, I hear the reporters dissecting what we've just seen, as if we need their help to understand it. The one thing I want to know is the only thing they can't tell me.

# CHAPTER 21

*Ava*

The next few hours pass in a blur of tears and confusion and panic. I'm an absolute disaster.

At some point, Eric must've called my sister, because she and Rob arrive, even though it's the middle of the night at that point.

Camille sits with me while Eric confers with his brother.

"Can I get you anything?" she asks.

I shake my head. I wouldn't know what to ask for. I'm numb and terrified and anguished and afraid that my reaction to this latest news will ruin my relationship with Eric. That last part has me sobbing again. I can't lose him, too. I just can't.

"Ava, honey," Camille says, sounding desperate. "We don't know anything yet. He could be fine for all we know."

"Eric…"

"What about him?"

"This is too much for him. I know it."

"No," she says. "No way. He adores you. He'd walk through fire for you."

I'd like to believe that, but a little more than twenty-four hours since I accepted his proposal, I'm crying over my ex-boyfriend. Again. That might be more than any man can handle, even one who adores me.

He comes over to sit on the coffee table in front of me, his face lined with tension, his eyes red with weariness. "Rob has an idea I want to run by you," he says.

"Wh-what idea?" I wipe my face and try not to think about how red and swollen I must be. Did we really make love right here on this sofa only a few short hours ago?

"Our dad knows the vice president. They've campaigned together in the past and have remained in touch. Rob wants to call Dad and ask him to reach out to the VP to see what we can find out for you. But only if that's what you want us to do."

Is that what I want? I don't know.

"Ava," Camille says in the gentle voice she's used on me since she arrived. "Let Rob make the call. It'll be better when you know one way or the other."

"Will it?" I ask her in a tone she doesn't deserve. But I can't help it. "Will it be better if I know?"

Camille looks to Eric, looking for answers none of us has.

"I'm sorry," I say to her. "I don't mean to be short with you."

"You be whatever way you need to be. Don't worry about me."

Someday, many days from now, I'll have to thank her for her support.

"What do you want us to do, sweetheart?" Eric asks, holding my hands.

"I… Call your dad. See what he can find out."

He kisses my forehead. "Okay." Releasing my hands, he gets up to talk to Rob.

I lean into Camille, wondering how long I'll have to wait before I know what happened to him.


Answers are hard to come by when the whole world is closed for the holidays. With my office shutdown for the week, I have nothing to occupy my restless mind as I wait to hear something, anything from the queries Governor Tilden has made on my behalf.

One thing that hasn't shutdown for the holidays is social media. Twitter goes wild with speculation about the raid, the men whose faces were made public and the ravenous desire for information that's so prevalent in the digital age. On the advice of my sister and Eric, I steer clear of all social media.

While I wait, I'm surrounded by well-meaning family and friends who want to help, but there's nothing they can do to ease the tension that makes it impossible for me to eat or sleep or function normally.

Sky calls Jessica on my behalf, and she takes time away from her family to spend a couple of hours with me, trying to help me through this latest setback. As always, it helps to talk to her, but it doesn't alleviate the awful stress that's with me every waking moment. Even when I'm sleeping, I'm haunted by disturbing dreams in which I'm trying and failing to find John in a maze without end.

I spend an inordinate amount of time envisioning the possible scenarios.

In the first scenario, John was killed that night in Afghanistan.

In the second, he survived but was so badly injured, he's been unable to contact me.

In the third, he was injured but has recovered in the subsequent months, having chosen not to contact me.

Oddly enough, it's the last one that causes me the most consternation. That he could be out there somewhere, back from the five-year deployment, and never bothered to let me know, is somehow worse than the possibility that he might be dead.

I'm so tired of running the scenarios. I'm sick to death of being obsessed with him. I'm sick of thoughts of him drowning out everything else. I should be planning a wedding and anticipating the future with my wonderful fiancé, and here I am once again mired in the nightmare of the past. I drag myself out of bed and into the shower for the first time in days.

The hot water relieves the strain and tension that've overtaken me. I wash and condition my hair, shave my legs and emerge feeling more like myself than I have since Christmas night.

Eric and I had plans for this week off together, the "staycation" we called it. We have a list of movies we want to see, restaurants we want to try and wedding plans to begin making. I dry my hair, apply a minimal amount of makeup to be presentable and dress in a sweater and jeans that Eric once told me do wondrous things for my ass.

I leave the bedroom and find Eric sitting at the bar, his laptop open and a cup of coffee next to him. I can tell I take him by surprise when I wrap my arms around him from behind and kiss his neck.

"Hey, babe. You smell good."

"I'm sorry."

"For what?"

"Losing my shit, hiding out, not showering, sleeping all day… To start with. I've ruined our staycation, and that ends right now. Let's go to the movies."

"We don't have to, Ava. If you don't feel up to it."

"I feel up to it. I want to get out of here and see to the plans we made for this week. Sitting around dwelling isn't helping anything. Will you please go to the movies with me?"

He turns to me and caresses my face. "I'd go to the ends of the earth with you."

I smile for the first time in days. "And when we get home, I'll show you how much your love and support has meant to me."

His brow lifts. "Show me how, exactly?"

"You'll have to wait and see."

"That's not fair."

Pleased by his reaction and the return of some semblance of normalcy between us, I saunter away from him, looking back over my shoulder. "The sooner we go to the movies, the sooner we get to come home…"

He jumps off the stool, which topples over with a huge crash. "Motherfucker," he mutters while I lose it laughing.

It feels good to laugh, to joke with him, to be with him. He makes me feel good—all the time. Even in the worst of times.

"Do me a favor?" I ask after he fixes the stool and joins me to put on his coat in the foyer.

"Anything."

"Leave your phone at home?" I power mine down and put it on the table where we keep our keys.

"Happy to." He turns his off, puts it next to mine and follows me out for a few hours away from the stress of waiting.

Eric lets me pick the movie, and I go for the funniest thing I can find. The humor is sophomoric, but the laughter is therapeutic. We go to dinner afterward, trying out a new Italian place in the neighborhood that we've heard great things about. Laughter, food, wine and good company go a long way toward fixing what ails me. Over dinner, we have the first real conversation about our wedding. I'm not surprised that we're in agreement about wanting a small, intimate affair, perhaps on a beach, by next summer at the latest.

We return home in good spirits. Wanting to stay in the bubble we've been in since we left earlier, we leave our phones on the table and go to bed, both of us eager to reconnect physically as well as emotionally.

Eric is incredibly tender with me, as if he knows how fragile I still am despite the effort I made today. He worships me with his hands and lips and words that have me clinging to him, my rock in the storm.

"I promised you a reward, so this hardly seems fair," I tell him.

"Making love to you is the only reward I'll ever need." He grasps my hips and enters me slowly, his gaze hot with love and affection and desire so intense, it takes my breath away. "I love you so much. More than you can imagine."

"I love you, too."

He seems relieved to hear that, and it pains me to know that he's suffered along with me these past days, but in a different way. He's had reason to question whether I'm still committed to him, to us. I want him to know that I am, that I always will be, that nothing or no one could ever change how I feel about him.

I give him everything I have. It's all his. Every part of me is his.

We come together, gasping and clinging to each other, holding on to the only thing that makes sense to either of us. Afterward, safe in the comfort of Eric's loving embrace, I fall into a deep, dreamless sleep.

*Eric*

I wake to someone pounding on my door. I was so dead asleep that it takes a second for my body to catch up with my brain. Then I extricate myself from Ava and pull on a pair of sweats before going to see who the hell is banging on my door—and how the hell did they get in without me buzzing them in?

In the peephole, I see my brother's surly face and disengage the locks to let him in.

"What the *fuck*, Eric?" He storms by me into the loft. "Why are your phones off?"

I rub my face, still trying to wake up. "We shut them off yesterday. Ava wanted a break from it all."

"I've been trying to call you since last night."

My stomach drops with dread. I want to back up, shove him out the door and reengage all those locks to keep out whatever he's come here to tell me.

"Her guy… He's alive."

I want to scream that he's *not* her guy. *I'm* her guy. But I don't say that. I don't say anything as I try to process what it means that he's alive but hasn't tried to reach her. What will that mean to her? More important, what will it mean for *us*?

"What else?"

"That's it. That's all they'd tell us. Dad tried to get more, but the VP said everything about the raid is still classified even though the other side released that video. Apparently, the VP had to make a special plea to the Joint Chiefs to get that much."

"So they won't tell her where he is?"

Rob shook his head. "No."

"That's fucked up."

"Agreed."

I glance at the bedroom, where Ava is sleeping. I dread having to tell her this. It was such a relief to see her somewhat back to normal yesterday. This will set her back—again—and I can't bear that for her or for me.

"Are you okay?" Rob asks, looking at me with the kind of awareness that comes from a lifetime spent looking out for each other.

"I'm... I don't know what I am. I want to be supportive of her, you know?"

He nods. "Of course you do."

"But I'm so fucking scared that he's going to come waltzing back into her life and she'll take off with him, like I never happened." It's the first time I've given voice to my deepest fear, and I hate how selfish I am to be worried about myself when all my attention should be on her and what she's dealing with.

"Eric... My God. That's not going to happen."

"And you know that how?"

"She *loves* you. That's apparent to anyone who knows you guys. She's crazy about you. She's not going anywhere."

"She was crazy about him, too, once upon a time."

"There's a lot of rough water under the bridge between then and now. She can't possibly feel the same way she used to."

"The guy's a national hero. How can I compete against that?"

"You don't have to compete against him. There's no contest. He left her. You didn't. You win."

"If only it were that simple. He didn't leave her because he wanted to. He's devoted *years* of his life making this world a safer place for everyone. Hell, I'm half in love with him myself for what he did for all of us."

Rob snorts with laughter.

"Tell me this isn't going to turn into Brittany two-point-oh," I say, needing his reassurances.

"No fucking way. Ava is nothing like that bitch. If the worst thing possible happened, she'd at least have the decency to tell you to your face."

His words are like a sharp arrow to my heart, which he immediately realizes.

"That's not going to happen, bro." He says what I need to hear, but I can see that he's worried, too, and that doesn't help. Not one bit.

"Thanks for coming over, and sorry to worry you."

"No problem. What happens now?"

"I'll tell her what you found out, and we go from there." I hope I sound strong and confident, because I'm quaking on the inside.

I can fool a lot of people. Rob isn't one of them. He places his hands on my shoulders and forces me to look him in the eye. "She loves you. It may get worse before it gets better, but at the end of the day, it's going to be okay. You got me?"

I nod because that's what he needs me to do so he'll be able to leave me.

In a very un-Rob-like moment, he hugs me and kisses my cheek. "I'm right here if you need me."

"Thank you." I'm ridiculously moved by his unusual show of affection.

Heading for the door, he says, "Oh, and turn on your fucking phone." The door slams shut behind him, leaving me alone with my fears. I make a Herculean effort to get them under control before I return to the bedroom. I don't want Ava to know how unnerved I am. I want her to see confidence and strength when she looks at me, not fear. I can never show her the fear.

In the bedroom, I slide into bed next to her, curling up to her warm body and kissing her shoulder. I hate that I have to do this, but I can't spare her the truth, even if it will hurt her.

"Where were you?" she asks, her voice gruff with sleep. She hadn't slept—really slept—in days until last night, when she didn't stir for nine hours.

"Rob came by."

"How come?"

"Our phones were still off, and he had some news."

As if she's been electrocuted, her body goes rigid. She turns to face me, pushing the hair back from her lovely face. "Whatever it is, just say it. Say it, Eric. Please…"

"He's alive."

# CHAPTER 22

*John*

Pain is the only constant in my life. Every part of me hurts, especially the part that's gone now. The phantom pain, something I once would've dismissed as bullshit, is the worst of the physical agony, but even that has nothing on the emotional despair that plagues me like a fever I'll never shake.

*Five years, nine months and eighteen days.*

That's how long it's been since I've seen Ava, held her in my arms, kissed her lips, lost myself in her sweet body and felt complete in a way I never have before or since.

I'm trapped in a nightmare of my own making that began the night I met her in a dingy bar off base and has continued every night since then, especially the more than two thousand nights I've spent away from her, having to worry every minute about whether she's okay, if she hates me, if she has someone else. I wouldn't blame her if she hates me. I deserve that, and I own it. But the thought of her with someone else kills me in a way that an enemy's bullet didn't, even if it came close.

The night of the raid, I was shot in the thigh, the bullet nicking my femoral artery. From what I was told much later, I nearly bled out on the chopper. A tourniquet applied by one of the medics saved my life, but in the end, I'd lost the leg and nearly died a second time from an infection that ravaged me for a full month.

I have no memory of any of it. I'm told that's a blessing. We got Al Khad. That's the first thing they told me when I regained consciousness. It should be the only thing that matters, but it doesn't matter anymore. I've given that son of a bitch as much time as he's ever going to get from me. I hear we let him live, but he's dead to me.

Another month passed before I was strong enough for physical therapy, which has been pure torture, worse than anything I've ever endured, even leaving Ava, knowing I might never see her again.

I refuse to contact her until I'm strong enough to stand again. I'm getting closer all the time. My strength is coming back, slowly—so fucking slowly. But it is returning. Every day that passes, I feel less like an invalid than I did the day before. Every day that passes takes me one day closer to the day where I'll be ready for her.

The Navy liaison assigned to me brought a new cell phone, and it sits on the table in my room at the rehab hospital, torturing me with how easy it would be to pick it up, punch in the number I know by heart and hear her voice, like light at the end of the longest, darkest tunnel.

But I don't want her to see me like this, a shell of the man I once was. I want to return to her whole—or as whole as I'll ever be after losing a leg. I want to be strong and capable and ready to plead my case to her.

I suffer from no illusions. I face an uphill battle when it comes to her. I did a terrible, awful, horrible thing to her by getting involved when I knew I might have to leave her someday. I certainly never expected a more-than-five-year mission in the rugged hills of some of the most hostile space on earth.

If I knew six years ago what I know now, I would've walked by the sweet girl in the hallway outside the restrooms. I would've apologized for my clumsiness and gone on with my life, none the wiser to what I'd be missing. I would've spared her me and what I put her through.

But I didn't walk past her. Instead, I subjected us both to the kind of torture usually found at the hands of the enemy. I can't imagine what she's had to deal with in my absence, but I sure as hell know what I've endured worrying about what became of her, what she did when I left and never came back.

She owes me nothing. Less than nothing, if I'm being truthful. I'm prepared for everything and nothing, or so I tell myself. She may refuse to see me, and I think I can handle that, or so I tell myself. But in the meantime, she's my inspiration, the sole reason I'm fighting so hard to regain my mobility.

Everything I do is for her. For the possibility that maybe, just maybe, she still feels a shred of what she once did, before I destroyed us. I refuse to return to her until I'm able to take care of myself. I've already been enough of a burden to her.

I'm in bed with the shades drawn against the late-afternoon sun, my eyes heavy as I try to relax muscles that tremble violently. The ache in my missing limb is almost unbearable, but I've been refusing narcotics for the last few weeks. I don't like the way they make me feel or how ardently I began to look forward to more of them.

A knock at the door has me opening my eyes. They don't usually bother me after grueling daily PT sessions. Many nights, I sleep right through dinner because I'm so exhausted.

"Come in."

The liaison, a dark-haired lieutenant commander named Muncie, sticks his head in the door. I don't recall his first name, though he told it to me once. He's a nice enough guy and has tried to be helpful, but more than anything, he annoys me with his upbeat optimism and rah-rah company-man bullshit.

The United States Navy can suck my dick for all I care. Even if I hadn't lost a leg and hadn't been facing medical discharge, I would be so done with my naval "career." From what I'm told, I got promoted twice while I was gone, and apparently, I'm a captain now. A freaking O-6. At one time in my life, that rank would've been a dream come true. Now, I couldn't care less if I tried.

"I thought you went home for the holidays," I say.

"I did, but I came back early, sir."

I experience a trickle of unease at wondering what brought him back early and what it has to do with me. "What do you want?"

"You got a minute, sir?"

The question pisses me off. I have *all* the minutes, and he fucking knows it. "Quit your hovering and come in or fuck off."

He comes in. "They said you're in a good mood today, sir."

"This is me in a good mood, and quit calling me sir when it's just the two of us." I make him nervous, and a sick part of me enjoys that. I take my thrills where I can get them.

"I'm sorry to bother you, um, sir, but we need to talk."

"About what?"

"There've been a few developments in the, ah, situation, and they asked me to update you."

I don't like the sound of this, but I refuse to make his job easier, so I wait for him to continue.

"Al Khad's camp released a video," he says, obviously pained for reasons I can't comprehend.

"So?"

"It showed the raid. *All* of the raid."

As if a bolt of lightning has descended from on high and struck me square in the chest, I realize what he's saying. I have a TV in my room, but I don't ever turn it on, which Muncie knows. It's all I can do to eat, sleep and breathe between PT sessions.

*Ava... Oh God, no.*

Gritting my teeth, I ask, "How long ago was the video released?"

"Four days."

Closing my eyes, I breathe through my nose as pain ricochets in every space inside me, leaving a breathtaking new ache in my chest. "I assume I can be seen on the video?"

"Yes, sir."

"Does it show me go down?"

"Yes, sir."

I suck in a sharp breath, imagining Ava seeing me for the first time in years and then watching me get hit by gunfire. Has she seen it? Could she tell it was me? Did she care that I was shot? Is she wondering where I am? Does she still think of me every minute of every day the way I think of her?

"An inquiry was made about you through official channels."

That info nearly stops my heart. "What kind of inquiry?"

"It came from the governor of New York via the vice president and the Joint Chiefs."

I try to wrap my mind around what he's saying. "What was the response they were given?"

"That you're alive."

"That's it?"

"The mission remains classified despite the release of the video."

Ava is the only person in my life who would care enough to ask, so the inquiry had to come from her. And now she knows I'm alive, that my mission was completed months ago, and I haven't bothered to contact her.

*Motherfucker.*

I couldn't add her to my empty list of people to be contacted if anything should happen to me, because I was never supposed to get involved with her in the first place. But she cares enough to ask about me. That thought buoys my spirits like nothing else ever could.

"Is that it?" I ask Muncie, wanting him gone.

"In light of the video's release," he says hesitantly, "the chain of command has decided to embrace the opportunity to shine a positive light on the Navy."

"What the fuck are you talking about?"

"The American public is clamoring for more information about the brave SEAL team that took down Al Khad. Multiple media outlets have filed Freedom of Information requests for more about the three service members who were seen in the video. Since you've already been compromised, they're going to release your names, ranks and hometowns in the next few days, and the Pentagon is preparing to declassify some details of the mission, enough to celebrate the victory without compromising other, ongoing operations."

"In other words, they're going to throw me and the others to the sharks to get the media off their backs."

"Something like that, sir."

"What if I say no?"

"Unfortunately, that's not an option, sir."

The Navy still has me by the balls, and we both know it.

"I'm really sorry about this. If it was up to me, I'd never ask you for this on top of everything you've already sacrificed."

It takes everything I have not to shoot the messenger, to remind myself that it's not his fault. None of this is his fault. Al Khad's organization, an offshoot of Al-Qaeda, had been seen as a low-level threat until the mastermind sent a message to the world by blowing up a US-based cruise ship.

"What else?"

After weeks of him being my only connection to the outside world, I know his tells. When his left eyebrow twitches, there's more, usually things he wishes he didn't have to tell me. Like when he brought news I was finally strong enough to hear that Jonesy and Tito were killed in the raid. I kicked him out, not wanting him to see me sobbing helplessly over two of the few people in this world I love.

"So, um, your face has become somewhat of a social media sensation since the video was released. People want to know who you are. They want to know your story. It's so rare for Special Forces to be able to speak publicly about an operation such as this one."

It's not *rare*. It's *unheard of*. We're trained to never speak to *anyone* about what we do, let alone the media. It goes against everything I believe in to even consider such a thing. But apparently, it's not up to me.

After a long, uncomfortable silence—at least I hope it's uncomfortable for him—he clears his throat. "Um, sir?"

"What?"

"What do you want me to tell them?"

"We're going to pretend I have a choice? Because if I do, my *choice* is to say nothing to anyone." The thought of talking about any of it makes me physically ill, and I'm already sick enough.

"It's, um, going to be very... difficult... for you to move around freely after you get out of here. You'll be recognized." He clears his throat again. "Everywhere you go."

*Goddamn it...* All I want is to go home to my girl and try to pretend like the last six years never happened.

It takes me longer to organize my thoughts than it did before I lost half my blood and fought a life-threatening infection. I try to process everything he's told me and put it into some semblance of order that makes sense.

I've been outed. The Navy wants to capitalize on the "success" of our mission, if you can call it that when two of our best were lost. They probably want to turn me into a recruiting video for other hapless youth seeking "direction" in their lives that only the Navy can give them.

Muncie shifts from one foot to the other. "Sir?"

I close my eyes and turn my head to face away from him. "You can tell them I'll do one interview with the outlet of their choice, and then I'll never again speak of it publicly. The interview can take place no sooner than thirty days from now."

That will give me one month to work toward standing and track down Ava before I'm forced to go public with my story.

"They're going to want—"

"That's my only offer. They can take it or leave it."

After a long pause, he says, "I'll let them know." The soles of his Boondockers squeak against the tile as he leaves the room, the door clicking shut behind him.

When I'm alone, I stare at the phone on the table, my anxiety spiking the way it would if the phone were a live grenade.

I would give my life to hear her voice and experience her gentle touch. She was the first person to show me tenderness, to ever truly love me, and the thought of her kept me alive more than once since I last saw her.

I wish it didn't matter so much to me that I be strong enough to deserve her before I reenter her life. I also need to be strong enough to survive if she doesn't want me anymore. I'm not sure another month will be enough time to prepare myself for that possibility, but it's all I've got.

# CHAPTER 23

*Ava*

John is alive. John is alive and hasn't contacted me. In the three weeks since I found out he's alive, those thoughts have plagued my unproductive days and sleepless nights. I'm grief-stricken, the same way I would've been if I'd been told he died that night in Al Khad's compound. The man I spent six years mourning doesn't care enough about me in return to have the decency to let me know he's alive.

Along with my grief, I'm filled with rage and bitterness over the years I devoted to him, years I'll never get back. His name and that of the other two men shown in the video were released, along with their ages and hometowns, but no other information about them was made public. John, who is thirty-seven now, listed his hometown as San Diego.

While the world goes mad trying to figure out who he is, I hate him with a ferocity that frightens me. I've never hated anyone or anything the way I hate him.

I'm at work, counting the hours until my badly needed appointment with Jessica, who's been away with her family on an extended trip to Europe. Since I found out John is alive, we FaceTimed once, but the session was interrupted several times by her children, who needed her. I need her badly, and I can't wait for two uninterrupted hours with her after work.

Carlos appears at my desk holding a skinny latte that he presents with a flourish and I accept with a grateful smile. He knows something's up with me, but he doesn't know what. Other than Miles, he's my best friend at work, but I've never told him about John.

"You look like hell."

"Gee, thanks." Though I've gone to great lengths to keep my grief to myself, I'm not surprised that people are noticing the toll it's taking on me.

Throwing myself into work and wedding planning has helped. I've made it clear to those who know that I don't want to talk about John or the raid or the video anymore. I've had enough. Thankfully, those closest to me respect my wishes and haven't brought it up.

But they know I'm suffering, especially Eric, who watches me like a hawk when he thinks I'm not looking. He's worried, and I hate that. I hate John for doing that to the man who has been my rock since the day I met him and who doesn't deserve to live in the shadow of someone who never cared about me the way I cared about him.

That's been the hardest thing of all to accept. I find myself once again reliving every minute I spent with John, picking apart things he said and did, looking for signs that he was using me or passing time with me. The memories are beginning to get fuzzy around the edges. I suppose that's bound to happen after nearly six years apart, and while part of me wants to forget, the forgetting only adds to the grief.

"I hope you know I'm here for you if you need a friend," Carlos says, his brows knitted with unusual concern. Carlos doesn't do serious, so the look is nearly comical on him.

"I appreciate that, but I'm fine. Really."

"Okay, then."

"Thanks for the latte."

"Any time."

Determined to get something accomplished today, I dive into the press briefing I'm preparing on behalf of the family group. Though I have other clients now, I still spend most of my time working with Miles and the family group. The civil litigation is moving with unusual speed, and interest in the case is at an all-time high since the video was released. After working closely with the group for so many months, I can answer questions for them without having to think too hard. I spend a couple of hours deeply engrossed in my work, which is a welcome relief from my own thoughts.

I'm stretching out the kinks from sitting for so long when the extension buzzes on my desk with a call from Miles.

"Hey, what's up?"

"Can you come in for a minute?"

I gaze at the clock and see I have ninety minutes until my appointment. "Sure. Be right in." I print out the briefing, grab a notebook and pen and head for his office. Keith isn't at his desk, so I knock on the open door.

"Come in, Ava."

Miles gets up and comes around his desk, gesturing to the seating area in front of the window. "Can I get you anything?"

"I'm good, thanks."

He's like a totally different person since he got together with Sky, and I like seeing this new side to him, the lighter, happier side. I also admire that even as he fell for Sky, he's never backed off his work on behalf of Emerson and the family group. He sits next to me but doesn't say anything.

"What's up?"

"That's what I wanted to ask you."

With that one sentence, I realize my friend Miles—and not my boss—has requested this meeting. I look down at the floor.

"Ava…"

"I'm trying to move past it, Miles. I'd rather not talk about it, if that's okay with you." Talking about it to Jessica will be enough torture for one day.

"I'm worried about you. You haven't been yourself since you found out…"

"That the man I once loved with all my heart is alive and didn't have the decency to tell me that himself?"

The look he gives me is full of empathy—and pity. I hate the pity almost as much as I hate John.

"I just wondered if maybe it's possible that he *can't* contact you for whatever reason."

I've thought of that. Of course I have, but it's been weeks since the video was released, and if he has any kind of soul left, surely he must know that seeing his face would send me reeling. How could he *not* try to get word to me after that video went public? "Anything is possible," I say to Miles.

"I wish there was something I could do for you. I've exhausted every contact I have trying to get more information, but the Pentagon is locked up tighter than a drum when it comes to details about the men involved in the raid."

"I… I didn't know you'd done that. Thank you for trying."

"It was nothing."

"It's not nothing to me."

He seems pained when he adds, "If I found out Emmie was out there somewhere and hadn't contacted me…" He shakes his head. "I can't even imagine what that would be like."

"It's torture," I say bluntly. "I wish I could just forget about him and go on with my life, but…"

"You can't. You never will."

"No, I won't."

"At least I have closure, knowing she's gone and won't be back. You've been stuck in this horrible state of purgatory for so long."

"I hate him for that," I say softly. "He said he loved me. How could he do this to me?" I hate myself for shedding more tears for someone who's proven he's not worth them.

Miles puts an arm around me and tries to offer comfort. "I'm sorry, Ava. Everyone who cares about you would do anything to help you find some peace."

"That would be nice." I wipe my face and struggle to regain my composure. "Let's talk about the briefing."

"We don't have to if you don't feel up to it."

"I'm fine, and I made good progress today." We spend the next thirty minutes fine-tuning the family group's response to the latest round of media inquiries. Every time there's a development, our workload triples. It's been crazier than ever since the capture of Al Khad and the release of the video.

"This all looks great. Just run it by Dawkins to make sure he's good with it before you release it."

"Will do."

"Let me know if he has any unreasonable requests, and I'll rein him in."

"Sometimes I think managing him is your biggest role in this organization."

"It definitely is."

Miles is the voice of reason on behalf of the families, who respect him greatly.

"Is there going to come a day when this story is no longer the story of our lives?" I'm not sure where the question comes from, but I've asked it before I can ponder whether I should.

"Yeah, I think that day will come, but it won't be any time soon." What he means but doesn't say is that with Al Khad facing a trial in the next few years, the civil case against the government proceeding and a renewed interest in a permanent memorial to the victims, the story has "legs," as we say in our business.

"I know," I say, sighing.

His hand on my arm has me looking at him, noting the intense expression on his handsome face. "It doesn't have to be the story of *your* life, Ava. We can take you off this account so you don't have to deal with it every day anymore. As much as I'd hate to lose your valuable contributions, I'd totally understand if it's too much for you."

"I might take you up on that at some point." The work that was so meaningful to me when I didn't know John's fate has lost some of its luster now that I know he's alive. I've lost the personal connection to the cause that fueled my passion for it.

"Just say the word and we'll make a change. No questions asked."

"Thank you, Miles. You've been such a great friend to me these last few months. I can't thank you enough for the professional opportunities and the personal support. It's meant everything to me."

"I could say the same to you—and I owe you forever for introducing me to Sky."

"I'm so glad you're happy with her."

"I'm beyond happy. I'm madly in love, and it feels so good to be moving on with my life after such a long period of terrible darkness."

His words penetrate the fog of grief that's surrounded me for weeks, reminding me that I've already moved on with my life and finding out that John is alive doesn't change anything that truly matters for me. I'm madly in love with Eric, and it's time to put the past where it belongs and focus fully on the future with him.

"Yes," I say to Miles. "It does feel good to be moving on." I can tell I surprise him when I lean in to kiss his cheek. "Thank you."

"For what?"

"For saying exactly what I needed to hear."

"Okay…"

"I've allowed the past to suck me back into the rabbit hole these last few weeks. Enough is enough. It's time to move past the darkness to focus on the future."

"I'm glad to hear you say that."

"I'm glad I finally realized it. See you tomorrow?"

"I'll be here."

I leave him with a smile and head back to my cubicle, where I pick up my phone and send a text to Jessica.

*So sorry—something came up, and I can't make it tonight.*

*You want to reschedule? I can fit you in tomorrow same time.*

I think for a long moment before I respond. *No, thank you. I've decided I don't want to talk about it anymore. I'm done.*

*Ava… Are you sure that's wise?*

*It might be the wisest thing I've ever done. I'm okay. I promise.*

*Call me if that changes?*

*Absolutely. Thank you for everything. You've been a big part of the team that put Ava back together.*

*It's been a pleasure. You should know that I admire you more than just about anyone I've ever known, and I'll be right here if you ever need me.*

Her kind words bring tears to my eyes. *Not sure I deserve that, but thank you just the same.*

*You deserve every good thing. Be kind to yourself and be happy.*

*That's the plan! I'll be in touch.*

*I'll look forward to that. xo*

I leave the office and splurge on a cab, eager to get home to Eric. I text him on the way. *I'm making you dinner. Anything you want...*

*Thought you had Jessica tonight??*

*Canceled.*

*Everything okay???*

*Yep! So dinner...*

*What's the occasion?*

*No occasion.*

*That's my favorite kind.*

Smiling, I type my reply. *When will you be home?*

Leaving now because my fiancée is making me dinner.

You're a lucky man.

*And I know it.*

*What do you feel like eating?*

*Surprise me.*

*Okay, see you soon.*

*Love you.*

*Love you, too.*

# CHAPTER 24

*Eric*

Her text is the best thing that's happened in weeks. She sounds like her old self and not the shattered woman who's tried so hard to hide her pain from me and everyone who cares about her. I text her sister.

*Ava seems better… Not 100 percent sure yet. But I'll let you know.*

*Thank God. Keep me posted.*

This is what it's come to. I'm talking to her sister and friends behind her back because we've all been so worried. Finding out that John is alive but didn't contact her broke something in her, even if she's never said so. She didn't have to. Despite her efforts to hide it from me and everyone else, it's been as obvious as the button nose on her face that her heart is broken—again.

Watching her nurse a broken heart caused by another guy has been excruciating for me, but I keep telling myself it's not about me. It's about her. It's all about her.

Rob says some of it is about me, but I don't care about myself. I only care about her and trying to get her past this setback so we can return to our life already in progress.

Rob has decided to run for Congress and has asked me to manage his campaign. I told him I'd think about it, but I've been so focused on Ava that I haven't had even two seconds to ponder his offer. Part of me wishes he wouldn't run, but I'd never say that to him. From the time we were very young, he's had big political ambitions, and I don't want to hold him back. But after the scandal of our parents' divorce, I think the public could use a break from the Tildens.

I take the subway home, and I'm walking toward my building when I see Ava coming from the bodega on the corner, her arms laden with colorful reusable grocery bags. I jog toward her, and when she sees me coming, her face lights up with pure pleasure that's such a welcome sight to me, I nearly trip over my own feet. I haven't seen anything resembling joy from her in longer than I'd care to admit. I began to wonder if she might be lost forever in her grief and despair. Seeing her smiling and putting in the effort to plan a meal for us… I can't find the words to describe how happy that makes me.

I relieve her of the bags and then kiss her. Her gorgeous face is red from the cold, and her eyes are bright with excitement. I want to know what happened today, but I'm so afraid to burst the fragile bubble that I refrain from asking. While she handles the locks and doors, I carry the bags inside, up the stairs and deposit them on the kitchen counter.

"Thank you so much," she says. "Your timing, as always, is impeccable."

I smile at the inside joke that stems from the fact that we've gotten very good at achieving simultaneous orgasms. Because she's smiling and happy and referring to our simultaneous orgasms, I put my arms around her and bring her in for a better kiss than the one on the street. My heart soars when she opens her mouth to my tongue and wraps her arms around my neck.

I lose myself in her and the kiss, thankful to have her back in my arms after dwelling in the terrible distance that formed between us after I had to tell her the news about John, or He Who Shall Not Be Named (HWSNBN), as I think of him. I become aware of the fact that I'm getting warm and not just from the kiss.

With my lips still on hers, I remove my coat, drop it to the floor and then see to hers, first unwrapping the colorful scarf from around her neck and then removing her coat and adding it to the pile on the floor.

"Eric," she says, sounding breathless.

I open my eyes to study her, noticing her swollen lips and flushed cheeks. "What, honey?"

"Let's go to bed."

"What about dinner?"

"Later?"

"Later sounds good." We should put away the groceries, but I feel an urgent need to roll with it while she's present and in the moment with me. "Hold on to me."

"Why—"

Cupping her sexy ass, I lift her, making her squeak with surprise as she wraps her legs around my waist. She starts to laugh, but I drown out her laughter with more deep kisses while I walk us to the bedroom. She kisses me back with the enthusiasm I've come to expect from her.

I've tried to give her space and room to process her grief, but it's been hard to keep my distance from her, especially right after we made a huge commitment to each other. Having her back in my arms is the only thing I need to be happy. I undress her slowly, touching her reverently, hoping I'm conveying everything she means to me with every caress and kiss. She's become my whole world, and seeing her suffer has been brutal for me, especially because there isn't a thing I can do to make it better for her.

I've made daily phone calls to my father, begging him to use every contact he has at his disposal to get us more information about HWSNBN, so Ava can finally have the answers she needs to fully move on with her life. Dad has called in every favor owed to him, but he hasn't been able to learn anything more than what everyone else knows. My frustration has never been higher than in the last few weeks as I watched her slip further from me with every passing day.

I've been feeling increasingly more desperate to reach her, which reminded me far too much of the aftermath of the Brittany disaster.

I release the front clasp of her bra and push the cups aside to reveal full, round breasts and light pink nipples that tighten as the cool air washes over them.

Bending my head, I take her left nipple into my mouth, pin it against my teeth with my tongue and suck.

Her hips come off the bed, her fingers grasp my hair, and her nipple gets harder under my tongue. "So sweet," I whisper. I love everything about her—the soft silk of her skin, her taste, her scent, her enthusiasm. I've never wanted any woman the way I do her, and I set out to prove that to her by kissing her until she's writhing in a fever of need beneath me.

I raise her legs to my shoulders and open her to my tongue, exploring her sensitive flesh while I move my fingers in her, triggering an orgasm that comes as sweet relief to me because she's still with me, still able to let go with me. It fills me with hope that she turned a corner today and left the darkness behind.

"Eric," she says, breathless in the aftermath of release.

"What, sweetheart?"

"I need you. Please…"

Hearing she needs me sparks something primal in me. I shed my clothes with fumbling fingers and come down on top of her, gazing into her wide, open eyes as I push into her tight wetness. "I love you. More than anything in this world."

"I love you, too. Just as much."

The words are a balm, soothing the fears that have kept me awake night after night, torturing me with what-ifs. She's here, right here in my arms where she belongs and giving herself to me without reservation.

Gazing into her eyes as I move in her, I feel a connection with her that's soul-deep. It touches every part of me and makes me wish I had the words to tell her what she means to me, how essential she's become. Since I don't have the words, I try to show her, giving her everything I've got until she's coming with a strangled cry. I know the signs by now and when to let go of my closely held control so we can come together.

That moment of total unity is the closest thing to religion I have in my life. It makes me believe in higher powers and heaven and angels right here on earth.

For a long time after, we remain joined, arms around each other, bodies cooling, desire sated for now. It feels like a homecoming of sorts, to be close to her again after so many weeks of uncertainty.

"I've been thinking about our wedding," she says, breaking the long silence.

"You have?" It's the first mention she's made of our plans since that awful morning three weeks ago.

"Uh-huh. What would you think about a tent on the lawn at Croton?"

I notice her use of our family's shorthand word for "home," and it gives me pleasure to hear her speaking "Tilden."

"Would it be weird to have it there after what happened with your mom last summer?"

"Nah. That's one of a million memories there, most of them good." None of us has spoken to our mother in months. I hope her new life is worth what she gave up for it, but otherwise, I rarely think of her.

"What would we do about parking?" Ava asks.

I run my hand up and down her arm. "We could use the high school parking lot and shuttle them over."

"So you like the idea?"

"I love it."

"I looked at the town's website, and if we do it on the third of July, we'll get fireworks, compliments of the town."

"That'd be fun."

"Are you busy on the third of July?"

"It's starting to sound like I might be."

Her smile lights up her face and my world. "So it's a date?"

"It's a date."

"I… I just want to say thank you for your patience with me these last few weeks and even before that. I know it hasn't been easy… You've been my rock."

I'm deeply moved to hear her say that. "I always want to be there for you, Ava. It's been so hard to watch you struggle with this."

"I know, and I'm sorry if I left you out of it or checked out on you or—"

I kiss her. "Shhh, you have *nothing* to be sorry about."

"It's going to be better now. I promise."

I still want to know what changed, but I don't ask. Whatever it was, she seems to have made peace with the situation, so what does it matter how it happened?

"The only thing that matters to me is you and your well-being. If you're happy, I'm happy."

"I feel really lucky every day to have been matched up with you at my sister's wedding, but never more so than I have in the last few weeks."

"No matter what happens, sweetheart, I'm right here with you, and I'm not going anywhere."

She tightens her arms around me. "That means everything to me."


*Ava*

With our date set and Eric's dad fully onboard with our plan to take over his home and yard, I go full steam ahead into wedding planning, to the exclusion of everything but Eric and work. I avoid the news and the internet and anything that might trigger a setback. I feel strong again, focused, determined to keep moving forward and to leave the pain of the past behind.

A week after we set the date, we invite Rob and Camille to dinner at a five-star restaurant that requires suits, ties and cocktail attire for women. We're all dressed up and in high spirits as we discuss the wedding.

After we're served a round of drinks, I glance at Eric, who nods. "So the reason we asked you here tonight is because we'd like to ask you both to return the favor as our best man and matron of honor."

Camille lets out a squeal that draws the perturbed attention of other diners and the tuxedoed waitstaff.

Rob clamps a hand over her mouth.

"You owe me fifty," she says to her husband, her words muffled by his hand.

"You guys bet on why we wanted to see you tonight?" Eric asks.

"Duh," Camille says. "We bet on everything. I usually win, and I've never been happier to be right than I am now."

"Does that mean you'll do it?" I ask.

"Duh," they say together.

"Of course we will," Rob says. "It'd be an honor."

"We should all go somewhere together for the bachelor and bachelorette weekend," Camille suggests.

"Not happening," Rob says. "No chicks at the bachelor party, except the strippers."

Eric laughs, and his brother offers a high five.

"Do it and you're dead," I tell him.

"Sorry, bro. I'm gonna leave you high and dry on that one."

"Already whipped, and you're not even married yet."

"Shut up, Rob," Camille says, "or you'll be high and dry. Emphasis on the *dry*."

Rob offers his wife a shit-eating grin. "Yes, dear."

Camille rolls her eyes at him and raises her glass. "To sisters marrying brothers!"

"To our kids being double cousins," Eric adds.

I hadn't thought of that, but how cool will that be? We touch our glasses and offer other silly toasts that keep us laughing. I'm afraid they're going to kick us out before we eat at this rate.

"Speaking of sisters marrying brothers," Rob says, "I told one of the *New York Times* reporters who covers Dad that my brother is marrying Camille's sister, and they want to do a *Vows* article about the governor's sons marrying sisters."

"That's so cool!" Camille says. "You didn't tell me!"

"Truthfully, I forgot about it until right now. What do you guys think?"

I glance at Eric.

"It would be some positive publicity for the family and your campaign after the parental scandal from hell," he says.

"That's my thought, too," Rob says.

"But only if Ava is in favor," Eric says, looking at me. "I know how private you are."

"I'd be okay with it," I tell them. "How soon do they want to do it?"

"The reporter said they'd jump on it if we give the go-ahead," Rob says, "so probably fairly soon. I'll let you know."

The next day, Eric and I interview two caterers and choose the second one because he seems to totally get the relaxed vibe we're going for, whereas the first one wanted to turn our wedding into a society affair.

My mom comes into the city the following weekend to go wedding dress shopping with me and Camille. I find the dress I want in the first place we go and refuse to try on any others after finding "the one." It's simple and elegant and classy, with intricate bead work on the bodice that transforms it into a wedding dress.

"You don't have to decide anything today," Mom says.

"This is the one. It's exactly what I want." I try to picture myself walking toward Eric wearing that dress, and I can see it so clearly. He'll love it as much as I do.

"Well," Mom says. "That was easy."

"You can say it, Mom," Camille adds. "She's nothing like me."

"You said that," Mom replies, smiling. "Not me."

"Since we have the rest of the day, we can spend it helping Camille pick her dress." I've told Camille, Jules, Amy and Sky to pick navy-blue cocktail-length dresses in any style that works for them.

"One day won't be enough," Mom says, making us laugh.

We have such a great time that Mom decides to spend the night in Eric's guest room so we can choose invitations on Sunday before she goes home.

In bed that night, Eric refuses to come anywhere near me because my mom is sleeping in the next room. Naturally, when presented with a challenge, I bring my A game to convince him he's being silly.

"She knows we sleep together and that we have s-e-x."

"Hush. Leave me alone and go to sleep."

I suppress the urgent need to giggle madly. He's so damned cute and funny and sweet. Sitting up in bed, I tug at the hem of the T-shirt he told me I had to wear to bed because we have a guest. He wore a T-shirt that he tucked into flannel pajama pants.

"What're you doing?" he whispers.

"I'm hot." I fan my face for effect.

"You who are cold in the middle of summer are suddenly hot?"

"I'm *roasting*." I lift the T-shirt up and over my head and toss it aside. "That's better." Gathering my hair into a ponytail, I hold it up with one hand and continue to fan myself with the other. "Did you crank up the heat?"

"You think I don't know what you're up to."

"What am I up to?"

"You're trying to break me."

"Why would I do that? I love you. I don't want you broken."

Laughing softly, he says, "Yes, you do."

I release my hair and crawl across the wide expanse of bed he put between us for the first time ever.

His eyes, illuminated by the street light coming in from outside, flare with desire. "Go away."

Smiling, I lean over him and begin to kiss his neck. "No."

"Yes," he says, sounding more desperate as I move toward his abdomen.

"Make me."

He buries his hands in my hair but makes no move to relocate me. "Ava…"

"Hmm?"

"What're you doing?"

I tug on his T-shirt. "Breaking the seal."

"Not with your mom here."

"Yes, with my mom here."

"You know I can't resist you."

"So why do you try?"

He gasps when I take him into my mouth. "*Ava.*"

"Shhh, you wouldn't want her to hear, would you?"

"I thought you loved me?"

"I love you so much. More than anything." Sensing his surrender, I set out to show him just how much.

# CHAPTER 25

*Eric*

Ava has thrown herself into wedding planning with a feverish urgency that alarms me. I worry she's using our wedding to deal with the *other* thing we never talk about. Don't get me wrong… I'm thrilled she's excited about the wedding and caught up in the details of planning it. All I care about is her happiness and to see her eyes sparkling with joy as she devours bridal magazines and checks items off her massive to-do list. But underneath it all, I worry that the thing we never talk about is lying dormant like a creature in the deep, dark ocean, waiting to come surging to the surface and turn our lives upside down again.

I worry incessantly about her, enough that I take the unusual step of asking Camille to meet me for lunch because I need to talk to someone about it—and I need to know if I'm the only one who's concerned that the wedding frenzy might be a front.

Camille comes into the restaurant looking windblown, her cheeks red from the brisk March breeze.

I wave to her, and she winds her way through the tables to reach me. Standing, I kiss her cheek. "Thanks for meeting me."

"No problem."

"How's the job?" I ask, not wanting to hit her with the reason for this meeting the second she arrives.

"It's very… rewarding. I like it a lot. I'll be able to truly enjoy it once I pass the bar and can put the incessant studying behind me."

"You've got this."

"I guess we'll see, won't we?"

Our waiter comes to take our order. I get a pastrami sandwich that I don't really want, and she orders a salad.

"What's going on, Eric? Is everything okay?"

"Yeah, everything's great. I just…" I fiddle with my water glass and force myself to say it out loud, to express my concerns to someone who knows her almost as well as I do. "How does Ava seem to you?"

"Really good, actually. I was just saying to Rob last night that she seems like her old self again. She's super excited about the wedding."

"I know." I glance at the window, where people rush by, moving fast the way they do when it's cold. This winter is holding us in its grip until the last possible second.

"You don't think that's a good thing?"

"It is. It's just I wonder if maybe she's using the wedding to avoid dealing with the other thing." There. I said it. My fear is no longer a private thought. It's on the table to be picked apart and analyzed.

She stares at me, mouth agape. "You honestly think that?"

"I don't know what to think."

"Every bride goes crazy planning her wedding. Ava is no different."

"Ava *is* different, and we both know that for her to be totally embracing every second of planning the wedding is somewhat out of character for her. I could see you doing that—no offense."

She waves a hand. "None taken. It's true."

"But it's not like Ava to care so passionately about centerpieces and lighting that she stays up all night to thoroughly research her options."

Camille ponders that, and when she looks up at me, I see concern. "She did that? She stayed up all night?"

"More than once."

"And you think it's related in some way to… the other thing?"

"I'm afraid it might be how she's chosen to cope with finding out he's alive. I don't think she realizes she's doing it, but it's like she's using the wedding to drown out her thoughts of him."

"Eric… She loves you. She can't wait to marry you."

"I know that. I don't doubt for a minute that she loves me and she's excited about the wedding. That's not what I'm saying." I take a minute to gather my thoughts. "I feel like her single-minded *obsession* with the wedding is unlike her, but then I wonder if I know her well enough to make that observation. Which is why I called you."

"You know her as well as anyone, but it is… *unusual*, I guess you could say, for her to care so much about the details."

"So you agree it's slightly worrisome?"

"Slightly."

Our lunch is served, and I pick at the pastrami while she pokes at the salad. My stomach hurts, and I couldn't be less interested in eating.

I take a sip of water, wishing it could wash away the lump that has taken up permanent residence in my throat. "When she found out he was alive, she was off for weeks, but then one day, it was like she decided not to give a shit that he survived the raid but hasn't contacted her. She came home that night, full of enthusiasm for making dinner, and seemed to make a concerted effort to get back on track with me and everything else. She's never again mentioned his name or said anything about him when she has to wonder where he is and why he never bothered to reach out to her, you know?"

Camille nods. "How could she not wonder?"

"Exactly."

Silence hangs heavy between us as we continue to pretend we're eating.

The waiter comes by and stops short when he sees we've barely touched our food. "Is everything all right?"

*No, not really.* "Yeah, we're good. Thanks."

"What do we do?" Camille asks in a small voice that's so unlike her. It tells me how concerned she is, which makes me feel bad for unloading my worries onto her.

"I don't know. It's not like I can come right out and ask her if she's using our wedding to mask her despair over him."

"No, you really can't do that." She taps her fingertips on the tabletop for a few minutes. "But what you *could* do is take her away for a weekend with no wedding planning, no nothing but you two spending time together."

"I like that idea. I like it a lot."

"There's an inn upstate that she loves. We went there once with our parents to meet up with some friends for a weekend. I'll send you the info."

"That'd be great. Thank you."

"Maybe you can get her to open up to you while you're away."

"I hope so." She's stuffed her feelings about John into a box full of wedding details that keep her so busy, she has no time to think about him. I'm sure of it, and while I love the idea of taking her away from it all for a weekend, I'm desperately afraid of what might happen if he gets out of that box.

*Camille*

"She's going to crush him," Rob says when I tell him about my lunch with Eric. "I feel it coming, and there's nothing we can do to stop it." We're in the back of an Uber on our way to a fundraiser for his campaign that was organized by longtime supporters of his father.

I recoil from his certainty. "She's *not* going to crush him. Don't say that."

"Why shouldn't I say it? Everyone else is already thinking it."

"*Who* is thinking it?" I ask, shocked to hear that.

"Jules, Amy, my dad. Ever since we heard that this guy she's pined for all this time is alive, we've been worried about her pulling the rug out from under Eric."

"It's not going to happen."

"How do you know that, Camille? What's she going to do if this guy… *John*… resurfaces and wants her back? He's been off fighting for our country all this time. He's a fucking national hero. How can Eric compete against that?"

"It's not a competition. She *loves* Eric. She'd tell you herself that he saved her life in more ways than one."

"I believe she loves him. I really do. We can all see that she does. But that doesn't mean she'll stay with Eric if the other guy wants her back."

I feel chilled to the bone by his certainty that Ava would walk away from Eric after everything they've shared and been to each other. "If nothing else, Ava has proven that she's a loyal person by staying true to the man she loved for more than *five years* when she didn't even know he was alive."

"She's a very loyal person, babe. That's my point."

"You've got this all wrong, Rob. She won't do that to Eric." The thought of it makes me shudder. What would it mean for my marriage if my sister breaks the heart of my husband's brother? The very thought of it makes me sick.

"I don't mean to be hard on Ava. She's a sweetheart. And she's been through so much. I admire her as much as I like her. But I'm scared for my brother in this situation. You saw him after Brittany…" He shakes his head, his expression grim. "You know how awful it was. If it goes bad with Ava…"

"It's not going to."

"I hope you're right. I really do."

So do I. The alternative is unimaginable.

## Ava

I'm bouncing with excitement as Eric drives us out of the city just after noon on a Friday in late March. We both took half-days so we could get out of the city ahead of rush hour. He won't tell me where we're going, just that he wanted to get away for the weekend and spend some time alone with me.

That sounds good to me. We've both been so busy in recent weeks that time alone has been hard to come by. Last week, we met with the *Vows* reporter from the *New York Times* and posed with Rob and Camille for the photographer they sent.

The feature is scheduled to appear in this Sunday's paper. Everyone at work is excited about the article, and Rob is thrilled about the positive publicity for his campaign after a tough year for their family. We also celebrated Camille passing the bar exam on the first try, not that any of us are surprised.

Eric has put me in charge of road trip music, and I've got Nirvana blasting.

He turns it down a smidge. "You're going to blow my speakers."

"Wimp."

His mouth falls open in shock that makes me laugh as I dance in my seat to the music of my youth. I adored all things Grunge in high school.

I love that Eric orchestrated this weekend for us and that I can say anything to him and not have to worry about him reacting badly. I've never had that with anyone, even John, who could be sensitive about perceived insults.

*John.*

Why am I thinking about him when I'm on a getaway with Eric? I have no space in my brain or time in my life for him. That phase is over. Finished. Ended. I have a whole new life now, and that's where my focus belongs.

"Are we there yet?" I ask Eric, feeling itchy about my thoughts straying into dangerous territory.

He rolls his eyes at me. "I told you it would be a few hours."

That's a long time with nothing to keep me occupied but music and scenery. My skin feels hot all of a sudden, like it did the one time in my life I broke out in hives. I was thirteen, at a sleepover with friends, when my skin suddenly revolted. Later, it was determined I'd reacted to the laundry detergent my friend's mother used on the blanket I was given, but now I wonder if that was the case. I've never had them again or experienced the distinctive prickly heat that led to them until now.

I take a sip from my water bottle, hoping the cool liquid will help. My throat feels tight—enough so that I begin to be concerned. "Eric."

"What, honey?"

"I don't feel good."

He looks over at me and does a double take. "What's on your face?"

I hastily pull down the visor and gasp at my reflection. I have blotchy red patches all over my face. "Benadryl." I recall what they gave me at the ER the first time this happened. "I need Benadryl."

Eric takes the next exit, finds a CVS and pulls into the parking lot. He jumps out of the car and runs inside while I focus on breathing and trying not to scratch my itchy skin. He's back momentarily and drops pills into my hand that I take with greedy gulps of water. I close my eyes and wait impatiently for the medication to take effect.

Eric strokes my hair and offers what comfort he can. "Do we need to get you to a hospital, honey?"

I shake my head. "I'm okay."

It takes about thirty minutes before my throat begins to clear and the violent need to itch recedes. I open my eyes to find him watching me with concern etched into his handsome face. I hate that I keep giving him reason to look at me that way. "Sorry."

"No need to apologize. Do you feel better?"

"Yeah. It'll take a while for the red patches to go away, though."

"What brought that on?"

"I don't know," I tell him, even though that's not true. I know exactly what brought it on, but I don't understand why. The last time, it was laundry detergent, or so we thought.

"Has it happened before?"

"Once when I was thirteen."

"Do you want to go home?"

"No! Not at all. Unless…"

"What?"

"I'd understand if you didn't want to be seen with me when I have welts all over my face."

"I don't give a shit about that. As long as you're all right, that's what I care about."

"I'm all right." I tell him what he needs to hear, but the incident has unnerved me. I've tried so hard to move forward with my life after learning John is alive, but the thought of a few days without frantic activity to keep me busy brought on an outbreak of hives. I can't deny the connection as much as I might wish to.

I hate the way I feel when I think of him. I hate knowing he's out there somewhere, back from his long mission, and couldn't care less about me, not that I want to hear from him. I don't. I want nothing to do with him. I want him to go away and leave me alone once and for all. I want to be free of him.

Free. What would that be like? I've been obsessed with wondering what became of him for so long, I can't remember what it was like to live any other way.

The Benadryl makes me drowsy. I want to spend this time with Eric, but I can't keep my eyes open.

# CHAPTER 26

*Ava*

I hear Eric calling my name. He sounds like he's far away, but then I feel his hand on my shoulder gently shaking me.

"Ava, honey, wake up."

My eyelids weigh a hundred pounds, or so it seems. I force them open and blink a large Victorian house into focus. Something about it is familiar.

"We're here."

"Where's here?"

"The Fairlawn Inn. Camille told me you've been here before and loved it."

"Yes! Once with our parents. I did love it. This is amazing, Eric. Thank you so much."

"I'm glad you're happy. Do you feel better?"

"Much better. Sorry about conking out on you. It was the Benadryl."

"No problem, but I did miss you." He smiles and kisses the back of my hand. "Want to go in and see if it's like you remember?"

"Uh-huh." I'm so touched by the thought he put into taking me somewhere that would please me. The inside is just as I remember, cozy and welcoming with antique furnishings. We're shown to our room, which features a sleigh bed with a floral quilt and canopy. "The last time I stayed here, I had to share a bed with

Camille." I rest a hand on his chest, feeling the steady beat of his heart beneath my palm. "I'm much more excited to share a bed with you."

"I should hope so."

His reply makes me laugh, and I vow to put all my focus and attention on him this weekend. That's the least of what he deserves after going to all this trouble to arrange a romantic getaway for us.

We spend that afternoon taking a hike on trails that surround the inn and have a delicious dinner at a nearby restaurant in downtown Hunter. It's a lovely, relaxing day that ends with a soak in the claw-foot tub in our bathroom. I'm facing him, and he's got my feet in his lap, massaging the bottoms of them.

"Thank you for this," I tell him. "I really needed it."

"You've been burning the candle at both ends lately."

"I know." I shouldn't be surprised that he's noticed. He notices everything where I'm concerned. "I'm sorry if you've been feeling neglected."

"I haven't. Don't worry about me. I have, however, been worried about you."

"Really? Why?"

He seems to choose his words carefully. "You've been very... *absorbed* by the wedding."

"Do you know that most people these days are engaged at *least* eighteen months? A six-month engagement is almost unheard of. It's a lot to do in a short amount of time."

"I realize it's a lot, and I want our big day to be perfect for both of us, but I worry that your enthusiasm for the wedding might be coming from a different place."

"What different place?" I play dumb, but a twinge of panic hits me. He knows. Of course he does. He knows everything.

Tipping his head, he looks at me imploringly. "Ava..."

I don't know what to say.

"You don't have to do this with me. I'm not going to be threatened if you want to talk about him—"

"I don't."

Eric doesn't say anything, but he looks at me without blinking for such a long time that he breaks me with his compassion.

"He's *the last thing* I want to talk about. I'm *sick* of talking about him. I'm sick of seeing his face *everywhere* after not seeing it *anywhere* for years. I'm fed up with the speculation about who he is and where he is. I've had enough of feeling like a fool for caring so much for so long when he clearly doesn't give a shit about me. Is that what you want to know?"

"It's a good start."

"I don't want to think about any of those things. I want to think about you and me and our wedding. I want to talk to you about going off the pill soon so we can try for a baby right away."

His eyes widen with surprise. "You do?"

"Yes, I do. I want to be a mom. I want a family with you. If you still want that, too."

"I want it. You know I do."

"If I'm overly focused on our wedding, it's because that's what I *want* to be thinking about. Not that other stuff."

"I understand, but I don't want you to ever think you can't talk about the other stuff with me or that you have to hide it from me."

"You've been so amazing through all of this. I don't know that I would've been able to handle it at all if I hadn't had you to hold my hand."

Sitting up, he takes my hand and kisses the back of it. "Yours is my favorite hand to hold, and I'll always be there for you, Ava. Good times and bad. That's what I signed on for."

"I don't want any more bad times," I whisper, my eyes filling. "I'm so tired of being sad. You make me happy. The wedding makes me happy. If I fill myself up with those things, there's no room for the sadness."

"You know that I'm always happy to fill you up with me."

I snort with laughter even as I brush away tears.

He stands and reaches for me. "Let's get out of here before you turn into an old prune."

"We can't have that. I'm getting married soon."

"Yes, you are, and the groom didn't sign on for an old prune."

We go back to bed and stay there until the following afternoon, laughing, talking, making love and making plans. In need of food and coffee, we go into town for brunch and spend the rest of the day checking out the antique shops, bookstore and galleries.

A movie we've both been wanting to see is playing in the town's movie theater, so we buy tickets to the five o'clock show and grab dinner afterward.

It's a relaxing, invigorating getaway, and as we leave to head back to the city around noon on Sunday, I do so determined not to let the wedding become more important than my relationship with Eric. On the way out of Hunter, we pick up a copy of the Sunday *New York Times* and pore over the flattering story about the four of us.

"That's a great picture of us all," Eric says. "We should frame it for them."

"And for us."

"Two of everything, for sure."

Rob and Camille text us to share their delight with the story and the photos. *Nice change in the narrative about our family*, he says.

I text back for both of us to tell them we loved the story and the photos.

"Thank you for this weekend," I tell Eric when we're on the highway headed back to the city. "It was just what I needed."

"You're welcome, and it was definitely my pleasure." He waggles his brows at me so I don't miss the double meaning.

"After this weekend," I say, patting his leg, "you should be set for sex for the next month or two."

"Ummm… Wait. What?"

I lose it laughing. His expression is absolutely hysterical. I'm laughing so hard, I almost don't hear my phone ringing. I grab the call from my mother right before it goes to voicemail.

"Hey, Mom. What's up?"

"Ava…"

"Mom? Is something wrong?"

"Honey, agents from the NCIS were just here."

"What? Why? What'd they want?"

"It's John, honey. He's trying to find you."

*John*

It took twenty-seven days, but I'm now able to stand for up to five minutes at a time thanks to the prosthesis I'm learning to tolerate. I'm told I'll be able to stand for longer periods over time, but for now, five minutes is all I can handle. They also tell me I'm well ahead of schedule in my recovery. All I know is the pain is excruciating, I still look like absolute hell and I'm out of time.

The interview with *60 Minutes* is set for a week from Sunday.

I have to see Ava before I go on national TV to tell my story. About three weeks ago, I decided I can't call her out of the blue after nearly six years. More than anything, I'm afraid she'll tell me to go to hell, hang up and never speak to me again. I can't take that chance.

I used the phone to look her up online and found no sign of an Ava Lucas in San Diego. She was never into social media for her personal life because she had to deal with it so much at work, so that's a dead end. I asked Muncie to go to our apartment building and find out if she's still there.

Muncie came back with a report from the super that she left almost a year ago and didn't leave a forwarding address. This is the best news I've had in years.

"I want you to find her," I tell Muncie, buoyed by the fact that it took her *five years* to move out of our place.

"How am I supposed to do that, sir?"

"Get the NCIS on it."

"I don't think they're in the business of tracking down ex-girlfriends."

"They want me to do that interview with *60 Minutes,* right?"

"So you're saying…"

"If they don't find my girl, there's no interview."

That's how I got the NCIS involved in tracking down Ava. It didn't take long because I knew she was from Purchase, New York, and her parents were lifers there, at least they were when I knew her.

"She's in New York City, sir," Muncie reports late on a Sunday night by phone.

"What else?"

"You asked us to find her. We found her. That's all I've got. You want her address?"

"Yeah."

He rattles it off, and I write it down so I have it. "I want you to go there."

"*What?* You want me to go to New York and find your ex? Er, um, sir?"

"She's not my ex." Or at least she wasn't when I last saw her. No, she was the sun, the moon, the stars, my whole life. The best thing to ever happen to me. There was nothing "ex" about it. "Didn't you say the Navy made you available to tend to whatever I might need?"

"I did, but—"

"I *need* to see her and talk to her before I go public with my story. There're things… that she should hear from me." I need *her.* I have to see her, to find out if what we had is still there. I have to know if she still loves me the way she once did.

"Why can't you call her? Don't you have her number?"

"I do, but…" I can't tell him I'm afraid she won't take the call. "It would be better if you went there and told her I need to see her. That it's urgent."

He is silent for such a long time that I fear he's ended the call.

"Muncie?"

"Yeah, I'm here."

"Please. I wouldn't ask this of you if I didn't really need to see her."

"I'll go tomorrow," he says reluctantly.

"You will? Really?"

"Yes, sir. I said I would, and I will."

"You'll tell her I need to see her? And arrange to get her here?"

"I'll do what I can, sir," he says with a deep sigh. "That's all I can promise until I talk to my chain of command."

"Of course, there's that interview they've got me doing…"

"I understand your position, sir."

"I don't want her to see me in the hospital. Set it up for a hotel or somewhere other than this place. In fact, I know just the place." I give him the name of the hotel I want. "Get a suite."

"Is there anything else, sir?"

"No, that'll do it. Just hurry up about it, will you?"

"Yes, sir. I understand your urgency."

"You can't possibly understand my urgency, Muncie."

"No, sir, of course I can't. I'll call you tomorrow night."

"I'll be waiting." I'm so excited by the possibility I might see her—soon—that I can't sleep that night. I lie awake the entire night, staring at the ceiling, reliving every minute I spent with her, the bliss I knew in her arms, the overwhelming love I felt for her and received from her in return. I've never experienced anything like it, and living without it, without *her*, for all this time has been the worst form of torture. I'd do it again to bring Al Khad to justice, but I paid a hefty price for that victory, and so did Ava.

I need the chance to apologize to her, to try to explain… I just hope and pray she'll see me and give me the chance.

# Chapter 27

*Eric*

She's in a state of shock. Since she got the call from her mother and heard that John is looking for her, she has barely said a word to me or her sister or any of the friends who came to be with her after I shared the news with them.

We don't know what to do for her.

Leaving her in the care of her sister, I take her phone into the bathroom and call her therapist, Jessica, and fill her in on the latest development.

"I don't know what to do for her. None of us know what to do."

"I'd come there, but I've got two kids down hard with the stomach bug, and the last thing you all need is to be exposed to that."

"True."

"Wait her out, Eric. Let her talk to you when she's ready."

"I'm trying not to make this about me, but I'd be lying if I said I'm not a little freaked out by this development."

"That's totally understandable."

"I know you're her therapist and not mine, but tell me this—what the hell am I going to do if she goes back to him?" Saying it out loud, giving voice to my greatest fear, makes me sick.

"You're getting way ahead of yourself with that."

"Am I, though? This is what she's waited almost six years for—a chance to see him again. What if she takes one look at him and forgets all about me?" That I'm unloading on a woman I barely know is a sign of desperation I'd never dare show anyone else. I need to be strong for Ava, and I will be. As soon as I stop freaking out about what it means for me.

"As difficult as it may be, you have to take this one minute at a time. Deal with what's right in front of you, and not what might happen. I'm not permitted to speak about Ava's treatment, as you know, but one thing I can tell you—she loves you very much and frequently talks about how critical you've been to her putting her life back on track."

"That's nice to hear." It's nothing I don't know, but I begin to wonder if all I've been to her is a diversion until the one she really wants comes back to her.

"It's the truth, Eric. Hold on to that, no matter what happens."

"I will. Thank you for your time."

"Please ask Ava to call me if I can help. I'm available to her at any time, and I'm sorry I can't come there."

"It's all right. I totally understand, and she will, too. We'll be in touch."

Long after we end the call, I remain seated on the bed, forearms on my knees, head bent to relieve some of the pressure that's formed at the base of my neck. *John is looking for me*, she said. Five words that turned my world upside down and plunged her back into the nightmare she's tried so hard to escape.

It's not fair to either of us. What right does he have to come back after all this time, thinking he can snap his fingers and she'll come running? Does it occur to him that she has a life? That people love her? That she's no longer sitting around waiting for him?

I no sooner have those thoughts than I feel like a monster. The man has given *years* of his life to protect the rest of us. He's sacrificed more than I or anyone I know ever will. He should have whatever he wants. Except Ava. He can't have her. She's mine.

My phone buzzes with a text from a number I don't recognize. I click on it.

*Heard u r engaged. Sooooo happy for you. No one deserves to be happy more than you do.*

My fingers fly over the keyboard. *Who is this?*

*Brit.* She's included the kissy-face emoji and a heart.

I delete the text and block the number. The last freaking thing I need right now is to hear from her. What would've been a bombshell in my life only a few months ago barely registers now.

"Eric?" Amy is at the door. "Are you okay?"

I want to tell her what she needs to hear, but the words get stuck in my throat, wedged against that gigantic lump that won't go away no matter how hard I try to get my emotions in check.

Amy steps into the room, closes the door behind her and sits on the bed next to me. She puts her arm around my shoulders, and I lean my head against hers. "I hate this for both of you."

"Thanks."

"Ava is asking for you."

The words are like a jolt of electricity that have me straightening, marshaling my defenses and standing to go to her.

Looking back at my sister, I say, "Brittany texted me."

"*What?*"

"She wanted to congratulate me on my engagement."

"What'd you say?"

"I deleted the text and blocked her."

"The bitch has got some nerve. That's for sure."

"Yeah. Her timing is exquisite, too."

"Always was."

"I can't do this again, Ames. I just can't."

She gets up and comes to me, her hand on my back, propping me up the way she has all our lives. "Everything about your relationship with Ava is different."

"But will the outcome be the same?"

"Don't do this to yourself, Eric. She's engaged to *you*."

"For now." My stomach aches and my head pounds, as if I'm hungover. But Ava is asking for me, so I push aside my own concerns to tend to her.

Camille is sitting with Ava on the sofa. She gets up to give her spot to me.

I sit with Ava and take her hand, which is freezing. I cradle it between both of mine, my gaze drawn to her engagement ring. "What can I do?" I ask her.

"I... I don't know what's going to happen now. But whatever it is, I want you right here with me. Is that okay?"

"Yeah, baby. That's okay." Her sweet words fill me with relief. He's looking for her, but she wants me. I put my arm around her and hold her close to me while Camille, Rob, Amy and Jules look on. They want to help, but there's nothing any of us can do yet.

Now that John knows how to find Ava, we wait for his next move.

It comes the following afternoon in the form of a Navy officer named Muncie at my door. Ava and I both called out sick from work, and we've spent the day in a restless state of suspended animation, waiting for something without knowing what we're waiting for.

Neither of us slept for shit last night, and we're tired and stressed. I buzz Muncie in and open the door to the hallway to wait for him.

He comes up the stairs, and the first thing I notice is the khaki uniform he wears under a blue wool coat. Extending his hand, he says, "David Muncie."

"Eric Tilden."

"Thanks for seeing me."

"I'd say it was no problem, but..."

He has the good grace to seem pained. "Is Ms. Lucas at home?"

"She is. Come in." I step aside to admit him and gesture to the sofa, where Ava is seated with her legs under her and a blanket over her lap. "Ava, this is David Muncie."

"Hi," she says tentatively.

"Thank you for agreeing to see me," he says, taking a seat on the chair next to her.

"I'm almost afraid of what you've come to tell me."

So am I, and I appreciate her saying it for both of us. I take a seat next to Ava, but I don't touch her.

"I'm here on behalf of Captain John West, United States Navy. I'm the liaison appointed to assist him after he was injured in the raid on the Al Khad compound."

"Wh-where has he been since then?" she asks.

"In the hospital, ma'am. I've been authorized to tell you he was shot in the leg, and the bullet nicked his femoral artery in a near-fatal injury. The leg was too badly damaged to be saved."

Ava whimpers, the sound so small as to almost be inaudible, but I hear it.

"About four weeks after his surgery, he contracted an infection that left him in a coma for more than a month. For a time, we weren't sure he was going to survive it, but he recovered, and he's currently in a rehabilitation hospital in the San Diego area."

*Oh my God.* He's been in the hospital. That's why she hasn't heard from him. She reaches for my hand and holds on tight to me.

"May I ask," Muncie says, "if you two are…"

"We're engaged," I tell him and watch his face fall with what can only be called disappointment.

"I see," he says.

*Do you?* I want to ask him. *Do you see that she's in love with someone else, and this guy from her past has no right to show up after all this time and want to see her?*

"Is John… He's all right now?" Ava asks tentatively.

"He's getting better all the time." After a long pause, he drops the bomb. "He would very much like to see you."

*Ava*

They're words I waited years to hear. *John wants to see me.* But they bounce off me like rubber bullets, painful but not penetrating.

Beside me, Eric's body is rigid with tension. He holds my hand so tightly, it hurts. This is killing him, and I hate that. I never want to cause him any pain, but hearing that the man I once loved nearly died not once but twice in service to our country and now wants to see me hurts him deeply.

I wanted to know why John hadn't called me. Now I know. It was because he couldn't, and that is so much easier to accept than thinking he didn't want to.

"Ms. Lucas," Muncie says gently. "I'm prepared to transport you to San Diego, tonight if possible, and arrange for you to meet with Captain West tomorrow. He's scheduled to give an interview to *60 Minutes* later this week, and he would like the opportunity to speak with you before he goes public with his story."

I could see John tomorrow.

I look to Eric, who's staring at the wall behind Muncie. "Eric."

He glances at me.

"What should I do?"

"I can't tell you that, sweetheart, but I'll support whatever you decide to do."

"Would you come with me if I go to San Diego?"

"If you wanted me to."

"Of course I would."

"Would you mind excusing us for a minute?" Eric asks Muncie.

"Certainly. Take all the time you need."

Eric gets up and gives a gentle tug to bring me with him.

My legs are rubbery under me as we go into our bedroom and close the door.

He puts his arms around me and brings me into his warm, sturdy embrace. "I needed this, so I figured you might, too."

"I need it so much."

"I can't imagine what you must be thinking and feeling."

"My mind is racing, and so is my heart."

His hand glides over my back. "You don't have to do anything you don't want to do, Ava."

"I know."

"And you don't have to decide anything this minute. You could ask Muncie to call you in the morning, so you have time to process everything he told you."

"That would be good."

"You want me to let him know?"

I nod. "Thank you."

"Whatever you need." He kisses my forehead. "I'll be right back."

Eric leaves the bedroom and closes the door, but I hear their voices in the next room. I hear the door to the apartment open and then close.

He's gone, but he's left me reeling from the information he provided about John, information I craved for such a long time. And now... Oh God, I don't know what to do with it.

Eric comes back into the bedroom and sits next to me, taking my hand and holding it the way he has for almost a year now. He doesn't say anything, but I know he has to be reeling, too.

"Tell me what to do."

"I wish I could, but this has to be your decision. All I can do is tell you I'm right here, and I'm not going anywhere."

"You won't be mad if I want to see him?"

"God, no, Ava. I'd totally understand."

He says and does all the right things, but I can see the toll this is taking on him.

"Could we lie down for a while? I need to put my head down."

"Whatever you want." He helps me up and holds the comforter for me until I'm settled under it.

I can't seem to get warm no matter what I do.

He gets in next to me and holds out his arms.

I curl into him, resting my head on his chest. The steady beat of his heart calms and soothes me. "I'm sorry this is happening, especially now."

"Don't make it about me, Ava. This is about you. And him."

"There is no me and him, not anymore." I mean that, but every time I think about what it would be like to see John again, my heart pounds. I'm not sure if it pounds with excitement or fear, but what does it matter? "It might be better... If I just don't see him."

"Is that what you want?"

"I don't know. Part of me wants to leave the past in the past, but then I think about what happened to him and how the least I could do is give him the courtesy—"

"Don't mention courtesy in regard to him." Eric's tone is sharper than I've ever heard from him. "He didn't give *you* the most basic of courtesy, so you don't owe him that. If you want to see him or need to see him to get closure, that's one thing. But don't do it out of courtesy to him."

His tense words tell me a lot about how he's feeling, and his pain kills me.

"I'm sorry."

"Please don't be, Ava. This isn't your fault—and it's not his, either. It's just a tough situation no matter how you look at it."

"I'm not going to see him."

"Really?"

"Really. It's not in my best interest or yours."

"It's not about me."

"It's about *us*. I worked so hard to get over him and move on. Seeing him would be a huge step backward."

"But it might also give you closure that you haven't had before now."

"I know he's alive and he's safe, and that's more than I've known up to now. That's all the closure I need."

"Don't you want to know *why* he did the things he did?"

"What does it matter now? It won't change anything for me." I raise my head so I can see his face. "You agree with me, don't you?"

"I want to."

"What does that mean?"

"As much as I want to protect you from ever being hurt again, I'm afraid you'll always regret not seeing him. Why not give him half an hour so you can go forward into the rest of your life with that chapter firmly closed and left behind where it belongs?"

Returning my head to his chest, I mull that over. If only the thought of actually seeing John didn't terrify me. Would thirty minutes with him undo all the hard work I've done to move forward? That's my greatest fear, but Eric makes a good point. Will I ever truly be at peace if I don't see him?

# CHAPTER 28

*John*

I wait all day to hear from Muncie and pounce on the phone when he finally calls at ten. "Did you see her?"

"I did."

I want to ask him everything—how she looks, what she said, where she lives. "And?"

"Sir…"

My heart sinks at the way he says that single word. "*What?*"

"She's engaged to be married."

I want to howl. *No, no, no.* She can't be engaged to someone else. I can't hear that. Although… What did I expect? Ava is a beautiful, wonderful woman. Of course she didn't sit around waiting for me. But still, I held out hope that maybe she had—hope that's now been dashed.

"Sir? Are you still there?"

"I'm here." I grit my teeth. "Who's the guy?"

"His name is Eric Tilden. Seems like a nice enough guy. I did a search on him, and he's the son of the New York governor. There was an article about them in the *New York Times* because her sister married his brother. That's how they met—at the wedding last June."

Last June. She was single as recently as last June. They haven't been together that long. "Does she... Is she... happy?"

"I was only with her for a short time, but I would say she seems happy—albeit rattled to hear that you want to see her."

My heart sinks to the floor and crashes. "She's not coming, then?" Earlier in the day, I got someone to cut my hair, and I shaved off the beard I allowed to flourish during my hospitalization. I sent word to my unit that I wanted my dress blues updated with my new rank and brought to me so I could meet her in uniform. She's never seen me in my dress blues.

"She asked for the night to think about it."

I had this picture in my mind of her screaming with joy at the news Muncie brought and begging him to bring her to me right away so we could get on with the rest of our lives. I feel like I've swallowed a ten-ton boulder now that I know she didn't exactly jump for joy at hearing I want to see her.

"I'm really sorry to not have better news, sir."

I can't bear his pity. "Don't worry about it. Let me know when you hear from her tomorrow."

"Will do."

I end the call before he can say anything that'll make me feel worse than I already do. I'm like a balloon that's been deflated. Every minute I've spent in this hellhole trying to get back my mobility has been with her in mind. She was the light at the end of the tunnel, the pot of gold at the end of the rainbow.

The possibility that she wouldn't want to see me never occurred to me. Maybe it should have. I know what I did to her was unconscionable, but I never in a million years expected the deployment to last as long as it did. However, when I accepted the assignment to the task force, I knew years-long deployments were a remote possibility.

That was before Al Khad came into our lives and changed the ballgame.

I roll my chair to the window to look out on the world that's gone on without me. Six years is a long time to be gone. I feel like a foreigner in a country I no longer recognize. And without Ava, I have no idea where I belong. She's my home, the only real home I've ever had, the only home I've wanted to come back to since the day I left.

Without her, I have nothing.

Less than nothing.

Tears burn my eyes as the worst pain I've experienced yet attacks my heart, making it almost impossible to breathe. I can't conceive of going on without her. She's been my reason for living.

I haven't shed a single tear since I lost my leg. Even during the painful rehab, I haven't cracked. But this...

This guts me.

I wheel the chair to the table next to my bed and push the nurse call button, keeping the chair facing the windows so they won't see my face or my tears.

"Hi there," a nurse says cheerfully when she comes into my room a few minutes later. "What can I do for you, Captain West?"

"I'd like something for the pain, please."

"I thought you weren't accepting pain medication any longer."

"I changed my mind." I want to scream at her to *get me the fucking pills*, but I don't. I somehow manage to contain myself. Just barely.

"I'll be right back."

She's not gone long, but it feels like an eternity before she returns with a medicine cup full of relief. This time she comes around the bed, hands the cup to me along with a glass of water while taking a too-close look at my face.

I take the pills, chase them with the water and close my eyes to pray for respite from the grinding ache in my chest.

"Are you okay?" the nurse asks.

I nod.

"I like the haircut and shave. You look great."

It was all for nothing if Ava doesn't come. "Thank you."

She squeezes my shoulder. "I'll let you get some rest. Give a ring if you need anything else."

I nod to let her know I've heard her. The only thing I want or need is the one thing she can't get me.

## Ava

I'm up all night, tossing, turning, pacing. One minute I'm positive I've made the right decision not to see John, and the next I'm questioning myself again. The facts run through my head like a movie I can't escape:

He lost a leg.

He nearly died from blood loss.

He nearly died a second time from an infection.

He wants to see me.

After all he's endured, how can I *not* honor his request?

But what about what I've endured? That counts for something, too.

And then I'm back to not going. For this minute, anyway.

Dawn peeks through the buildings that make up our neighborhood, a place where I've felt safe to get comfortable and start over. Where will John be comfortable now? Where will he start over?

God, I have to see him, even if it's not in my best interest. I need to know he's all right and that he'll *be* all right. How will I ever have any peace to call my own until I reckon with the past?

I'm standing in front of the big windows that look toward the Hudson and New Jersey in the distance when Eric joins me, placing his hands on my shoulders and his chin on my head.

"Did you sleep at all?" he asks.

"No. You?"

"Not much. What're you thinking?"

"That I have to see him, even though I probably shouldn't."

After a long pause, he says, "Then that's what we'll do."

*

Three hours later, Eric and I are loaded onto a sleek military jet and preparing to depart from Teterboro. We've been treated like VIPs, which is somewhat surprising. I say as much to Muncie, who jumped into action as soon as Eric called him this morning. I couldn't bring myself to pull the trigger, so Eric took care of that as well as letting Trevor know I'll be out of work and notifying our closest friends of where we're going and why.

"You are VIPs," Muncie says. "The Navy has instructed me to see to whatever Captain West needs."

Before I can process that information or the fact that one of Captain West's needs is *me*, my phone chimes with a text from Miles. *You are in my thoughts as you make this difficult journey. Whatever happens, you have my love and support.*

His words bring tears to my eyes, but then again, everything does. My emotions are so raw that when Eric made coffee for me, his unwavering kindness nearly made me cry. He can tell I'm on the razor's edge between holding it together and falling apart.

When the pilot announces we're next for takeoff, Eric takes my hand and holds on tight. As we lift into the air, I'd give anything to be on my way to work. There is so much to be said for a boring, routine day in which nothing out of the ordinary happens.

I no sooner have that thought than I immediately feel selfish. So many people, including my dear friend Miles, would give anything to be able to see the people they lost on the ship as well as the military members who've died fighting Al Khad's organization. I recall the sales clerk at Bloomingdale's, and how she touched the pin on her lapel that she wears in honor of her late parents. I think of Dawkins and his tireless pursuit of justice on behalf of his daughter and son-in-law.

What they wouldn't give for the chance I've been given. I have no right to be undone by the opportunity to see John. I need to celebrate it for the blessing that it is and take this moment to celebrate the great victory John helped to achieve for our country as well as those who lost loved ones on the ship and in the war.

I've nearly got myself convinced that it'll all be fine. That I'll be able to see him, talk to him, get answers to my many questions, thank him, maybe hug him and then go on with my life—my new life, the one I was forced to create for myself after he left and never came back.

Eric is so tense, his body is rigid in the seat next to mine. He stares straight ahead without blinking while chewing on the inside of his cheek, something he does when he has a lot on his mind.

I touch his face to let him know he's doing it, and he offers a small smile of gratitude. It always hurts after he does it, but he says he doesn't know he's doing it until it hurts. I don't want him to hurt, and this roller coaster I've been on since the night Al Khad was captured has hurt him. It's filled him with insecurities and concerns about me and our relationship—and I hate that for him. I hate it for both of us, but mostly I hate it for him.

I want him to feel confident about me. We're planning our wedding. This should be the happiest time of our lives, but here we are on a plane flying three thousand miles to confront my past. It's too much to ask of anyone, especially someone who's survived what he has.

"I hate that this is happening now," I whisper so only he will hear.

"What do you mean?"

"This is supposed to be a happy time for us."

He touches his index finger to my cheek. "I'm happy to be wherever you are."

"You always know what to say to me."

"Because I love you."

"I love you, too."

"I know you do, babe," he says, sighing as he rests his head against the seat.

"Will you tell me how you're feeling? The truth?"

"I'm kinda tired after a restless night."

"And?"

"That's about it."

Across the aisle from us, Muncie is wearing headphones and has his eyes closed, but I keep my voice down anyway. "Tell me the truth."

He's quiet for a long time, but I never look away. "What do you want me to say? That I'm freaking out over the thought of you taking one look at him and forgetting about me? Because I'd never add to your burden by admitting something like that."

I blink back more goddamned tears. "That's not going to happen."

"How do you know?"

"Because that's not what I want." I squeeze his hand. "I have what I want right here."

"I hope you still feel that way after you see him."

"I *will*, Eric." After hearing his concerns, I want to tell the pilot to turn the plane around and take us home.

*John*

She's coming.

Muncie woke me before dawn with the news that he is bringing her to me today. I don't know what changed between yesterday and today, but I don't care about anything other than seeing Ava.

I've already showered and shaved, and I'm waiting for one of the nurses to come help me with my uniform. I can do most of it myself, but I need help with the prosthetic and my pants, which makes me crazy. I never pictured a scenario in which I'd need someone's help to get my pants on, but that's my reality. For now, anyway.

The act of bathing leaves me exhausted. With hours to wait until someone from my unit will come drive me to the hotel where I'll meet Ava, I move to the recliner chair and try to relax so my muscles will stop trembling so violently. I don't want her to see me as sick or feeble. I want her to see the strong, steady warrior who helped capture the world's most wanted man.

I'm so excited that I don't expect to sleep, but I doze off anyway and awake when the nurse I asked to help me comes into the room.

"Heard you're getting out of here for a while today," she says.

Her name is Hailey, and she's my favorite among the nurses because she never treats me like I'm less than I used to be. Her matter-of-fact approach to my situation is a welcome relief from the others, who act like I'm something special when I know I'm not. I was just a guy doing his job. I didn't ask for notoriety or fame or any of the attention I'm getting since the video was released by Al Khad's scumbag disciples.

I don't want any of it. I only want Ava. I want to return to the life I had before the hell of the last six years. I want a time machine.

"Yeah," I reply to Hailey. "Going to see my love, Ava, for the first time in six years."

"Oh my goodness! I didn't know you had someone special. Where's she been while you were in here?"

"I waited to contact her until I was stronger."

"You must be so excited to see her."

"I am." I don't tell her that my Ava has a fiancé. He doesn't exist to me. My focus is on her and only her.

"Well, let's get you tricked out, then." She gets the uniform that my unit sent over out of the closet and helps me into it.

For the first time, I see the fourth stripe on my sleeve and know a moment of pure pride at having achieved the rank of captain. I gaze with pleasure at the trident that identifies me as a SEAL as well as the ribbons that tell the story of decorated service.

"I want my leg," I tell her, my face heating with embarrassment.

"Of course you do."

It takes about fifteen minutes that leave me further depleted, but being back in uniform does great things for my morale. This uniform saved my life in more ways than one, and I will never look at it with anything other than pride, despite how my career is ending.

I look up at her. "Could I ask you something and will you be honest?"

"Of course."

"Do I look like hell? It's okay. You can tell me."

"Not at all. You look very handsome."

"I don't look sick or weak or…"

"None of those things. I don't think you have any idea how invested in you we've all become. Not just here but the whole country is talking about you and what you did."

"I hate that." I shake my head. "I was just doing my job. I never signed on to be anything more."

"You're a national hero, Captain West. You may be a reluctant hero, but you're a hero nonetheless." She pauses, seeming to try to get her emotions in check. "When I think back to that day… when the ship was bombed and the sheer horror of it, I remember the poor families who lost loved ones and their terrible grief. My heart broke for them. What you and your comrades did… You got *justice* for them, for the people who died. We owe you a debt of gratitude that can never be repaid."

"Thank you," I say, moved by her words and the passion behind them.

"Everyone in the country feels the same way I do."

"I don't know how to deal with that."

"You're going to figure it out one step at a time. The first step is seeing your Ava." She brushes lint off my uniform jacket and takes an assessing look at me. "I think you're ready."

I have butterflies the size of seagulls in my stomach as she helps me into my wheelchair. "I need my crutches, too. I want her to see me standing, not sitting in this chair."

Hailey gets the crutches and hands them to me to hold. "I'm going to check to make sure your ride is here, and then I'll be back to get you."

"He'd better be here," I say of the ensign Muncie assigned to transport me. "He's supposed to be waiting for me downstairs."

"I'll confirm that and be right back."

She leaves me alone with my thoughts for a few more minutes. I close my eyes and think of Ava, going back to that first encounter outside the bathrooms in that awful bar Sanchez picked to celebrate his advancement, to the last time I saw her the day of the attack and everything in between. I recall so precisely the first time I saw her precious face. It's a moment I've relived every day since I saw her last.

The two years I spent with her were the best of my life, but I have regrets, too. So many regrets, and I'll share them with her today. She has a right to know the truth, even if it'll kill me to say words that will break her heart—and mine.

I never should've gotten involved with her.

I told her things about me that weren't true and withheld other things she had a right to know. I loved her so much that it made me selfish. I'm still selfish where she's concerned. I don't give a flying fuck that she has a fiancé or a new life that doesn't include me. I want her back, and I'm prepared to fight for her as hard as I fought to find Al Khad. This fight, the fight for the love of my life, is the most important fight of all.

# CHAPTER 29

*John*

Hailey returns a few minutes later. "Ensign Bidlack is here. You ready?"

"Yeah." I'm as ready as I'll ever be. I tuck my uniform hat under one arm and hold my crutches with the other hand.

Hailey props open the door and then comes for me, pushing my chair into a corridor lined with doctors, nurses, physical therapists and other hospital staff who break into applause at the sight of me.

Several of them are in tears as I go by.

I'm blown away. I can't believe they did this, especially since I was a raging asshole to many of them over the last couple of months. That doesn't seem to matter now as they give me a send-off I'll never forget.

The sound of their applause follows me all the way to the elevators.

I look up at Hailey and catch her wiping away tears. "You did that."

She shakes her head. "Everyone wanted to be here for you."

"Thank you so much." My voice is gruff with emotion. I'm like a live wire these days, experiencing so many emotions in the span of a day that I can barely process them before another day is upon me with a million new emotions. And this day promises to be the most emotional one yet.

In the lobby, we meet up with Ensign Bidlack, who shakes my hand and thanks me for my service before loading me into the handicap-accessible van. This is my life now, I think as I'm raised into the back of the van on a lift.

I immediately reject that thought. It's my life until I get used to the prosthetic and can stand for more than a few minutes at a time. The chair is temporary, as are the crutches. My PT team tells me I'll be able to run, ski, ride bikes and do all the things I used to before I became an amputee. It's hard to imagine that when I'm still working on standing, but they know better than me what to expect.

On the ride to the hotel, I soak in the scenery, hungry for the sight of familiar landmarks in San Diego, the place I've lived longer than anywhere else in my nomadic life. Ava and San Diego are home to me.

We arrive at the Fairmont Grand Del Mar, and the memories come flooding back. We'd had to vacate our apartment for three days while it was painted, and I surprised Ava with a mini-getaway to the five-star hotel. I'm unprepared for the rush of emotions that overtake me as the Spanish details come into view, reminding me of being here with her.

Something like that never would've made me choke up before, but now…

"Captain?" Bidlack has the doors open. "Are you ready, sir?"

"Yeah, let's go." After he's lowered me to street level, I say, "Straight to the elevators. Don't stop for any reason."

"Yes, sir."

Muncie took care of checking me in under his name and instructed Bidlack to pick up the key before he came for me. I don't want anyone to know I'm here, so I keep my eyes down and my gaze averted, hoping no one will recognize me. We get as far as the elevators when a woman gasps.

"You're that Navy SEAL!"

"Ma'am, please give Captain West his privacy," Bidlack says, shocking the hell out of me.

"Of course," she says, backing off. "My apologies. Thank you for your service."

Bidlack rolls me in, and the doors close behind me.

I look up at him. "Well done, Ensign."

"Commander Muncie told me he'd have me demoted to seaman apprentice if I let anyone bother you."

That makes me laugh. Good old Muncie. I owe the guy after what he's done for me these last few days.

"He wasn't joking," Bidlack says earnestly. He's so young. I don't recall ever being that young—probably because I wasn't.

When we arrive on the floor, he backs me out of the elevator and steers me toward the room. The suite is just like the one we had the last time we were here.

"Is this to your liking, sir?"

"Yes, thank you, Bidlack." I point to a chair. "Let me sit there, and then stash the wheelchair in the bedroom if you would."

"Yes, sir."

When I'm settled in the chair with the crutches propped against the arm, he rolls the chair into the bedroom and out of sight.

Someone knocks on the door, stopping my heart. It's not time yet. She shouldn't be here yet.

Bidlack goes to admit a room service waiter who delivers a pitcher of ice water. He brings the pitcher to the table, pours me a glass and leaves a second empty glass next to the pitcher. That's for Ava.

Ava.

*God, Ava… Hurry. Please hurry. I need to see you so badly.*

"Commander Muncie thought you might appreciate the water. He said to order anything else you might want."

"The water is good. Thank you."

"Is there anything else I can do for you?"

"Not now."

"You have my number to call when you're ready to return to the hospital?"

"I do."

"I'll wait for your call, sir. And may I say while I have the chance that it's an honor and a privilege to have met you." He salutes and spins to leave before I can raise my arm to return the salute. I can't remember the last time I was saluted. The courtesies we take for granted here in the States were the least of our concerns in the field.

Ava's flight is due to land in the next few minutes. It's a thirty-minute ride from the airport to the hotel. Muncie is supposed to text me when they land. I take my phone from my pocket and hold it in my hand, staring at it until it comes to life ten minutes later.

Landed. The fiancé is with her...

"Fuck. No." I text him back. *Please ask her to come to me alone.*

*I'll do what I can.*

*Give me a heads-up when you're close.*

*Will do.*

I want to be standing when she comes into the room.

The half hour passes so slowly, I wonder if the clock is moving backward instead of forward. I stare so hard at my phone that my vision blurs. After nearly six years, the last thirty minutes are the most difficult because I know she's close—closer to me than she's been since the last time I saw her.

The phone lights up with a text from Muncie. *Lobby. She's coming alone.*

I put the phone in my pocket and reach for the crutches, straining to pull myself up with muscles that don't work the way they used to. Something that once would've been so easy now takes all my strength.

I keep most of my weight on my good leg and grasp the high back of an easy chair until I have my balance. I carefully prop the crutches on the front side of the chair, keeping them in reach. I brush the wrinkles out of my uniform as my heart pounds and my mouth goes dry.

With my gaze fixed on the door, I wait.

*Ava*

Muncie hands me a key card and the room number. "He won't be able to answer the door, so use this."

"Why can't he answer the door?"

"He's not really walking yet." He hesitates, seeming to decide something. "It was vitally important to him that he be able to stand before he saw you. That's all he can do so far. Eventually, he'll be able to do everything he did before, but right now... Standing is a huge accomplishment."

As I take the key card from him, I realize my hands are shaking. I glance at Eric. Ever since Muncie told me John wants to see me alone, Eric hasn't said a word. His body is so tight with tension that I'm afraid to touch him.

Muncie hands him a key card for a room on another floor. "Your bags will be delivered there. Whenever you're ready," he says to me, "you can go on up. Captain West is waiting for you." He walks away.

*Captain West is waiting for you.*

It's surreal that John is in this hotel waiting to see me and that he chose this of all places for our reunion. I don't tell Eric that we're here because John and I once spent a beautiful weekend here while our apartment was being painted.

I look up at Eric. "I'm going to go now. I'll meet you at the other room after?"

He nods and places his hands on my shoulders before leaning his forehead against mine. "Are you okay?"

"I don't know what I am. You?"

"Same. I wish I could go with you."

"I do, too, but it might be better if—"

"I understand. Don't worry. Just go do what you have to do and come to me after, okay?"

"Okay." I have a lump the size of Texas in my throat.

"I love you, Ava."

"Love you, too." I'm afraid to move, afraid to leave him, afraid to see John and confront the painful memories. I'm afraid to breathe.

"Go while I still can let you." His hands drop to his sides, and he takes a step back.

I want to cling to him, beg him not to let go, but I can't do that to him. This is already excruciating for him. I try to imagine how I would feel if we'd come here so he could see Brittany. I wouldn't be able to handle it, certainly not as gracefully as he's handling this.

I swallow the lump in my throat and force my feet to move, to walk toward the elevator, to push the Up arrow, to get into the car and push the number I need. I keep my gaze down so I won't see Eric, but I know he's watching me.

I feel shredded by his pain. This is killing him, but he came with me anyway, held my hand for six hours on the flight and left me only when he had to. I thought I understood the word *agony*, but I've never experienced the emotion as acutely as I do right now, watching the numbers ascend on the panel above the doors. Each number takes me closer to John.

The doors open and nearly close again before I notice and step forward to get off. I panic for a second, thinking I've forgotten the room number, but then I remember and follow the arrows. Standing in front of the door where John waits for me, I'm unable to move or breathe or think or do anything other than stare at the door.

*He won't be able to answer the door...*

*Standing is a huge accomplishment.*

I hold the key card up to the black circle on the door and watch the green light come on. Green means go. I push open the door.

He's standing about ten feet from me.

The first thing I notice is the uniform. I'm not sure what I expected, but it wasn't the stark reminder of why we're here, why this happened, where he's been, why he had to go. In the span of seconds, my eyes travel from his chest to his face, and then I'm crying and moving toward him, drawn to him the same way I've always been.

I'm in his arms, and he holds me just like he used to—firmly, lovingly, perfectly. He buries his face in my hair and breathes me in.

"Ava," he whispers, "my beautiful Ava. I'm sorry. I'm so, so sorry. I love you so much. I never stopped. Not for one second." The words pour out of him, as if he's afraid I won't give him the chance to say everything he needs to. "I thought of you every day. Everything I did was about getting home to you."

I'm sobbing and clinging to him and listening. I listen to every word he says, each of them arrows to my battered heart.

His face is wet, too, and the realization nearly brings me to my knees. I've never seen him cry before, whereas he used to tease me about weeping over sappy commercials.

We stand that way for a long time. I have no idea how long it is before I begin to sense that he's tiring. I don't want to let him go, but his body is trembling.

"Sit," I tell him.

"I need help."

The three little words seem to cost him greatly.

I keep an arm around his waist and support his weight as we move the short distance to the sofa.

When he's seated, I notice his face has gone white with pain. "What can I do?" I ask, sitting next to him.

He shakes his head. "Didn't want you to see me this way."

"The only thing that matters is that you're alive."

"Does it matter, Ava? Does it still matter?"

"It matters very much." It occurs to me that this isn't going to be as simple as I wanted it to be. This isn't going to be about closure, but rather, about reopening recently closed wounds that never really healed.

"I have so much I want to say to you." He takes my hand and looks into my eyes, his blue-eyed gaze as familiar to me as anything in my life. "Beginning with I'm sorry. I hate that I did this to you, the last person who should ever be treated the way I treated you, the most precious thing in my life."

Tears run freely down my face. I'm powerless to stop them. He's saying everything I've longed to hear for years, that I wasn't crazy to wait for him or to mourn him or to yearn for him.

"That first night we met... I never should've left with you or stayed with you or fallen for you. But it was already too late. That first instant in the hallway outside the bathrooms... After that, it was too late."

"For what?"

"To walk away. It happened that fast for me. Like being hit by lightning."

I can barely see through my tears.

"I wasn't allowed to have a girlfriend, Ava. It was against the rules. And I broke every one of them because I couldn't bring myself to leave you." After a pause, he says, "I tried a couple of times."

That stuns me. "When?"

"Remember that weekend I went to Mexico with my unit?"

Nodding, I wipe tears from my face.

"I didn't go to Mexico. I went apartment shopping. I came this close to signing a lease, but I couldn't bring myself to do it. I went home to you. Another time, I packed my stuff while you were at work. I was going to leave you a note and tell you I'd met someone else. I wanted you to be so angry you wouldn't come after me."

"I... I don't understand."

"We weren't supposed to have entanglements, but you were never that to me. You were *everything*. I couldn't bring myself to leave you until I had no choice but to go."

"I tried to find you. After you left... I went to the base, and I asked people, but no one had ever heard your name. I couldn't find you anywhere, not even online."

"I don't exist online—or I didn't until the Pentagon released my name after the video was made public." The words are tinged with bitterness. "They're making me do an interview with *60 Minutes* that'll air in the next week. That's why I wanted to see you now, so I could tell you before I have to tell everyone else."

"After the video, I thought I might hear from you. Why didn't you call me?"

"At first it was because I was really messed up, and then it was because I was afraid you wouldn't take my call."

"That was months ago." I force myself to look at his face. He's gaunt and hollowed, but it's the same face that's haunted my dreams. "What took so long?"

"I didn't want to come back to you as a cripple."

"Because you thought that would matter to me?"

"No, because it mattered to *me*." He reaches for my left hand and zeroes in on my engagement ring. "Muncie told me you're engaged."

I nod, my heart beating so hard, I can hear it echoing in my ears.

"Who is he?"

"Eric... He's..." I pull back my hand and pour a glass of water from the pitcher on the table. I take a sip and then another.

For the longest time, he stares down at the floor while I wonder what he's thinking.

"I stayed in San Diego until last May. I... I gave it five years. I gave *you* five years, and then... I couldn't do it anymore, John. I just couldn't."

He nods but doesn't say anything.

"John..."

Turning those piercing blue eyes on me, he says, "I'm too late, then?"

The shattered expression on his face breaks my heart all over again. "I... I love him. He was there for me."

"And I wasn't."

I can't remain seated any longer. I get up and begin to pace as his gaze follows me. "I didn't know if you were even alive! Every day for years, I scoured the news looking for something—*anything*—that would give me hope or closure or something, but there was never a single thing about you. I waited for five years. *Five years*, John." My voice catches on a sob. "I was by myself with this for all that time, until I thought I'd go *mad* if I didn't make a change."

"Come here," he says.

I shake my head. I'm afraid to go anywhere near him. He's taking apart my carefully reconstructed life one sentence at a time.

He holds out a hand to me. "Please. I can't come to you."

I return to my place on the sofa, but I don't take his hand. I keep my arms crossed as if that'll protect me somehow.

"I get it. I've put you through hell. I'll always be sorry for that. Everything that happened is a hundred percent my fault."

"No, it was Al Khad's fault."

Shrugging, he says, "A big chunk of it was mine, too."

"Not everything that happened was bad," I whisper, wiping away more tears. "For a long time, it was the most beautiful thing to ever happen to me."

"Until it wasn't."

I can't think of a thing to say that wouldn't be wrong. It wasn't like he left because he wanted to. "Did you know you could be gone more than five years?"

"Hell no. We were told extended deployments were possible, but nothing like this."

"Your... your father must be very proud."

His face loses all expression. "I don't know who my father is, Ava."

"But you said he was a general, that you grew up all over."

"I did grow up all over, because I was in the system. The foster system. I was in a lot of trouble as a kid, and a judge told me I could go to jail or the military. He made it my choice. I chose the Navy. I have no family to speak of. Just you and the people I've served with. My lack of attachments made me an ideal candidate for the job I was asked to do."

*Just you...*

*Just you...*

*Just you...*

Hearing he has no one else breaks something in me. "You lied to me about so many things."

"Only because I had to. Never because I wanted to."

At some level, I understand that, but I don't like it. "My therapist said you're a national hero for what you did and sacrificed for the rest of us. But what you did to me wasn't heroic at all."

"I freely admit that. I watched the early coverage of the attack, and when I got the call from my command, all I could think about was you and what would happen to you. I was sick about it, but our mission, my role in it, everything about my professional life was and is classified. I couldn't have told you even if I wanted to."

"You could have. You chose not to."

"No, baby," he says gently. "I chose to protect you by not giving you information that could be used against you by the people we were trying to capture."

Hearing that, I recoil. "How could they have used it against me? They didn't even know I existed."

"I was unwilling to take even the slightest chance with your safety."

"Instead, you nearly ruined my life."

"I'll always regret the pain I caused you, Ava. You have every right to hate me. I wouldn't blame you if you did."

"I wish I did. That would make it so much easier to tell you to go straight to hell."

"If that's what you want to do, I'll try to understand. But if there's any chance… Any chance at all that you might still love me as much as I love you, that you might find it in your heart to forgive me and to give me another chance… There's nothing I want more than the opportunity to make things right with you. All the time I was gone, I dreamed of the life we might have when I came home. I'm being medically discharged from the Navy with a full pension. We'd have the resources to do whatever we want wherever we want. All I need to be happy is you, Ava."

"No." I shake my head as if the word isn't enough on its own to make my point. I keep my gaze fixed on the four gold stripes on his sleeve. "You don't get to do this to me. I'm finally in a good place in a healthy relationship with a man who adores me. He put me back together and helped me find a whole new life. I'm sorry, but no. I can't go backward."

After a seemingly endless silence, he says, "Okay." From his pocket, he withdraws a piece of paper that he hands to me. "My new phone number."

"I won't need this, John."

"Take it anyway. If you change your mind…"

I take the paper and put it in my pocket. "I… I should go."

He nods but doesn't look at me.

I'm not sure if I should hug him or if he would even welcome the gesture.

"Could I ask you one thing?" he says.

"Okay…"

"If you didn't have him, would you still be leaving?"

"It's not about him, John. It's about *us*, and too much water under the bridge to go back to who we were six years ago." Here come the goddamned tears again. "For a very long time, I would've given anything to hear the things you said to me today. But now… I had no choice but to move on."

"Thank you for coming all this way to see me."

"Thank you for your extraordinary sacrifices in service to our country. I'll never forget you or the time we spent together." My voice breaks. "I… I loved every minute of it." I rush toward the door because I need to be out of here before I break down. And I need to move quickly before I lose my resolve.

"Ava." His anguished cry is more than I can bear. "Please don't go. Don't leave me."

I open the door and wait for it to close behind me before I slide down to the floor, my heartbroken sobs echoing in the empty hallway.

# CHAPTER 30

*Eric*

This is what torture must be like. Almost an hour goes by, and Ava doesn't return. I'm like a caged animal as I move around the hotel room, trying to resist the urge to throw a large paperweight through the plate-glass window.

I can't take it. I can't stay in this room for another minute. If she comes back and I'm not here, she'll call me.

I take the elevator to the lobby and find the bar. "Maker's Mark," I tell the bartender. "Neat."

"Coming right up, sir."

He puts the drink in front of me, and I pounce on it, downing half of it in the first swallow.

"Would you like to charge that to your room or start a tab?"

I withdraw my wallet and hand over a credit card. "Start a tab, please."

I'm so tense, my muscles feel like they were carved from concrete. Not even the dreadful aftermath of my breakup with Brittany can compare to this hell. What'll I do if she tells me she's going back to him?

I take out my phone, make sure I don't have any new texts and then call Rob.

"Hey," he says, answering on the first ring. "How's it going out there?"

"She's with him now."

"Ah God, Eric," he says with a loud sigh.

"I'm dying, Rob. I can't handle this. The guy is a fucking national hero. I can't compete with him."

"*You* have been *her* hero."

The phone beeps. It's her. "I gotta go. She's calling me."

"Hang in there."

"Thanks." I switch over to take Ava's call. "Babe."

"Where are you?"

"In the bar. I'll be up in a minute."

"I want to go home, Eric."

I signal the bartender for my check. "Then that's what we'll do. I'll be right there." I scribble my signature, grab the card and run for the elevator. I walk into the room a few minutes later and stop short at the sight of her eyes red and swollen from crying. "Baby."

She comes to me, and I wrap my arms around her.

I have so many questions, but I don't say anything. I need to take my cues from her.

"Can we go home? Please?"

"Yeah. Let's go." I grab her bag and mine and keep an arm around her as I walk her to the lobby, where I ask the bellman to get us a cab. I wonder if I should let Muncie know we're leaving but decide he's not my problem.

"Are you checking out?" the bellman asks.

"Yeah, we're done here." I give him our room number, and he makes a note before signaling to a cab.

"Airport, please," I tell the cabbie.

In the car, I put my arm around her, and she snuggles up to me. There's traffic this time of day, and I'm not even sure we can get on a flight, but since we're going to the biggest city in the country, I'm optimistic. Every airline flies into New York.

If I stay focused on the details, I won't go mad trying not to ask her a hundred questions she won't want to answer. Instead, I do what I do best. I hold her and I love her and I take care of her. I've never been better at anything in my life than I am at loving Ava.

We end up on a red-eye flight to freaking JFK. I hate flying in there and having to battle traffic into the city, but LaGuardia wasn't offered, and my fiancée wants to go home. We'll arrive at five thirty in the morning Eastern Time. Hopefully, we can sleep on the plane.

"Any chance of an upgrade?" I ask the ticket agent.

She pokes around on the computer and finds us two seats in first class.

I hand over my credit card.

Ava stands by my side, and I catch the ticket agent making surreptitious glances at her, probably wondering about her ravaged face. I reach for Ava, bring her into my embrace and level a stare at the ticket agent that I hope encourages her to hurry the fuck up.

"Is there a lounge or somewhere we can go to wait?" I ask.

She gives me a day pass to the airline's club, and we wait there until our flight is called.

Ava never says a word until we're buckled into seats at the front of the plane. "Thank you."

"Whatever you need." I raise the arm between our seats and make her comfortable on my chest.

"I don't have the words yet."

"That's okay. You just hold on to me, and everything will be okay." But as I say what she needs to hear, I worry that nothing will ever be okay again.

*John*

After Ava leaves, I unbutton my uniform coat and remove it, tossing it on the chair that kept me upright while I waited for her. I pull at my tie and release the top button of my shirt. It was all for nothing. That's all I can think now that she's been here and gone, leaving her scent behind to torment me.

Everything I did to recover my health so I could get back to her doesn't matter now. Will anything ever matter again now that I've lost her?

I text Muncie. *Get me a bottle of vodka and bring it to the room.* I have no idea where he is, but he'd better be somewhere in this hotel or I'll have him court-martialed.

The phone chimes with his reply. *Coming right up, sir.*

Fifteen minutes later, I hear the door click before it opens to admit him. He's carrying the requested bottle, and I see his expression change when he realizes Ava is gone. He puts the bottle on the table.

"Now go away."

"Sir…"

"Muncie, I said to go the fuck away. That's an order."

He goes the fuck away.

When the door clicks shut behind him, I crack open the bottle and drink directly from it. I haven't had a drink in six years, except for the rotgut Tito brewed up in the field that'd nearly killed us all. The vodka goes down easy—and goes straight to my head. I feel the buzz almost instantly, but the relief… that takes longer. Half the bottle, in fact.

I feel like I just stepped out of a plane without a parachute, and the ground is rushing up to meet me. The landing is going to hurt like hell.

What do I do now that I don't have thoughts of her to keep me going? Where do I find hope now that she's given me her answer—and not the one I prayed for all this time? Even after I heard she was engaged, I still held out hope that once she saw me, it would be like the six years we were apart never happened.

Wishful thinking. They happened, and she moved on without me. What choice did she have when I wasn't able to give her even the slightest reason to keep her faith tied up in me?

The second half of the bottle goes down easier than the first.

I have no memory of ending up facedown on the sofa, but that's where I am when Muncie shakes me awake the next morning.

Memories of yesterday come flooding back, reminding me that I've lost Ava forever. I don't want to go on without her. "Leave me alone, Muncie."

"I can't do that, sir."

"I'm ordering you to leave me alone."

"I understand that, sir, but I'm not going to leave you. People are worried about you."

"What people are worried about me?" I have no people.

"The doctors and nurses at the hospital, for one. Your command, for another."

"They don't care about me. They just want me to do that interview."

"Sir, the entire country cares about you. The Pentagon has received more inquiries about you than anyone else in years. People care very much about you."

I don't care about those people. The only one I care about doesn't want me anymore, and now I have to find a way to live with that—to live without her.

I can't do it.

Closing my eyes, I yearn for the oblivion the vodka gave me. "Please go, Muncie."

"No, sir," he says gently. "I'm not leaving you."

I'm well aware that I'm setting an awful example, and that my conduct is highly unbecoming of an officer of my rank and stature. I don't give a flying fuck about anything now that Ava is gone forever.

My head is pounding and my mouth tastes like roadkill, but the ache in my chest might do what a bullet to the leg failed to do.

It might very well kill me.

*Ava*

We land in New York to snow flurries and howling wind that makes for a bumpy descent into JFK. Eric holds my hand the way he has all night as we flew across the country toward home. I appreciate that he hasn't asked me any questions. I can't talk about it. Not yet.

I'm haunted by my hour with John. I close my eyes, and I see his face, his distinctive blue eyes, the ravages of his illness. I hear his voice, pleading with me to give him the chance to put us back together.

*Please don't go. Don't leave me.*

I thought I knew what heartbreak felt like, but turning my back on him while he begged me to stay ruined me. I'm hollowed out, gutted. I don't know how to go on from here, how to function. I can barely breathe through the pain.

I thought I'd gain closure by seeing him, but that's not what I got.

*I'll always regret the pain I caused you, Ava.*

*I was unwilling to take even the slightest chance with your safety.*

*If there's any chance… Any chance at all that you might still love me as much as I love you, that you might find it in your heart to forgive me and to give me another chance…*

*There's nothing I want more than the opportunity to make things right with you.*

*All the time I was gone, I dreamed of the life we might have when I came home.*

*All I need to be happy is you, Ava.*

*Please don't go. Don't leave me.*

"Ava?"

Eric's voice brings me back to the present to realize we've arrived at our gate, and it's time to get off the plane. I fumble with my seat belt until it releases.

Holding our overnight bags, he waits for me to gather my things and gestures for me to go ahead of him.

The flight attendant tells us to have a great day.

I have nothing to say to that.

"Thank you," Eric says. "You, too."

His hand on my lower back keeps me moving forward in the crowd at JFK to the curb, where we wait in a long line for a cab.

Icy wind whips at my face, bringing tears to my eyes, but I'm so numb, I barely feel the cold.

Rush-hour traffic makes a long ride longer.

We arrive at Eric's place at seven thirty and trudge up the stairs like two refugees returning home after a trek through the desert without water. I want a shower and a bed. I take the time to text Trevor to let him know I'll be out again today.

He knows what's going on and texts right back. *Take all the time you need.*

My phone is full of texts from my sister, my mother, Jules, Amy, Miles and Skylar, all of them checking on me. They want to know how things went with John, but I can't deal with their questions. Not now.

Eric follows me into the bedroom and deposits my bag inside the closet. "What do you need?"

"A shower and then I'm going to sleep for a while. If you need to go to work, that's fine."

"I'm not going anywhere."

"I… I'm sorry I can't talk about it…"

"You don't have to." He caresses my face and then kisses my cheek. "Do whatever you need to. I'll be right here."

"It meant everything to me that you took this trip with me."

"I'm with you, kid," he says, forcing a smile. "All the way."

"Thanks." I go into the bathroom and turn the water on to heat up while I remove the clothes I wore to see John. I'll never be able to look at the tunic I used to love again without hearing him pleading with me not to go.

As I step into the shower, I give into emotions that boil over into anguished sobs.

# CHAPTER 31

*Eric*

Camille has been trying to call me all night, which is the only reason I take her call now, while Ava is in the shower.

"Hey."

"Oh, Eric. Thank God you finally answered. I've been losing my mind worrying about you guys. How is she?"

"Not good, Camille. Not good at all."

"What happened?"

"I don't know. She hasn't said much of anything since she got back from seeing him."

"So you don't know what happened?"

"No. All I can tell you is she said she wanted to come home. So we came home."

"What now?"

"I don't know. I don't know anything."

"I'm sorry. I'm just so…"

"I know. I am, too."

"Will you let me know if there's anything I can do?"

"Yeah. I will."

"Okay, then. Give her my love."

"I'll do that, too. Talk to you soon." After ending the call, I turn off the phone. I can't do that ten more times with everyone who'll want to know how Ava's meeting with John went. Camille can take care of updating everyone. I don't know what to do with myself or the tension that grips me like a fist. I want to be there for Ava, but she's so closed off that there's no way to reach her.

The shower goes off, and a few minutes later, the bedroom goes dark when she closes the blinds against the early morning sunlight.

I go in, change into sweats and a T-shirt and stretch out next to her in bed. "Is there anything I can do for you?"

"No, thank you."

I don't know what else to say, so for a long time, I lie there and stare up at the ceiling as daylight peeks in around the blinds. I'm too keyed up to sleep, so I get up and do some work, things I can do without thinking. Around noon, I turn on my phone and begin to deal with the slew of texts from friends and family, asking about Ava, asking about me.

I'm not sure what to say, so I just tell them we're both okay and thanks for checking on us.

Ava sleeps all day and into the night.

I order pizza that I eat alone, while wondering if I should wake her to eat something. But I decide not to bother her.

She never stirs when I get into bed around ten, exhausted in more ways than one. She's right next to me in bed, but she's so far away, she may as well still be in California.

I don't expect to sleep, but my alarm wakes me at six thirty like it does every weekday. I glance over to find the bed next to me empty and get up to see where she is. I find her in the kitchen, dressed for work in a slim-fitting skirt and tailored blouse. Her hair hangs in shiny waves that fall down her back as she makes her usual bowl of workday oatmeal.

When she sees me, she looks up and offers a small smile. "Morning. I made coffee."

"Thanks." I pour myself a cup and study her, looking for chinks in the armor, but there aren't any. She looks like she always does on work mornings. "So you're going to work?"

Nodding, she says, "I have to. I'm so far behind. Don't forget we have the meeting with the cake baker at six. You can still make that, right?"

It's surreal, at least to me, to be talking about our wedding after what's transpired in the last forty-eight hours. But if she wants to play it like nothing is wrong, then I guess that's what we'll do. For now, anyway.

"I'll be there."

## Ava

Staying busy has saved me in the past, so I dive into work with a single-minded focus that keeps my brain from straying into unhealthy areas. Trevor has asked me to put together a proposal for a potential new client, a chain of local jewelry stores that's hoping to make a run against the national brands.

I'm compiling ideas on how to differentiate theirs from some of the better-known brands when Miles appears at my desk. The change in him over the last few months can only be called remarkable. He smiles more often and laughs and cracks the occasional joke. On the lapel of his suit coat, he still wears the family group pin to remember Emmie, but his demeanor is considerably lighter than it was when I met him.

"What's up?" I ask him.

"That's what I want to know. I didn't think you'd be here today."

"Why not? I work here." I can't talk about it. I won't talk about it.

When he seems to realize that, he clears his throat. "I have news about the lawsuit."

"What kind of news?"

"The kind in which the government offers a settlement."

"Seriously? Is it a decent settlement?"

"It's got our attention."

"I'm really happy to hear that. It's the right thing for them to do."

"You should feel very proud of the work you've done that helped us get here, Ava. It made a difference."

"It was an honor to be involved. Thank you for the faith you had in me."

"My faith was well placed. I've spoken to Trevor, and we both agree that we'd like to promote you to senior account executive. If you're interested, that is."

Not that long ago, a promotion of that magnitude would've been huge news. Today, it barely permeates the numbness. "Wow, that's… It's amazing. Thank you."

"Don't thank me. You've worked your ass off and shown us you've got the stuff for much bigger things around here. If that's what you want."

"It is. I love working here, and I appreciate the new opportunity." Last week, I would've taken a second to gloat about being promoted over Catty Caitlyn. Now? I don't care.

"Great. I'll get with Trevor and set up a meeting with both of you for later this week to move some things around and get you started. Congratulations."

"Thank you, Miles. For everything."

"Same to you. I owe you an enormous debt of gratitude on a number of different fronts—and if this settlement happens, we're going to celebrate."

"That sounds good."

"I'll let you get back to work."

"Keep me posted."

"I will."

I watch him walk away, noticing that he carries himself differently than he did when I first met him, which pleases me greatly. He deserves a second chance at happiness.

I try to get back into what I was doing with the proposal, but my mind wanders. *Please don't go. Don't leave me.*

Where is he now, I wonder. Is he okay? Does he have friends or comrades or someone to support him? Or is he alone? I can't bear to think about him or the things he said or the way he begged me to stay. Staring out the window, I spin the engagement ring around on my finger without realizing what I'm doing.

Carlos appears, puts a takeout cup on my desk and backs away slowly, as if he's afraid I might bite or something. I gather that he's heard about my involvement with the celebrated captain who helped bring down a monster.

"Thank you."

"Welcome. If there's anything I can do…"

I smile and shake my head.

"Okay, then." He gives a little wave and takes off.

He's brought me a skinny latte that goes down easy. I'm blessed to have friends and family who care about me the way they do, but the attention makes me uncomfortable. I can't bear to think about the conversation with John, let alone relive it a hundred times sharing it with everyone who is interested.

I want to go back to who I was and what I was doing before Muncie showed up at Eric's the other night. I want to focus on my wedding and Eric and my job and our life in the city. That's what makes sense to me.

At five thirty, I leave the office and grab a cab to take me to the bakery where I'm meeting Eric to choose our wedding cake. Only last week, I was so invested in every detail of the wedding. Now, I'm forcing myself through the motions while hoping the numbness lets up eventually.

If I keep pushing forward the way I have since I came to New York, I'll move past this latest setback, or so I tell myself.

*Please don't go. Don't leave me.*

I slump against the cab door as thoughts of him come rushing back to me. The way he looked in his uniform. The intense blue eyes that gazed at me with such love. The effort he made to stand and greet me. The words he said. The pleas he made.

I can't get him out of my mind, no matter how hard I try to stay focused on my new life.

"Ma'am?"

The driver's voice drags me out of my thoughts.

"We're here."

Out the window, I see the entrance to the bakery. I pay for the ride with a credit card.

"Do you need a receipt?"

"No, thank you." I gather my belongings and get out of the cab. Inside, Eric is waiting for me in the reception area. He seems relieved to see me, and I hate that I've given him reason to question whether I'd show up.

"Hi, babe," he says, greeting me with a kiss. "How was your day?"

"Busy. You?"

"Same."

There may as well be a two-ton elephant standing between us. The elephant comes with us into the conference room, where a wide variety of wedding cakes are on display for our perusal. Samples of the actual cakes are on plates.

"You're Amy's brother, right?" the owner, Deborah, says to Eric.

"One of them."

"I know her through the Bensons."

While they catch up, I walk around the room, trying to focus on the cakes and not the voice in my head that begs me not to leave. I stand for a long time, staring at a cake decorated with live flowers. It's the most gorgeous cake I've ever seen, but I'm not thinking about my wedding or the cake or Eric.

No, I'm back in a San Diego hotel room with a man in uniform who can't stand for long on his new prosthetic. He's begging me to forgive him for what he's done to me and asking me not to go. I see his blue eyes, so focused on me the way they always were when we were together.

"Ava?"

I realize Eric is speaking to me and has been trying to get my attention. "I'm sorry," I say, smiling at him. "What did you say?"

"Deborah was going to explain the various options. Do you want to come sit?"

No, I don't. I don't want to sit or talk about cake or think about anything as trivial as a wedding when John is out there somewhere, trying to learn how to walk again. Nothing in my life makes sense to me after seeing him.

But I don't say those things. Rather, I walk around the table and take a seat next to Eric, who looks at me with concern and maybe a hint of dread, as if he can feel me coming apart and doesn't know how to stop it.

Deborah's presentation is thorough, and it would've interested me greatly a week ago. Today, I can't work up the enthusiasm.

She suggests we taste each of the various flavors, but I can't. I just can't.

"I'm not feeling well," I tell her.

"Oh, sorry to hear that."

"Would it be possible to reschedule the tasting?" Eric asks.

"I'm booked for the next six weeks."

That's how long we waited for this appointment.

"We might need to find someone else, then," he says. "Our wedding is the third of July. We need this sewed up long before six weeks from now."

"Let me check with my assistant and see what we can do." She gets up and leaves the room.

"What's wrong, Ava?" Eric asks when we're alone.

"I don't know, but the smell in here is making me sick."

"Do you want to wait outside while I set up another appointment?"

"Yes, please." I grab my coat and purse and head for the door, stepping out into cool fresh air that's a welcome relief from the overly sweet air inside the bakery.

I lean back against the building and take deep, cleansing breaths.

Eric comes out of the bakery, pulling on his coat as he walks. "What was that in there? I thought you were excited to pick out the cake."

"I was. I *am*. It was hot in there, and the smell… It was overwhelming."

"No, it wasn't. It smelled the way a bakery should."

I realize he's angry with me, which is a first.

296 | MARIE FORCE

"Are we going to talk about what's really going on here, or are we going to pretend that the smell of cake made you sick?"

"I… I told you…"

"You haven't actually told me anything. Instead, you've left me twisting in the wind for two days wondering what happened in San Diego while you try to pretend everything's fine when we both know it isn't."

I can't think of a single thing to say that.

Huffing with disgust—or what I take to be disgust—he waves down a cab and holds the door for me.

I slide across the cracked vinyl seat to make room for him.

Eric gets in and gives his address to the driver.

We take off like a shot into traffic.

Eric sits a foot from me, but he stares out the passenger side window the whole way home. When we arrive in Tribeca, Eric pays for the cab, holds the door for me and follows me up the stairs.

Inside the loft, we hang up our coats.

"I need to know one thing," he says, breaking the long and unusual silence.

"What?"

"Do you want to be with him? Is that why you've shut down on me since you saw him?"

"No! That's not what I want, and I haven't shut down on you."

"Yes, Ava, you have. You're here, physically, but you're not here in any other way. You're a million miles away from me."

"I'm trying to process it all. I'm sorry that I've been unable to talk to you about it or that you thought what you did."

In a softer, more conciliatory tone, he says, "You have to tell me about San Diego. I'm going crazy trying to figure out what's happening to us."

"I'm sorry to have done that to you. It was really… hard to see him again and to see him diminished by his injury."

Eric takes my hand and walks me to the sofa, where we sit together.

"He said some things…"

"What kinds of things?"

I look down at the floor. "He's sorry for what he put me through. He said he never should've gotten involved with me and actually tried to leave a couple of times but couldn't bring himself to do it."

Blinking back tears, I force myself to continue because Eric deserves to know these things. "While he was gone, he thought about me every day, he still loves me and wants a chance to make things right with me. I told him about you and our relationship and that we're engaged. I told him how you put the pieces back together for me and that my life is here with you now. And then when I had to go, he said… He asked me…"

"What, honey? What did he say?"

"He begged me not to leave him." I feel dead inside as I say those words and hear his voice in my head, pleading with me as I walked away.

"God, Ava." Eric puts his arm around me and encourages me to rest my head on his chest. "No wonder you've been so upset since we came home."

"I don't want to be upset. I don't want to think about him anymore. I want to think about you and the wedding and our life, but all I can hear is him begging me not to go. I… I didn't know that he was raised in the foster system. I don't think he has anyone else." I squeeze my eyes shut against the threat of tears. "He broke my heart all over again."

Eric holds me close to him and rubs my back. "We're going to find a way through this together. It's going to be okay. I promise."

"How? How is it going to be okay?"

"I don't know, but we're going to figure something out. Maybe we should get with Jessica. She might be able to help."

"Okay."

"You want me to call her?"

"Would you mind?"

"Not at all."

He takes my phone and punches in the code I gave him a long time ago. Eric and I don't have secrets from each other, so it's a relief to have told him what happened with John even if it hurt us both.

I sit back against the sofa and close my eyes. I can hear him on the phone, but I don't pay attention to what he's saying. I already know the story. I don't need to hear it again. I'm so tired, I could sleep for a week and it wouldn't be enough.

Eric returns to the sofa. "She's coming here in thirty minutes."

"She is? Really?"

He nods. "She said you're one of her VIPs. If you call, she drops everything for you—and she said her husband is at a movie with the kids tonight, so she's free anyway."

"And she probably has better things to do than listen to my sob story."

"It's not a sob story, Ava. You've survived one of the most difficult things anyone I know has confronted with grace and class and determination. Everyone who knows you admires the way you've handled an unimaginable situation."

"That's very nice of you to say, but I don't feel worthy of that kind of admiration."

"Well, too bad," he says with a teasing smile. "You're stuck with it."

"I don't want to feel this way anymore, Eric."

"I know, sweetheart."

# CHAPTER 32

*Ava*

We sit together until the buzzer sounds to announce Jessica's arrival. Eric gets up to let her in.

Jessica comes in and makes a beeline for me, hugging me like an old friend.

"Thank you for coming."

"I told you before—any time you need me, I'm here."

"Eric told you the latest?"

"He did, and on the way over here, I tried to imagine what it must've been like for you to see him again and to hear the things he said." She sighs. "I couldn't imagine it."

Eric sits next to me and takes my hand.

"I can't get it out of my head."

"And you won't, probably for quite some time."

That's not exactly good news to me.

"Tell me what happened. I need to hear the details."

I relive my hour with John, from the moment I arrived until the second I left. "I found out things about him I didn't know before. He'd told me his father was a high-ranking military officer, but that wasn't true. He grew up in foster care and went into the Navy out of high school when a judge offered him that or jail. They put him through college and recruited him for special assignment because of his lack of personal attachments. I never knew, until I saw him the other day, that I was all he had."

"And now you're feeling guilty for leaving him when he's facing a long, arduous recovery. Am I right?"

Leave it to my Jessica to zero in on the heart of the matter. "Yes, you're right. I feel awful."

"He's not your responsibility, Ava."

"I know, but—"

"No buts. He is not your responsibility. I want you to say that back to me. He's not my responsibility."

"He's not my responsibility."

"Say it again."

"He's not my responsibility."

"Do you need to say it again, or is it sinking in?"

"It's starting to sink in."

"And you understand that no one is at fault here except for the terrorist who decided to blow up a cruise ship and the lives of thousands of people, including you, along with it, right?"

Placing the blame on Al Khad is much better than blaming John for doing his job and serving his country. "I'm trying to understand that. It's a work in progress."

"You wondered what became of John. Now you know. You wondered how he truly felt about you. Now you know. You wondered how you'd feel when or if you saw him again. Now you know. What else do you need to know?"

"N-nothing. I have all the answers I needed."

"Then it's time to move on. Unless..." She glances at Eric. "I'm not quite sure how to say this..."

It's so unlike her to waver. "Just say it. Whatever it is."

"Unless you'd rather be with John than Eric," she says, grimacing in Eric's direction. "Sorry."

He looks like he's been punched.

"That's not what I want."

"You're sure of that?" Jessica asks.

"Yes." John is the past. Eric is the present and the future. I have no question in my mind about that.

"Are you really sure, Ava?" Eric asks. "I don't want you torn between me and him while we're planning our wedding. If you want to postpone it, we can do that, but I need you to be absolutely certain that I'm what you want before you commit to me."

I look at him and see everything he's been to me since that day last June when he saved my life with a slice of cheese pizza. He's held me up, supported me, helped me put the pieces back together and never wavered in his devotion to me, even when a lesser man surely would've said enough already.

I see him down on one knee with the Christmas tree lights twinkling behind him, asking me to spend the rest of my life with him. I see him holding my hair back when I was sick when Al Khad was captured and calling in favors to find out whether John was still alive after the video surfaced. I see him buying first-class tickets to get me home as quickly and comfortably as possible and not asking a single question even when he must've been full of them. He's already proven himself to me in every possible way. It's time now for me to return the favor.

"I'm absolutely certain that you're what I want," I tell him.

His relief is obvious and palpable.

"I'm sorry I ever gave you reason to doubt that."

Eric hugs me tightly. "Don't be sorry. If you're here with me, I have everything I want and need."

Jessica dabs at her eyes.

I close mine and thank my lucky stars that Eric Tilden found me when he did and loves me like he does. I hope that in time, I'll stop hearing John's voice begging me to stay and give him another chance. Sharing my dilemma with Eric and Jessica has helped me to put it into perspective and to free myself from the shackles of the past.

I want to focus on the lovely present and the beautiful future that's ahead for me and Eric.

"I think," Jessica says as we continue to hold each other, "that my work here is finished. Don't get up. I'll let myself out, and I'll check in with you tomorrow."

She ducks out, and still I cling to Eric, my port in the storm, my love. "I love you so much," I whisper. "I'll never have the words to properly tell you the full extent of it."

"I think I know, because I feel the same way about you."

I'm not under any illusions that the path forward will be easy or that I'll suddenly stop thinking about John or aching over the things he said to me. But I've made my decision, and there is peace in that.

# EPILOGUE

*Ava*

Four days before my July third wedding, I get home early after work—my last day for two weeks. Miles, Trevor and Carlos threw a shower for me this afternoon that involved far too much champagne. I'm a little buzzed and super excited for the festivities to begin.

Work has been insane since the family group settled with the government. Numerous officials were forced to acknowledge that they could've done more to possibly thwart the attack, which was the primary goal of the lawsuit. The two hundred million in damages they were awarded is almost beside the point to the families.

I moved in with Eric in May—the same week Sky moved in with Miles—but Eric's loft felt like home long before I officially moved in.

I'm stronger now than I was a few months ago. I've been amazed by how freeing it is to not have to wonder about John anymore. A thousand-pound weight has been lifted off me now that I know he's safe and on the road to a full recovery. I still think of him frequently and hope he's doing well, but my heart and mind are no longer held prisoner by a past I had no control over.

My heart and mind are fully engrossed in Eric, our wedding and our upcoming honeymoon to Spain and the Canary Islands. As Jessica predicted, it didn't happen overnight, but as the weeks went by, I found myself thinking less and less about the things John said to me in that hotel room. I'm not haunted anymore by his parting words. I've successfully moved on by reminding myself over and over again that as much as I once loved him, he is not my responsibility.

My phone rings with a call from a number I don't recognize. I almost ignore it, but because of the new frenzy of media attention for the family group since the lawsuit was settled, I take the call. "Ava Lucas."

"This is Lieutenant Commander David Muncie. We met a few months ago..."

"Yes, I remember." As if I could ever forget. "What can I do for you?"

"I'm sorry to bother you, but I wasn't sure who else to call. Captain West doesn't really have anyone else."

My heart sinks along with the rest of me when I sit on the sofa. "What's wrong?" *Not my responsibility. Not my responsibility. Not my responsibility.*

"He's given up on his PT. He won't talk to anyone, and most days he doesn't get out of bed. He refused to do the *60 Minutes* interview. He's in a bad way."

I wondered why the interview he'd told me about never aired. But I can't hear this four days before my wedding. I just can't. "What does that have to do with me?" *Not my responsibility.*

"I wondered if you might be willing to give him a call. It might help if he heard from you."

*Not my responsibility.* "I... I'm getting married. In four days."

"I'm so sorry. Never mind. We'll figure something out on our end."

"Wait..." My mind races when I contemplate the implications of talking to John again, especially right now. *He's not my responsibility, but how am I supposed to hear that he's in a bad way and do nothing?* "You really think it would help if I call him?" I wish Eric was here to tell me what he thinks I should do.

"I really do, or I wouldn't ask. He hasn't been the same since he saw you."

My eyes burn with tears, and I'm scared—truly terrified of a setback after I've worked so hard to get to a good place. "I'll call him. When would be a good time?"

"What're you doing now? I'm at the hospital and could encourage him to take the call. He's been so overwhelmed with media and other inquiries that he's stopped answering his phone."

I have no idea if I'm doing the right thing or not, but I can't take the time to think it all the way through. "Now is good."

"You have the number?"

"Yes." I get up to retrieve the paper John gave from my wallet where I put it after I saw him. All this time, I've known it was there, but I've never touched it.

"Give me five minutes," Muncie says.

"All right."

The line goes dead, and I return to the sofa, where I sit staring at my phone for five of the longest minutes of my life. Then I punch in the number and listen to it ring twice before Muncie picks up. "Please hold for Captain West." In the background, I hear arguing. I hear Muncie say, "Take the goddamned call."

"*What?*" John growls.

"It's me. Ava."

"Ava?" He sounds like a little boy on Christmas, and my heart aches for him and for me and for everything we once were to each other.

I force myself to stay focused on the purpose of this call. "I hear you're giving everyone a hard time."

"Ava…" A world of agony is conveyed in the way he says my name.

Fighting the emotional overload, I focus on the purpose of this call. "John, listen to me. You have to do what the doctors tell you so you can get better and get out of there. Don't you want to get out of there?" The question is met with silence. "John?"

"I'm here."

"Don't you want to get out of there?"

"Yeah, I do."

"Then you have to do what they tell you to. Can you do that?"

"Yeah. I can do it."

"Are you saying what I want to hear so I'll leave you alone?"

"I don't want you to leave me alone. I spent six years trying to get back to you. The last thing I want is for you to leave me alone."

Maybe I played this all wrong. Maybe it doesn't have to be all or nothing. "If I call you once in a while to check on you, will you get out of bed and go to therapy?"

"You'll really call me?"

"Only if you do what you're told."

"I'll do it."

"This doesn't mean… I'm still getting married. In four days, actually."

"I know. I saw the thing in the paper."

Oh God, the *Vows* column. He saw it. "I want you to be okay."

"Everyone wants something from me since they released my name. I don't know how to handle it all. The press… They're relentless. I've even had endorsement offers. I keep thinking you'd know what to do."

"Do you want me to find someone who can help you manage that?" I think immediately of Jules. It can't be FergusonMain. It just can't.

"Would you? That would be great."

"I'll have someone call you from New York next week. You'll take the call?"

"I'll take the call."

"I have things of yours. Do you want me to send them to you?"

"Could I get with you about that when I get out of here and figure out where I'm going?"

"Sure."

"Ava…"

"What?"

"You're happy with him? Really happy?"

My life with Eric runs through my mind like the best movie I've ever seen. "I really am."

"Okay," he says with a sigh.

"Be well, John."

"Be happy, Ava."

I press the End button and wipe away tears. I feel like I did the right thing making the call. If that's all it takes to get him back on track, it was the least I could do.

I take a deep breath and release it. I'm okay. Better than okay. I'm happy and in love with an extraordinary man who will soon be my husband.

I can't wait.


I marry Eric four days later, on the lawn of his family's home on the Hudson. We get the gorgeous summer day we hoped for, and the wedding is just what we wanted—casual, relaxed and fun. We're surrounded by the people we love best, and I don't have a single reservation or doubt as my father walks me down the aisle to my new husband. He is everything I could ever want or need.

When Eric spoke to his mother about the wedding, she said the only way she would attend was if she could bring her new man. Eric replied that since her new man wasn't invited, he was sorry she wouldn't be able to make it.

After the ceremony, Eric surprises me with a piece of cheese pizza on a plate that makes me laugh even as our guests look on in confusion. That's okay. They don't have to get it. It's our own inside joke, and the reminder of the first day we spent together, just over a year ago, makes today even more special.

After I told him about Muncie's call and how I talked to John, Eric said he was fine with me referring John to Jules. She was thrilled by the possibility of working with the man of the moment and promised to take good care of him. I asked that she spare me the details, which she agreed to do. It's better that way.

Eric and Amy have taken leaves of absence from their jobs to run Rob's campaign. The media has eaten up the fact that the Tilden Triplets are back together again to get Rob elected, and there's been a lot of positive coverage of their individual successes. No one talks much about how their parents' marriage ended anymore, which is a relief to us all.

Rob stands a good chance of being elected to Congress in November, and no one is more pleased by that than the governor. Last night at the rehearsal dinner, he toasted Eric and me, calling us survivors who deserved every good thing that comes our way. I was more than happy to drink to that.

Our first dance as husband and wife is to "You Are the Best Thing," a jazzy song we both love by Ray Lamontagne. My *husband*, Eric, gazes down at me, his smile lighting up the gorgeous eyes that look at me with love and adoration.

"Are you happy, sweetheart?" he asks.

"So happy. You?"

Nodding, he says, "I've got everything if I've got you."

"You've definitely got me."

And I have my happy ending, finally.

\*\*\*

Thank you for reading *Five Years Gone*! The idea for Ava's story came to me at the beginning of 2017. I thought about it so much that I had to stop my regular programming at the end of 2017 to WRITE the book that was demanding my attention. Sometimes that's how the muse works! I can tell her—but the readers want more Gansett or Fatal—and she says, "Too bad, this is what we're writing now. Get over it." She's the boss, and I do what she tells me to. Since she rarely leads me astray, I wrote FYG in November and December of 2017. Then I got the big idea to translate it into French and German so my readers in those countries could have it the same time as everyone else, pushing the release date to October of 2018. I want to thank my amazing publishing partners at Kensington Books for handling the distribution of the trade paperback editions as well as Andi Arndt and Joe Arden for narrating the amazing audio edition, which is well worth a listen whether you're an audiobook fan or not. They are two of the most popular voices working in romance today, and I'm thrilled to have them attached to this project. To have a book out in print, ebook, audio, French and German ON THE

SAME DAY is the holy grail of indie publishing, and I couldn't be more excited to get *Five Years Gone* out to my readers and listeners around the world. I hope you love Ava's story as much as I enjoyed writing it, and watch for the sequel, *One Year Home*, featuring John, out next summer.

So many people help me to do what I do, including my husband, Dan Force, and my amazing team behind the scenes, Julie Cupp, Lisa Cafferty, Holly Sullivan, Isabel Sullivan, Nikki Colquhoun, Anne Woodall, Kara Conrad, Linda Ingmanson, Joyce Lamb, Jessica Estep and Jules Bernard. I always say that I couldn't do what I do without them, but it's 1000 percent true, especially with this book in which we knocked the collective cover off the ball to make it available in three languages, print, ebook and audio on the same day. GO TEAM JACK!

The biggest thanks of all go to my readers, who make my dreams come true every day with their love for me and my books. Having reader friends all over the world is a gift I never take for granted. I've never felt the love of my readers more profoundly than I did this past summer after I lost my beloved dad. Thank you for always supporting me—and my muse—on this incredible journey.

Much love,

Marie

Keep reading for a sneak peek of John's book, *One Year Home*

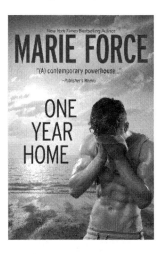

# One Year Home
## Chapter 1

*John*

Nothing has gone according to plan. From the second I was shot while capturing Al Khad, the most wanted man on earth, my life has spun out of control. I lost half my leg. I lost a month of my life to an infection and then… And then I lost Ava, the love of my life, who is now married to someone else and on a European honeymoon. *Eric*. The guy's name is *Eric*, and supposedly, she fell in love with him after I'd been deployed more than five years. Weeks after I saw her and learned that she'd fallen for someone else during my interminable six-year absence, it still hasn't completely sunk in that we're over for good. Thoughts of her, of *us*, of the life I wanted so badly with her, sustained me during the long years we spent apart.

That she's gone forever is inconceivable. I've loved her from the moment I first laid eyes on her, eight years ago in a bar off base in San Diego. We ran into each other—literally—outside the restrooms, and that was that. We were together from then on, even when I wasn't supposed to have entanglements or relationships that would keep me from doing a job that very few service members are ever chosen to do. My unit and its mission is so top secret that I can never share the details of what or how we do what we do with anyone. And since I returned to the US, a reluctant hero after Al Khad's camp outed me in a video of the raid that led to his capture, *everyone* wants the details.

I'm overrun with media requests, so many that the navy public affairs officer assigned to me has stopped taking their calls, which means they come directly to me. How they got my number, I have no idea. I've got no choice but to hire someone to deal with it. That someone, recommended by Ava, happens to be her new sister-in-law, Julianne Tilden, who also happens to be the daughter of the New York governor. Good times. Not only do I get to deal with someone from Ava's new family, the governor's daughter is probably a pampered, privileged princess pain-in-the ass who has no concept whatsoever of what I'm dealing with.

I'm prepared to hate her on sight.

Her brother married my Ava. What else do I need to know about her than that?

If I wasn't so desperate for relief from the relentless media demands, I would've wanted nothing to do with Ava's new sister-in-law. Besides, what does it matter who deals with the press? As long as someone other than me does it.

While I continue daily PT as an outpatient at the base hospital, I'm living in an apartment that Lieutenant Commander David Muncie, the liaison assigned to me by the navy, arranged when I was released from inpatient treatment. I'm told being released to outpatient status is a victory to be celebrated.

Whoo. Fucking. Hoo.

I don't give a shit about anything now that Ava is gone. She was my reason for being, and I'm left with half a leg and a heart so broken, it might never beat normally again. What's the fucking point? I don't know anymore, and I'm self-aware enough to realize I'm profoundly depressed. The medical professionals who deal with me on a regular basis see it, too, and have referred me to a shrink. I have his card. I just haven't bothered to make an appointment.

What can he do? Unless he can dissolve Ava's marriage and get her to come back to me where she belongs, I can't see the benefit to wasting his time or mine.

The doorbell rings, and I drag myself off the sofa to let Muncie in, moving slowly on the crutches I'm still reliant upon.

At least he brought coffees, one of which he hands to me after I'm back on the sofa. He's learned the hard way not to speak to me until after I've had at least one, preferably two, cups of coffee. I'm a real joy to be around lately.

I never used to be this way. Before the deployment from hell, I had a nice life with Ava. She was all I needed to be happy, and I was all she needed. Until I disappeared without a word to her for six years, giving her no choice but to move on without me. I blame Al Khad for screwing up the loveliest thing in my life. I certainly don't blame Ava for surviving. I just wish she hadn't fallen for someone else. Eric. Her husband's name is Eric. I hate his fucking guts, and I've never even met him.

I had this picture in mind of what it would be like to see her again. I didn't imagine her telling me she'd found someone else, that she was in love and engaged and planning a life with him. Six weeks after that fateful meeting with her, I'm still reeling from having to let her go because that was what she wanted.

Life is so fucking unfair. I gave more than six years and half a leg to the quest to bring a ruthless terrorist to justice, and what do I get as a thank-you? The rest of my life without the only woman I've ever loved.

"Are you going to shower before Julianne gets here?" Muncie asks from his post at the dining room table where he's set up his laptop.

"What time is it?"

"Nine thirty."

Julianne is due at ten, and I haven't showered or shaved in days. I look nothing at all like the well-groomed naval officer I used to be before life kicked me in the balls. Maybe she ought to see the new me, the me who doesn't give a shit about anything, even personal hygiene, so she'll know what she's getting if she decides to take me on as a client.

Because I'm still unsteady on the prosthetic, it'll take me every second of the thirty minutes I have if I'm going to shower and change. I pull myself up on the crutches and hobble into the bedroom.

Muncie follows, puts the coffee on the counter and then leaves me to shower in the handicapped-accessible stall. I'm technically handicapped now. Heartbroken and handicapped. That's me. Oh and heroic, too, if you believe the bullshit being spewed about me from coast to coast. The country is grateful. I appreciate that, but I wish they'd leave me the fuck alone to wallow in my depression.

Only because it's possible that I stink, I take the goddamned shower. I shave days' worth of scruff and wash my hair. It's gotten long—longer than it's been since Afghanistan, when it grew past my shoulders for the first time ever. When I woke up in the hospital after I lost my leg, the hair was gone, too. I never asked who decided it needed to go. I'd had much bigger problems then, like figuring out how I was supposed to live without my leg.

Now I have to figure out how I'm supposed to go on without Ava. Standing under the warm water, I think about that first night with her, my favorite memory to wallow in when I was deployed. I could transport myself out of whatever hell I was in at the moment and be with her, my favorite place in the world to be. After I talked her into leaving the bar with me that first night, we drove around in my truck for a couple of hours, talking, laughing, listening to music and swapping life stories. She told me hers. I told her the version of mine I was allowed to share, ninety percent of it complete bullshit, such as the part about my father the general, who'd moved us from one town to another as kids.

There was no father and no "us." I was raised in the foster system and have no family. My lack of personal connections, coupled with my former physical agility, made me an ideal candidate for the elite team of special forces that deployed to hunt down Al Khad. And we finally got the slippery bastard who'd eluded us for years before that fateful night.

But I don't want to think about him. I want to think about *her*. And *us*. The first thing about her I noticed was that she was young. Just barely twenty-one at the time, whereas I was twenty-nine. She was way too young for me, and I should've kept walking right on by her. That's the only regret I allow myself where she's concerned—that I sucked her into my life without all the information she needed to decide for herself. I never told her, for example, that I could be deployed for years at a time, and that if that happened, I wouldn't be able to contact her at all while I was gone.

I realize that makes me sound like the biggest dick who ever lived, but I wasn't *allowed* to tell her. I wasn't even supposed to have her in my life. And yes, I struggled with the deception. I agonized over what would become of her if the worst should happen to our country. My only excuse is that I loved her so fucking much—and loved being loved by her—that I would've done anything to have her in my life, even if that meant lying to her every day of the two years we spent blissfully together.

I told myself then that I was doing it for the right reasons. I was protecting her from having to worry about something that might never happen. But that's a bunch of bullshit. I was protecting myself from the possibility of losing the only person who'd ever truly loved me, the only person who ever belonged only to me and me to her.

I run my fingers through my hair until all the soap is out and then turn my face up to the water. I should've fucking married her when I had the chance. What were they going to do? Drum me out of the SEAL Team or out of the navy itself? After spending hundreds of thousands of dollars to train me for the kind of mission that led to the capture of Al Khad, they wouldn't have let me go easily. However, they could've demoted me or even court-martialed me for failing to stick to the rules that were spelled out to me very clearly when I agreed to join this particular team in the first place.

It would've gutted me to be demoted or court-martialed. Until I met Ava, the navy and the SEAL Teams had given me the first real family I'd ever had, and the thought of disappointing my commanders had been unbearable to me. That's why I didn't marry her when I knew I should have. I worried so much about her being left unprotected that I'd given myself an ulcer, which was another thing she never knew about. I'd told her I had reflux, and that was why I had to watch what I ate.

Whenever I need to escape from my new reality, I let my mind wander back to the most perfect night of my life, the night I met Ava in that nasty bar that Sanchez had chosen to celebrate his promotion. She'd been there with a friend who was interested in one of the navy guys who hung out there. Never in my wildest dreams had I expected to meet the woman of my dreams in such a place. But there she was, walking into the ladies' room as I came out of the men's room and nearly took her down.

She'd been so fresh and pretty and perfect. I told her when I saw her again recently that I knew I should've let her go and gone on with my life that night. The reason I didn't was because the first second I laid eyes on her, I was a goner. One second with her and it was already too late to go on as if I'd never met her.

That first night had been like something out of a dream or a movie or someone else's life, because perfect things didn't happen to me. At least they never had before. But everything about Ava and me together was utter perfection, the kind of thing that comes along once in a lifetime if someone is very, very lucky. I was lucky once, and sometimes, the loss of her, of her love… I wonder if I'll survive it. Losing my leg was nothing compared to losing her.

I talked her into coming home with me that night, and we fell into bed like we'd been together for years rather than hours. She said she'd never done anything like that before, she'd never gone to bed with a guy she'd only just met, but we both knew right away that this was different. The first time I sank into her sweetness, I was ruined for anyone else. I haven't been with anyone since her, and I can't imagine ever again wanting a woman the way I still want her. I'm hard as stone just thinking about that first night and the way we came together like two meteors on a collision course with destiny. The next day, I did something I'd never done before in twelve years in the navy and have never done again since—I called in sick to work so I could spend the entire day in bed with her.

She skipped her Friday classes, and we stayed in my bed for days, sending out for food so we could fuel up and go back for more. By the time we reemerged on Monday morning to rejoin our lives, she had become my life and I had become hers. That's how fast it happened. I went from single to committed to her over the span of one momentous, sexually magnificent weekend.

I wrap my hand around my hard cock and lose myself in the memories of what it had been like to love her. I remember every nuance of her body, every reaction

I could draw from her effortlessly, because I spoke Ava fluently. I knew her better than I knew myself. I knew what made her sigh and what made her scream and could make her come so many times, she'd be left all but senseless afterward. I close my eyes and vividly remember the snug fit of her pussy around my cock as it contracted with one orgasm after another. She was so fucking responsive.

Muncie knocks on the door, interrupting the beautiful images in my mind with a cold, harsh dose of my new reality. "What're you doing in there? She's going to be here in ten minutes."

"Fuck off," I tell him, all but admitting to what I'm doing. The moment is lost and so is Ava. The memories have retreated into a past so sweet, I wonder what point there could possibly be in trying to go on without her. It's occurred to me—on more than one occasion since she made her choice—that I could take too many of the pain meds I was given when I left the hospital and make it all go away. Who would care? Ava is gone, and my two closest friends in the world were killed in the Al Khad raid. It would be so easy to take the pills, to slip away, to finally find some peace.

I haven't done it for one very important reason—Ava. I'd never do that to her. I wouldn't ruin the rest of her life by taking mine and leaving her to think it was her fault. So even though losing her nearly killed me, I force myself to continue on so my death won't destroy her happy new life.

Fucked up, right? Believe me, I know.

I get out of the shower and fumble through the process of drying off and getting dressed, which I've had to relearn along with just about everything else since I lost my leg. Even with the prosthetic, my balance is precarious, and I still have a great deal of pain—real and phantom—in my missing leg.

By the time I'm dressed in jeans and a button-down that's come from a dry cleaner thanks to Muncie, I'm completely depleted and sweating. So much for the shower.

I hear Muncie talking to someone in the next room, which means she's here. Though it's the last fucking thing I feel like doing, I drag myself up on the crutches and make my way to the door to meet this woman Ava swears is the best at dealing with the media and the staggering amount of bullshit that has become my life lately.

I pull open the door, and the first thing I see is a red dress and three-inch black fuck-me heels at the end of a stunning pair of legs. I may be heartbroken, but that doesn't mean I don't notice great legs when I see them. I let my gaze travel up the front of her until I connect with big, startled doe eyes.

I can't believe Ava sent me Mary Fucking Poppins.

\*\*\*

*Look for One Year Home, releasing August 20, 2019!*

# OTHER BOOKS BY MARIE FORCE

A Gansett Island Christmas, Novella

Book 19: Mine After Dark *(Riley & Nikki)*

Book 20: Yours After Dark *(Finn McCarthy)*


**The Green Mountain Series**

Book 1: All You Need Is Love *(Will & Cameron)*

Book 2: I Want to Hold Your Hand *(Nolan & Hannah)*

Book 3: I Saw Her Standing There *(Colton & Lucy)*

Book 4: And I Love Her *(Hunter & Megan)*

Novella: You'll Be Mine *(Will & Cam's Wedding)*

Book 5: It's Only Love *(Gavin & Ella)*

Book 6: Ain't She Sweet *(Tyler & Charlotte)*


**The Butler Vermont Series**

**(Continuation of the Green Mountain Series)**

Book 1: Every Little Thing *(Grayson & Emma)*

Book 2: Can't Buy Me Love *(Mary & Patrick)*

Book 3: Here Comes the Sun *(Wade & Mia)*


**The Treading Water Series**

Book 1: Treading Water *(Jack & Andi)*

Book 2: Marking Time *(Clare & Aidan)*

Book 3: Starting Over *(Brandon & Daphne)*

Book 4: Coming Home *(Reid & Kate)*


**Single Titles**

Five Years Gone

Sex Machine

Sex God

Georgia on My Mind

True North

The Fall

Everyone Loves a Hero

Love at First Flight

Line of Scrimmage

### *The Erotic Quantum Series*

Book 1: Virtuous *(Flynn & Natalie)*

Book 2: Valorous *(Flynn & Natalie)*

Book 3: Victorious *(Flynn & Natalie)*

Book 4: Rapturous *(Addie & Hayden)*

Book 5: Ravenous *(Jasper & Ellie)*

Book 6: Delirious *(Kristian & Aileen)*

Book 7: Outrageous *(Emmett & Leah)*

### Historical Romance from Marie Force:
### *The Gilded Series*

Book 1: Duchess By Deception

### Romantic Suspense Novels Available from Marie Force:
### *The Fatal Series*

One Night With You, *A Fatal Series Prequel Novella*

Book 1: Fatal Affair

Book 2: Fatal Justice

Book 3: Fatal Consequences

Book 3.5: Fatal Destiny, *the Wedding Novella*

Book 4: Fatal Flaw

Book 5: Fatal Deception

Book 6: Fatal Mistake

Book 7: Fatal Jeopardy

Book 8: Fatal Scandal

Book 9: Fatal Frenzy

Book 10: Fatal Identity

Book 11: Fatal Threat

Book 12: Fatal Chaos

Book 13: Fatal Invasion

Book 14: Fatal Reckoning

**_Single Title_**

The Wreck

# ABOUT THE AUTHOR

Marie Force is the *New York Times* bestselling author of contemporary romance, including the indie-published Gansett Island Series and the Fatal Series from Harlequin Books. In addition, she is the author of the Butler, Vermont Series, the Green Mountain Series and the erotic romance Quantum Series. In 2019, her new historical Gilded series from Kensington Books will debut with *Duchess By Deception*.

All together, her books have sold 7 million copies worldwide, have been translated into more than a dozen languages and have appeared on the *New York Times* bestseller list 29 times. She is also a *USA Today* and *Wall Street Journal* bestseller, a Speigel bestseller in Germany, a frequent speaker and publishing workshop presenter as well as a publisher through her Jack's House Publishing romance imprint. She is a two-time nominee for the Romance Writers of America's RITA® award for romance fiction.

Her goals in life are simple—to finish raising two happy, healthy, productive young adults, to keep writing books for as long as she possibly can and to never be on a flight that makes the news.

Join Marie's mailing list for news about new books and upcoming appearances in your area. Follow her on Facebook at *https://www.facebook.com/MarieForceAuthor*, Twitter *@marieforce* and on Instagram at *https://instagram.com/marieforceauthor/*. Join one of Marie's many reader groups. Contact Marie at *marie@marieforce.com*.

Made in the USA
Columbia, SC
06 October 2020